Praise for *New York Times* bestselling author Lindsay McKenna

"McKenna provides heartbreakingly tender romantic development that will move readers to tears. Her military background lends authenticity to this outstanding tale, and readers will fall in love with the upstanding hero and his fierce determination to save the woman he loves."
—*Publishers Weekly* on *Never Surrender*

"Talented Lindsay McKenna delivers excitement and romance in equal measure."
—*RT Book Reviews* on *Protecting His Own*

"Lindsay McKenna will have you flying with the daring and deadly women pilots who risk their lives… Buckle in for the ride of your life."
—*Writers Unlimited* on *Heart of Stone*

Praise for *USA TODAY* bestselling author Merline Lovelace

"Merline Lovelace rocks! Like Nora Roberts, she delivers top-rate suspense with great characters, rich atmosphere and a crackling plot!"
—*New York Times* bestselling author Mary Jo Putney

"Lovelace's many fans have come to expect her signature strong, brave, resourceful heroines and she doesn't disappoint."
—*Booklist*

"Ms. Lovelace wins our hearts with a tender love story featuring a fine hero who will make every woman's heart beat faster."
—*RT Book Reviews* on *Wrong Bride, Right Groom*

NEW YORK TIMES BESTSELLING AUTHOR

LINDSAY McKENNA

USA TODAY BESTSELLING AUTHOR

MERLINE LOVELACE

SOLITAIRE
&
TEXAS HERO

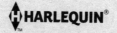

ISBN-13: 978-1-335-00694-3

Solitaire & Texas Hero

Copyright © 2019 by Harlequin Books S.A.

The publisher acknowledges the copyright holders of the individual works as follows:

Solitaire
Copyright © 1987 by Lindsay McKenna

Texas Hero
Copyright © 2002 by Merline Lovelace

Recycling programs for this product may not exist in your area.

This edition published by arrangement with Harlequin Books S.A.

For questions and comments about the quality of this book, please contact us at CustomerService@Harlequin.com.

Printed in U.S.A.

www.Harlequin.com

CONTENTS

Lindsay McKenna is proud to have served her country in the US Navy as an aerographer's mate third class—also known as a weather forecaster. She was a pioneer in the military romance subgenre and loves to combine heart-pounding action with soulful and poignant romance. True to her military roots, she is the originator of the long-running and reader-favorite Morgan's Mercenaries series. She does extensive hands-on research, including flying in aircraft such as a P3-B Orion sub-hunter and a B-52 bomber. She was the first romance writer to sign her books in the Pentagon bookstore. Visit her online at lindsaymckenna.com.

Visit the Author Profile page
at Harlequin.com for more titles.

SOLITAIRE

Lindsay McKenna

Chapter 1

"Don't go in there. It's too dangerous." A large hand splayed across on the blueprint of the emerald mine in Hampton, Maine, that Cat was studying. Her concentration broken, she blinked. Thinking it was the owner of the gem mine, she slowly stood up and turned.

Normally, she barely had to lift her eyes to look into those of a man, so she was momentarily disconcerted to find herself eye to eye with a khaki-covered chest. She brought her gaze up and looked into dark blue eyes the color of midnight sapphire and equally breathtaking. The man's stubborn jaw accentuated the intensity of his gaze, and if it weren't for the laugh lines bracketing his mouth and the crinkles at the corners of his eyes, she would have bet he never smiled.

"I beg your pardon," Cat said coolly.

"I've already been in that mine. It isn't safe."

Her mouth curved into a knowing smile. "What mine is?"

Impatience flared in his eyes. "This is no time for jokes, Ms. Kincaid. I was in that dump this morning and the owner is crazy to ask anyone to actually inspect that worthless pit. The timbers are not only rotted, but there's water in the sedimentary manging wall above those timbers that's weakened the entire crosscut."

"You're obviously not Mr. Graham," Cat returned testily. "So perhaps you'd be good enough to tell me who you are, and how you know my name."

"No, I'm not the owner of this worthless excuse for a mine. And everyone in our business knows the name Cat Kincaid." His eyes grew warm and he extended his hand. "My name is Slade Donovan. I'm a geologist."

Cat shook his hand, finding his grip firm but not overpowering. "I don't understand, Mr. Donovan. Has Mr. Graham hired you to help assess the condition of the Emerald Lady Mine?" She stole a look at her watch. She didn't have much time and she couldn't waste what she had on social amenities.

Slade had the good grace to look sheepish. "Well, not exactly, Ms. Kincaid. Oh, hell, do you mind if I call you Cat? That's what most people call you, right? I don't like standing on formality any more than I have to."

Wariness returned to Cat's eyes. "Slade Donovan. Where have I heard that name before?"

He colored slightly, heightening the ruddy glow already in his cheeks. "Mining engineers and geologists are a pretty close group on the international circuit," he parried. "I've worked a few gem mines in Africa and South America."

Cat pushed a few dark brown strands of hair from

her forehead and took a step back, gauging him closely in the interim. "I know I've heard of you…"

"That's not really important right now; you are." He pointed out the grimy window of the old shack. "Lionel Graham has a poor reputation among geologists. You can't trust him." His voice, naturally low and with an obvious Texas accent, deepened with urgency. "He's waited too long for a mine inspection into that crosscut. Those post and stull timbers would crack if someone were to breathe on them the wrong way, Cat."

"Ms. Kincaid, please, Mr. Donovan. If the owner hasn't hired you, then what are you doing here?" It was on the tip of her tongue to ask just who he thought he was to be telling her, a mining engineer, whether she should go into a mine or not. Staring at him critically, she guessed his age to be around her own thirty-three years. He managed to look both rugged and boyish, a combination helped by the lock of rebellious brown hair lying on his broad brow.

He suddenly offered her a devastating smile, obviously meant to melt the heart of any woman he wanted to charm. The smile, however, had the opposite effect on her. Placing her hands on her hips, she stood waiting for an explanation.

"Actually, I flew in from Bogota when I heard you were coming here." Slade brushed the errant lock back in one quick motion. "I've been trying to track you down for days. I got in last night and—"

"Ah, there you are, Ms. Kincaid." Lionel Graham, a portly man dressed impeccably in a gray suit, entered the office. His balding head shone beneath the naked light bulb suspended above them, and his brow wrinkled as he turned to the tall man standing beside her.

"What are you doing here, Donovan? I thought you were still in South America."

Slade scowled back at Graham and drew himself up to his full six-foot-four. "I was in Tunnel B this morning, Graham, the crosscut. I can't say I liked what I saw."

Graham frowned, sucking in his potbelly. "Now see here, Donovan, I don't know what you're doing here, but no one is allowed inside the Emerald Lady unless I authorize it."

"I can see why," Slade shot back. "That mine's back is broken. Someone hasn't been following proper pumping practices, and you've got nothing but rotting posts and stulls weighed down by a ceiling ready to collapse on anyone stupid enough to go in there."

Graham colored fiercely. "What does a geologist know about engineering matters?" he challenged.

"A damn good geologist, Graham." Slade glanced over his shoulder toward Cat. "I know emerald mines, Graham, and you have no business sending anyone down in that shaft."

Cat moved forward, her anger finally at the boiling point. She didn't have time to stand there listening to these two. "Mr. Donovan, your opinion is not wanted or needed. That's why I'm here. I troubleshoot bad mines for a living. Do you?"

Struggling to contain his temper, Slade asked, "Ever hear of taking a bath, Ms. Kincaid?" Although not a common practice, some unscrupulous mine owners would put very little money into a supposedly rich gem site, then declare it a catastrophic business loss to collect a healthy tax return. Well, the Emerald Lady was a lost cause and both Slade and Graham knew it. The only one who didn't was Cat Kincaid, and he wasn't going to let her find out the hard way if he had anything to say about it.

"I fail to see what that has to do with this situation, Mr.—"

"My friends call me Slade. And the Emerald Lady is nothing more than a nice, juicy business loss just waiting to be picked up by Graham."

Graham flushed scarlet. "You've gone too far this time, Donovan," he sputtered. "Unless you're suddenly working with the U.S. Mine Safety—"

Slade turned conspiratorially to Cat for a moment. "That's who ought to be called in to handle this situation. Tunnel B is just begging to fall. But then, Graham—" he turned to the red-faced man "—you wouldn't stand to get as much of a tax loss if you didn't have someone of Ms. Kincaid's stature sign on the bottom line, stating that your mine is not only inoperable, but a disaster of the first degree."

"Look, Donovan, you've no right," began a riled Graham.

Slade, ignoring him, swung his attention back to Cat. "You've been a mining engineer for over ten years. And there isn't anyone in our business who doesn't respect or admire your work in constructing mines under almost impossible circumstances." Slade jabbed a finger toward the Emerald Lady mine. "But your life and your knowledge, not to mention your neck, aren't worth risking for that pit. I'm telling you, that shaft is deadly. Don't go in there. Let Graham get the U.S. mining officials to do it instead."

Cat was momentarily swayed by the fervor of his request; Donovan's deep Texas accent flowed through her like a cool breeze on a hot jungle night. Then she blinked, realizing that he had literally spun her into his web with his husky, coaxing voice. Irritated that she had let him affect her at all, she said, "Mr. Donovan, I think Mr. Graham and I can handle this. In case you forgot, mine inspection is part of being a mining engineer."

Graham pulled out a white silk handkerchief and mopped his perspiring brow. "It most certainly is! Ms. Kincaid's specialty is troublesome mines; that's why I called her. And I resent your inference, Donovan, that I'm doing this for a business loss. Nothing could be further from my mind. The Emerald Lady is the best, and we'll hire only the best if we get into trouble."

Slade snorted. Graham was lying through his perfectly capped teeth. Slade wondered briefly why Cat couldn't see through Graham's ploy. Who had raised her to never question another person's motives?

"Please—" he opened both his callused hands out toward Cat in a final, pleading gesture "—don't go in there. There was a heavy rain here last night. Give the mine another day to settle down. Water's leaking like a sieve in there, and in the crosscut. The supporting timbers are rotted. A day. Just one."

There simply wasn't enough time for this, and Cat stepped up to Donovan, her jaw set. "My schedule doesn't permit the luxury of an extra day. I intend to inspect this mine right now, Mr. Donovan. I don't have time to stand here and discuss this issue. By this afternoon—" she looked at the gold Rolex watch on her darkly tanned left wrist "—at 2:00 p.m., to be precise, I have a flight back to New York City. I have to be in Australia by tomorrow evening."

Rain began falling at a steady clip, spreading a gray

pall over the heavily forested area that surrounded the mine. Slade interpreted this as a warning. Cat merely regarded it as an inconvenience.

She picked up her white miner's hard hat, which had accumulated scratches and dents from many years of use. Each depression was from a rock large enough to have injured her. Cat tested the light strapped to the front of the hat before settling it on her sable-colored hair. Then she plugged the jack into a battery pack that she carried on a web belt around her waist. As she finished her preparations, Cat tried to ignore Donovan, whose tightly throttled energy had the room in a state of electric tension.

"Donovan," Graham began, "I don't care who you think you are. You're trespassing on private property." He glanced around. "If you don't leave, I'll call the sheriff on my car telephone and have you booted out of here on your—"

"Save your threats, Graham. I'm staying until Ms. Kincaid is safely out of that mine." His blue eyes narrowed on Graham's porcine face. "And there's not a damn thing you can do about it unless you think you're big enough to throw me out of here."

Cat shook her head and picked up a safety lamp. Lighting the regulation-size lantern, she watched with satisfaction as the yellow flame grew. She straightened up.

"You going in with her, Graham?" Slade prodded savagely.

"Of course not. She's the mining expert."

Slade's mouth twisted into a lethal line. "You wouldn't be caught dead in there because you know just how unsafe that pit is."

Cat opened the door and nailed both men with a look of authority. "You two can stay here and argue about the mine's merits, but I'm going into it." She looked directly at Slade. "And don't follow me in. Understand?"

He grimaced and nodded. "Whatever you say, lady." Then his icy composure gave way to concern. "But I'd like to see you come back in one piece."

Cat tilted her head, a question in her eyes. What had the scuttlebutt been about the man named Slade Donovan? Later, after the mine inspection was over, she'd search her memory. The name sounded familiar, but was he tied to good news or bad? Judging from his bull-in-the-china-shop tactics, it probably wasn't very good.

"I'll be out in about an hour, Mr. Graham, unless I find something, then it will take a bit longer."

"Fine, fine. Take your time. I'll be waiting."

Slade took a step toward her. "Get in and then get the hell out. Any miner with an ounce of brains could tell twenty minutes after entering it that the mine's broken."

Cat gave him a cool look, then pulled the miner's hat brim a little lower across her eyes. "In about an hour, Mr. Graham…"

Helplessly Slade watched her leave and move out into the downpour. The lightweight pale blue canvas jacket she wore darkened immediately with splotches of rain. Muttering a curse, Slade elbowed past Graham. Cat was halfway across the empty, muddy expanse, heading toward the yawning dark hole of the mine shaft, when Slade caught up with her.

"Ms. Kincaid—Cat—here, take this with you." He thrust a portable radio into her hand. "It's waterproof," he quickly explained. The rain slashed across his face, and his hair darkened as it became plastered against his skull. "Just in case, okay? Don't give me that look, either. This is a safety measure. There's no one here to help you in case something does go wrong." He drew to a halt just inside the shaft. Slade gave her a pleading look, knowing he couldn't intimidate or push Cat into doing what he wanted. He'd heard she had a mind of her own and now he had to deal with that.

Cat stuffed the radio inside her jacket to protect it. The damp, stale air flowing out of the mine swept around them and a chill worked its way up her back. "Okay," she said, "I'll take it with me. But you stay here. I've had enough of your strong-arm tactics, Mr. Donovan. You're just lucky Mr. Graham didn't call the sheriff. You could be in a lot of hot water. He's a fairly influential man in mining, even if his reputation is less than virtuous."

"Lady," Slade confirmed, grinning, "Graham's sunk more worthless pits around the world than I've sampled ore."

"Let me get on with my business, Donovan."

"Yeah, go ahead. How about if I buy you a steak for lunch when you're done?"

There was something intriguing about Slade Donovan that Cat couldn't quite put her finger on; her sixth sense—or was it female curiosity—urged her to accept. "Lunch," she grudgingly agreed. "But a short one."

"I know, you've got a plane to catch." He smiled, the tension in his face easing momentarily.

Cat flipped on her helmet light, holding the safety lamp out in front of her. "See you later, Donovan." Watching where she placed her rubber-booted feet, Cat began her trek down the gentle incline of the adit, or main shaft. Darkness closed around her like a consuming embrace, and the only light was the muted yellow glow of the safety lamp. She inhaled the dankness of the silent shaft. Like most emerald mines, it wasn't deep; it ran shallow, following either sedimentary or pegmatite veins that hid the green rock in calcite nests. The floor was littered profusely with limestone slabs, evidence that the mine hadn't been worked in quite a while.

Cat stopped at every few timbers and studied them carefully with her practiced eye. The overhead roof, or manging wall, of pale green limestone dripped constantly. Most of it was due to the dampness inherent in a mine. But Slade had been right: trickles of water had followed fissures in the sediment and wound their way down into the mine itself. Rock bolts should have been placed in the wall to strengthen it. Without them the wetness would weaken the wall. As Cat ran practiced fingers across the stull, or timbers, supporting the limestone roof, she saw that the main shoring points would have to be immediately replaced and new ones installed.

The thin beam of light from her helmet probed the blackness as Cat raised her head to assess the damage to each post and stull. The adit split into a Y, known to miners as a crosscut. This was the beginning of Tunnel B. The air leaving the shaft was desultory and pregnant with a stale, musty odor. Cat wondered if the dew point was high enough for it to actually rain within the mine. Again, Slade had been right: Graham hadn't even begun to put the necessary care into this mine to make it a decent place to work. If Graham was as knowledgeable as Donovan had said he was, he had no excuse to have skimped on proper ventilation and pumping equipment. Moisture was eating away at the powerful oak and hardwood beams that kept the walls from collapsing and the roof from dropping, and some unlucky miner could lose his life beneath it. She turned down the crosscut, a secondary tunnel off the main adit, and carefully inspected each support. The limestone had turned a rust color where water had leaked through from above, indicating iron in the sediment above the exposed vein. Cat smiled grimly. Slade had accurately predicted the condition of the shaft: there was no way emeralds were going to be found in this kind of rock. The only type that held emeralds was calcite limestone, and none was in evidence here. Even though she wasn't a geologist, she'd seen plenty of rock, and she was knowledgeable enough to make the assessment on her own.

The deeper she went, the more oppressive the air became. The incline became vertical—what miners called a winze. Cat halted at the lip of the winze. She held the safety lamp high, looking for the reason for the vertical descent of the shaft. Normally, it was because the vein of calcite or pegmatite went off in an unexpected direction. But judging from the iron-marked limestone, Cat could see no discernible reason for it. She ran her fingers lightly over the hardwood timber; the surface was slick with algae and wet from the constant leakage of water. Above, the main horizontal stull was fully cracked and sagging. Again, Slade's words came to her about the back of the mine being broken.

Cat's lips tightened and she stood quietly. All around her, she could hear the plunk, plunk, plunk of water. The passage gleamed from the liquid seeping in through the walls. Should she go on? Chances were, if one timber was cracked, the others would be, too, indicating that the entire roof was caving in. It was only a matter of time until the limestone, weakened by water flow through the natural fissures, would collapse. Why did Graham want her to investigate the worthiness of this mine? It was a total loss. So much money would have to be poured into shoring up the crosscut alone, she wondered if the mine's calculated yield was worth that kind of expense. Cat thought not, but that wasn't any of her business; that was Graham's decision to make.

The floor of the mine was slippery with mud and slime. Cat took each step carefully, for she had no wish to cause any undue vibration that might further weaken the supports. Automatically, she pressed her wet fingers against her jacket where the radio lay next to her heart. Slade was turning out to be a pretty decent person after all; his advice had been good, and the radio was a definite asset.

Pushing thoughts of Slade aside, Cat concentrated on the overhead stulls. She stopped every ten feet and examined each one thoroughly. About three hundred feet into the winze, Cat crouched by the left wall. The limestone had cracked, and a healthy spring of water gushed through the opening, running down into the shaft. That wasn't good. It indicated a major structural weakness in the rock wall glistening beneath her fingertips. Slowly rising, Cat cautiously moved to the other side of the mine and continued her inspection.

She had gone another two hundred feet, almost to the end of Tunnel B according to the map, when a sickening crack echoed through the shaft. In one motion, Cat turned, sprinting back toward the beginning of the crosscut. Suddenly, a rumbling sound began. The hollow, drumlike roar rolled through the shaft like mounting thunder. She couldn't tell whether the winze was caving in behind or in front of her. Water several inches deep rushed down the shaft, and she splashed through it. She leaped to the lip that signaled an end to the winze. Slipping, Cat skidded to her knees in the muck and mud of the crosscut. The safety lamp bounced twice and then the flame went out.

Loud snapping and groaning noises followed. Cat's breath tore from her as she scrambled to her feet; the only light left was the one on her helmet. Water was rapidly rising from foot to ankle level; she knew a crack in the wall up ahead had given way. Had the entire wall caved in, leaving her no escape?

Behind her, Cat heard the limestone manging wall grate, and she automatically ducked her head, keeping one hand on her helmet as she raced toward the intersection of the adit. Only two hundred feet more, she guessed, gasping for breath. A crash caromed beside her, and rocks began falling. She halted, breathing hard. Should she retreat or—fist-size pieces of limestone began raining down around her. She was trapped! Cat shielded her face and lurched forward, dust and rock hailing down as she slogged forward, staggering and stumbling.

Suffocating dust filled Cat's mouth, nose and lungs. She coughed violently, unable to breathe. Blinded by the dust, which was thicker than smoke, she tripped. As she did, the manging wall where she had stood seconds before dropped to the floor. A rock the size of a baseball crashed onto her hard hat, knocking it off her head. The hat and light bounced crazily, sending a skittering beam of light through the dense grayness. Another rock struck her shoulder, spinning her around. Cat threw her hands up to protect her head as she pitched backward. She slammed into the jagged rocks, the breath ripped out of her. Seconds later, more than a ton of rock and soil filled the chamber where she was trapped. A cry tore from her as the rest of the other wall collapsed, nearly burying her. Pain lanced up her right side and Cat sank back, unconscious.

With a violent oath, Slade raced down the mine shaft. He had heard the ominous crack of timbers, sounding one after another like breaking matchsticks. He shouted for Cat, but his voice was drowned out by a deep roar that sent icy fear up his spine. A rolling cloud of dust engulfed him and he turned back, hacking and coughing, his hand across his nose and mouth as he stumbled out.

Lionel Graham came lumbering out of the mine shack, his eyes round with shock. Slade ran toward him and grabbed him by the lapel of his expensive English raincoat.

"Damn you, Graham, it's happened! Now you get on that car phone and call for help. Now!"

"Y-yes, of course. Of course," he sputtered, and hurried toward his car.

Slade spun around and ran back to the mine opening, pulling out the radio he kept in a leather carrying case on his hip. The red light blinked on, indicating that the battery was sufficiently charged and ready to be used.

"Cat? Cat, can you hear me? This is Slade. Over." He released the button. All he could hear was static. His mind whirled. Was she dead? Buried alive? Or had she been given a reprieve, and been trapped in a chamber? If so, how much air was left? He knew from his own grim experience that dust could suffocate a person. He ran into the mine and went as far as he could before the choking wall of limestone dust stopped him. Again, he called her. Again, no answer. Damn it to hell! He wanted to wrap his fingers around Graham's fleshy throat and strangle the bastard. He might as well have set Cat up to be murdered. But right now, Slade needed Graham's influence to get local miners together to begin excavating the mine to search for Cat.

Slade wasn't one to pray often, not that he didn't believe in God, but he more or less used Him in emergencies only. Well, this was an emergency, and as he pressed the radio's On button once again, he prayed that Cat would hear him this time.

"Cat? Cat Kincaid, can you hear me? This is Slade Donovan. If you can hear me, depress the handset. Show me you're alive. Over."

The constant static of the portable radio now lodged between her rib cage and the wall of rocks slowly brought Cat back to consciousness. Blood trickled from her nose and down her lips. She tried to lick them, but her tongue met a thick caking of dust. Suddenly a sharp, riveting pain brought her fully conscious; it felt as if her right side were on fire. Dully, Cat tried to take stock of herself. She was buried up to her thighs in rubble. The weak light from her helmet lay to the left, barely visible through the curtain of dust that hung in the chamber.

The radio static continued, and dazedly Cat reached into her jacket. It hurt to breathe. It hurt to move. Dizziness washed over her and she knew that she was injured. How badly she didn't know. Not yet. And maybe never. She had no idea how large or small was the chamber where she was buried. If it was too small, and there wasn't sufficient oxygen, she would die of suffocation sooner, rather than later. If she was lucky, oxygen might be trickling through the walls blocking her escape, and she wouldn't suffocate.

Her fingers closed over the radio. Twisting slightly, she pulled it out of her jacket. A gasp tore from her and a tidal wave of pain caused her to black out for several seconds. When she came to, she took light, shallow breaths of the murky air. To breathe deep meant suffering a knifelike pain ripping up her right side. Busted ribs, she thought, slowly pulling the radio out of the jacket.

The light from her hard hat was slowly dimming, but she focused on first things first: the radio. Would it work? Was Donovan still out there? Her hand trembled badly as she fumbled to turn the radio on. The red light blinked on, and a rough, scratchy noise greeted her. Finally, she fine-tuned it with the other dial.

Her fingers, now bruised and bloodied, slipped on the button she hoped would link her with the outside world. Cat depressed it and tried to speak, but the only sound that came from her throat was a low croak. If only she could have some water! She could hear it all around her, the same rushing sound as before. Had that wall collapsed behind her where the limestone had cracked and separated?

"D-Donovan..." Her voice was barely a hoarse whisper. Dust clogged her throat and she wanted to cough, but didn't dare for fear of disturbing her broken ribs. Then the radio crackled and an incredible surge of relief flowed through her as she heard Donovan's Texas baritone come scratchily over the handset.

"Cat! I can barely hear you. Give me a report on your condition."

"I—I'm trapped between a double cave-in. My legs

are under rubble, but if I can move off my belly, I can free myself. Chamber is—dust too thick to tell how small or large it is yet."

"Injuries?"

"Right lung hurts…can't breathe very well. Legs are numb but I think if I get the rocks off, they'll be okay."

Terror leaked through Slade's voice. "Head injury?"

Cat had to wait a minute to assess herself. She slowly raised her hand, feeling her dust-laden hair, and met warm stickiness as she felt across her scalp. Her head was throbbing as if it might split into a hundred pieces, like the limestone around her. "Maybe a mild concussion. Dizzy—"

"Oxygen?"

"Let me radio back. Got to try and reach my hard hat."

"All right, just take it easy. We're going to get you out of there. Just hang on. Graham's phoned for help. We expect miners and excavation equipment within the next hour. Get back to me on the size of the place you're trapped in. Over."

Just the reassuring sound of Slade's voice kept her panic from exploding. There was something about him that instilled faith in his promise to get her out of there. Gently, Cat set down the radio. What she would do for some water now! Dizziness came and went and Cat felt nausea clawing up her throat—she had all the symptoms of a concussion. Stretching her left hand out, fingers extended, she reached for her hard hat. There! Her fingers closed over the hat and she pulled it back to her.

As the dust slowly settled around her, Cat got an idea of the chamber's size. Rocks ranging from the size of her fist to huge sheets that easily weighed half a ton were lodged all around her. She had been lucky: if she had not tripped and fallen where she now lay, a sheet of limestone nearby would have sheared right through her. She'd be dead. The drenching reality washed through her and she closed her eyes, exhausted. *I shouldn't be tired. Got to get these rocks off my legs and move around. Maybe I can find some water...* Then drowsiness overwhelmed her.

Slade paced back and forth in front of the mine like an infuriated lion. He gripped the radio tightly in his fist. The rain was continuing to fall at a steady rate; the sky had become a dismal gray. Angrily, he shook off the thought and the feeling. Cat was alive, and that was all that mattered. No one should die alone in that god-forsaken place. He wanted to vent his anger on Graham, who sat in his silver Mercedes looking pasty from the turn of events. The frightened mine owner had gone to extraordinary measures to call in local workers who had once toiled in the worthless mine, and to order heavy equipment from a nearby town. The local fire department would arrive shortly with oxygen tanks, masks and rescue apparatus. As soon as they came, Slade was going to borrow a tank and mask and make his way down the shaft to locate Cat's chamber. He halted. Cat should have called in by now.

Slade called her five times and there was no answer. Was Cat unconscious? Had she died because of oxygen deprivation? Torn between staying and going deeper, he stared down the black maw of the shaft. Maybe her radio was on the blink. He tried to ignore his memory of the slur of Cat's words and the pain he'd heard with each breath she had taken. He had a gut feeling she was in a lot more serious condition than she was revealing.

He called again. This time, he got an answer. "Cat, how are you?"

"Uhh, dizzy. Sorry, didn't mean to black out."

Slade's mouth thinned, his eyes reflecting his anxiety, but he kept it out of his voice as he depressed the On button. "You're doing fine. Did you get a look at the chamber?"

"Twenty feet long and ten feet wide. The manging wall is holding. I'm under a stull that's stopping it from falling on top of me."

Relief flowed through him. "Great. Any indication of air supply?"

"Dust still too thick. I'm turning off my light to conserve it. Need water worse."

"I know. Look, you just rest."

"C-can't. Got to try and get rocks off legs."

Slade nodded. "The fire department is coming with oxygen gear. As soon as they arrive, I'm going to find you, Cat. For now, just conserve your energy."

She knew Slade was right, but she was shivering from the overwhelming dampness around her. As dry as her mouth and throat were, the moisture was seeping through to her bones. She shut off the light and slowly began to remove one rock at a time from the back of her legs. Only her left hand was undamaged. Movement of her right arm sent such a spasm of pain up Cat's side that she lost consciousness.

Cat was used to darkness; when she constructed a mine shaft, she was constantly in the darkened earth with only a safety lamp and lighted hard hat to illuminate her way. But rarely had she gone without any light at all, and now the dark was as suffocating as the dust that hung around her. A shiver rippled through her, the darkness like fingers of fear closing around her throat. Cat tasted her panic and concentrated on removing the rocks from her thigh, gradually releasing herself from the entrapment.

Minutes dragged by. *And each minute seems like a lifetime,* Cat realized. She clung to the hope that Slade would call again. Just to hear another human voice eased the terror that was intensified by the dark. Her breath came in painful, ragged gasps; each one feeling as if a knife was being plunged through her lungs. Sweat mingled with dust as it trickled down her face, stinging her eyes. Resting until the dizziness passed, Cat knew she would have to use her right hand to start removing the debris from her right leg. An involuntary cry tore from her contorted lips as she pushed the first rock off her thigh. Blackness closed in on her and she rested her brow against her left arm, sobbing.

"Over here!" Slade motioned the first of two arriving volunteer fire department pumpers toward the opening of the mine. Graham reluctantly got out of his car and met the chief, who was dressed in a white helmet and turnout gear. *Finally,* Slade thought, moving toward the fire chief. In moments he had established his identity and was given an air pack and mask. He took a safety lamp and settled the hard hat on his head, then entered the mine. His heart rate picked up. How far down the crosscut had the cave-in taken place? He mentally began to calculate the possible scenarios he might find. If there was a huge wall of debris, it might take days before they could reach Cat. He prayed it was the opposite—that the bulk of the cave-in had occurred behind her and only a thin wall stood between her and freedom.

Chapter 2

Slade found the wall of rock near the second timber support in the crosscut and carefully examined the timbers around him. They were sturdy and did not appear stressed. That meant mining equipment such as drills and augers could be moved into the mine to begin removing the debris without fear of another avalanche. The dust was still thick as Slade breathed in the sweet flow of oxygen through his face mask. Sweat trickled down his temples, following the line of his jaw. Some of his fear for Cat slipped away; most of the rock and dirt that had fallen was in small chunks, and easily handled by picks, shovels and wheelbarrows. Rescue would come more quickly.

Slade crouched by one wall of the crosscut, watching as a constant stream of water disappeared into the wall. He knew that if it was getting through, life-bearing oxygen could also be carried into the chamber where

Cat was trapped. Pulling out the radio, Slade attempted contact with her. He waited patiently, repeating his call three times before she answered. Cat's voice was tight and hoarse, and Slade knew she was in a hell of a lot of pain.

"How's my girl doing?"

A choked sound came over the radio. "Hanging—in there."

"Mining engineers always did have more guts than brains," he told her wryly. "I'm outside the wall where you're trapped, Cat. Give me a status report."

"Oxygen level seems the same. There's—running water to my left."

"Outstanding. How about you?"

"Would it do any good to tell you?"

"Don't play that game with me. I know I can't get to you yet, but I want to know the extent of your injuries and if you're feeling worse."

"I'll bet you use that line on every woman you meet, Donovan."

He grinned, but it didn't reach his narrowed eyes as he continued to appraise the wall of debris before him. "With you, I wouldn't use a line. Come on, level with me. How are you doing?"

"I've got the rocks off my legs and I managed to turn over. The right side of the tunnel wall looks weak and the stull above my head keeps creaking and groaning."

Slade scowled. That meant that even Cat's chamber could cave in, burying her under tons of rubble. Urgency thrummed through him. "How's that concussion you're sporting?"

"Not—good. I keep passing out. Very sleepy when

I shouldn't be. I was sleeping until you called. The scratchy sounds from the radio woke me up."

Damn it! She had suffered a worse head injury than he had first thought. "Okay," Slade soothed, keeping his voice steady. "How's your ribs?"

"If I don't breathe, I feel great."

She had spunk, he'd give her that. "And when you do?"

"Feels like someone's shoved a knife up under my right rib cage."

"Think you've got compound fractures?" If she did, the broken bone could conceivably puncture the lung if she moved around too much.

"I can feel blood there. I don't know. It hurts too much to touch the area and find out."

"Stay still if you can." It was either busted ribs or a punctured lung. Or both.

"Right."

"Do you have a water source?" If she had oxygen and water, Cat could last a long time. But if she had undetected internal injuries, time could prove to be their enemy. Cat needed immediate medical attention.

"Y-yes, a small stream along the left wall. All the amenities, Donovan."

"Except you don't have me. And I intend to remedy that situation shortly. Tell me, how many posts are in your chamber?" There was a post for every ten feet of spacing.

"One, Donovan. And it's not looking very healthy."

"You know enough to place yourself under it, with your back up against it, don't you?"

"Y-yes. Once I feel up to crawling over there, I'll do it."

"Can't you walk over to it?"

"Too dizzy. I'd fall and skin my knees."

He almost smiled. "Wouldn't want you to skin up those pretty knees."

"You're full of Texas baloney, Donovan."

He laughed. "I told you before, Cat, with you, I'm honest."

"Sure, an honest geologist. That'll be the day."

"Guess I'll have to prove it to you, won't I?"

"Right now I need a knight on a white charger. Come and get me, Donovan."

"Would you settle for thirty firemen, fifty miners and some drilling equipment instead?"

"Sounds wonderful."

He heard the sudden wobble in Cat's voice, as if she were close to tears. Slade tightened his grip around the radio. "Look, it appears that about ten feet of earth and rock are separating us, Cat. Unless we run into some limestone sheets weighing a ton or more, we ought to be able to reach you within twenty-four hours."

"Slade?"

Slade blinked the sweat from his eyes, hearing the fear in Cat's voice for the first time. "What is it, sweetheart?"

"C-could you contact my parents? Tell them what's happened? Especially my brother Rafe? They live in Colorado. The Triple K Ranch. If I give you the phone number, could you call them? Please?"

"Sure, anything you want."

Relief cracked her voice. "T-thanks. Here's the number."

Slade committed it to memory. "I'm signing off, Cat. The miners will be here any minute. I've got Graham's permission to organize and run this rescue operation. If you need anything, call. Otherwise I'll contact you in about an hour."

"Just let me know if you can reach my family."

"I'll personally make the call. Graham's got a phone in his car."

"Thanks, Slade. It means a lot to me…."

"I can tell." As he left the dankness of the mine, his mind shifted to another matter. Slade knew very few geologists or mining engineers who had sunk roots and had a family or children. He also knew from reading articles on Cat Kincaid that she wasn't married. As Slade got to his feet and began his trek to the adit, he wondered what man in his right mind would let someone as rare as Cat Kincaid out of his sight, much less out of his life. There was a special quality about her that he longed to explore. She was like an emerald mine waiting to be discovered: enticing, mysterious and filled with rich promise.

Gray light filtered through the adit, telling him he was near the opening. Well, he'd discovered one thing about Cat: family meant a great deal to her. Rafe was obviously a brother she could look up to, admire and lean on in times of trouble. Lucky guy, he told himself enviously.

As Slade walked out into the pall of rain, he glared at the gray sky overhead. They didn't need more water; it would loosen more dirt and the rain would trickle through the weakened limestone, making the rescue effort even more precarious than before. Slade had good instincts, and his gut sense had often saved his life in the past. Now, that voice screamed out that another cave-in was near. His instincts also warned him that if this was Cat's first cave-in, she would need emotional support to get back the courage to someday walk into the darkness of another mine.

* * *

Cat could barely move her head. She sat with her back against the rough, splintered surface of the post. Five hours had elapsed. Slade had called once an hour and sweet God in heaven, how she came to rely on him; he was her support system against the fear that threatened to consume her. Each passing hour made it become harder to control her rising panic.

Her spirits had plummeted when Slade had not been able to raise anyone at her parents' ranch right away. Cat felt alone and vulnerable in a way she'd never before experienced. Rafe—she needed Rafe's steadying presence. He was always the one to get them out of a jam when they were kids growing up in the Rocky Mountain wilderness. There had been times when she was scared to death, but because Rafe reassured her that it would be all right, she took dangerous chances with him. When Slade informed her he couldn't reach anyone at the Triple K, her fears loomed up again.

Slade had told her he had the first shift with the miners clearing away the debris. Cat couldn't hear the strike of pickaxs or the grind of huge auger drill bits boring holes to loosen the soft base so it could be shoveled away. The wall, Slade had said, was at least ten feet thick, perhaps twenty. It could, at worst, be days before she could be rescued.

At 10:00 a.m., Slade was able to make contact with the Kincaid Ranch. After a tense conversation, he made his way to the wall and called Cat. After four tries, she still didn't answer and Slade grew worried. Another five calls. Nothing. Had Cat passed out? Was she sleeping because of the concussion? Slade tried to contain his apprehension.

* * *

Cat finally floated out of unconsciousness and weakly raised her left arm. The luminous dials on her Rolex told her she had been asleep for nearly six hours. She lay on the hard pebbled floor on her left side to ease the pressure on her right. Experimentally, Cat lightly ran her fingers over her ribs, feeling how swollen her flesh had become beneath her damp canvas jacket. Not good, she thought blearily. The radio clicked, telling her that Slade was trying to contact her.

The radio lay near her head and she depressed the button. "S-Slade?"

"Cat? My God, are you all right?"

A grimace pulled at her lips. "Fine. Went to sleep, didn't I?"

"Yeah. Six hours. You scared the hell out of me."

"S-sorry."

"Don't worry about it. Listen, I got hold of your family and everyone's flying out here to see you. They'll be landing soon and I've arranged to have someone meet them at the nearest airport. Your parents, brother, sister and her husband are coming."

Tears leaked down her face and she couldn't trust her voice.

"The whole family's coming?"

He laughed. "Yeah. I'm impressed. Not many families would fly to the rescue."

"We're close."

"How are you holding up?"

"I've had better days, Donovan. How are things out there?"

"We've got thirty men on line for you, sweetheart. We're hauling about a ton of dirt and rock an hour. I'm shoring the shaft up with new post and stull every three feet as we go."

Cat nodded, trying to lick her dry lips. "How many tons do you figure is between you and me?"

Slade's voice was apologetic. "About fifty tons of material. If we can keep up the pace I've set, we'll have you out of there in roughly fifty hours."

Fifty more hours in the damp darkness. It seemed like an eternity. Could she control her fear? It was so black, she couldn't even see her hand if she held it up in front of her nose. And she was thirsty. Her tongue felt swollen, her throat rough as sandpaper. She would have to crawl the width of the footwall to sip that trickle of life-giving water along the opposite wall.

"You're doing a good job, Donovan. I'm going to owe you a lot by the time you get me out of here."

"Don't worry, I intend to collect for my services, lady."

Cat smiled, allowing his voice to cover her like a blanket of balm. "Whatever you want, Donovan, within reason."

Slade chuckled indulgently. "Don't worry, the price won't be so high you won't want to pay it. Look, I'll check in on you an hour from now."

Panic nibbled at her crumbling control and Cat gripped the radio, dreading the return to silence. "For some reason, I trust you, Donovan. I shouldn't, but I do."

His voice came back, husky but velvet to soothe her shattered composure. "Hold that thought, Cat. I'll be here for you, that's a promise."

Two things happened in the next hour. The entire Kincaid family arrived at the Emerald Lady, and Slade could not raise Cat again on his radio. Rafe Kincaid, the brother, was close to exploding, firing questions faster than Slade could answer them. The tall, strapping Colorado rancher took off his Stetson, rolled up his sleeves, grabbed a hard hat and went into the mine to help in the rescue effort. So did Jim Tremain, Dal's husband. Slade liked Cat's family; Sam and Inez Kincaid, Cat's parents, and Dal Tremain, Cat's younger sister, helped to set up a place where coffee could be dispensed in the nearby shack and sandwiches could be made for the hardworking rescue crews. Millie, the Kincaid's housekeeper, who was apparently an integral part of the family, watched Dal's months-old baby, Alessandra, while Dal worked.

Within an hour of their arrival, the Kincaid family had organized chow lines for the hungry miners. Meanwhile, Slade had returned to the mine to continue directing the rescue. Slade tried to reassure Rafe that his sister had probably lost consciousness again due to her concussion. Rafe glowered at him, as if it were his fault, but Slade shrugged it off. Let the rancher expend his anger on the pickax he was wielding, instead of blowing up at him.

Cat tasted blood. She lay on her left side, shivering. What time was it? How many hours had passed since she had last lost consciousness? The luminous dials of her watch blurred and she blinked. Her vision was being affected and that frightened her. The radio was pressed protectively to her breast and she shakily turned it on, the red light glowing brightly in the darkness. Almost immediately, Slade's voice came through, soothing her fragmented nerves.

"Cat?"

She heard the anxiety in Slade's voice and was grateful for his undiminished caring.

"I'm alive," she announced, her voice weaker than it had been earlier.

"Thank God. What happened? You've been out ten hours."

"I can't hang on to consciousness, Slade. Keep blacking out."

"Don't worry about it. Let me go get your parents. Your family arrived some time ago. They're helping in the relief efforts. Rafe and Jim Tremain have been using a pickax and shovel the last ten hours. That's quite a family you've got. Hold on…"

Tears began to stream down her grimy cheeks when she heard her father's gruff voice, and then her mother's. Cat tried not to cry. She tried to sound brave and calm and steady, everything she wasn't. But when Rafe was put on, her voice cracked, betraying her real emotions. Whether it was the avalanche of tightly withheld feelings or the strain of her entrapment, Cat was barely coherent. There was so much she wanted to say; instead tears flowed in a warm stream down her cheeks, and her voice was wobbly and fragmented.

"S-Slade…" she choked.

"He's done a fine job, Cat," Rafe came back. "He knows what he's doing. Look, you just hang on. We've got an ambulance and paramedic crew standing by to take you to the closest hospital. Keep your chin up, Baby Sis. We all love you. Just remember all the times you and I dared danger and won. It'll be the same this time. I promise you."

Rafe grimly handed the radio back to Donovan. Neither man looked at the other; if they had, they would have seen tears forming in the corners of their eyes. Slade's face was slack with exhaustion and streaked with dirt and mud. He took the radio from Rafe.

"Cat?"

"Y-yes?"

"Thirty-five hours to go, sweetheart. You've got a passel of people out here who love you. Just remember that."

Grim, unshaven men, their eyes bloodshot and red-rimmed from too much dust, their hands bruised and bloodied with scrapes and cuts, continued on. Day had turned to night and then day again. The rain had stopped and so had Cat's infrequent radio exchanges. Yet, the Kincaids' courage inspired the rescuers, and there wasn't a man among them who slept more than a few hours between the mandatory six-hour shifts at the end of a shovel, a wheelbarrow or pickax. No one complained, and Slade found that phenomenal.

Rubbing his bleary eyes, Slade held up his watch. A portable generator provided light in the damp expanse of the mine. Five hours…five hours before they broke through and made contact. Was Cat on the left wall near the stream? No stranger to cave-ins, he worried about her dehydrating. The people who knew of his escapes had said he'd had nine lives. Well, Cat had better have nine lives; she'd need them to survive this one.

Cat wasn't sure what pulled her from her floating state. Was it the whoosh of fresh air into the staleness of the chamber or the frantic sound of steel-bladed shovels tearing a hole through the last of the wall that held her captive? Or was it actually recognizing Rafe's hushed voice, and Slade's? Whatever it was, she pulled on the last of her reserves and turned her head, which was now lying in a trickle of water, toward the men's urgent voices.

The light from Slade's helmet slashed through the thick silence of the chamber. His eyes widened as he found Cat covered with filth and dust, her hair caked with mud around her pale, translucent face. She lay on her left side, stretched out across the stream of water. Thank God she'd had the foresight to move to the water; all she had to do was turn her face and sip from the shallow stream. His admiration for her survival instincts rose. Next, Rafe came through the six-foot opening, followed by a paramedic with a thin oak body board and a neck brace.

Slade reached her first, his hand closing protectively over Cat's shoulder. He leaned over from his kneeling position, his face close to hers. He whispered her name twice before he saw her long dark lashes flutter and barely open.

Cat saw a lopsided smile pull at Slade's mouth; his face was tense, his eyes burned out with bone-deep exhaustion. She saw a flame of hope in them, too. She tried to form his name on her parched, cracked lips, but only a hoarse sound issued forth.

"Shh, sweetheart. Your knights in shining armor have arrived. All I want you to do is lie very still while we get you on this body board and truss you up like a Christmas goose."

She wasn't able to comprehend all that Slade said as he leaned over her. The warmth of his breath coupled with his husky voice flowed like balm across her, filling her with new strength. A small smile tugged at Cat's mouth. She felt Slade's long fingers close gently across her shoulder, and she knew he understood.

An incredible aura of care surrounded Cat during those twenty minutes when the three men worked on her. She was conscious for minutes at a time, lapsing in and out of the arms of darkness. Rafe's voice or his familiar touch on her hair would draw her back to consciousness. She began to anticipate Slade's knowing, professional touch as he and the paramedic turned her over, placing her on the body board. She had grown used to the pain in her right side, but the callused pressure of Slade's fingers as he fitted the brace around her neck brought tears to her eyes.

The jab of a needle brought her to greater awareness, but once they had her strapped securely to the thin oak board Cat lost consciousness again.

Slade handed Sam Kincaid another cup of coffee as they stood in the waiting room of the surgical floor of the hospital. He wasn't sure who looked worse: he or Rafe. They were muddy, their hair plastered down from untold hours of sweat. Every muscle in Slade's body screamed for rest and the luxury of a hot shower. He wrinkled his nose; the brackish odor of the mine and his sour sweat smell surrounded him. He glanced at his watch. An hour ago Cat had been taken to the emergency room, attended by a number of physicians and nurses. None of the family had been allowed to go with her. Why didn't someone come out and tell them how she was?

Slade hadn't tried to hide his own emotions as he'd sat alongside Rafe in the ambulance. Cat had been chalk white; even her freckles had looked washed out. Her once-beautiful sable-brown hair was a stringy mat of mud and blood. There'd been a three-inch gash across her scalp, and she had bled heavily, but he was more worried about the skull beneath her scalp. Just how bad was her concussion? Judging from Cat's pallor and her prolonged bouts of unconsciousness, it was serious.

A doctor came through the double swinging doors, his face unreadable. He headed for the elder Kincaid. The entire family, with Millie and Slade, surrounded the doctor before he drew to a stop.

"Mr. Kincaid?"

Sam Kincaid nodded. "Doctor? How's my girl?"

"I'm Dr. Scott," he said, extending his hand. "Cathy is in serious condition, Mr. Kincaid. She's suffered two broken ribs. She's extremely dehydrated and we've got her on two I.V.s to restabilize her."

Slade closed his fist. His voice was strained. "And her head injury, Dr. Scott?"

Scott's narrow face became impassive. "Severe concussion. She keeps lapsing in and out of consciousness." His brow furrowed. "Is your name Slade?"

"Yes. Slade Donovan."

"Cathy is asking for you. We need to try and keep her awake. I want to keep her from going into a coma."

Inez Kincaid's thin face grew still. "A coma, doctor?"

"Yes. If I can keep Slade with her, she might rally enough to fight back and stay awake. We've got that portion of her head packed in dry ice to reduce the swelling." He looked up at Slade. "Let's get you cleaned up a little, son, and then, if you don't mind, I'd like you to remain with Cathy for a while."

Slade nodded. He followed Dr. Scott down the immaculate hall to a lounge. A nurse gave him a green surgical shirt and a pair of trousers to replace his filthy clothes. Slade took a quick hot shower and fought the deep drowsiness that tried to claim him. It wasn't yet time to sleep off the past forty-eight hours he'd been awake.

The nurse, a petite blonde with blue eyes, smiled once he emerged from the lounge. "Now you look like a doctor, Mr. Donovan. Follow me, please." She took him to the intensive-care unit, where each patient's room was enclosed on three sides with glass panels. Cathy looked dead. She matched the color of her sheets. Her hair had been washed clean and an ice pack placed carefully against her skull. The sigh of oxygen and the beeps of the cardiac unit made Slade grow wary. So many machines to monitor her fragile hold on life, he thought.

The nurse drew up a chair alongside Cat's bed. "You can sit here, Mr. Donovan."

Slade thanked her, but moved to the bed. He reached out and slipped his hand across Cat's limp, cool fingers. They had washed her free of all the filth.

"You look a little on the thin side, Mr. Donovan. They said you and the Kincaids worked but didn't eat. I'll have someone run down to the cafeteria and bring you dinner."

Slade smiled, grateful for the nurse's thoughtfulness. "Thanks," he replied. Then he shifted his attention to Cat. Funny, Slade told Cat silently as he cupped her fingers between his to warm them, you were a stranger to me three days ago. A lump rose in his throat. What is it about you that touches me so?

Perhaps it was the vulnerability of her features. Or

the lips that reminded him of a lush, exotic jungle orchid he'd seen in Brazil—cherry red, even now in her present condition. Or perhaps it was her heart-shaped face, or the wide cheekbones that gave her eyes an almost tilted look. A smile eased the taut planes of Slade's face as he followed the coverlet of freckles from one cheek across her broken nose to the other cheek.

Slade reached over, lightly tracing the bump on her nose. How did she break such a pretty nose? And when had she broken it? He had so many questions to ask her, so much he didn't know about her that he wanted to know. "Cat?" he said softly. "Can you hear me? It's Slade. I've come for you. I want you to fight back." His fingers tightened against hers as he reluctantly straightened up. He blinked. Was he imagining things, or had her lashes fluttered in response to his hushed request?

When Cat awoke, she was clear at once as to where she was. The murmuring of the equipment caught her attention first. Then she forced open her weighted lids. She became aware of the broken snore of a man nearby. And then she felt the warm, callused fingers that enclosed her hand. Despite the pain, Cat turned her head to the right. Her eyes widened. Slade Donovan lay slumped in a chair, snoring, his chin sagging toward his chest and his hand gripping hers. A flood of warmth coursed through her and Cat closed her eyes. She was alive. Slade had dragged her back from the depths of the mine.

Her voice cracked when she tried to call his name. Cat used what little strength she had in her hand and squeezed Slade's fingers. She watched him awaken from the heavy sleep. Her heart wrenched as she saw the darkness shadowing his red-rimmed eyes. His face was gaunt and she saw the stress plainly carved on the stubbled, angular planes of his face.

Slade blinked, his hand tightening on her fingers. "Cat?" He whispered her name unbelievingly. Standing, he leaned over the bed, one hand cupping her cheek as he gazed disbelievingly into her barely opened eyes. "I'll be damned, you're awake."

She gave him a weak smile. "I-is this a dream?"

Slade laughed unsurely, his blue eyes burning fiercely with happiness. "If it is, sweetheart, then we're dreaming together." He reached over and pressed a buzzer to alert the nurse's desk. "Hold on, there's a whole passel of doctors who are anxious to see you awake."

Cat was thirsty, her mouth gummy. "What about my family?"

"They're here, waiting for you to open those beautiful emerald eyes of yours." He pressed a kiss to her cool, damp brow. "Welcome back to the world of the living. This calls for one hell of a celebration."

In the next two days, Slade was absorbed into the Kincaid clan. He ate with the family and shared rooms with them at a local motel. At breakfast on the third morning, Sam Kincaid sat with his family, a frown marring his features.

"Dr. Scott says Cat will need a place to recuperate. He's worried about her concussion and thinks she ought to be under some kind of supervision for at least eight weeks." Sam gave his wife a tender look. "With your hip operation coming up in two weeks, we won't be able to give Cat the care she needs."

Rafe's mouth twisted. "I've got the room; it's just the timing, Dad. We've had these Bureau of Land Mines investigations going on for the past few months, and they've thrown off our schedule for a while. Family comes first. I'll take Cat in; she's more important. If I made the time for the BLM, I can sure as hell make time for my sister."

Slade suddenly brightened. "I can help. I think, under the circumstances, Cat would be better off with me." The corners of Rafe's mouth turned down and Slade knew instinctively that Rafe felt this was strictly a family matter; outsiders weren't needed. Slade directed the remainder of his proposal to Rafe to win his approval, knowing the family would then agree to Cat's staying with him. He folded his large hands on the table. This reminded Slade of poker games. Some he had lost; others he had won. This time, the stakes were high, and he had never wanted to win more. Slade didn't question why he wanted Cat on his ranch to recuperate. Since the beginning, Cat had touched some inner chord of his. He wanted—no—demanded the opportunity to get to know her. His reasons for meeting her in the first place would take secondary importance. He put on his most serious expression and spoke in a low voice.

"I know you've only been allowed fifteen minutes at a time to visit with Cat. And she may or may not have been conscious enough to mention our relationship. I have a small ranch in southwest Texas. Del Rio, to be exact. In addition, my next-door neighbors, Matt and Kai Travis, can be of great help, if we need them. Kai's a physiotherapist and a nurse for the local grade school. I have a qualified nurse three miles down the road from my ranch and the perfect place for Cat to stay." Slade's voice dropped. "I think Cat's going to take a lot of attention in order to get back on her feet. I've been in three mine cave-ins myself and I know what they do up here," he said, pointing to his head.

"I care a hell of a lot for Cat. Those hours spent with her while she was buried were some of the worst of my life." He felt a tinge of guilt for implying that he and Cat had a relationship. But it wasn't a total lie, he rationalized. "Having been buried myself, I'm in a pretty good position to help Cat." His voice grew tight with undisguised emotion. "I can help her. I can get her up and over some of the reactions she's going to have because of this experience."

Rafe rubbed his recently shaven jaw. "Kinda like falling off a horse and getting scared to mount up afterward?"

Slade nodded, sensing the subtle shift of acceptance to his proposal. "Yes, only worse. Cave-ins affect everyone differently. Nightmares are common, and with her concussion, someone is going to have to monitor her closely so she doesn't sleepwalk or something. And that does happen." He looked at father and son. "I realize this is a family matter, but in this case, I think I can provide the type of care Cat is going to need."

Sam glanced over at his son. "Why don't we let Cat have a say in this before we decide for her?"

Slade held up his hand. "I really don't think that's necessary. I'm positive Cat will want to come home with me. Besides, I've got my twin-engine plane at the airport ten miles from here. I could fly her back in comfort while you'd have to make an awful lot of special arrangements to try the same thing. I'm sure Cat would like to be with me. I know how close she is with the family, but each of you have a lot of things going on right now. Hell, I'm between job assignments. And even if I wasn't, I'd drop what I was doing to come and take care of Cat."

Rafe looked hesitant, but shrugged his powerful shoulders. "Sounds like it may be the best thing for Cat, and that's the most important thing right now, Dad."

Sam Kincaid stared at Slade for a long time, mulling over the request. "It's settled then. Cat will go home with you, Slade."

Slade felt heat rise in his cheeks as he grasped the rancher's hand. "Thanks, Sam. None of you will regret your decision, believe me." A fierce wave of protectiveness nearly overwhelmed Slade as he rose from the table. He was shocked by his offer to care for Cat, yet nothing he'd ever done had ever felt so right. Gratefully, he shook each man's hand.

Inez kissed her daughter's cheek. Cat had been transferred to a private room and the entire family, minus Millie, who, since the baby wasn't allowed in the room, was in the lounge, stood around her bed.

"You take care, honey," Inez said. She patted Cat's hand gently.

Cat blinked up at her mother. "You're all leaving?" There was a catch in her voice. She saw Rafe nod, his cowboy hat clasped between his roughened fingers.

Slade went to the other side of the bed and grasped Cat's left hand, while giving her a devastating smile meant to neutralize her questions. He hadn't talked to her about the arrangements and he knew the Kincaids hadn't either. Cat wasn't even aware of the agreement, but in all honesty, Slade felt Cat would thrive in the environment he could provide her. His initial reason for contacting her had been to offer her a lucrative business deal. Now, that all seemed unimportant.

"Everything's been taken care of, Cat. All you have to do is just lie there, look beautiful and heal up." He patted her hand, giving her a conspiratorial wink. Her green eyes widened as she stared blankly up at him.

Rafe leaned down, kissing her hair. "I'll be in touch, Cat. Slade's given us your phone number and I'll give you a call every couple of days to see how you're coming along." He smiled. "I'll keep you posted on what Goodyear and Nar are up to. They've had a lot of run-ins with each other lately."

Sam Kincaid was next, giving his daughter a slight smile. "You're in the best of hands, Cat."

"But—"

"Now, now," Slade soothed, "just relax, Cat." He wished they would hurry through their farewells and leave before Cat upset his carefully constructed applecart. Dal and Jim Tremain came over, saying goodbye.

"Slade promised us you'd be in good hands," Dal told her sister. "We'd love to have you stay with us, but I don't think you'd get any rest with the baby around. I hope you understand."

Cat looked from Dal to Slade. His features looked suspiciously beatific.

"Well, uh, sure I understand. And Alessandra probably takes up all your time, anyway."

Dal looked relieved that she understood and pressed another kiss on Cat's waxen cheek. "Listen, we'll call you once you get to Texas. Slade's ranch sounds perfect for you."

Slade's ranch? Cat turned too quickly, pain causing

her to gasp. She shut her eyes, all the questions purged from her mind. Slade gave her a game smile and waved goodbye to the departing family.

"Well, we'll be seeing you, Cat," her dad said, opening the door. "We'll call you once a week and see how you're comin' along. Bye, honey…"

Cat tried to speak, to beg them to stay. When the pain finally subsided, the door had shut and silence filled the void. She looked up at Slade, her eyes narrowed. Slade was still holding her left hand, his fingers warming her cooler ones. She wanted to jerk out of his grasp but had better sense than to try it, knowing what the movement would cost her in terms of pain.

"All right, Donovan, what is going down?"

"Donovan? You were calling me Slade before."

Cat compressed her lips, and set her jaw in a well-known Kincaid line that spelled trouble. "What cards do you have up that sleeve of yours? Everyone thinks I'm going to your ranch. No one's asked me. If you think you can shanghai me, you've got another thing coming."

Slade tried to look properly chastised and continued to run his thumb in a feather-light circle on the back of her hand. "Shanghai you?" He groaned and raised his eyes dramatically to the ceiling. "Cat, I simply volunteered my plane and my ranch as a place where you can properly recuperate." He stole a glance at her to see what effect his teasing was having. Absolutely none, he realized with a lurch. Slade girded himself for battle as spots of color came to Cat's cheeks and an emerald flame leaped to life in her eyes. She might be sick, but she wasn't helpless.

Slade tried to nip her reaction in the bud. "Listen to me, this is no time to get upset, Cat. I told your family that a nurse is three miles away from my ranch. Kai Travis and her husband, Matt, are good friends of mine. Dr. Scott said you'd need a warm, dry climate and the help of a nurse from time to time. Plus," he went on quickly, trying to stay ahead of her opposition, "your brother, Rafe, has been under a BLM investigation for the past few months and he's got his hands full trying to catch up on the ranch work. He wouldn't be able to devote enough time to you. Your mother's hip operation is in two weeks." Slade shrugged and managed a hopeful smile. "I offered my ranch because I can take good care of you, Cat, while you convalesce. I did what I felt was best for us at the time."

"Us?" came the strangled response. "There is no 'us'!"

Looking contrite, Slade released her hand and walked to the end of the bed, holding her outraged stare. "Yes, us."

Cat's mouth dropped open. And then she quickly closed it into a thin line. "You and I are complete strangers."

Slade had the good grace to look embarrassed. "Maybe we were a week ago, but I don't feel that way about you now. Not after everything we've gone through together." His voice became husky. "Before, I respected your work as a mining engineer. And then, when you were trapped, I saw and felt your courage. We both know the chances of your surviving that cave-in were pretty slim."

At the mention of the cave-in, a chill wound through Cat. She tried to throw it off, but a suffocating fear rose up into her throat, choking her. Panic followed on its heels and Cat struggled to pretend nothing was wrong. My God, she was breaking out in a cold sweat! What was wrong with her? The fear she felt was all-consuming as it flowed darkly through her. Shakily, she wiped her sweaty brow, refusing to look at Slade.

Finally back in control, she spoke. "That still doesn't give you any right to tell my family that they aren't needed, Donovan!" Her voice cracked. "I want my family, not you."

His face softened and Slade came to her side, brushing his knuckles lightly against her tear-stained cheek. "I know how fragile you really are, Cat, remember? I've been in cave-ins myself and lived to tell about it. I told your family that I knew what you were going to go through and I felt I was the best one for the job."

"I'm not your responsibility, damn it!"

"Don't get excited, Cat. The doctors want you to rest."

"Then you shouldn't have bullied your way into a family situation and taken over like you did!" She was breathing hard, each expansion of her ribs a fiery agony. Sweat glistened on her taut features and she lay back, her fists clenched. She turned her stormy green gaze on him. "You're not doing this out of the kindness of your heart. I wish I could remember where I'd heard your name before. Then, I could put this together."

Slade winced. He wasn't sure himself why he was doing it. Sure, there was his business proposition, but that wasn't his primary reason for wanting her nearby. He felt like a greedy robber, stealing time to get to know Cat on a personal level. "You've a right to be upset and angry," Slade said, choosing his words carefully. "Rafe wanted to ask you if you wanted to go with me or come to the Triple K. For that, we owe you an apology. Rather, I do. Because I persuaded them that you'd be happy to come to Del Rio, Texas, with me." He held her angry gaze. "I may kick around the world, Cat, but I do have some roots. The ranch is nothing fancy, but it's nice. You're not out of the woods yet with your injuries, and I convinced your family that with qualified medical help nearby, my ranch would be better for you. Besides, when you get better, there's a business deal I'd like to discuss with you."

Cat eyed him suspiciously, somewhat mollified by his explanation. "I don't know… Let me think for a moment, Donovan."

He shrugged shyly. "All I'm asking is to be allowed to help you for eight weeks, Cat. Hey, this isn't a jail sentence. If you don't like the place, you can leave. No hard feelings. It's just that you can't be by yourself and I have the time plus the room."

Cat could have cried with frustration, but she had to admit that Slade was right. He had saved her life, and if she hadn't been so arrogant, she'd have listened to his warning.

"All right, Donovan," she muttered, "you saved my life. I didn't realize my mother was going to have an operation so soon." She rubbed the tears out of her eyes. "I hate feeling like an invalid! I don't like to be a burden on anyone, especially you. I don't call getting a crabby, sick mining engineer just payment for all that you've done for me."

His serious face creased in a boyish smile. "I happen to like crabby, sick mining engineers. For the next few months you're going to rest and get plied with a lot of stories told by one of the best storytellers in west Texas: me. You're to be a guest at my ranch, Cat. I just hope you like my company as much as I'm going to enjoy yours."

Cat refused to look at him. "I'm not a small child that needs to be told bedtime stories."

Slade's grin was wide, revealing white teeth. "We'll see," was all he said. He glanced at his watch. "Time for a nap. You close those beautiful eyes, and I'm going to talk with Dr. Scott about what time we can get you out of this godforsaken cell."

Cat wrinkled her nose. "Why should I be so anxious to trade one kind of prison for another?"

Slade came around and pressed a quick kiss to her fragrant hair. "It's really me who is your prisoner."

"Want to bet?" And yet, another part of her relaxed. If nothing else, the cave-in had taught Cat how alone a person could really be. Slade had reached her during those terrible hours, and her heart knew it even if her mind tried to tell her differently. "Don't mind me," she muttered in apology. "I'm not normally this crabby. I do appreciate your offer to take me in."

Slade enjoyed her pout; her lower lip was full and petulant. The urge to capture her mouth and gentle it beneath his was growing, but Slade gently tucked the desire aside. "I understand your apprehension, Cat. Things have moved mighty fast today. But you sit back and concentrate on getting well. Let me take care of you for a while."

With a merry look, Slade opened her door. "Rest. You're getting dark shadows beneath those lovely eyes of yours. Just dream of the Mourning Dove Ranch."

Cat watched Slade leave, enjoying his irrepressible, little-boy spirit that magically coaxed her out of her darkest moments. She shut her eyes, aware that the monstrous fear she had wanted to bury had miraculously vanished. Was it because of Slade? With a groan, Cat tried to look objectively at her motives for capitulating to him. He had vaguely mentioned discussing a business deal with her when she was better. Cat clung to that bare-branch offering and turned away from other feelings toward him.

Since when had she ever backed down from the demands of life? Only once. When she and geologist Greg Anderson had called off their relationship. But this was different, a voice whispered to Cat. Not only that, she reluctantly conceded, she didn't have the emotional fortitude it took to wage the necessary battle to get out of Donovan's clutches. And clutches they were, Cat thought grimly. Or were they? She couldn't ignore the tender light that burned in his sapphire eyes every time he looked at her. Right now, as never before in her life, Cat needed help from someone other than herself. And Slade had offered that help to her. Instinctively, Cat knew that Slade could help rebuild her strength from the rubble of the mine cave-in.

Chapter 3

"**W**ell, Cathy, you're certainly going to be in good hands." Dr. Scott smiled as he looked through the release forms, while Cat sat patiently on the edge of the bed. With the help of one of the nurses, she had awkwardly pulled on a pair of cinnamon-colored slacks and a white tank top. Maine's summer weather was usually on the cool side, but at eight o'clock this bright August morning, it was already a sunny seventy degrees.

"We'll see about that, doctor," she told him dryly. Cat automatically touched her tightly taped ribs. Two of the lowest had been broken and if the break had been any higher, her breasts would have prevented the elastic torso wrap from being applied.

"Mr. Donovan's a paramedic, you know," the physician said, hurriedly scribbling his signature on the last paper.

"Is he?" Cat looked up with interest.

"Yes, a very capable one. I've given him a list of all the prescriptions you might need, Cathy. He's going to be watching you rather closely for the next couple of weeks because of your head injury. Let him know if you ever get dizzy."

Dizzy? The first time she'd sat up, she'd nearly keeled over. If it hadn't been for Slade's quick action, she would have fallen off the bed. At first, Cat had retreated from his watchfulness; she was unused to being confined by an ailing body and resented being taken care of. But after three days, Slade had remained his cheerful, positive self and Cat had had to beg him not to tell any more jokes. She had feared she would laugh out loud, and that awful, ripping pain would take her breath away. Slade's normally ebullient personality had sobered slightly, then shifted into a new gear—that of charming conversationalist.

A nurse arrived with the wheelchair for Cat's ride to the front doors of the hospital. "The dizziness may or may not be permanent," Dr. Scott warned, helping her into the chair. "The next two weeks will tell us quite a lot. Off you go, now. I understand you've an air trip ahead. Mr. Donovan's quite a good pilot."

Cat couldn't resist a smile. "Did he tell you that?"

"No, I saw his flight logbook sitting with some other items. Being a pilot myself, I got him talking. He's not only multiengine rated, he's up on all the instrumentation demands, too. Judging from the hours he's flown, I'll lay you odds he flies around the world. He certainly has a lot of stories to tell."

"Slade Donovan is a born storyteller, I suspect. Thank you, doctor, for everything."

"Have a good flight, Cathy. We'll be eager to hear how you're progressing."

At the curbside outside the hospital, the nurse eased the wheelchair to a halt. Slade was waiting next to the rental car for her. He was dressed in a freshly pressed blue shirt with epaulets on each shoulder. The shirt matched the color of his eyes, Cat thought. She had to stop herself from staring as if she were a gawky teenager instead of a woman older than thirty. His hair was dark and shining from a recent shower, his skin smooth of the stubble that always gave him a five o'clock shadow by four o'clock.

As Cat took his large hand and stood up, she suddenly saw Slade in a new light. His touch, as always, sent a warm rush through her. He had brought sunshine to her during her recent exile to Hades. She closed her eyes, allowing a fleeting feeling of dizziness to pass. Slade, observing her hesitation, moved closer to her left side, in case she should fall. Cat opened her eyes and raised her face to the sun.

"Do you know how good it feels to be outside again?" she asked, drawing in a deep breath of fresh air.

"Spoken like a true tunneler," Slade replied. His fingers tightened on her elbow. "Ready? I've got Maggie all fueled and waiting."

"Maggie?" Cat looked up at Slade tentatively.

Slade helped her into the front seat of the rental car and then shut the door. "Yeah, Maggie's my twin-engine Cessna. And she's as pretty as her name."

The sun shone warmly through the windows and a fragrant scent of pine drifted in, making the day magical for Cat. As Slade eased into the car, he flashed her a heart-stopping smile. "You'll like Maggie. She's built like a sleek greyhound. Red and white, lean and mean."

"The way you like your women, Donovan?" Now why had she made that remark? He had looked absolutely elated, as if flying were going to release him from his captive state on earth. Cat felt like a genuine wet blanket, but Donovan cheerfully snapped the safety belt across his lap and chest.

"Jealousy will get you nowhere. Maggie's big-hearted enough to embrace both of us. Now, young lady, we've got a light westerly wind and clear skies waiting for us. Ready?"

Yes, she was ready, Cat realized. Perhaps it was partly relief that they were putting miles between her and the mine that had almost claimed her life, but another part of her was ready for a new adventure. Cat closed her eyes, allowing the wind to flow across her, moving her hair languidly against her temple and neck. Slade's hand settled momentarily on her own.

"Okay?"

The concern in his voice soothed her. "I'm fine. Just enjoying my freedom, Donovan."

There was hurt evident in his voice. "My friends call me Slade."

Cat opened her eyes and studied his clean profile, from his straight brows to his finely shaped nose and mobile mouth. "After all we've been through together, I guess friend is a good word to use for us."

His hand left her fingers and he concentrated on his driving. Friend was only one term he applied to Cat. He also wanted to explore other possibilities. She affected him as no woman ever had before. "Friends," Slade murmured. "That's a good place for us to start."

"I hope you have a lot of patience," she warned, feeling suddenly awkward.

Slade pinned her with an intense look. "Why?"

"Because I'm not myself, Slade. I'm jumpy and I snap when I don't mean to."

He smiled. "Lady, I've been snapped at by the best of them. I regard our two-month vacation at my ranch as just one more adventure."

"Normally I'd agree with you. But I'm afraid you're getting the raw end of this deal, Slade. I'll give you one more chance to back off from your offer to let me use your ranch as my hospital for two months."

The road spilled out of the small town, a narrow gray asphalt ribbon among the pine-clad hills. "Not on your life, Cat. I like a woman who has wanderlust in her soul!"

A smile shadowed Cat's mouth as she met Slade's merry glance. "Folks like us have it in their blood, don't we? What's so surprising about finding someone like yourself?"

"You try so hard to hide what's deep inside you, Cat Kincaid. I keep trying to figure out who closed you up like a book under lock and key. But I know you're not like those rocks I hunt, without feeling." He laughed, a deep, resonant laugh. "You're like an elusive emerald: hard to find, dangerous to extract and fragile when being cut and polished into a gem."

Cat felt the heat rise in her cheeks. "It's the nature of my work that makes me quiet. You're a geologist, you should know that."

Slade knew, but he couldn't resist teasing her. She responded so quickly to the slightest amount of goading. He really shouldn't, because she was far from well and Dr. Scott had warned him about overtaxing Cat. "I know what you're saying, Cat, but I like to see that green fire leap into your eyes. I'll let you off the hook, though. Dr. Scott gave me a stern lecture about not picking on you…for now."

Cat closed her eyes, resting comfortably despite the tightness of the rib wrap. "That's big of you," she parried. "I suppose I ought to count my lucky stars for the reprieve."

"It's going to be a short one," he warned, shooting her a mischievous look.

Cat smiled. She knew he was baiting her again. He's good for me, she suddenly realized. But if the big, arrogant Texan knew that, he'd gloat. "What kind of pilot are you?" she asked, changing the subject.

"I got my license at Disneyland. Does that impress you?"

Laughter bubbled up in her throat but she squelched it, trying to avoid the subsequent pain. "You're so full of baloney. Come on, level with me."

"And if I did, would it make any difference?"

"My level of comfort would increase markedly if I knew more of your nefarious credentials." She suspected his credentials were far from nefarious, but enjoyed turning the tables on him for a change.

Slade appeared momentarily wounded. "Well, I have exactly 3,212 hours on my multiengine and I.F.R. ratings and have been qualified in twelve different aircraft during my short experience of flying."

"My comfort level is increasing," she admitted with a smile.

"Let's see. What else? The pilot is thirty-five, six feet four inches tall, single, roughishly handsome, makes a decent living, doesn't have any outstanding debts to speak of and currently is unattached." He looked squarely at her. "How's your comfort level now?"

"It just nosedived."

"Oh."

"I'd have felt better if you'd told me that you've flown around the world and are an excellent navigator."

"Well, I'm that, too."

"But for some reason, you thought your personal stats would be of more interest to me?"

"I don't want you to worry that you'd be a third wheel at the Mourning Dove Ranch. You're lucky— you'll be the only woman there besides Pilar, my manager's wife."

"Somehow, I don't quite know if that's lucky or unlucky, Donovan."

He grinned. "It's definitely lucky, Ms. Kincaid. Wait and see."

"Is that a threat or a promise?"

"Your choice. Which do you want it to be?"

"You're impossible, Slade, certifiably impossible."

"Yeah, that's what I've been told. But then, because of my impossible qualities, I did discover a couple of gem deposits over in Brazil." His voice grew softer. "Ever heard of the El Camino Mine, Ms. Kincaid?"

Cat blinked. The El Camino Mine had been splashed across all the mining and geology magazines two years earlier. It was, according to most geologists, one of the finest tourmaline discoveries in the world. The quality of the precious stones was almost flawless, and had sent excitement through the gem community. One fine deposit of watermelon tourmaline had set everyone on their ears. The pink stones without fractures were as rare as emeralds without flaws. She saw Slade's smile widen.

"Don't tell me…wait…you discovered that deposit! That's where I've heard your name before." Her thumping heart underscored her awe. "I almost ended up working at that site," Cat added in disbelief.

"I know. I was the one who tried to persuade the owners to hire you to sink the shafts." Slade shrugged. "But contracts are contracts; you were still building a mine shaft in Austria at the time. Just think, we almost rubbed elbows two years ago."

Cat was still shaking her head. "You discovered El Camino. I can't believe it."

"You'll wound my poetic soul with barbs like that."

"Somehow, I think very little penetrates that thick skin of yours."

"Mmm, careful. The right woman has open access to my tender heart and loving soul."

"You're going to make me laugh whether I want to or not, Slade. Now stop it."

He saw the faint smile at the corners of her lush mouth, an unspoiled mouth that needed taming. Cat wasn't like most women, he suspected. But then, he didn't expect her to be. She lived in a world of brawny miners, skilled in the reshaping of the earth, but resistant to women who chose to be more than bed partners and housekeepers. Slade knew by the set of Cat's jaw that she had endured much to succeed in her career, and he admired her for that. Like the roses that grew wild behind his ranch house, Cat had not only flowered, she had blossomed in the harsh environment.

Slade cornered the car gently, turning into the flight-service area of the airport. He pointed toward the tarmac. "Say hello to my number-two gal, Maggie."

Cat's eyes widened in appreciation as she stared at the sleek, aerodynamically designed Cessna. Slade might appear laid back, but he took good care of his airplane. Its gleaming white surface looked recently waxed, and the graceful red stripe running from the tail to the nose was a dark ruby color. The name on the fuselage read: Donovan's Services, Inc.

"Just what services do you perform?" she couldn't resist asking.

Slade put the car in park and pulled the key from the ignition. His grin was infuriating. "What service would you like rendered?"

Cat clamped her mouth shut, fiercely aware of the innuendo in his voice.

"If Maggie's number two, who's number one?" she persisted.

Slade released his seat belt and opened his door. Still grinning, he replied, "I'm holding that position open for a woman who wants to share my name and put her shoes under my bed and has as much wanderlust in her soul as I do."

"Chances are, like every other engineer and geologist I've met, you've got a woman in every port."

Donovan winked. "Maybe," was all he said, before he walked off to the flight office. Within ten minutes he had returned with his flight plan in hand. Then he helped Cat out of the car, remaining close beside her, their bodies almost touching.

"Maggie's beautiful," Cat told him admiringly.

"I knew you had a fine eye for beauty. Ready?"

Cat was as excited as if she were heading off to a

new mining site in a new land. Slade's smile told her he understood the tremor of excitement in her voice when she said, "Yes, I'm ready."

Some of Cat's initial exuberance turned to gratitude when she entered the spacious cabin of the aircraft. Slade had taken out three seats on the starboard side. In their place was a comfortable-looking cot, complete with a pillow, blankets and sheets. He motioned her toward it.

"Dr. Scott said that you wouldn't be able to withstand a trip sitting up all the time. It's going to take us ten hours to reach the ranch."

She slid him a glance. "Do you spoil all your women this way? So much attention to detail?"

"Just for you, Cat. Just you."

"One part of me believes you; the other doesn't," she said lightly. Her expression, however, was thoughtful.

"You wound my Texas spirit," Slade complained. "Perhaps I'm your knight in shining armor carrying you off to my castle to live happily ever after. Would that be so bad?"

His wistfulness moved through her like a lover's caress. My God, the man could weave a spell with his intimate talk—something Cat had not often found in men she'd met during her travels. She'd been handed most of their lines, but Slade was different. The feeling was good, however, so she didn't really want to fight it.

"You have been my knight, Slade," she admitted shyly. "You saved my life."

He preened beneath her compliment, his careless grin spreading across his face. "Well, my lady, you have a choice: sit up in the copilot's seat for a while and keep me company, or lie down and enjoy the scenery."

"I'd like to sit up in the cockpit."

"Ah, to be with me. Good choice."

"No, I want to see how you handle this plane." Mustn't let him get too cocky, she reminded herself.

"Oh." A shadow crossed his face.

Cat had never run into a man who showed such a range of feelings so easily. Most men stonewalled their emotions and responses, which was why she had found little incentive to establish an enduring relationship with any of them. With Slade, it was just the opposite. He was so obviously rattled by her reason for coming into the cockpit. Feeling more than a little guilty, Cat muttered, "I don't feel like being relegated to the rear just yet. I'm hungry for some good conversation."

Slade brightened and motioned her to move in front of him. "So, you'll even settle for me, hmm?"

Choosing not to reply, Cat sat down and observed Slade's attention to detail as he checked her seat belt before revving up the aircraft's two engines. Once he put on the headset, with the slender mike close to his lips, Slade was in another world. But even then, he made Cat feel as though they were a team, putting a headset on her and showing her where the volume dial was located.

She was entranced by Slade's hands: despite their size and roughness, there was a touching grace to their movements as they went through the preflight check. Heat unexpectedly moved through her. Slade was affecting her on levels she hadn't anticipated.

Meanwhile, Slade was receiving clearance to take off, and launched into a nonstop commentary about how Maggie was just as alive as they were, in her own way. Cat noticed how his fingers wrapped gently around the twin throttles positioned on the console between them, and she wondered what it would be like to be similarly stroked by this man. A slight smile hovered around her mouth as a fantasy began to take shape.

Suddenly, they were lifting off. All else was forgotten as Slade shot her a joyous look. She smiled back. Maggie sliced through the blue skies of Maine, her nose pointed in a southwesterly direction, toward Texas. Slade adjusted the fuel mixture and the engines began their deep, throbbing growl. Then the vibration minimized and peace blanketed the cabin.

"Maggie's crew will now ask their esteemed and illustrious passenger if she would like some coffee."

"I don't know about the esteemed and illustrious part—" she grinned "—but yes, the passenger would love a cup of coffee. Where is it? I can get it."

Slade held up his hand. "No, don't move." He reached down and retrieved a battered aluminum thermos from behind his seat. Setting the plane on autopilot, he expertly poured a cup and handed it to her. Cat's otherwise pale cheeks flamed as their fingertips met and touched. "You look more relaxed," Slade commented. "Is it because we didn't crash on takeoff or because you're on another adventure?"

"You have the disturbing ability to read my mind," she muttered, disconcerted.

Slade poured himself some coffee and recapped the thermos. Then, taking Maggie off autopilot, he wrapped his fingers lightly around the yoke. "Why does that bother you?"

"In my experience," she said thoughtfully, "few men look farther than the wrapping."

"You can't blame any of us poor males for looking, after spending months in some foreign jungle or godforsaken desert. Especially when someone as exotic-looking as you comes along."

Heat flowed up her neck. "I'm hardly exotic." Cat held up her left hand, showing him the calluses on her palm. "That's not exotic, Donovan. I've got hands like millions of women in Third World countries who wash and beat their family's clothes on some rock in a stream. I've got more muscle than women who work out daily at a health spa." She touched her hair. "I have to wear my hair so short that sometimes I'm mistaken for a man from the rear." She grimaced. "I'm hardly exotic, as you put it."

"So you think I'm handing you a line?"

Cat sighed, then admitted warily, "The way you talk, I almost believe you mean it."

Slade gave her a smoldering look. "I do mean it. Someday," he drawled in his thick Texan accent, "I'll show you why you're such an incredibly exotic woman."

Cat avoided his gaze as molten weakness again flowed through her like light refracting through a diamond. "If there is an enigma here," she said, laughing, "it's you. Tell me about yourself. And none of your Texas tall tales."

Slade laughed good-naturedly, then finished off his coffee and set the cup aside. "Now, there isn't a Texan alive who can resist embellishing the truth a bit."

"Try."

Slade scanned the instrument panel. They had climbed to fifteen thousand feet, the skies were azure and the sunlight bright. He pulled a pair of aviator's sunglasses from the pocket of his shirt and put them on. "I was born in Galveston, Texas, thirty-five years ago. My Irish father emigrated to the U.S. when he was a lad and he's still a fisherman in Galveston. My mother—she's the native-born Texan—owns a small shop at an exclusive mall, importing products from Ireland."

"Sisters? Brothers?"

"Seven. I'm the fifth-oldest, with three brothers and three beautiful sisters."

"Not exotic sisters?"

He tilted his head toward her and his voice lowered to an intimate tone. "No, you're exotic. They aren't."

He had such a convincing line, Cat thought, secretly delighted with his opinion that she was exotic and, of course, keeping in mind that it was just that. "I see. How did you get into geology?"

"I decided I didn't want to fish for a living like the rest of my family. I used to stand in the boat and watch the waves and wonder where they had come from. What far shore had they left? What ships did they encounter on their journey? Or what fish or mammals had graced them with their presence?" Slade shook his head. "No, my father told me when I was only this high—" he pointed to his knee "—that I was like my great-grandfather, who was the family adventurer. He could never stay in one place more than a few months at a time, either."

"And you have that same restlessness?" Cat offered. She handed him her empty cup.

Slade shrugged. "Restlessness? No. Life to me is one constant, nonstop adventure. I always want to know what lies over the next hill or wander through the next valley to see what and who is living there."

"Why the fascination with geology then? You could have been in the merchant marine instead, sailing the seas."

Slade smiled at her question. "Rocks held a special fascination for me. As a kid, when I finished my fishing chores, I used to pick stones up from the beach and study them. I'd wonder why one was black and another striated with pink and white. I used to hold them in my hand, trying to communicate with them and asking them their names and where they had come from."

Cat closed her eyes, resting against the seat. She could imagine a dark-haired boy crouched on the ground, holding in his palm a rock that stirred his curiosity, staring at it with intense fascination. Slade was like a child who had never closed off his ability to dream and spin stories. He was special, Cat admitted, a rare being who still had the ability to fantasize, to ignore the limitations in a rationally constructed society. "And did any of them talk to you?" she asked softly.

"Of course they did," he said with a laugh. "That was what led me to ask my teachers about the life of a rock. Eventually they got tired of all my questions and ordered special books on rock hunting for me."

"And are you still like that little boy, always asking questions?"

"I haven't changed at all," Slade confirmed with satisfaction. "Today, I drive mining engineers to the edge of distraction."

"Where did you take your geology schooling?" she asked, curious to know more about his past.

"Is there any other place? Colorado."

"Like me. I'm impressed."

He feigned drama, his hand across his heart. "Finally! We have something in common."

"Oh, come on, it's not that bad."

"You made it seem that way, Ms. Kincaid."

She shot him a wry glance. "Despite any possible ulterior motives, you did save my life. The least I could be is a decent guest."

"Did I slip something into the coffee?"

Cat chortled. "Come on, I'm not always a stick-in-the-mud."

"Did I accuse you of that? No way, sweetheart. You're a risk taker because your career demands it. It makes you an interesting and exotic woman. One of a kind."

"Oh, please! Get off the exotic kick, Slade."

"I can't help it if you're not a regular hothouse flower. That's your fault."

"Let's steer the conversation back to you. A four-year degree out of Colorado and then what?"

"Just kicked around the world prospecting like any other crazy rock hound."

"What kind of rocks? Is your specialty igneous?" she asked, remembering his tourmaline discovery.

"Why? Do I remind you of an igneous type?"

She smiled. Geologists usually chose one of three of the different rock types to specialize in: igneous, metamorphic or sedimentary. "You know what they say about the igneous type: they run hot and molten."

"So that's how you see me, eh?"

"I see you being bored by sedimentary exploration. You're strong and robust; you're the sort who would challenge igneous rock and tackle it with ease. Although we both know sinking mine shafts into rock that doesn't want to be penetrated isn't easy."

"Granted. Or should I say: granite."

"Slade, I'm not even going to laugh because that's a sick rock joke you'd use on a freshman in geology."

"Nobody said my humor was always in top form."
He gave her his innocent little-boy look.

"Do people always forgive your transgressions?"

"More importantly, will you?"

"I don't hold grudges."

"But you'll remember."

Her voice grew soft. "I'll remember."

"Well, enough of me," Slade countered. "How about
yourself? I had the pleasure of meeting your entire family, so I got an idea of what you're like."

"I'm sure Dal and Rafe gave you an earful about me."

"Don't sound so wary."

With a grimace, Cat pretended to pay more attention to the sky around them. "All right, you tell me
what they said."

"Let's see, what adjectives should I use?"

"If you use exotic, I'm going to take everything
you're saying as one-hundred percent baloney, Donovan," she warned him.

"Texans can be serious at times, too," he reassured
her, attempting a somber look.

"We'll see. So what do you think of me, now that
you've learned all from my family?"

"You're a daredevil. Rafe told me how you two
jumped your horses between two cliffs."

"Did he also tell you that my horse stumbled on the
other side and fell? I broke my arm and nose."

Slade shook his head. He saw and felt Cat relaxing.
She had been so long in isolation with men that she was
closed up. He saw the softening of her lips, heard new
life in her voice and saw more color stain her cheeks. If
nothing else, during the next eight weeks of recupera-
tion, Slade would remind Cat of her decidedly female

side, gently drawing all of it to the surface. He knew he could do it; there was a chemistry between them.

"Rafe said you and he made the jump, but that Dal had chickened out. I'd probably be with Dal." Slade paused and looked at her. "What you did matches the kind of career you chose. Mining engineers have to be a blend of conservatism and daring."

"What I did didn't take much brains—is that what you're saying?"

"Hey, we were all young once and we all pulled our share of foolish stunts. I'm chalking up your wild ride to youth."

"If the truth be known, I was scared spitless. Rafe was angry because Dal wouldn't go and he—well, I let him coerce me into doing it."

"But you didn't want to?"

"Are you kidding me? That was an eight-foot leap. I was riding a green four-year-old quarter horse who'd never seen a cliff, much less jumped one. I didn't know if he was going to jump it, skid to the edge, fall into it or what."

Slade pursed his lips, going for a second cup of coffee and offering her some. She declined. "Interesting," he murmured.

"Oh?"

Slade put the plane back on autopilot and sipped his coffee. "That gives me a useful piece of information about you."

"Uh-oh…"

He grinned. "It's not bad. What it tells me is that despite an overwhelming fear, you did what had to be done and carried it out successfully. I call that courage."

"That particular stunt was called stupid. What took

courage was to tell Dad how I broke my arm and nose. Rafe got the belt on his behind. I would've gotten a licking, too, if I hadn't gotten broken bones."

Savoring the hot liquid before he spoke, Slade commented, "You can still take that basic premise about yourself and apply it like a formula to any other type of situation. No, there's a basic vein of courage in you. I like that."

Cat warmed beneath Slade's compliment; the obvious pleasure in his voice was like a physical caress. She rarely enjoyed men in the field. But she wasn't in the field; her contract assignment had been delayed because of her injury. Cat's brows dipped.

"What's bothering you?" Slade asked.

"Hmm? Oh, I was just thinking that because of this accident, I've blown my next assignment." She had talked briefly to Ian Connors, the man who had hired her. Technically, because of her unexpected injuries, she didn't have to honor the contract. Cat had managed to hold off giving him an answer on whether she'd fulfill the contract or not. Just the bare thought of entering another mine made her break into a cold sweat.

"In Australia?"

"Yes. A two-year contract."

"You needed a vacation anyway, Cat."

He was right. She hadn't walked away from work for five years now. "Work is play for me," she tried without enthusiasm. How could one mine cave-in turn her lifelong love into a terrorizing nightmare she never wanted to experience again?

"Still, we all need time away, Cat."

"Do you?" Cat asked, trying to deflect talk of her going back to work. Specifically, into a mine.

"Sure, I'm only human. I can stand the jungle or being a sand rat for only so long and then I have to get back to civilization and get human again."

"Are you between assignments?"

"Yeah. I was heading home to Texas for a couple of months."

"How long since you were home?"

"One year. I think you'll like Mourning Dove. For west Texas, it's a nice spot."

"A lot of sand, scrub brush, jackrabbit and deer?"

"That, too."

"Tell me about the ranch. Is it a working one?"

"Not anymore. I've more or less created a deer preserve out of it and sold off all the cattle. I have a Mexican family who lives nearby who takes care of it during my absences. Carlos and his wife, Pilar, are the caretakers." His voice grew warmer. "Pilar is the best cook this side of the Mexican border. I can hardly wait to get home and fatten up on her cooking." He patted his hard, lean stomach meaningfully.

Cat understood; she was underweight as well. Perhaps the Mourning Dove Ranch wasn't going to be all that bad after all. Slade wasn't the womanizer she had first thought. As a matter of fact, she was going to have to reevaluate many things about Slade. Cat couldn't apply her earlier experiences to him because he didn't fit into the categories of men she had known before. She slid him a warm look.

"Has anyone ever accused you of being different?"

Slade laughed solidly, flipped a switch to take the plane off autopilot and resumed the task of flying. "Many times. Why? Does it bother you?"

"You are a bit disconcerting." And disturbing. Every

movement he made reminded Cat that Slade was a consummate athlete; there was never a wasted motion and he had a coordination that at times took her breath away.

"But not threatening?"

She paused a moment before answering, "No."

"What took you so long to answer my question?"

Cat refused to be baited by him. "Nothing."

"You were trying to decide whether to be wary of me or not, weren't you?"

"Quit being such a know-it-all."

"Your brother, Rafe, spoke a lot about you." He added in a gentler voice, "Good things. How you love the land and the animals. How easily you were moved by a sunset. Or by a foal being born. I like my woman to be easily touched by everything around her."

A tremor vibrated through her and Cat discreetly did not ask what Slade meant when he called her his woman. His ability to put everything, including their conversation, on intensely personal terms rattled her. "Life, to me, is a continual blossoming," she admitted, her eyes darkening with fervor. "All we have to do is keep our hearts and minds open to receive its gifts."

Slade's mouth curved into a knowing smile. "Why are you so afraid to show that side of yourself?"

"I think all of us hide parts of ourselves," Cat said defensively.

"I'm an open book."

"Sure you are. That's why you unexpectedly dropped into my life."

Slade glanced quickly at her. "Best thing I ever did."

Cat shook her head. "So, if you aren't an igneous type, what are you?" she asked, ignoring his innuendo.

"I'm a sedimentary man. Ah, the eyebrows lift and

the eyes go wide. What do you know, I finally got a rise out of you."

"You get a rise out of me every time we spar," Cat parried.

"I don't see us as sparring."

"Call it whatever you want."

Slade scratched his head. "Somehow, I'm going to have to instill some trust into our relationship."

Cat almost blurted out, "What relationship?" But she bit back the response. "Why sedimentary rock? Most geologists are bored stiff by that type."

"You find a fair amount of gem-quality stone in sediment, that's why."

"Ah, now you're beginning to make sense. You're more a gem hunter than a geologist." Cat eyed him speculatively. "You're a prospector in search of the mother lode, aren't you?"

Slade checked the instruments, a smile pulling at his mouth. "You mean a treasure hunter? A modern-day gold miner?"

"You said it; I didn't."

"I hear distaste in your voice." Slade's voice was deceptively noncommittal.

Cat tried to evade his comment. Greg had done this to her; he had placed the mining of precious gems over their love for one another. And it had killed their relationship. Struggling not to let her past experience taint her idea of Slade, she said, "There's nothing wrong with finding the world's major tourmaline deposits. It can make you a very rich man."

Slade looked at her a long time. He saw the discomfort in every line of Cat's mobile face. "And you think that's why I go chasing after gem mines?" he probed.

"I don't know. Why do you? You don't strike me as the typical treasure hunter." Which was true. Slade was unlike Greg in many ways, and for the better.

Slade was glad that Cat had asked instead of just assumed why he specialized in precious stones. Even he had to admit that most of the gem hunters he knew were like the old-timers during the gold rush. They were loners to begin with, shaped by the roughness of their life-style. Most of the men he knew carried pistols on their hips and knives in their belts. And they all had one driving force in common: they wanted to get rich. Money took precedence over anything else that life might offer them.

"Gems hold a special fascination for me, Cat. In a way, they're like people: when you first discover them, put a miner's light on them, they're rough and unpolished. Then, as you take the time to gently loosen them from the matrix of pegmatite or sediment, you can carry them to the surface. It's exciting to realize that what you carry in the palm of your hand hasn't ever seen sunlight. As you bring it to the surface to watch the light refract through it for the first time, you're the first one to ever witness it." Slade gave her a soft smile. "It's much like watching a person unfold in front of you, watching how they react and respond. Later, a jeweler will look at that rough specimen with a knowing eye, spot its inclusions and watch how the light refracts through it. He'll cut it to bring out all of the natural fire and brilliance that has waited millions of years to be brought to life."

"That's an inspiring view." At least he hadn't mentioned money as his prime goal, Cat thought.

The corners of his eyes crinkled and he shared a look with her. "I'm comfortable with it. Although there are some people who are always going to be as impenetrable as iron ore."

"How many diamonds have you met in your life, as opposed to plain old iron ore?" she asked curiously.

Slade laughed, enjoying her easy acceptance of how he saw the world. "I've met many an uncut gemstone in both men and women."

"And a few iron-ore types?"

"Sometimes. In my business, as you already know, we're a pretty interesting lot to begin with."

Cat closed her eyes, suddenly exhausted for no reason.

"Tired?" Slade guessed. "Or bored with this piece of iron ore?"

"You're hardly iron ore, Slade Donovan. But right now I think I'd better get some sleep before my opinions get me in trouble. I feel so tired all of a sudden."

"Maybe it's the company you've been keeping."

"Now, Slade," she reassured him, her eyes sparkling mischievously, "you're hardly a bore, and you know it."

A slow smile touched his strong mouth. "Just wanted to make sure."

"You're such an egotist," Cat said, yawning, and slowly rose, then made her way from the cockpit to the cot in the cabin. Carefully, she lay down on her left side, then closed her eyes and spiraled into sleep.

Chapter 4

There was a mild bumping. Cat heard a change in the aircraft's engines and stirred. She had fallen asleep just as they had flown over Pennsylvania's border. Now they seemed to be landing. Probably refueling, she thought groggily, closing her eyes once again. With a sigh, she slid back into sleep.

Slade quietly made his way from the cockpit. It was early evening and the shadows were long as the sun edged toward the western horizon. Cat lay on her back, still sleeping soundly. He'd made a feather-light landing, the wheels gently kissing the parched Texas airstrip. Now they were home. Home... The feeling moved powerfully through him as he gazed down at Cat. Yes, they were home.

He approached the cot, noting that Cat's skin was stretched tautly across her cheekbones and dark shadows lay beneath her thick lashes. It was her mouth, however, that made his body tighten with sudden, almost painful awareness of just how much this woman affected him. He felt the same kind of excitement that thrummed through him when he was close to finding the one rock leading him to a vein of hidden treasure.

Cat was a treasure, Slade had decided. He crouched down, one hand resting near her head and the other on her slender arm. Hungrily, he brought her close to him, breathing in her sweet scent. How vulnerable she was. Leaning over, Slade gently caressed her parted lips with his.

Cat's lashes fluttered as she felt the warmth and pressure of Slade's mouth molding to hers. Heat spiraled through her like a ribbon, flooding upward on its dizzying course. Slade's breath fanned lightly across her cheek. Her heart pounded as his mouth coaxed her lips open, and she responded to him unquestioningly.

The instant Slade felt her returning pressure, his mouth worshipped her as if she were a fragile gift that would shatter if mishandled.

Cat drowned in Slade's honeyed invitation, her nipples hardening against the confines of her blouse. He was strong and good and tasted wonderful. Her nostrils flared as she drank in the scent of his special blend of male aroma combined with a slight hint of shaving cream.

"Sweet," he whispered against her wet, responsive lips. "God, you're sweet emerald fire."

Cat forced her lashes open, and became hotly aware of the naked desire in Slade's face. His eyes held her captive with a look that went straight to her heart. This man was supremely confident of his masculinity.

"Did I turn into a frog or something while I slept?" she asked huskily, smiling.

Slade caressed her hair. "Hardly. You're more like Sleeping Beauty!"

It was too much for her and Cat could barely think. Suddenly aware they were on the ground, she glanced around. "Where are we?"

Slade slowly moved out of his crouched position, knowing that if he didn't, he'd be sorely tempted to kiss Cat again. "We're in Del Rio, Texas. We've landed at Mourning Dove Ranch in time to see the sun set in a couple of hours."

"We're at the ranch? Already?"

"Sure." Could she be as shaken as he was by that kiss? he speculated. Or was it simply that her bearings were off?

"How long did I sleep?" Cat looked at him shyly. Slade had his answer.

"A long time." He reached out, brushing her flushed cheek. "But you needed it. Come on, I'll help you up."

Cat took his hand, biting back a cry of pain when Slade carefully levered her into a sitting position. Her face ashen, Cat thanked him and gripped the edges of the cot. Slade went to the hatch and opened it. The early evening sun and a slice of blue sky showed through the door. Dry Texas heat flowed through the cabin. Cat took a deep breath, then released it, feeling the tension pour out of her.

Slade grinned and lifted his hand in welcome as Carlos, his manager, came down the long, narrow dirt strip in a beat-up Jeep. "Our chariot has arrived, my lady," Slade announced to Cat. "Are you ready to go to your castle?"

"Lead on, my prince," she said with a flourish, moving to the door. "I'm rather curious to see this castle you've hidden in the desert."

And desert it was. The earth was the color of bone, and was strewn with twisted, jade-green sagebrush. A few long-eared, black-tipped jackrabbits were in evidence, and the sun was strong and bright.

Cat gripped Slade's hand as he led her down the stairs. She stood back and watched as Carlos climbed out of the olive-colored Jeep. He greeted them in Spanish, waving his straw cowboy hat exuberantly. As the men heartily embraced each other, Cat smiled. Carlos and Slade acted more like family than employer and employee.

With one arm around Carlos, Slade turned and introduced her to his number-one man. Carlos bowed grandly, then took her hand and kissed it.

"Señorita Kincaid, welcome to Mourning Dove. We've been expecting you for some time now." Carlos's coffee-colored face beamed with genuine sincerity as he released her hand.

Cat slid Slade a glance. "You've been expecting me for some time?"

Slade shifted awkwardly.

"Si, señorita," Carlos confirmed, seemingly unaware of his friend's discomfort. "Come! My wife, Pilar, has your room ready. Señor Slade told us of your injuries and Pilar can hardly wait to mother you as she has our other six children. She even has chicken soup waiting."

Cat smiled and walked with Slade toward the Jeep. "Six kids?"

"Si. Señor Slade has sent two of them to college al-

ready. He's practically their uncle. The other four are helping with the ranch when they're not in school."

Cat's luggage, which had once been destined for Australia, was carefully placed in the Jeep. Slade sat in back, perched precariously between all the bags, while Cat sat in front. She was grateful that Carlos carefully negotiated the dirt road leading from the airstrip to a rambling adobe brick ranch house surrounded by sturdy cottonwood trees. Cat tried to ignore the aggravating rib pain that seemed to be settling in for good, and concentrated on the ranch instead. The house was a testimonial to Texas's tradition of spaciousness. She noticed solar reflectors on the roof, and the number of windows made her gape. She turned her head slightly to Slade, who sat behind her.

"You wouldn't have had something to do with the design of this house, would you?" she asked sweetly.

His teeth were white against his tanned skin. "Why? Does it show?"

"Yes. How much reconstruction did you do after you moved in?"

"After I made my fortune from the El Camino, I was able to afford the walls of windows facing east and west. There's more, but you'll see it all when we get inside."

Cat guessed that there were at least fifteen rooms in the house. Four chimney stacks rose from the roof. It would be fun to tour this house, she thought. What would it reveal of Slade?

Carlos parked the Jeep beneath a cedar-topped garage with no sides. Next to it stood a woman who looked to be in her forties, and whom Cat assumed to be Pilar. Her black hair was tightly wound into a crown of braids and she wore a simple white peasant blouse and a scarlet skirt. Her welcoming smile reminded Cat of Slade's, and she smiled in return, feeling lighter and happier than she had in a long while.

Pilar gripped Cat's left hand and squeezed it gently, introducing herself in halting English. Her warm brown eyes sparkled as she motioned for Cat to follow her.

If Cat could have taken a deep breath, she would have. The ranch reminded her of a geode: plain, gray and undistinguished on the outside, but once opened, a crystalline palace of shimmering beauty. Cat walked from the foyer and into the expansive living room. A slanting cathedral ceiling rose skyward with windows facing west to catch the late-afternoon and setting sun's light. In one corner a floor-to-ceiling granite chimney, glinting with feldspar and mica, rose like a speckled black-and-white giant.

Trees and jungle foliage grew along a waterfall and stream winding through the living room. The wall opposite the windows held ten long shelves with a gem collection that took her breath away. Cat automatically held her ribs as she walked to the wall. Strategically placed lights brought out the rough, unpolished gems that ranged in size from as small as her fist to as large as a watermelon.

"Oh, Slade…" she whispered, entranced as she stood staring at them. She felt him come to her side.

"Like the collection?"

"Like it? This would rival some of the better museums I've been in."

"Each specimen is from one of my trips."

Cat couldn't resist stroking a cantaloupe-size blue topaz crystal growing out of brown colored lepidolite rock. "And I'll bet each one is a story," she said, grinning, and returned the gem to its niche.

Slade tried to look serious. "I told you, I'm a master spinner of tales. True tales, I might add."

"I intend to take you up on some of them, believe me," Cat said, while inwardly estimating that this gem collection was easily worth at least a quarter of a million dollars.

"Not today, however." He led her across handwoven Navaho and Hopi rugs and out of the living room. "Pilar's already giving me dirty looks because I haven't taken you to your room and gotten you into bed to rest."

"Slade, I'm not an invalid. As a matter of fact, I hate being sick and I can't stand being bed bound. Busted ribs might prevent me from riding one of those horses in the corral, but they can't stop me from being mobile."

He motioned down a wide hall and opened the first door on the left. Sunlight spilled into the room and one wall was composed all of glass supported by weathered cedar spars. Palms, their fronds grazing the slanted ceiling, graced each corner. A handwoven multicolored quilt covered the cedar double bed. The dresser and drawers were also of cedar and, if Cat wasn't mistaken, hand carved. The room was spare, but homey.

"Over here is a desk, should you feel the urge to write a letter," Slade said, motioning toward it, "or make phone calls. There's also a stereo and a TV hidden in the cabinet over there, should you get bored with our company."

"Slade, what a thought!"

"Carlos will bring your luggage in a minute. In the meantime, the bathroom's over there and if you want to sweat out anything, the spa is directly outside the glass doors, across that brick patio and straight ahead. I'll see you later."

Cat turned as Slade quietly slipped out the door, leaving her to get adjusted to her new surroundings. She was grateful for this act of consideration. In fact, she felt better already. A knock on her door announced Carlos with her bags. Pilar arrived moments later to put all her clothes away for her, leaving Cat feeling extremely pampered and a little helpless. To remedy that feeling, she decided on a hot shower. Stepping to the dresser, she chose a pair of pale blue cotton pants and a dainty, short-sleeved turquoise blouse. Now that she was between jobs, she could allow herself to dress more femininely. On the job she always wore khaki pants, a T-shirt or a short-sleeved blouse.

Alone again, Cat stripped down, gently pulling apart the Velcro binding around her rib cage. The cloth bandage that had surrounded her torso fell away, leaving a weltlike imprint on her flesh. She reveled in the hot shower and wrapped herself with a white towel afterward. Relaxed, she padded into the bedroom to face the chore of getting dressed. No longer was she in the hospital where one of the nurses could help her get into her bra and then expertly wrap the elastic bandage around her ribs. Slade had discussed it with her earlier, saying that he was sure Pilar could do it for her instead.

Pilar was eager to help and understood Cat's instructions fully. She hooked Cat's lacy white bra and helped her into her slacks. Despite all her well-meaning attempts, however, Pilar could not rewrap the torso bandage properly. By the fourth try, Cat was sweating from the pain while Pilar tried futilely to maneuver and close it.

"I'm so sorry, *señorita*. Perhaps you can go without it?"

"I wish I could, Pilar. Would you go get Slade, please? He knows how to close it."

Pilar's eyes widened slightly as she set the wrap aside, but she said, "I'll get him right away, *señorita. Uno momento,* eh?"

"*Si,*" Cat agreed. Already, she could feel a flush crawling up her neck and into her face. Slade would see her blushing. Well, what else could she do? Wear the bandage, not bathe and smell? No way. Slade was a paramedic: he would know how to rewrap her quickly and expertly.

There was a brief knock at the door and Slade entered. "Pilar said you're in trouble," he said, slipping through the door. He saw Cat's red cheeks, and knew at once that she was having problems.

"Pilar gave the bandage the old college try, but it didn't work. Would you mind wrapping it around me?"

Slade nodded, deliberately keeping his gaze above her neck as he approached her. "I'd ask Kai Travis to do this, but I just called their ranch and they won't be home for two more hours, according to their maid, Maria."

Cat watched him pick up the bandage and she stood, carefully raising her arms so that he could place it around her. "That's all right. Pilar did her best. I guess we both should have expected this. Wrapping ribs is an art."

Slade leaned down, perusing the large black-and-blue bruise that covered most of her right side. He gently touched the outer edges of the area. Cat inhaled slightly. "Hurt?"

"It's okay."

"Lie to anyone but me, Cat."

"It hurts like hell."

Slade grimaced. "And Pilar's handling of the situation hasn't helped, has it?"

"Hindsight. Don't be upset with her. Can you get it on?"

"I'm not upset with Pilar. Grip my shoulder with your left hand and hold on." He noticed a thin white scar that traversed the left side of her rib cage. "Looks like you've taken your share of rib injuries before," he commented. "All right, exhale. I'll make this as fast as possible."

Cat did as Slade requested, her fingers sinking into the folds of his blue chambray cotton shirt. She tried to steel herself against the coming pain. Slade was quick and efficient. She felt his other arm go around her shoulders the instant he closed the Velcro on the left side of her ribs, below her bra.

"You're a good patient, Cat Kincaid," he praised huskily, watching all the color drain from her face. Despite the pain, she hadn't moaned or complained. Slade guided her to the edge of the bed to sit down. Picking up her blouse, he helped her slip it on. Then he crouched down in front of her, buttoning it for her.

Cat forced a slight smile. "Thanks…" Each touch of his fingers on the pearl-shaped buttons sent a tremor through her, erasing the pain, fanning a liquid flame higher and brighter within her.

"We can do one of two things," he told her. "I can try to teach Pilar the art of wrapping or do it myself." He glanced up at her. "Frankly, I don't think your ribs need extra punishment while Pilar learns. You have any qualms about me doing this for you once a day?"

Cat shook her head. "No. Anything's better than having someone learn to do this right now. It's just too painful for me."

"It's my fault. I thought anyone could wrap ribs."

Relaxing as the pain lessened, Cat managed a slight smile. "It's nobody's fault, Slade. I'm not upset if you aren't."

Slade captured the top button, just above the slight swell of her cleavage. "We'll manage this together," he promised, noting that his voice had thickened. He couldn't react like this to Cat, or she'd choose to suffer through Pilar's attempts, no matter what the cost to herself. No, when he kissed her again, Slade wanted her to know it wouldn't be an occasion for pain. He wanted her to be totally willing and if he had read the sultry look in her half-closed green eyes correctly, they were both anticipating when it would happen again.

"You're done," he said briskly. "Now, I was making a pitcher of 'welcome to Texas' margaritas out at the bar. Care to join me?" Slade stood and held out his hand to her. He saw disbelief in Cat's eyes, as if she'd expected him to take advantage of the situation. His smile broadened.

Cat gripped his hand, watching as her fingers were swallowed up in his palm. Tiny shivers raced up her arm as she rose.

"Do you make a mean margarita, Slade?"

"How mean do you want it?"

"Make mine a double."

"For the pain or for the embarrassment?"

Cat wondered when he was going to let go of her hand as he led her to the door. He seemed reluctant to relinquish her fingers. "You're less of a brigand than I first thought," she confessed.

"Didn't you know? Texans are the epitome of discretion. Not to mention being gallant gentlemen."

"Careful, or you'll start believing your own tales."

His laughter floated down the hall as they walked toward the living room. "Caught. Again."

Cat followed him to a cedar bar that sat opposite the huge fireplace. Sunlight lanced through the area, setting the honey-colored cedar aglow. She took a seat on one of the leather-upholstered black bar stools while Slade went behind the bar and finished making the promised pitcher of margaritas. Pouring two, he placed them on a tray then motioned her to follow him out to the screened-in porch.

The breeze was dry and lifted a few errant strands of her damp hair. Slade pulled out a chair and she sat down, taking the proffered drink.

Slade sat opposite her, crossing one leg over the other. A hundred feet from the porch, a slender ribbon of water wound its way through a line of cottonwoods. He sighed happily. Everything he valued most was right here before him—including this slender young woman he had promised to nurse back to health.

"What did you use, 150-proof tequila?" Cat grinned, a sweet shiver rippling through her.

"You asked for a double," he reminded her innocently. "I took you at your word."

Cat eyed the cold, beaded glass. "This would neutralize a tank," she grumbled good-naturedly.

"Drink it slowly. Texas is like the Caribbean or South America; you're living at a different pace than most Americans."

She sipped the tart drink and nodded. "I've served

my fair share of time on those kinds of jobs, too. I call it Bahama time."

Slade grinned. "Yeah. If you ask, 'How far is it?' they'll say, 'Not far, not far.' And if you ask, 'When?' they'll say, 'Soon, soon.'"

"Maybe those people have the right attitude, Slade. Maybe we westerners are too driven and don't know how to relax." She stretched luxuriously.

"Do you know how?" he asked, holding her amused gaze.

"No. I keep looking at this enforced eight-week convalescence and see myself going crazy. What will I do?"

Slade gave her an eloquent shrug. "I've got plenty of work waiting—assay reports, charting, core samples to check." Slade slid her a careful glance. "If you get bored, you might want to pitch in…" he baited.

Cat chuckled and raised her glass in toast. "Not a chance, Slade. Not a chance."

Cat couldn't get to sleep, no matter how hard she tried. Each time she closed her eyes, images of her entrapment in the mine loomed before her. Thank God, Slade had kept her going, or she'd have given up all hopes of rescue. Slade. Almost immediately, she felt relief from the terror gnawing away at her. She drifted off to sleep, remembering how his lips had felt….

Toward 4:00 a.m., Cat jerked awake. Shakily she got up and pulled on her white cotton robe. Making her way through the still house, Cat stood at the screen doors. Although she was cold, sweat bathed her brow. How long she stood there, her forehead resting against the cool aluminum molding, she didn't know. Only when she heard a door open and then quietly close did she straighten up, her attention drawn to the hallway.

Slade rubbed his face wearily as he padded into the living room. Seeing Cat standing forlornly near the doors, he halted abruptly.

"Cat?"

"I'm all right," she replied faintly.

He heard the strain in her voice and walked over. Even in the dim light, he could see the tension etched in Cat's somber features. "Bad dreams?" he guessed, moving toward the bar.

With a shaky laugh, Cat followed him. "Yes. In it, my Australian contractor was calling me to find out where the hell I was. What about that contract we signed, he kept saying." That was one of her dreams. The one that had awakened her involved the mine cave-in. Pride stopped her from admitting as much to Slade. She sat down on the bar stool and watched as he began making a small pot of coffee. Just having him nearby eased some of the fear ripping through her.

Slade pushed the errant strands of his hair off his brow and turned around to retrieve two earthenware mugs. Then he leaned against the counter that stood between them.

"How can you fulfill your contract now?" he demanded. Concern was evident in his voice. "You're going to be laid up for two months solid. Isn't there a clause somewhere that refers to acts of God or some such thing to get you off the hook?"

Cat turned away. Right now, Slade looked endearingly mussed and she had a powerful desire to slip her arms around his broad, capable shoulders and seek the solace he was offering. Without a doubt, Slade would hold her if she wanted and give her the peace she sought. Torn by so many conflicting emotions and her fears of ever entering a mine again, Cat remained silent.

"Hey..." Slade gently touched her arm. "What is it, Cat? Come on, you can tell me..."

Cat hung her head, not wanting Slade to see the stinging tears blurring her vision. "I, uh..."

"Great start," he teased, "what else?"

With a loud sniff, Cat managed a half laugh and half sob. "You'll think it's stupid. Childish."

As much as Slade wanted to continue touching her soft, warm skin, he forced his hand to drop away. Leaning against the bar, his head bent forward almost touching hers, he said, "Okay, straight-arrow, shoot. I don't think a contract is the reason you're crying." His voice lowered to a velvet coaxing. "Fear of entering a mine is probably more like it. Right?"

Cat nodded slowly. "Oh, I feel so damn stupid, Slade." She raised her head, dabbed away at the evidence of the tears and stared at him. "Here I am, a grown woman—not a scared little child. So I was in a mine cave-in; big deal. I ought to be able to face my fear of going in again instead of shriveling up and dying inside whenever I think about it. Or dream about it."

With a slight smile, Slade shook his head. "As a kid, I was always afraid of thunderstorms. I still am to this day. Get a lightning strike too close and this guy cringes and ducks."

"I doubt you're afraid of anything, Slade."

"Think I'm fibbing?"

"I don't know. These days, I'm one knot of confusion." Cat smiled slightly at him. "Maybe you'd say something like that just to make me feel better. I don't know..."

Slade had to physically stop himself from pulling Cat close to him. Right now, she was very, very fragile. "Look," he began softly, "you're going to go through all kinds of daily and nightly hell with this fear. Get used to it. More important, don't close up. Talk about those fears, Cat. That's one of the reasons I wanted you with me: I've survived more than my fair share of cave-ins. I know what you're going through and I can help you if you'll let me." He reached out, capturing her tightly knotted hands on the bar. Gently, he pried each of her fingers free until they were relaxed between his own larger hands.

His warmth spread through her, enveloping her pounding heart. Cat met his tender expression. "Was anyone there to help you through nights like…this?"

"Most of the time, no. And I'm not ashamed to admit that after the first cave-in, I hit alcohol to escape from the same type of hell you're going to experience." Slade grimaced. "After a few bad weeks, I got off the booze and cleaned up my act. I crawled through it and survived, just like you will."

Her heart wrenched at his admission. "I don't know how you stood it, Slade. Right now I don't want to be alone. That's a first for me; practically all my life I've been alone or lived in remote places. I liked it. But now…"

He squeezed her hands. "We all have barriers we can't overcome alone, sweetheart. And I promised you, you won't have to go through this alone…"

She mustered a tender smile. "I told you I was a bad patient. Thanks for being here for me, Slade. The next step is to stop having nightmares about Ian Connors trying to pressure me into fulfilling that contract."

Chapter 5

A week later, Cat's worst fears came true when she received the dreaded call from Ian Connors, owner of the Australian mining company. She had been drinking her third cup of morning coffee, reading a book Slade had written on sedimentary gemstones, when the phone rang. Pilar answered it and pointed to the phone sitting near Cat's elbow.

"A Mr. Connors, *señorita*?"

Cat felt a sharp stab in her stomach as all her carefully hidden fears exploded within her. Pilar shot her a look of concern as Cat picked up the extension.

Closing her eyes, Cat took the call, too occupied to see Pilar quietly slip from the kitchen and hurry across the patio toward Slade's hobby shop. Mouth dry, heart pounding at the base of her throat, Cat barely got out a civil hello to Ian.

Pilar, alarmed by Cat's unexpected behavior, rushed out to Slade's shop to tell him that Cat had turned alarmingly pale. He followed her back without delay. Folding his arms against his chest, he grimly watched Cat as he eavesdropped on the heated conversation.

"Look, Mr. Connors," she was explaining, a hint of tremor in her voice. "I simply can't come. I'm under doctor's orders to rest for two months. There are a number of other highly qualified mining engineers who can take my place. You don't need me."

Slade's eyes narrowed as he saw Cat nervously wipe her perspiring brow. In the past week, she had tried so valiantly to fight her inner battle with fear. And yet, he had sensed her aching need to lean on him, to trust him to help her. His mouth flattened into a thin line as he pondered the situation.

"I know what my contract says, Mr. Connors. You don't need to remind me. Look, there's no use shouting! That's not going to get us anywhere. I'm no happier than you are that that mine caused me so much injury." She twisted around on the stool, uncomfortable. "And no, I'm not going to fulfill the terms of the contract. You what? Are you joking?" Cat rolled her eyes and stifled the urge to swear. "You're going to sue me?" She clenched her teeth momentarily. "Okay, you go right ahead and try. But before you do, let me give you the phone number of the surgeon who saved my life! He can fill you in on all the gory details."

She was breathing hard by the time the call was completed. Slamming down the phone, Cat regretted the action instantly. Holding her right side, she slipped off the chair and headed out of the house and onto the screen-enclosed patio.

A few minutes later, Slade ambled out with two glasses of cool, frosty lemonade. Cat's lower lip was compressed into a tight line, and her eyes flashed with emerald fire as she glared over at him.

"I suppose you heard?"

"He's just upset. Here, this is nice and cool. Come and sit down with me here and let's discuss it."

Unable to contain her anger, Cat put the lemonade down and began pacing the entire length of the porch. "Of all things, Slade. Ian Connors thinks he's going to sue me for breach of contract!"

Slade rose to his feet, holding out his hand to her. "Come on," he coaxed, "let's go for a walk down by the stream."

It seemed natural for Cat to slip her hand into Slade's. As they wandered down the stone path toward the stand of cottonwoods and the ribbon of water, she relaxed even more. She gave Slade a warm look.

"You're good for me."

"I try to be, Cat. You deserve it."

She shook her head. "I wish Greg had felt that way." Then she added, "We almost got married."

Slade slowed down as they neared the stream. Multicolored rocks peeked out from just below the water's surface and shimmered in the early-morning sun. He motioned for Cat to sit against the trunk of a cottonwood and then joined her. "Want to tell me about it?"

Cat chose two stalks of grass and plucked them. She handed one to Slade and then put the other into the corner of her mouth. Tipping her head back, she stared up through the dark green, sunlit foliage.

"It's the closest I ever came to marriage."

"You make it sound like a disease." Slade watched as the tension drained from Cat's features.

"I don't mean it to sound like that. I fell head over heels in love with Greg. Imagine, at twenty-seven taking the blind nosedive of an eighteen-year-old girl."

Slade smiled slightly. "There must have been some chemistry there to have done it."

With a painful nod, Cat said, "There was. Or I thought there was."

"What went wrong?" Slade resisted taking the small, graceful hand that lay so close to his. Was she even aware of her sensuality? He loved the feminine swing of her hips and the luscious mouth that begged to be kissed. And sometimes her breathless laughter sent a keen ache through him.

"Greg was a geologist, like you. He was thirty, single and had been knocking around in the industry since he was twenty-four. His whole life revolved around finding the mother lode."

Slade heard the disgust in her voice. "A treasure hunter?"

"Of the first order. Gold, platinum or any kind of precious gem mining. It didn't matter to him. He lived for that find of a lifetime."

Slade suddenly recalled their conversation when they had flown in from Maine, and remembered how Cat had reacted to the possibility that he might also be a treasure hunter. He certainly didn't want Cat to place him in Greg's category. Had she already? Clearing his throat, he asked, "Greg put money before people?"

Throwing the chewed stalk of grass away, Cat picked another. A frown creased her brow. "Yes. Only I didn't realize the depth of his treasure fever. The whole thing came to a head when he found gold on some land he had purchased near the Kalgoorlie mines."

With a whistle, Slade turned around, facing her. "The Kalgoorlie gold mines are among the best in Australia."

"Overnight, Greg became a very rich man," she recalled, bitterness staining her words.

Slade picked up her hand. "But?"

"What we had became second best," she admitted hoarsely. "Greg put gold above us. He really didn't need what I had to offer him. Gold fever became his wife, friend and lover."

Slade ran his thumb across her soft cheek. How he wanted to gather Cat into his arms and hold her! He could see tears glistening in her eyes and he gently placed his hands on her shoulders.

"Listen to me, Cat," Slade said in a low voice charged with emotion. "Greg didn't deserve you. Anyone who puts money ahead of the most priceless gift in the world hasn't got his head screwed on straight."

Cat fought back the tears and met Slade's level look. "Do you, Slade?"

He shook his head. "I may have green-fire fever, but it has never come between me and the woman in my life." His hands tightened momentarily on her shoulders. It was important that Cat believe him. "I do know what money can and cannot buy. Do you understand that?" *Please, say you do,* he begged silently.

Impulsively, Cat leaned forward, placing a kiss on his cheek. Slade smelled male, of sunshine and perspiration. "I believe you," she said huskily, smiling up at his surprised expression. Running her fingers down his left arm, she sat back.

Shaken by her spontaneity, Slade felt a molten heat

spread through his hardening body because of her touch. He gave her a shy smile, the words coming haltingly. "I hope, Cat, that you always know you're more important to me than any business concern." Gathering his courage, he added, "I like what you and I have. Money can't buy that."

Without a word, Cat rested her hand in his. "I like what we have, too, Slade. But I don't know where it's going."

"Is that important right now?" He tried to brace himself for an answer he did not want to hear.

"No," Cat said softly. "My entire life's in a tailspin professionally. The only good thing to come out of all this is what we share. And for that, I'm grateful. You're steady and you've offered me someone to lean on. And right now, I need that." She smiled tenderly. "Maybe this restless, globe-trotting mining engineer needed that all along and was too blind to realize it."

"Well," Slade said huskily, "a crisis has a funny way of putting things into proper perspective. Having you here is like sunlight to me, Cat. I don't know where we're going, either, but I like it. I like what you bring out in me, and the talks we have. You're important to me..."

Leaning toward him, Cat placed her arms around Slade's shoulders. She wasn't able to give very much of a hug because of her healing ribs. "You have a funny way of making yourself a part of my life, Slade," she whispered near his ear.

Gently, Slade placed his hands on her waist. "You're more valuable than any gold mine, sweetheart. Believe that with all your heart and soul." As he got to his feet and helped Cat to stand, a sweet euphoria swept through him.

* * *

Three days later, Slade was still remembering their conversation as he doodled absently on a note pad. There was plenty of work clamoring for his attention, but he had a hard time concentrating on anything except Cat. Slade turned around in his leather chair, staring out of the window toward the patio below. Suddenly Cat appeared, dressed in a pair of kelly-green shorts and a white tank top. She was slowly taking her afternoon stroll across the brick-topped patio. She looked lonely—just as lonely as he felt. Slade, restless, tossed the pencil onto the desk. Getting to see Cat for a few minutes each morning to help her with the rib wrap, and then for an hour at lunch, wasn't enough. Not anymore. The eight hours a day demanded of him to coordinate the opening of the Verde mine held less and less interest for him.

With a snort, Slade got up, moving to the window to watch Cat as she wandered aimlessly on her way. Questions raced through his mind. When should he broach the fact that he wanted Cat to work for him? Right now, she wasn't even sure she wanted to continue being a mining engineer. Cave-ins had a way of forcing one to look at fear. How each individual handled it was another question. The past weeks had effectively erased Slade's original reason for wanting Cat to recover at Mourning Dove. No, more and more, Slade wanted *her*. Each morning he awoke he was happy as never before because of Cat's quiet presence.

Glancing down at his watch, he saw it was two-thirty. To hell with work; he wanted to spend the rest of the afternoon with Cat. It was too late for the picnic they had talked about earlier. But there was still time to take her to a fishing pond nearby. Whistling softly, pleased with the idea, Slade shut off the light and strolled out of his office.

"There you are," he greeted her cheerfully.

Cat lifted her head. She sat in a lounge chair beneath a trellis shelter of bougainvillea vines. Her pulse began to pound as she met Slade's blue gaze. She closed the magazine on her lap as he approached.

"Uh-oh, you look like you're on the prowl." She eyed him with wary appreciation.

Slade sat down at the end of the chair, staring admiringly at her long legs, now tanned gold from days in the sun. He longed to run his hands all the way up them and feel her response. Tucking his torrid thoughts away, he met her teasing look.

"I am," he warned her. "I was hunting for you." He gestured toward the Travis ranch in the distance. "Figured the day was too nice to waste working. How'd you like to catch our dinner tonight?"

Cat hesitated, wanting to contain her eagerness. "Fishing?"

"Sure. Matt and Kai have a nice little river that's filled with bass. I've got the fishing tackle. All I need is my favorite lady to come along. Game?"

Cat gave up trying to disguise her delight. "You bet. But I'm not a good fisherman. My brother Rafe's an ace at it. If I hook anything, it's by sheer dumb luck."

Slade grinned and stood, offering Cat his hand. She took it without hesitation. The sun had tanned Cat's once-pale face, and her green eyes sparkled with good health once again. He hoped part of her happiness was due to his presence. "I suspect you're a lot better than you let on," replied Slade, gently pulling her up. "Come on, you can help me get the tackle and we'll be on our way. Maybe if Kai's home, she can join us."

"Wonderful!"

As they drove to the Travis ranch, Cat confided, "I'm glad you can pull away from work every once in a while."

The wind was hot and dry against his face. "I'm not a workaholic like some people you might have known."

Cat recognized the reference to Greg, but made no comment.

"Gold fever has a way of demanding your body and soul," Slade continued. He caught her thoughtful expression. "So, you like your man to be spontaneous and not hooked into the work harness all the time. What else do you like?"

Caught up in his expansive mood, Cat relaxed as they drove slowly down the dirt road. "My dream man would cherish our relationship above anything else."

"Even if you were pauper poor?"

"Poor in one way, but rich in another," she agreed with a laugh. "But this is a fantasy, remember? There's no such thing as a dream man—or woman, for that matter. But I'd like him to take me on picnics out in the wilderness where we could share a bottle of cold white wine or join me in the kitchen to bake chocolate-chip cookies."

"Hey, let's do that when we get back. I love chocolate-chip cookies."

Cat went warm inside. She could barely tear her gaze from Slade's wonderfully shaped mouth. She longed to have him kiss her again, but he'd been treading so carefully. His touch was nearly impersonal when he helped her with the rib wrap. Only lately had he even held her hand and, once, embraced her briefly. She wanted more, Cat realized. Much more. "Are you serious?" she challenged.

Giving her a hurt look, Slade held up his hand, as if swearing to his statement. "No kidding, I'm a sucker for cookies. And ice cream. And one particular exotic woman…"

Heat flamed into her cheeks and Cat allowed it to sweep straight through her. "Thank you," she managed, unable to hold his penetrating look. Both of them were tautly aware of the tension that crackled between them. Never had a man made Cat feel more like a woman.

Slade, unable to resist, picked up her hand and placed a gentle kiss on her palm. "You're welcome…"

Unstrung by Slade's sudden shift in mood, Cat fished quietly beside him at the river. The tall, stately pecan trees hugged their side of the bank, providing welcome shade. Kai Travis had greeted them when they'd arrived, provided icy lemonade, but had declined joining them. If Cat had looked closer, she would have seen a merry look in Kai's wide eyes that spoke volumes. Why did she feel Kai was deliberately leaving them alone?

"Hey! There goes your bobber!"

Cat jerked upright. She had been lounging half asleep against a pecan tree, rod in hand, when the red-and-white bobber at the end of her line was pulled down beneath the jade depths of the river. Slade's excitement sizzled through her and Cat scrambled to her feet. He was at her side as she gave a firm jerk upward on the pole. Immediately, the rod tip bent nearly double as the fish on the other end was hooked.

"I got him, Slade!" She struggled to flip off the safety

on the reel. It had been years since she had gone fishing and she was rusty and clumsy. Slade stood nearby, excitement in his voice.

"Looks big. Hold on, I'll get the net. Keep tension on that line or he'll flip out of the water and shake the hook loose."

Cat looked out of the corner of her eye as Slade swept the net into his hand and walked to the edge of the bank. "What a fighter," she gasped, slowly reeling the fish closer.

"You're doing fine, sweetheart. Hey…he's a grandpappy. Why, that bass must weigh close to five pounds. Okay, bring him in nice and slow…"

With a triumphant laugh, Cat set the rod aside after Slade had captured the bass. He expertly slid the hook out of the paper-thin mouth of the fish. Proudly he held the fish up for her to examine.

"For someone who hasn't fished much, you've got some kind of luck," he congratulated her. Slade put the bass on the stringer, then placed it back into the water to keep it alive until they were ready to go home. He knelt down and washed his hands. Cat stood beside him, her cheeks flushed with victory. Her smile went straight to Slade's heart.

His sapphire eyes darkened with intent as he stood up. Sweeping Cat into his arms, he held her gently against his damp, hard body. "You," he whispered thickly, "are something else." Then he claimed her parted lips.

Instinctively, Cat slid her arms across his shoulders. Slade's mouth was strong, cherishing. He ran his tongue in an outlining motion, placing small kisses at each corner of her lips. A soft moan welled up within her and

Cat trusted her full weight to Slade, lost in the growing fire of their mutual explorations.

"Sweet," he said in a rush, framing her face, lost in the tide of her returning kiss. The smoldering heat exploded violently within Slade as her mouth met and equaled the pressure of his own. Gripping her shoulders, Slade drowned in Cat, all thoughts taking flight. Feelings were what counted with him. He followed the inner yearnings of his heart, drinking deeply of Cat, losing himself in her womanliness.

Disappointed when Slade's mouth left hers, Cat looked up and was enveloped in the cobalt intensity of his gaze as he stared down at her. The world swayed and she gripped his arms.

"Cat? Are you all right?"

All right? She was delirious. Trying to smile, she nodded. "D-do you always catch a woman off guard like this, Slade?"

He groaned softly, cupping her chin, holding her dreamy expression. "There's just one woman I want to catch off guard, and that's you, sweetheart. No one else...just you..."

Waves of tidal strength rocked through her and Cat closed her eyes, pressing her cheek against his palm. "No one has ever made me dizzy, Slade Donovan. Ever."

Dizzy himself, Slade reveled in her openness and honesty with him. Here was the woman he had always known existed, and she was sharing herself with him. Light-headed and a little shaky, Slade gently drew Cat into his arms. The day was hot, their shirts damp from perspiration, but he didn't care. "It's your fault, you know."

"What is? The kiss?"

Slade rubbed his jaw against the softness of her sable-colored hair. "Definitely."

Cat pulled away, laughing at his teasing. "How could it be?"

Mirth danced in his features. "You promised me chocolate-chip cookies, remember? I go crazy when a woman offers to bake me cookies."

With a playful look, Cat stepped out of his arms. "You're so full of it, Slade Donovan."

He recaptured Cat's hand, pulling her to a halt before she could escape completely. "Now wait a minute, I was kidding about the cookies, not the kiss."

"Really?"

Slade gave her a measuring look, wondering if Cat was serious or if she was just giving him a good dose of his own medicine. "I can do without the cookies, but I can't do without you."

"That's nice to know, Donovan; I rate higher than a chocolate-chip cookie."

He wanted to throttle her. "You rate a hell of a lot higher than that and you know it."

Merrily, Cat slipped from his grasp and retrieved her rod. "Really? Well, we'll see." She gave him a look filled with challenge. "I'm going to put you to the test, Slade."

"Oh?"

Satisfaction wreathed Cat's smile as she baited the hook and then tossed the bobber back into the river. "Tonight, after dinner, I'm going to bake you three dozen chocolate-chip cookies. I'll use my mom's recipe, and they're better than any other kind you've ever eaten."

He brightened. "Great."

"There's only one catch to all this, Donovan."

He frowned. "What?"

Cat sat back down, her back against the pecan tree, grinning. "You have a choice: a kiss from me or those three dozen cookies tonight. Which will it be, I wonder?"

Slade gave in to her teasing. There was no question in his mind that he'd rather have the kiss. Still, he couldn't resist playing Cat's game. "Cat, how can you do this to me? Do you realize how rare it is that I get homemade chocolate-chip cookies?"

Choking back her laughter, Cat tried very hard to keep a straight face and appear to concentrate on fishing. "Didn't you just say I rated higher than a cookie?"

"This isn't fair! Of course you're more important than a cookie." Slade stood over her, hoping to intimidate her into thinking twice about the choice she offered him.

Cat looked up, giving him an innocent look. "If that's true, then you'll settle for a good-night kiss instead of those cookies I'm going to bake."

"What will happen to those cookies, then?"

"I'm sure Pilar's children would love them, aren't you?"

Groaning, Slade stalked over to his rod. "You don't fight fair, you know that?"

Barely able to keep the smile from pulling up the corners of her mouth, Cat nodded. "Neither do you. You're just getting a taste of your own medicine, Donovan. How does it feel?"

Slade sat down, balancing the rod on his knees, and gave her a devilish look. "You're going to pay for this, Ms. Kincaid."

"Uh-oh, threats! Threats!"

Joy swept through Slade as he watched Cat laugh like a delighted child. She was beautiful in so many ways. And grudgingly, he admitted he'd finally met his match. The little vixen. Well, he'd win the last round in this sparring between them. And what sweet, luscious revenge it would be.

That evening, after Pilar had left for the night, Cat went to the kitchen to bake. Slade hung around, watching closely as she made her mother's recipe for chocolate-chip cookies. Every now and again, Slade would lean over her shoulders and swipe a bite of the dough. And then he would steal a light kiss from Cat. Tinkering with the cappuccino maker, Slade worked nearby on the tile drain board. Cat looked soft and feminine in a pale pink sundress. The square neck on the dress showed off her recent tan to a decided advantage.

"Did I tell you how pretty you look in that dress?"

Cat began to drop the cookie dough onto the sheet. The corners of her mouth lifted slightly and she pinned Slade's longing gaze. "Is this your way of getting a cookie? Flattery?"

Slade placed the lid on the cappuccino machine, screwing it down tightly. He met her smile. "Cookies can't hold a flame to you."

Laughing lightly, she murmured, "Why, thank you. Can I help it if I think you have ulterior motives designed to weaken my resolve?"

"Sweetheart, if I want to weaken your resolve, I'll be a hell of a lot more straightforward about it."

"Uh-oh, Texans are rather brash, aren't they?" Cat walked around Slade and moved to the oven. He leaned petulantly against the drain board, watching her through half-closed eyes. She found it hard to fight the attraction he always generated in her. Eyeing the oven's temperature control, Cat straightened up. She brushed away strands of damp hair from her brow.

"Texans are honest," Slade defended, eagerly absorbing her every movement.

Placing the sheet of cookies in the oven, Cat closed the door. "Even if it kills them," she agreed. "There. In about ten minutes, the first dozen will be ready. How's our cappuccino coming?"

Slade roused himself from staring at her. Her flushed cheeks and the serenity surrounding her made her just that much more enticing. Everything was happening so quickly. He didn't want to rush Cat or make her feel as if he was stalking her.

"Here," Slade said, handing her a large mug of the steaming brew, frothy with hot milk. Then he joined her on the living-room couch. The last of the cookies had been baked and were set out to cool. The merriment in Cat's eyes as she took the cup made him smile. With a contented sigh, Slade sat back, his shoulders almost touching hers.

"How are you doing?" Cat asked, sipping contentedly at her cappuccino.

Slade rolled his head to the left, drinking in her smiling features. "Okay."

"You're holding up amazingly well for a Cookie Monster."

"Yeah, I know it."

"I've got them counted, Slade. So don't come sneaking out here in the middle of the night to steal one. Or two. Probably half a dozen."

Slade joined her laughter and picked up her hand. "I've got something even better than that, Cat."

"What?" She loved the feel of his big, firm hand.

"I was privileged to see you working in the kitchen."

"Being a mining engineer doesn't mean I can't do anything else."

"Now, don't go getting contrary. That was a compliment. You looked kind of pretty and at home in there. I liked the feeling." His voice lowered. "For the first time since I bought this place, it feels like a home." And then he met Cat's sober gaze. "Do you know what I mean?"

Her voice was barely above a whisper. "Yes, I know…"

Reluctantly, Slade released her hand. "What we… share…is so good, Cat."

Cat set her mug on the coffee table. Slade gave her a puzzled look as she rose and walked to the kitchen.

"Now what did I say?" he demanded, sitting up. "Cat?"

Cat returned with a saucer stacked with cookies. She handed them to Slade. "Nothing's wrong," she told him, sitting back down beside him. "Everything's right…"

Delighted with her change of heart, Slade picked up a cookie. He was about to take a bite out of it, then hesitated. "Does this mean I still get my kiss?"

"I hereby release you from having to make a choice," Cat said, her eyes sparkling.

"Here, this one's for the cook. She's one hell of a fine lady."

Cat took the proffered cookie, giving Slade a tender smile. Holding up her cookie in a toast, she murmured, "And here's to one hell of a fine man."

Happily, Slade touched her cookie with his. He consumed four of them without another word.

Laughing, Cat snuggled into the couch, her legs tucked beneath her. The beatific look of pleasure on Slade's face made her feel good. She reached out, resting her hand against his shoulder. "You're such an easy person to please, Slade Donovan. Does it always take so little to make you happy?"

He glanced over at Cat, matching her smile. "That's me in a nutshell, sweetheart. Small, simple things in life are the best. Like that kiss we shared this afternoon…"

"Or the cookies…"

"Yeah, them too. But the kiss was sweeter. Better." And then he brightened. "This is pretty good—not only do I get these great-tasting cookies, but I also get to give you a good-night kiss."

"Don't gloat, Slade."

"Was I gloating?"

"You know you are. You're as bad as Rafe when it comes to getting everything your way."

Rafe called her less than a week later. Joyfully, Cat picked up the phone when Pilar told her who it was. The early-afternoon sunlight spilled through the windows as Cat took the phone into the living room, making herself comfortable on the apricot-colored couch.

"How are you?" Cat asked, barely able to contain her happiness.

"Things could be going a hell of a lot better, Cat."

Her brows dipped. "Oh, no. What's wrong, Rafe?"

"You remember I told you about Jessica?"

"The lady investigator from the Bureau of Land Mines?"

"Same one," he said gruffly.

Gripping the phone, Cat felt her brother's unspoken anguish. "Oh, Rafe, what happened? I know how much you love her. Didn't you fly up to Wyoming to see her?"

"Yes…but…things just didn't work out for us, Cat.

Not the way I wanted, at least. Listen, enough of my troubles. How are you? You sound better. Happier."

Her heart bled for Rafe. How many times had he talked of Jessie to her? Any fool could see that Rafe was head over heels in love with the woman. Shutting her eyes, Cat had no defense against her brother's pain. "Oh, I'm surviving."

"Isn't Slade Donovan treating you right?"

The threat in Rafe's voice made her laugh softly. "Now don't go getting growly like an old bear just waking up from hibernation. Slade is—well, he's wonderful, Rafe."

"Then what's the problem? You're worried. I can hear it in your voice."

"It's just the calls I'm getting from mining companies who want to hire me. Seems like everyone knows I can't fulfill the terms of the Australian contract and they're trying to entice me into other jobs. They're like Nar hunting down a rabbit."

Rafe's laughter was explosive. "That damned eagle. Speaking of hunting, did you know he grabbed Goodyear the other day?"

Buoyed by Rafe's sudden good humor, Cat was swept along by it. "Oh, no. What happened? Did Millie get on her broomstick and fly after him?"

Chuckling, Rafe recounted the latest escapade of the golden eagle and the nearly-thirty-pound, overfed cat, Goodyear. "Well, you know how Nar dive-bombs the chicken coop every once in a while to keep everyone on their toes?"

"Yes, the little turkey."

"Now, Nar would be insulted if you called him a turkey."

"Jim Tremain calls him a flying pig and he's right! Well, go on. What happened?"

"Pig is right. Anyway, Nar spotted the Goodyear blimp outside the horse-paddock area. I guess Goodyear had caught his first mouse ever."

"As fat as that cat is, I'm surprised he's caught one. Sure the mouse wasn't crippled, blind and already dead from old age?"

"Who knows?" Rafe laughed. "Anyway, I was saddling Flight up to help herd some cattle to the south range when I saw Nar land about ten feet away from Goodyear. The cat hadn't hurt the mouse. He was just holding it between his front paws gloating over it. Frankly, I don't think Goodyear knew what to do with it. Millie feeds him so many table scraps he's never had to hunt a day in his life."

"What did Nar do?"

"He flapped his wings and came clucking and chutting up to Goodyear. The cat flattened his ears and crouched over his mouse. He wasn't going to give up his feast to that brazen bird."

Cat could barely stifle her giggles, and held a protective arm across her stomach. "Did Nar take the mouse?"

"No. He made a lightning strike for Goodyear's tail and picked him right up off the ground. You should have heard the racket. The mouse squeaked and ran. Goodyear was shrieking like a scalded cat. Nar lumbered toward the meadow, trying to get airborne, dragging Goodyear in a wake of dust. Can you imagine a thirteen-pound eagle trying to lift off with a thirty-pound fatso? I was laughing so hard, tears were running down my face. Goodyear was digging into the grass and dirt trying to stop Nar from moving forward. Nar kept getting jerked around until finally he crashed. Both he and the cat hit the dirt at the same time. You should have seen it—dust, feathers and cat fur were flying everywhere."

Crying with laughter, Cat couldn't speak for almost a minute. "Oh, no! What happened? Did Millie ever get wind of it?"

"Nah, I ran out of the barn to stop Nar from dragging the damn idiot cat around by the tail. There was a huge cloud of dust and all these screams from Nar and snarls from Goodyear. Just as I got there, Goodyear shot out like a fired cannonball with a couple of feathers in his mouth. Nar limped out the other side with a real hurt look on his face. I stood there laughing. That cat finally got even for all the times Nar teased and chased him. Last I saw, Goodyear was rolling at high speed toward the safety of the chicken coop, Nar's tail feathers in his mouth."

Wiping the tears from her eyes, Cat said with a giggle, "Finally, after all these years, Goodyear evens the score! Did you tell Dal that her eagle got the worst end of the confrontation?"

"Yeah, I did. I don't know who laughed harder, Dal or me."

Cat smiled tenderly, cradling the phone. "You're so good for me, Rafe. All I have to do is remember Nar and Goodyear's latest battle and I'll die laughing."

Suddenly shifting gears, Rafe asked, "Have you heard anything about the Emerald Lady Mine or what they were going to do with the owner?"

Cat sobered slightly. "Lionel Graham has been handed a large fine by the government."

"Well deserved," Rafe applauded.

"I don't think he'll be able to build any more mines in

the U.S. without the government watching him closely. He got what was coming to him."

"Slade had been right about him all the time," Rafe added.

Cat made a wry face. "Tell me about it. If I had listened to him in the first place, I wouldn't have gotten into my present bind."

"But then, you wouldn't have met Slade."

Rafe was right. Cat closed her eyes for a moment. "And I'm very glad we've had the time together."

"Good," Rafe rumbled, his voice warm and pleased, "you deserve some happiness."

"Between you, Slade and Kai Travis, I'm surrounded by people who make me smile and laugh."

"So, you like the Travis gal, eh?"

"Yes. She and her husband, Matt, are wonderful. Slade has had them over here for dinner once a week and we have a great time. You should see their one-year-old, Josh. I've never seen a cuter tyke." And then Cat cringed. Why did she have to bring up the subject of babies to Rafe? She knew how much he'd wanted kids before his wife had died in childbirth.

There were a few awkward moments of silence, then Rafe cleared his throat. "You sound better now, Cat. I'll give you a call in a week and see if you're still improving."

Trying to rally for his sake, Cat murmured, "Don't worry. Between Slade and Kai I have to get better."

Chapter 6

Kai loosened the blood-pressure cuff from around Cat's left arm. "Perfectly healthy and normal. Not bad after four weeks." She set the cuff aside and examined the nearly healed scar along Cat's scalp. "You're just as tough as Slade," she teased. "Are all you rock-hunting miners built out of the same genetic material?"

Cat met her smile. Kai had a genuine warmth emanating from her that made Cat feel good. "I'm not as tough as I look."

"Nonsense. Come on, let's go enjoy a late-morning margarita on Slade's back porch. It's almost noon and I can't stay long. Maria is watching Josh until I get back. Let's spend a few minutes catching up on what we've been doing the past few days." Kai reached for her hand, giving it a squeeze. "I'm really glad you're here, Cat. Out on this Texas desert, I get a little lonely for feminine company."

Cat followed Kai out into the living room and sat down at the bar. Kai made a mean margarita, almost as good as Slade's. "I don't know what I'd have done without you, Kai," Cat admitted.

Kai dropped the ice cubes into the blender, shut the lid and turned it on. "Slade would have been utterly lost without your help."

"What do you mean?"

Kai poured the margaritas into two long-stemmed glasses, her eyes sparkling. "I'm sure he's told you why he flew up to Maine to find you. After all, he wanted only the best engineer to build that mine of his down in Colombia. He'd talked for months of a way to lure you away from your other commitments. Believe me when I tell you that when Slade wants something, he doesn't take no for an answer." Kai added a slice of lime to the drinks. "But then, you've experienced his persuasive sales abilities, so you know what I'm talking about. I don't think I've ever seen Slade as intense as he was about hiring you. He wanted the best." Her eyes twinkled and she leaned forward, her long auburn hair falling around her face. "Just between us, I think Slade's enjoying your company so much he's forgotten about the mine. When I talk to him, he always speaks of you, never about the Verde."

Cat nearly choked on Kai's statement. She barely tasted the tart drink, thrown as she was into a maelstrom of powerful emotions. Slade had wanted to hire her to build him a mine? He had hinted about a business deal, but she had forgotten all about it. Maybe his offer to have her recuperate at the ranch was just part of his business plan. Why hadn't she questioned Slade more closely? But then, how could she? As badly injured as she was, she had willingly accepted Slade's offer to recuperate here. What an idealistic fool she had been.

"It's good," Cat forced out in a tight voice, all her focus on the unannounced business deal.

Kai smiled and came around to join her. The white slacks and bright green blouse did nothing but bring out her natural beauty. "Great! Hey, you know we should go shopping soon. Slade could fly us into Houston for the day. He always has business with Alvin, his partner, there. I'm sure he wouldn't mind if we tagged along."

Slade had a partner. A business partner. Cat didn't like what she was hearing. Was Slade's care and seeming desire nothing more than a means to get her to work with him on his mine? A knifelike pain tore through her. Had Slade's kisses only been a disguise for what he really wanted? No wonder he'd downplayed her problems with Ian Connors. If Slade wanted her services, he'd gladly tell her to drop Connors.

Her fingers tightened around the frosty stem of the glass. Shaken, Cat took another gulp of the margarita. *One way or another, I have to find out why Slade really brought me here. Maybe it wasn't out of the kindness of his heart, as I thought.* Inwardly, Cat died. Until that moment, she had never really gotten in touch with the depth of her feelings for Slade. And now it was sheer, aching torture to admit just how much he had come to mean to her.

After Kai had gone, Cat sat in the silence of the living room. *I've just found out why I'm here at Mourning Dove Ranch,* Cat grimly told herself. She gingerly ran her hands over her healing ribs and went to the kitchen, where Pilar was starting preparation for lunch.

"Did you want coffee, Señorita Cat?" she greeted her, lifting one soapy hand.

Cat managed a smile and went over to a large pot, pouring herself a cup of coffee. "I can get it, Pilar. Thank you." She needed time to think. "Is Slade in his office?"

"Either his office or hobby shop," Pilar replied. "Would you like an early lunch?"

"No, thank you. I'll just go out to the porch for a while." She had no appetite.

Cat sat down at the table, staring beyond the screened-in porch. Absently, she smoothed the burgundy skirt that was imprinted with a profusion of white, pink and lavender orchid blooms. Kai had insisted over the weeks that she have something other than pants to wear and had given her a gift of the Mexican skirt and blouse. Cat fingered the lace of the boat-necked white blouse she wore, her mind spinning.

Cat's mind focused on Slade. Was he planning to send men and machinery down to Colombia to gear up for the mine he wanted to build? For eight hours each day he would disappear into his office. Was Slade playing a waiting game with her? Cat tried to search her memory for some betraying facts. Slade would join her, like clockwork, at noon, for an hour-long lunch. She could never quite get used to his devastating effect on her—that special warmth flowing up through her, the added beat to her heart when she first saw him crossing the living room and moving to the porch where Pilar served lunch. Merriment was usually lurking in his eyes when he approached her. Cat frowned, the coffee tasting bitter. Right or wrong, she was drawn powerfully to Slade, and it was more than physical. How she felt about him and what he wanted from her warred within her. She had to talk to Slade and clear the air.

Cat rose, her mouth set in a determined line. She wanted to do something—anything—to settle what lay between them. In another few weeks she would be fit and ready to work again. Cat set the coffee cup on the drain board, gathering her courage. Padding silently through the house, she walked across the garden and patio. The palms of her hands grew damp as she followed the left fork. Cat tried out a number of opening lines in her head as she walked along the path to Slade's shop. She slowed, coming to a sliding-glass door that was partially open.

Slade was bent over what she recognized to be a multi-wheel gem polisher. He had a gem in a brown, waxlike substance known as dop, and was grinding the shape of the gem against the spinning wheel. His long workbench, to the right, was strewn with a can of dop sticks that would hold a rough-cut cabachon-shaped gem. Faceting equipment, which would shape a gem to blinding brilliance, was nearby. Cat stood in the doorway, tense.

Sensing her presence, despite the level of noise, Slade turned around. "Come in…if you can find a place to sit down." Taking off his safety glasses, Slade leaned over, pulling a stool toward him, motioning for Cat to join him.

"I—thanks." Cat sat down.

"Looks like you're a little bored."

Somehow, he looked more pulse-poundingly handsome than usual to her. Slade wore a faded red T-shirt that emphasized the powerful breadth of his chest and tight muscles. His jeans were streaked with dust and soiled across the thighs, where he obviously wiped his fingers as he worked.

"I didn't know you were a jeweler," Cat began lamely, unsure how to begin her preamble.

Slade grinned, putting the glasses back on and returning to the work at hand, turning on the polisher again. He expertly positioned the cabachon he held on the stick between his hands. "Making jewelry is my hobby."

Cat leaned forward, fascinated. "An unusual hobby for a man."

"But not a geologist," Slade corrected, lightly pressuring the stone against the wheel. A whirring sound continued for several seconds before he lifted the stone away. Slade dipped it into some water, and rubbed away the accumulated material that resulted when the rock was polished. There was satisfaction mirrored in his face. He held the stick out to her. "Take a look. That's pink tourmaline from the El Camino mine. Beautiful specimen, isn't it?"

Cat held the stick, observing the gem. Slade was no amateur in his fashioning of the stone. The tourmaline was at least four carats in size, and Slade had used the oval cut to bring out the breathtaking pink fire from the depths of the stone. "It's lovely," she whispered.

Slade smiled. "There's no color on earth like this," he agreed, running his callused finger over the gem.

"You're hardly a novice," Cat accused, handing the stick back to him.

His smile broadened as he set it down on the table next to the lathe. "No, but my mother taught me to be modest about my talents. So what did you think I was doing back here?"

"Working on the latest geology reports, collecting data for a place where you might want to go next," she hinted, waiting to see if he would take the bait.

"I wanted to get this ring finished in time for my mother's birthday. It's only ten days away," he murmured, taking off his safety glasses.

"It's a lovely stone. I'm sure your mother will be thrilled with it."

"I sure hope you're right. So, you're itching to get back into the mining mode?"

Cat froze internally. "Not yet."

"Let's change our schedule, then. How would you like to go on a picnic with me today?"

Caught off guard, Cat repeated, "A picnic?" It sounded wonderful and she knew the sudden catch in her voice showed her surprise. She saw Slade smile as he got up and rinsed his hands off in a basin nearby.

"Well—I—there's something we have to discuss, Slade."

"Great. I'm cashing in on that rain check I promised you, Cat. We can talk over lunch. Why don't you tell Pilar we're going? She'll be happy to fix something for us."

Cat slid off the stool. Maybe a picnic would be the right place to broach the subject. "Oh? Does she want to get us out from underfoot?"

"She's been after me for the past two weeks to take you on one. I couldn't because it's hell traveling with taped ribs any more than necessary. Now, you're almost as good as new and I think it's just what we both need."

Cat turned away, feeling heat in her cheeks. "Have you had broken ribs before, Slade?"

He chuckled. "Yeah, when I was at the university

I played football. One game I took three hits simultaneously and ended up under a pile of opposing players. I came out with four busted ribs. Needless to say, I didn't play the rest of the season." He lifted his head and turned toward her. "That's how I knew how much pain you were in this past month. You're a pretty brave lady, you know that?"

With a wan smile, Cat stepped out the sliding-glass doors. "Don't put me on a pedestal, Slade. I'll fall off before you can blink twice. I've got enough inclusions in me to match any emerald you find." Inclusions were the hairline fissures that could flaw the otherwise clear surface of a gem. In other words, they were mistakes, and she made her own fair share. And so did Slade.

"Inclusions make you interesting, sweetheart. Who wants a flawless gem? They're rather boring in comparison."

"You're a glutton for punishment, then. I'll tell Pilar of our lunch plans." Cat tried to stop the fear expanding within her. In the weeks they had lived together under the same roof, peace had reigned, not irritation or tension. No, Cat thought wryly to herself, the only tension her heart felt was a longing to draw closer to Slade. Toward the end of the picnic, Cat could talk to Slade about the mine.

Packing the wicker basket in the back of the Jeep, Slade guided Cat into the front seat. He wanted to tell her how beautiful she had become in the past month; her sable hair shone with gold highlights, and though it was a bit shaggy, it was more appealing as it grew longer. She was, by anyone's standards, a woman to be recognized. Pilar had given her a broad-brimmed straw hat to protect her face from the harsh sun overhead. Slade got into the driver's seat, and the Jeep started up with a cough and sputter.

"Where are we going?" Cat asked.

"A special place for a special lady," Slade answered. He pointed the Jeep down the flat expanse of dirt road, driving slowly and avoiding most of the holes in the road that might jar Cat. "It's on Kai and Matt's ranch. I only took you by one part of the river before. The part we're going to now has about four thousand pecan trees planted along it. And there's a beautiful spot near the water where they placed a picnic table. I thought you might enjoy a change of scenery."

The sun was warm and Cat held the hat on with one hand. "Kai wanted to know if I'd go into Houston with her to shop for a day."

Slade made a chortling sound. "Uh-oh. Women going shopping spells disaster. Houston will never be the same. Did you tell her you'd go?"

Cat shrugged. "I told her I'd think about it."

He heard the hesitancy in her voice, but didn't understand it. Usually, most women would give their right arm to go shopping in such a cosmopolitan and sophisticated city as Houston. But then, Cat wasn't the average female, Slade reminded himself. He almost sensed that Cat didn't want to leave the ranch, whatever her reasons. Had her nightmares dampened her otherwise keen traveling spirit? He decided to pursue that at an opportune time, later.

Slade spread the red cotton tablecloth across the green picnic table while Cat brought over the basket. Pilar had packed beef sandwiches, potato salad, some apples and a bottle of zinfandel, Slade's favorite white wine. The pecan trees rose straight and tall, already bearing a quantity of fruit. In the fall, they would be harvested during a five-day celebration. The noontime heat was well over ninety. Beneath the trees, with a cool breeze rippling off the small, quiet river that languidly flowed past them, it was an acceptable eighty degrees. Slade motioned for Cat to come and sit down. When she did, he sat next to her, something he rarely did at the ranch.

His move hadn't been missed by Cat, either. At first, she was going to say something, and then thought better of it. She wondered perversely if he had deliberately used reverse psychology on her so she would willingly welcome his advances. Cat shook her head, angry with herself. Slade had been the perfect host since she had come to his ranch. She decided to drop her wariness and simply enjoy him for the duration of the picnic.

"I didn't realize how skilled you were at jewelry making. Do you work on it every day?"

Slade handed Cat a plastic cup half-filled with the delicate white wine. "Yes. After I get caught up on paperwork, I head over to the shop. I use the samples I collect from my job assignments and play treasure hunter, stalking the gems I know are buried deep within the matrix."

"I'd like to see some of your finished work. Is that possible?"

"Sure. I keep all my fledgling attempts and mistakes in the back room."

"Knowing you as I do, I doubt if you've got any 'mistakes.'"

Slade set a plate loaded with food in front of her.

"I've got plenty of mistakes. I just don't go around showing them to everyone."

"Why to me?" she asked, meeting and holding his gaze.

"What if I told you I wanted you to know me with and without mistakes?"

Cat's heart pumped hard to underscore the implications of his question. "Then I'd ask why you're according me that privilege." Was he going to tell her about his mine?

"Would you?" He looked at her closely.

She nodded, sipping the spicy, clear wine. "I think it signals a certain change in a relationship when both people let down their guard and allow the other to see all their qualities."

Slade took her statement seriously, biting into a sandwich. He was having trouble keeping the conversation light. The past week had been pure hell on him. He wanted to do something about the longing in Cat's eyes as she looked up at him. Food was the last thing on his mind right now. "That's another thing I like about you, Ms. Kincaid; you don't play the games men and women play so well with one another."

"But you play games, Slade."

He winced inwardly at the sudden sadness in her voice. He wiped his mouth and then his fingers on a paper napkin. He captured her hand, squeezing it gently. "Not with you, sweetheart." He saw the unsureness in her emerald eyes as she studied him in the intervening silence.

Cat swallowed a sudden lump in her throat. Tears pricked her eyes. Angrily she shoved these unexpected feelings back down inside, to be dealt with later, and shook her head. "I just don't know what to think, Slade.

Ever since we met, I felt as though you wanted something from me. At first, I thought it was just because you were interested in me—as a woman. But later, once we developed a friendship, I changed my mind about that. Right now, I'm not sure what you want from me." She sat rigidly. "Kai mentioned you had a mine down in Colombia. By any chance does that explain why I'm here at your ranch?" She prayed it wasn't so. Slade's brows dipped. He shoved the plate aside, concentrating on Cat, hearing the pain in her voice. "I'm sorry, Cat. I really screwed up, then. Yeah, I had flown to Maine to try and persuade you to come and work for me. But—" he managed a shy smile "—when I saw you all my logic went out the door. I hadn't expected you to affect me like you did." He picked up her hand, cradling it gently. "I wanted you to come here for personal motives, not professional ones. Please, believe me." Slade refused to relinquish her hand. He reached out with the other, lightly tracing her cheek and delicate jawline. "And when it comes to you on a personal level…" His voice turned harsh. "Do you know how damned hard it's been to keep my hands off you so you could heal? As much as I wanted to put my arms around you, hold you tight against me and kiss the hell out of you, I knew I couldn't." He saw hope suddenly spring like an emerald flame into her widening eyes.

"Look, let's untangle our communication with one another. Yes, I came hunting you down." He halted, struggling with words. "I'm lousy at talk, Cat. Let me show you how I feel about you." Slade leaned down, wanting, needing to feel her lips once again beneath his. "I've been wanting to do this for so damn long…" He molded his mouth to hers. An explosion of need reeled through Slade as her soft, pliant lips yielded to him. He felt her arm sliding around his neck and he groaned as she lightly swayed against his chest. He had to forcibly stop his hands from following her curves upward to the small, firm breasts resting against him. Instead, Slade framed her face, cherishing her wine-bathed lips, using his tongue to probe the corners of her mouth.

"You make a man thirsty for more," he groaned as he probed the inner, moist recesses of her mouth. A column of need roared through him, his body hardening with a fire of its own. Cat's breath was moist and ragged against him and Slade reveled in her ardor. He allowed his hands to trail down her slender neck and cup her shoulders. Reluctantly, he eased away, then stared down hungrily at Cat. She was his, all of her.

As Slade drew back, his hands captured hers. "Listen to me," he told her roughly, his voice heavy with desire. "I want you like I've never wanted another woman, Cat. And it's not because of what I need from you professionally." Slade caressed her cheek, reveling in her luminous eyes. "Can you separate the issues? It's important to me that you can."

Cat was barely coherent after the branding kiss that had seared her lips. She hadn't been merely hungry for Slade's touch, she'd been starved, and her returning fervor had caught her totally off guard. Never had a man affected her so profoundly as did Slade. Touching Slade physically was merely an extension of everything else Cat already felt in her heart.

Her heart? Cat was careful not to place any emphasis on that unexpected and unknown quantity right now. If age had taught her nothing else, it had taught her that time would reveal what was real in their burgeoning relationship. Now, Slade was waiting for an answer from her. She stared into his eyes, seeing fear mingled with hope. Fear?

"I want to separate these things, Slade. Why don't you tell me what you want from me and then we can clear the air. I don't want to suspect your every move or intention. You can't blame me for reacting like this. Put yourself in my place."

Slade refused to allow Cat to reclaim her hands. He gave her all his attention. "Professionally, I want you to think about building a mine for me. That's all. The decision is up to you and I'm not going to pressure you about it." He gently squeezed her fingers. "But some of your reaction isn't warranted. At least, not with me and what we share."

She hung her head for an instant, wanting to believe Slade. "Maybe all the years of being in the field have made me more isolated than I wanted to be." She sighed. "Maybe I just need someplace I can go to when it all becomes too much to take."

"Don't you have a permanent address? An apartment on the coast? A condo?" Slade ran his thumb gently in small circles on the back of her hand.

Cat shook her head, relaxing beneath Slade's ministrations, wonderful tingling sensations fleeing up her arm as he lightly stroked her. "The Triple K is home."

"That's the family homestead. What about some place special for you?"

"No. The mine I'm building on my next assignment becomes my home. I live in a tent or trailer just like everyone else."

"Well, you apparently need more. I noticed you called the ranch your home today for the first time."

A shiver of longing moved through her and Cat acknowledged his statement. "I did, didn't I?"

"Yes."

Cat gave a rueful shake of her head. "I think I'm burned out and haven't even recognized my own symptoms."

Slade reluctantly let her go and brought their plates back over so that they could finish lunch. He wasn't hungry, but he recognized the need to step back and talk about their other problems. "I think this accident has helped open you up to some of your feelings," he said quietly, wanting to find a way to probe the content of her restless nights.

"I can't shake the nightmares, Slade."

He treaded lightly, sipping his wine. "Have you figured out why they're still with you?"

Cat picked up a ripe red apple, the surface slick and polished as she slowly turned it around between her hands. "As stupid as this sounds, I find myself standing at the opening to a mine. And then, I break out into a cold sweat."

"Afraid to enter it?"

Cat gnawed on her lower lip. "Yes. Of all things, Slade, I'm afraid to go down into an adit. I've spent the past ten years of my life in shafts, even those that miners were afraid to go into, and I never thought anything of it. Can you believe that? It's just blown me away." She looked down at her hands, closed tightly around the apple. "More important, it shouldn't affect me like it has. It's stupid."

"Ever fallen off a horse?"

"More times than I can count. Why?"

"Rafe said you can apply the same logic to a mine.

There isn't a miner, an engineer or geologist who's been trapped who hasn't experienced that same strangling fear."

Relief was mirrored in Cat's features. "You're using the right word: strangling. Sometimes, when I think about it, I can barely breathe. I feel as if an invisible hand is choking off my breath and I'm slowly suffocating."

"Like you were in that cave-in."

Cold fear took away the heat within her. "Yes."

"Well," Slade said slowly, "there are two things you can do, Cat. One is to never enter another mine and give up a good portion of your work. Or you can go face that fear by entering a mine again. It's like getting thrown off a horse and then climbing right back on. The sooner you do it, the quicker the fear recedes."

"Does the fear ever go away?"

"It's different for everyone."

"You've been trapped. How does it affect you when you go into a shaft?"

"There's always a thread of fear deep down in me," Slade admitted. "But then, I swing my focus to why I'm down there, and the fever of finding a gem outweighs my fear."

"What have three cave-ins taught you?"

A slight smile pulled at his mouth. "To value each minute of each day like there will never be another. I used to live in the future; I don't anymore."

Cat closed her eyes, relief washing through her. "I'm so glad you understand." Her voice held a tremor. "Every day I find myself enjoying little things I overlooked before. I used to ignore so much, Slade."

"But you don't anymore," he said softly, giving her a tender smile that promised so much.

They finished lunch and Slade repacked the basket, placing it in the Jeep. Cat stood near the river, watching a bass leap out at a dragonfly that had flown too close to his lily-pad home beneath the water. As he turned back to her, Slade read the sad expression on her face. She was allowing him to sense her feelings, no longer hiding so much of herself from him. He found himself smiling. Each time they shared an encounter, it was as if another petal of their relationship had opened.

Slade's feelings were strong toward Cat and he didn't fight them. How many nights had he lain awake, thinking of her? She was like him in some respects, always traveling the world in search of a new adventure. Cat was also strong and independent, and he liked that about her. Yet, as he studied her profile, he was achingly aware of her vulnerability.

Cat was pleasantly surprised as Slade gently drew her back against him. Her lips parted as he brushed her hair with a kiss. "Slade…" She whispered his name.

"This is what I wanted to do," he told her in a low voice, his fingers gently massaging her shoulders. Her skin was soft and firm beneath his explorations. "The sunlight dances off your hair and I can see the gold in it."

Cat's smile softened. "Pyrite. Fool's gold."

"No way, lady. You're a rare vein of gold that few are ever privileged to see."

Her nostrils flared as she inhaled his salty, masculine scent. "I'm afraid, Slade."

He opened his eyes, holding her a little more firmly,

disturbed by the tremulous quality in her tone. "Of what?"

"Of you."

"I won't hurt you."

"Not intentionally."

"Have you always run, Cat?"

She shook her head, glorying in his male strength, the tenderness he offered her. She needed it badly. "No, but you're different."

He rested his mouth against the silky strands of her hair. "Explain."

"You show how you feel. Most of the men I know are closed up like the mines we dig. I haven't had much experience with a man of your openness."

"Ah, I see." He pressed a kiss to her temple. "Never took on a Texan?" He deliberately teased her, feeling the tension in her shoulders. Then, almost as quickly, her tension dissolved beneath his cajoling tone.

"No. Never."

"What else bothers you about me?"

"Just that." Cat tilted her head, catching his teasing expression. "And what you wanted from me professionally."

Slade smiled, feeling the softness of her cheek against his sandpapery one. "I'm sorry I didn't discuss the matter sooner, Cat. The mine became secondary to your coming here to the ranch. You were what was important to me. I'm not lying, nor am I playing a game with you. If this has been on your mind, though, I wish you'd asked sooner."

"I was afraid of the answer, Slade," Cat admitted hoarsely. "No one likes to think they're manipulated or strung along."

Slade sighed deeply. "I guess I deserve that from you. My intentions were to discuss the mine when you were ready. Right now, you're still healing." He kissed her temple.

Cat leaned back against him. "What I want to know is, why aren't you married? A man with your attributes would turn any woman's head."

His smile disappeared and he gently folded his arms around her as they stood at the bank of the river. "Came close a couple of times," Slade admitted.

"But?"

"What woman was going to accept my traveling life-style and stay at home without me for months at a time?"

"She could go with you."

He shook his head. "Not the women I fell in love with. They wanted a home and a family. Until recently, I couldn't provide the kind of security they wanted. You know how geologists bum around the world. There aren't many women willing to make a home in the desert for a year, or live in a jungle in Thailand while you hunt for gems. Women get the worst end of the deal: loneliness. I can understand their position and that's the main reason I haven't married." Slade gazed down at her. "I told you before: I'm looking for a woman who's as footloose as I am."

Cat ignored the invitation in his voice. She was thinking along similar lines. Finding a man who would accept her vocation and allow her to travel had slimmed candidates to a bare minimum. "I don't find many men willing to let me roam, either."

"Just two old travel-weary vets of the rock industry, huh?"

Cat smiled. "With at least another couple of decades

of bumming around left in them." If she could control her fear of mine entry.

"I think when I'm eighty, I'll still be a rock hound at heart."

"The earth is too alive to us to ever walk away from," Cat agreed. And knowing that, she suddenly vowed to overcome her fear. The earth had always been good to her.

"I like your attitude, lady. Come to think of it, I haven't seen much not to like about you."

"Wait." Cat laughed. "I get in a blue funk every once in awhile."

"And when you do, what happens?"

"I get crabby and crawl into my shell."

"Retreat is the better part of valor, maybe?"

"You understand."

"I try," Slade whispered, pressing one last kiss on her temple before he released her. *Soon,* he promised Cat softly, *soon you'll be in my arms like I've been dreaming for the past month.*

As they walked back toward the Jeep, Slade stole a look at her. "How'd you like me to tell you about my mine, sometime? When you're up to it, that is."

Cat stared nonplussed at him for a moment, digesting his question. "Let me think about it."

Slade held up both hands in a gesture of friendly surrender. "Great. I just don't want any more misunderstandings between us, Cat. You tell me when you're ready, and I'll spill out everything."

Cat nodded and slipped into the seat of the Jeep. "Fair enough."

Slade accepted her dictate and turned the key. The Jeep roared to life and they followed the dirt road beneath the thousands of pecan trees, heading back to Mourning Dove Ranch.

Cat mulled over his explanation about the mine and was relieved. He hadn't asked her to the ranch just to get her professional services. The intimacy Slade had established with her after lunch had sent such sharp longing through her, it was worse than the pain she had experienced with her broken ribs. Cat forced herself to think of other matters. Casting a glance over at Slade, she decided to find out more about his mysterious mining project.

Chapter 7

As they got out of the Jeep and walked into the house, Cat gathered all that was left of her nerve and spoke up.

"Slade?"

"Yes?"

"I don't want to wait to hear the story of your mine." She came to a halt and rested her fingers lightly on his upper arm. "Do you have some time this afternoon?"

Pleasure shone in his eyes as he looked down at her. "That took a lot of courage, Cat. I was hoping you'd ask."

He guided Cat to the kitchen and gave Pilar the basket. Then Slade poured them some fragrant coffee and stole some date-nut bread that Pilar had just baked. He sat down next to Cat on the back porch, his long legs spread out in front of him.

She cast a glance over at him. "Why were you hoping I'd ask?"

"A long time ago, Cat, I found that people really didn't want something unless they asked for it. My mother used to shake her finger at me and tell me to hold my own counsel, opinions and advice unless someone asked for them." Slade gave her a little-boy grin as he polished off his chunk of warm bread. "Over the years, I've found my mother to be right—as usual."

"Wise words from your mother," Cat agreed solemnly. She wanted to rest against him and smiled to herself. "Tell me about your mine, oh weaver of spells and fables."

Slade nodded and settled back. "A long time ago, back in 1531, the Spanish conquistador, Francisco Pizarro, landed on the coast of Peru. To his delight and greed, he found fabulous emeralds there, and in Chile and Ecuador. He became entranced with where these emeralds had come from and tortured countless Indians to get this information.

"Finally, in 1537, the conquistadors had the answer they sought: Chivor, Colombia. There they found emeralds in feldspar-rich veins of yellow-gray shale or limestone. Chivor's crystal-clear emeralds made the conquistadors bend the backs of every Indian they could find and put them into slavery to work the mine. Twelve hundred Indians were kept caged in Chivor's tunnels on a food ration that even a rat couldn't subsist on. Spain's monarchy couldn't tolerate the conditions the Indians were placed in, and ordered them freed of further enslavement. Eventually, production dropped off and the jungle reclaimed Chivor. The mine became 'lost.'

"Then, in 1896, Chivor was rediscovered by a Colombian mining engineer who used a three-hundred-year-old map he had found in an old manuscript. Chivor now operates as one of the largest privately owned emerald mines in the world."

Cat smiled wistfully. "You sound as if you wished you had been that Colombian mining engineer to have found Chivor again."

Slade nodded, thinking how beautiful Cat looked when she was relaxed. "You'd better believe it. There's another well-known emerald site in Colombia. Chivor sits up where a breeze will stir and the temperature is cooler on the slopes of the jungle-capped mountains. The Muzo Valley, which sits in the Cordillera Oriental, an extension of the Andes Mountain chain, is hot, humid and insect-infested. The emeralds at Muzo are found in white calcite veins between beds of black shale.

"At Muzo, the emeralds are flawed heavily with inclusions, making them look cloudy. Chivor's emeralds are clear in comparison but lack the range of color that Muzo's hold. Muzo's emeralds are considered far more valuable because of this color range. Personally, I disagree. I'll take a less-inclusioned emerald over a cloudy one with color any day. Anyway, Muzo's reputation is that of greed, murder and thievery run amok. It got so bad that it was shut down in 1970 because of the number of murders and crimes. The mines of Muzo had been privately owned up until that time. The owners feared for their lives and the yield of their mines. They begged for government protection in the form of soldiers. The private companies agreed to lease their mines to the government in return for protection and guarding of their emerald treasure by the national police."

Slade glanced over at Cat. "The guaqueros, or treasure hunters, went on digging their rat tunnels into the emerald mines anyway. Cave-ins kill a lot of them. So does suffocation, because these rat holes aren't properly ventilated. The guaquero who manages to tunnel into one of the emerald mines then begins to steal. If he finds a stone, he must risk his own life trying to get it to an emerald dealer, known as an esmeraldero, who waits at the Rio Itoco, the river at the bottom of the Muzo Valley, to sell it."

"And have the police stopped some of the bloodshed, Slade?"

He grimaced. "To a degree, they have. But what has happened is that the police are either paid off by the guaqueros to look the other way while they steal from the mines or they just plain feel sorry for the tens of thousands of starving humans who have flocked from the squalor of Bogotá out into the field in search of their personal fortune."

"That's the history. How do you fit into this interesting puzzle?" Cat asked, watching his blue eyes grow warm with a smile. Slade made her feel good and she couldn't conceive of being away from his sunny presence.

"Let me tell you about my colorful partner who lives in Houston. Once upon a time, there was this grizzled old Texas diehard. His name was Alvin Moody and he made his fortune gambling on oil wells instead of dry holes. Pretty soon, his oil discoveries outweighed the dry holes he found, so he became one of the Texas elite money-wise. He's about six-foot-four and even taller in the stories told about him. Alvin's a meek name, and it doesn't fit him as far as I'm concerned. That aside, Alvin got restless with the gas-and-oil game. He wanted to stretch himself and had always had a fascination for gems. He'd heard of Chivor, Cosquez and Muzo in Colombia. And being the street-smart, junkyard dog that he was, he figured there were more emeralds than just in those three areas."

"How old is Alvin?" Cat asked, enjoying Slade's story.

Slade rubbed his jaw. "Let's see…somewhere around seventy-three. He's got snow-white hair, squinty blue eyes that'll drop you at thirty feet if you cross him the wrong way and a voice that booms like a bear."

"Sounds like a real character," she said with a chuckle.

"I think Texas glories in them," Slade agreed. "I was down in a sleazy bar at the bad end of Bogotá when I ran into Alvin."

"I won't ask what you were doing there," Cat said dryly.

"Same thing he was: looking for stories about the emerald-rich mountains of Colombia. I'd been there seven days and picked up quite a bit of bull. In between, I'd play rounds of poker with the emerald dealers, listen, learn and store it."

"You a good poker player, Slade?" Cat knew the answer to that without asking, but couldn't resist teasing him.

Slade grinned. "Wait and see. Alvin came into this dirty, smoky bar, twice as big as life, all decked out in a khaki safari suit, Texas cowboy hat and boots. He spotted our game and invited himself to sit down. There were four scruffy-looking esmeralderos who smelled of the Rio Itoco, plus me in my usual grubby geology gear and Alvin. Everyone in the bar stopped talking and gawked when he rolled on in and invited himself to our table. It was a hell of a sight."

"And so you all played poker?"

Slade hedged and held up his hand. "A fifth esmeraldero sat down. Juan Cortez was his name. He was a slimy-looking character; looked as if somebody was hunting him. He didn't have any money but we let him join the game because he said he owned three hundred and forty acres near Muzo and had a map where he knew emeralds were located. Whoever won, and believe me, he was planning on winning, would get the map. Cortez was hungry for some capital to start his venture into the area. That's why he wanted into the game."

"How did Cortez get this map?"

His eyes darkened. "Cat, you never ask an esmeraldero where he got anything or you're liable to be lookin' down the barrel of his pistol."

"Oh."

"The stakes got high. A lot higher than the cash I was carrying on me. I saw that glimmer in Alvin Moody's eyes. He, like I, believed that Cortez had the real thing by the way the guy was acting. I didn't want to fold my hand and Cortez wouldn't take my American Express credit card as a promise of cash."

Cat laughed. "Smart man! You might not be paid up or it could be stolen for all Cortez knew."

"Fortunately, Alvin came to my rescue. He didn't have to stake me but he said he'd loan me the money I wanted. If I won, he'd get half the mine." Slade's eyes twinkled. "Alvin had a busted card hand, so he was smart enough to sense that I was holding some pretty good ones or he wouldn't have made the offer."

"It wasn't out of the generosity of his heart, was it?"

"Hell, no. Alvin's a businessman. I'd have done the same thing."

"Cortez must have been holding some good cards, too."

"He was," Slade admitted, flashing a smile. "Alvin staked me. By this time, there was twenty thousand dollars on the table. Everyone in El Toro Posada was crowded around our table: farmers, miners and drifters. It was getting pretty tense, so I laid my pearl-handled Colt .45 revolver on the table close to my right hand where everyone could see it. The crowd stepped back a couple of paces. Alvin grinned. Cortez sweated. The other four esmeralderos all bowed out with a curse as the ante continued upward. In another ten minutes, there was forty thousand dollars lying on the table with just Cortez and myself still in the game. Alvin kept peeling off thousand-dollar bills from that wad of money he had pulled out of his pocket; cool as hell."

Cat sat up, rapt. "Well, what happened?"

Slade pushed an errant lock of hair off his brow. "I called Cortez's hand. He grinned that evil little smile of his. He had pointy teeth that reminded me of a weasel's. He said, '*Señores*, I'm happy to take your money,' and laid out a ten of clubs, jack of diamonds, queen of clubs, king of spades and an ace of clubs."

"A straight, ace high," Cat acknowledged, breath lodged in her throat. "And then what happened, Slade?"

"Cortez grinned wider and threw his hands over the pile of money and raw emeralds sitting in the middle of the table. Alvin said, 'Hold it, snake breath.' And he gripped both of Cortez's hands and then looked straight at me. 'Your turn,' he told me. So, I began laying out my cards one at a time. I started with a ten of hearts, jack of hearts, queen of hearts, king of hearts and finally, the ace of hearts."

"My God," Cat whispered, "a royal flush. What a

time to get one." And then she gave him a hard look. "You didn't cheat, did you?"

Slade looked momentarily wounded. "Me?" A devastating smile pulled at his mouth. Slade held up both his hands. "Sweetheart, I'm the luckiest damn bastard you've ever seen. Even luckier than Alvin, and he's not too shabby, either."

Cat laughed with him. "So what did Cortez do? Cry?"

Slade snorted. "I can tell you've got a lot to learn about these snake pits in Colombia. No, he lunged for my revolver. Alvin jerked him up like a rat out of a lab jar, holding him while he screamed all kinds of curses at us. I put all our hard-earned money into every pocket I had. I even stuffed it into Alvin's safari jacket and into that ten-gallon hat he was wearing. I knew we were in a hell of a lot of trouble. Any moment, any one of those men could jump us. I grabbed my revolver, firing it three times into the air. Everyone stepped back, eyeing us like a pack of wolves.

"Alvin held Cortez by his ragged clothes at each shoulder while I searched the little guy for his map. I found it, opened it up to make sure it wasn't a blank piece of paper. It wasn't. As far as I could tell, it was genuine. Cortez grudgingly signed the land deed over to us. We really didn't have the time to stop and check it out. We had to get out of there or we'd be dead meat. Alvin dropped Cortez and then unpacked that big, evil-looking .360 Magnum, Dirty Harry type of revolver he carries, and pointed it at the crowd while we backed out of the bar.

"Outside, we hightailed it for my Jeep and dug holes getting out of there. Alvin was staying at the Tequendama Hotel, so we went over there to rest up, have a tall, cool one and see if the deed had been worth all our efforts."

Cat stood, suddenly excited and unable to sit still any longer. "This is all true, Slade?"

"Yes. It gets better. Want a drink?"

"I could use one."

Slade slowly uncoiled from his relaxed position and guided her back into the house. Cat sat on the stool while he went behind the bar to mix up a pitcher of margaritas. She put both elbows on the polished cedar.

"How could you verify if the map was genuine?"

"We went to the deeds office in Bogotá and checked it out. Cortez had been as good as his word. As to the possibility of emeralds on it, we had to go to the location and find out. For all we knew, Cortez could have sold us a bunch of jungle with nothing but mosquitoes and anacondas crawling all over it. We packed up the Jeep the next day and took off for the Silla de Montar Valley."

"Where was it located?" Cat wanted to know, thanking him as he handed her a margarita.

Slade rested easily against the bar, sipping his drink. "How about two valleys over from the Muzo mines?"

Cat's eyes widened. "That close to another emerald field?" she gasped.

"Yes, ma'am. When we located Cortez's landholding, it was in the saddle between Caballo and Lazo Mountain. That's how the valley got its name. Alvin and I spent a month out there."

"What kind of rock base, Slade?"

He had her, he thought, seeing the sudden interest in Cat's eyes. Now she was starting to ask a mining engineer's questions.

"Calcite limestone. Prime sedimentary rock for emeralds. But then, you know that."

"Not the black shale of Muzo?"

"No. From the core samples I took, there is a thick base of limestone just beneath the topsoil and subsoil strata." He took a pencil from his pocket and reached for a small notepad, drawing her a quick illustration. "Perfect limestone for emeralds here," he said. "Beneath it, black shale. My guess is that it's the same stratum that has been pushed to the surface at Muzo." He tapped the limestone stratum with the pencil. "Here, at our location, it's still buried pretty deeply."

"Why are you saying calcite limestone when all evidence points to the shale bearing the emeralds instead, Slade?"

He straightened up. "Wait here," was all he said, and he disappeared out the door through the kitchen.

Cat sat there for what seemed a long time. By her watch, it was only five minutes, but it felt like hours. Slade came back, an enigmatic look on his face and a kidskin leather pouch in his left hand. He gently handed her the pouch.

"Open it."

She hadn't realized that she was holding her breath as she loosened the drawstrings. Then she drew out five uncut emeralds still embedded in the white rock known as calcite. They completely took her breath away. The perfect, six-sided green crystals were buried in the surrounding matrix, glinting with staggering color beneath the light at the bar.

"Incredible, Slade…"

"Green fire," he whispered, leaning close to her, their heads nearly touching as they both stared down at the matrix. "Gem of the gods, something mere mortals would murder their best friend for and sell their soul to the devil to possess. Green fire…"

"I—it's simply beautiful." She held it up to the light. "From what I know of Colombian emeralds, these uncut emeralds have far fewer inclusions than most." Cat leveled a look at him. "Emeralds of this quality are worth a fortune, Slade."

"They came from the land we won from Cortez, Cat. Take a good look at this, hold it and let it burn into your memory."

She didn't have to be told to hold it. Automatically, Cat could swear she felt a shimmering vibrancy that only a true gem possessed. What she held in her hands was priceless, the dark green vivid against the pure white calcite. "They're too beautiful for words," she whispered, turning them slowly, watching the light refract through the clear, near-perfect depths of each crystal.

Slade cupped his hands around hers, holding her gaze. "Your eyes are even more beautiful than they are, did you know that? Now, maybe you can appreciate what I see when I look at you."

Shaken by the intimacy of his voice, Cat's lips parted. She felt the roughness of his hands holding hers, sending flames of longing through her. "W-what are you going to do with this?"

Slade released her and straightened up. "Put it on the shelf over there. Another story to tell my next guest or visitor," he said. "What would you do with it?"

Cat carefully placed the matrix back in the pouch and sat it on the bar between them. "Most men would have sold it."

"I always save the first gems I find at a new site." He gave her an intense look. "Remember what I said before: money isn't everything. This may be worth two hundred thousand on the open market, but that doesn't matter."

Slade watched Cat nod in understanding. An odd smile tugged at his mouth. "I told Alvin I wanted the best for this project. The limestone deposit is almost a flaky kind of black shale. The chances of cave-in are great. I wanted someone who was used to dealing with unusual mine situations. You were the only one I wanted for the job, Cat." He picked up the bag that contained the matrix of emeralds and set it aside. "Your reputation far preceded you, and I told Alvin that we're dealing with a mine in a country that's used to volcanic and earth-quake potential. I didn't want just any mining engineer. There are special stresses and environmental items to be considered in how the mine will be constructed. That's where your special talents come in."

The idea was initially exciting to Cat. Seconds later, the pit of her stomach became a knot of cold, drench-ing fear. Yes, from what she knew of the rock strata of Colombia, earthquakes were always a hazard to a mine shaft sunk into the unstable earth. She broke into a sweat, focused on the fear that was now gobbling her up whole.

Slade frowned, noticing the sheen on Cat's forehead. The color had drained from her cheeks and the excite-ment he had seen in her eyes had flickered and died. Automatically, he reached across to close his hand over hers. "What is it?" he coaxed.

A lump grew in her throat. "I'm scared, Slade."

His fingers tightened. "Look at me, Cat. Come on now, listen carefully; the only way to conquer that fear is to face it. I know it's not easy. And it won't be pleasant. But I'll be there, if that makes any difference to you."

Oh, yes, that would make a difference, Cat wanted to blurt out. But the words were frozen in her aching throat.

Slade's low-timbred voice moved through her.

"Cat, if I didn't think this was best for you, I wouldn't even suggest it. Aside from my wanting you to sink that shaft, you have to enter a mine somewhere in the world. I'd rather it be ours. I can be with you. I can help you cope with that fear."

"I'll think about it," she whispered, taking her cold hands from his warm ones.

Slade measured Cat's hesitancy, trying to ferret out the reason for her behavior. He had seen the glow of adventure in her face minutes before, the promise of another challenge to be reckoned with and tamed. And he had also seen the fear swallow up that glow like dark thunderclouds rolling threateningly across the horizon. He placed both elbows on the bar and hunkered down.

"Cat, I don't have much time. While you've been recovering here the past six weeks, I've been in my office coordinating the leasing of heavy earth-moving equipment. Alvin's down in Bogotá right now directing the effort." Slade released a breath of air, his gaze moving over her pensive features. "You know as well as anyone what kind of effort it takes to get equipment, construction supplies and a host of other essential items into a jungle area."

Cat nodded, biting her lower lip. As much as she wanted to ignore Slade's persuasive words, she couldn't. She could no longer tell herself she was immune to

Slade on a personal level, either. "It's tough any way you want to cut it," she agreed.

Slade absently moved the pouch around on the polished surface of the bar. "We're trying to be discreet about the movement of the equipment. If word gets out in Bogotá about our possible find, we'll have hundreds of treasure-hungry guaqueros following us." He snorted softly. "And that's just the tip of the iceberg. Once they know we've got something, all hell will break loose. We're trying to keep a lid on it, but time's short."

Raising her chin, Cat met Slade's sober blue gaze. "As much as I would like to help you, Slade, I don't know if I can walk back into a mine. And I couldn't stand outside a shaft that's being built by laborers and not go inside to check their work." She bowed her head. "I feel so humiliated. I've never admitted I was scared to anyone."

"You've never been brought to your knees before, Cat," he began quietly. "Most of us get the hell knocked out of us long before you took your turn. It's not the end of the world, even though I know it looks like it to you. And as for having no guts or backbone, you've got more than most. The cave-in is going to show you how to reach down inside yourself and find a new wellspring of strength, Cat."

She sniffed, tears rolling down her cheeks. "I'm empty, Slade. How can you draw on nothing?" she whispered painfully.

His smile was gentle as he leaned forward, kissing her closed eyes, tasting the saltiness of her tears. "Trust me, it's there. And you can draw on it when you have to face walking into a shaft again."

A sob broke from deep inside her, and Cat felt Slade's

hands slide from her face. She sat there all alone on the stool, hurting and feeling more alone than she ever had in all her life. She had thought she knew what loneliness was, but she hadn't—not like this. When she felt Slade's arms go around her, drawing her against the warm hardness of his body, Cat abandoned herself to his strength. She had none of her own left; she took what he offered her of his, instead.

Slade pressed a kiss to her hair, aware of the subtle fragrance of jasmine around her. He held Cat while she wept, rocking her as he would rock a hurt child, allowing her to release the pent-up anguish she had tried to ignore. He felt his own eyes mist, and shut them, resting his jaw lightly against Cat's hair, murmuring words of comfort to her. The power of his emotions stunned even him; the protectiveness he felt toward Cat took him by surprise. He wanted to ease her hurt, absorb it so she could be cleansed of all the horror he knew stalked her twenty-four hours a day. Finally, her sobs lessened and Slade dug a handkerchief from his back pocket, lifted her chin and dried her face of tears.

Slade nudged stray wisps of damp hair from Cat's cheek and temple, easing them behind her delicate ears. His mouth worked to hold back a barrage of feelings. "When I first met you, something happened. And I know you feel it, too. There's a chemistry between us and I want a chance to explore that with you. Hell, we're not kids anymore, Cat. The rose-colored glasses were taken away from us a long time ago. I'm putting you between a rock and a hard place and I know it. I won't let you go, no matter how frightened you are of entering a mine. You can learn to trust me and lean on me. I won't let you down."

Cat let him hold her, unable to respond, yet desperate to believe him.

"I'll help you get back on your feet in two ways," Slade went on. "I'll provide a mine to work in and I'll be there to help you fight your fear." Slade caressed her flaming red cheeks. "Together, we're strong, Cat, and we both know that. Don't run and hide from this." Slade's heart fell when he saw that Cat remained numb in his arms. What else could he do or say?

Cat's eyes reflected the confusion she felt. Could her feelings for Slade heal this overwhelming fear of another cave-in?

Slade, feeling her slip away, groped to find something that would force her to stay. "If you can't agree to do it for the reasons I've just laid out for you, then do it because you owe me. I saved your life and this is what I'm asking in return: I want you to build me a mine in Colombia. An even and fair trade for saving your life. What do you say?" Slade held his breath, watching the shock register on Cat's face. He groaned inwardly. God, what had he done by blurting out the first thing that came to mind? Was he wrong to use her own sense of duty to blackmail her into conquering her fear?

Miserably, Cat looked away, far too uncertain of herself to deal with Slade's overture. She had to escape that wall of pain, run and hide in the quiet confines of her room. "Let me go, Slade. I've got to rest…"

He took a step back, allowing his hands to slip from her shoulders. Slade felt Cat withdrawing her temporary trust from him. He had blown it by telling her she owed him. Suddenly, he was afraid. Would he be willing to lose her to make her whole again? As he stood there, Slade knew the answer: he cared enough to risk everything to make Cat whole.

"Go ahead," he coaxed in a strained voice. "You're tired and you've been through hell today. Just lie down and sleep on it, Cat."

Sleep? How? Cat had walked to the sanctuary of her peaceful room, but despite the dizzying brilliance of the sun slanting through the trellis overhead, she felt as if she were again in the dark pit. Her conscience warred with her fear. Slade was right: she owed him. Then why had it hurt so much when he'd said it? Cat lay on her stomach, clutching the pillow between her arms, head buried in its goosedown folds. *I'm a mess inside. I can't think straight, I can't get a hold on my emotions. Why can't I just let my logic sort all this out?*

She lay there for almost an hour, an internal battle waging between her malfunctioning mental faculties and the tumult of emotions that refused to be ignored any longer. Cat cried some more, terrible animal sounds torn from her soul. They were sounds she'd heard others make, but never her. Finally, her eyes red-rimmed and the pillow soaked, Cat fell into an exhausted, dreamless sleep, an empty vessel floating aimlessly on a sea of dark, turbulent emotions.

Slade was frowning heavily, holding a tumbler of whiskey between his hands, when Pilar padded into the living room. She hovered near the bar where he sat.

"Señor Slade?"

He barely looked up. "Yes?"

"The *señorita*, she weeps like a woman who has lost everything." Pilar shrugged her delicate shoulders, then gave him a beseeching look. "I just passed her room on the way to the linen closet."

Slade's hands tightened around the heavy glass. "Thank you, Pilar."

She hesitated, tilting her head. "You are not going to see if she needs help?"

His mouth worked into a thin line, holding back the emotions that threatened to overtake him. "No," he said harshly, and then gave Pilar an apologetic look. He hadn't meant to take his anger out on Pilar because of his own stupidity. "No," he repeated more gently.

Pilar frowned, her huge brown eyes searching his for a long moment. *"Si, señor,"* she said, then turned away, going back to the kitchen.

Slade swore under his breath, scraping the stool loudly against the cedar floor as he moved. He stalked through the room, going out to the porch. Continuing outdoors, he opened the screen, striding down the slight incline toward the small stream winding lazily through the cottonwoods. Slade finally came to a halt at the edge of the clear green water, staring angrily down at the sun-dappled surface. Throwing down the last of the whiskey, his knuckles whitened as he gripped the tumbler. The whiskey was hot, searing, like the pain he felt for Cat.

I should go to her; she needs me. No, that's not true. If she needed me, she'd have stayed. She wouldn't have run to her bedroom. Slade snorted violently, his blue eyes icy with anger aimed at himself. *You blew it, Donovan. You dumb son of a bitch, why did you have to tell her she owed you?* He raked his fingers through his hair, unable to contain his inner fury over his desperate action.

Miserably, Slade allowed the full weight of what he'd

just done to Cat overtake him. *I did it for her,* he told himself. But his cartwheeling mind wasn't sure. Confused and upset, he knew he needed some counsel. Kai Travis had always been his sounding board when he got into a bind. He needed her common sense, because he didn't know how to untie the knot he'd just created between Cat and himself.

Kai met him at the sliding screen door as he walked up the steps.

"Slade? You look awful. What's wrong?"

Self-consciously, Slade thrust his hands into the pockets of his jeans, looking down at Kai. "I'm sorry to ride over unannounced, Kai."

She took him by the arm, leading him into the living room and to the couch. "Since when did you need an invitation? What's going on? Is something wrong with Cat?"

He shrugged and sat down. "I really screwed up this afternoon with her, Kai." He rubbed his face tiredly.

Kai sat on the small hassock in front of him. "Tell me what happened."

The quiet tenor of Kai's voice shook loose all his suppressed anxiety and worry. Slowly, Slade unwound the sordid chain of events. When he finished, Kai grimaced.

"I'm sorry, Slade. I didn't mean to mention your mine to Cat. I had just assumed that you had already discussed the possibility of her working with you." She reached over, apologetically squeezing his arm.

"It's not your fault, Kai. Cat thought I had brought her to the ranch just to use her professional talents."

"Does she still?"

"I took her on a picnic earlier today and we got that

issue straightened out." Slade shook his head. "And then I really blew it. I tried playing amateur psychologist by making her think she could repay me for saving her life by building the mine. How could I have been so stupid? Words were just pouring out of me. I was in such a panic, afraid that I was going to lose her. I didn't want to, Kai, I spoke without thinking. It had a devastating effect on Cat. She's probably still crying…"

With a sigh, Kai got up and went to the cabinet, pouring each of them a bit of brandy. She handed one snifter to Slade and sat back down. "Drink up, you need it."

Sorrowfully, Slade downed the stinging brandy. He sucked air between his clenched teeth, holding the delicate crystal in his hands. Slowly, the knots began to dissolve in his gut as he sat with her in the intervening silence.

"She's probably going to run," he muttered.

"You mean, leave Mourning Dove?"

"Sure, wouldn't you? Put yourself in Cat's place. I'm barely able to get her to believe that I didn't bring her to the ranch under false pretenses. And then I tell her she owes me." Slade suddenly stood up, unable to stand the anger he was aiming at himself.

Kai watched him pace for several minutes. "What will you lose, Slade?"

He halted. "Cat."

"You love her?"

"I didn't realize that I did until a half hour ago. I had all these feelings about her, Kai. I never thought there was a woman who could tolerate my life-style, but I know she can. Cat's just like me in many ways."

"And does she love you, Slade?"

He ran his fingers through his hair in aggravation. "Who the hell knows?"

"I think she does," Kai provided softly. "Slade, stop pacing for a minute and come and sit down."

Slade sat, staring at Kai. "Sometimes, I see longing in her eyes and I hear the emotion in her voice, Kai. Every time we're together, it's so damned special."

With a smile, Kai said, "I've been privileged to share a great deal with Cat since she's been here, Slade. I know you're very special to her, too."

"Well, I just destroyed whatever was there."

"Maybe, maybe not. Why don't you go home and talk with her? Iron this out and tell her how you feel. Let her know that you really didn't mean to make her feel guilty or hold her to building your mine. Tell her you were trying to make her address her fear."

"I just thought that she'd want to face up to it. I saw it as a perfect solution to all of Cat's problems."

Gently, Kai reached over and patted his sloping shoulder. "That's how you would have done it, Slade, if you'd been in her shoes. Let Cat tell you how she wants to handle her own healing process. Go on...go home and talk with her. I know it will do some good."

Slade caught Kai's hand, giving it a grateful squeeze. "We'll have that talk," he promised. "I've been wanting to make Cat a gift, anyway. Maybe, if I can persuade her to stay, I can get it done for her."

Kai's eyes twinkled. "Knowing how talented you are at making jewelry, I'm sure she'll be pleased."

"Better yet," Slade said, hope in his voice as he rose, "let's the four of us go to Houston in a couple of weeks. I can give it to Cat then. A sort of peace token for the way I've behaved."

Walking with Slade to the porch, Kai waved to him as he left. "Houston sounds like a good idea. And don't worry, your heart was in the right place, Slade. The words just came out wrong. Cat will forgive you."

Throwing his leg over his horse, Slade managed a thin smile. "I hope you're right, Kai. I'll let you know. Think good thoughts for us, will you?"

"Always."

Chapter 8

Cat tried to repair the damage that her crying jag had done to her face. Slade had knocked at her door earlier, but she had refused to answer. She had to get a hold on herself before she faced him. She put color into her pale cheeks with a brush, and a rose-colored lipstick actually made her look almost normal. She winced, avoiding the look in her eyes as she combed her hair. She had taken a warm, cleansing shower and changed into some of her more practical clothes: a peach shell and a pair of no-nonsense khaki pants. Now, she looked more like her old self, before the trauma of the cave-in. The only thing different was that her hair was longer, making her look more feminine. Cat didn't want to cut her hair even though she knew she was going into the jungle again.

No, I want it to grow. I don't care. And she didn't question why she violently fought the idea of a haircut. Wasn't that what Slade wanted? A mining engineer, not a feminine-looking woman? He'd made that very clear earlier. A life for a life. Okay, she owed him, and she'd pay up. Kincaids recognized that some things in life were sacred; you save a man's life, he owes you. It was that simple. She shut her eyes, allowing the brush to lie on the vanity for long moments.

Cat tried to ignore the ache in her heart. Was she so mixed up after the trauma of the cave-in that she hadn't read Slade accurately? She had thought she had seen and felt something special with him, but it had all been an act to maneuver her into going to Colombia with him. When she opened her eyes and warily stared at herself in the mirror, Cat could barely stand to look at the image that stood before her. There was hurt and pain in the depths of her emerald eyes, and anger. Yes, anger at being betrayed by Slade. He had deftly used her to get what he wanted—and he wanted a tough-minded mining engineer. Okay, he'd get it his way. She firmly placed the brush on the vanity, girding herself for the coming confrontation.

Cat allowed all the anger and hurt Slade had caused to rise and protect her. It gave her strength when she had none of her own to call on. Opening the door to her bedroom, Cat walked purposefully down the cedar hall to find Slade.

Slade heard a knock at his office door and he made a half turn in his chair. Cat was standing outside the sliding-glass door, and immediately he was on his feet.

"Come in," he said, opening the door for her.

The coolness of air-conditioning hit Cat as she stepped through the entrance. She saw hope in Slade's eyes, and his exhaustion, and tried to steel herself against feeling anything remotely human toward him.

As he slid the door closed and turned toward her, she said, "I'll pay off the debt between us, Slade. I've got another two weeks before I'm freed by the doctor to resume my normal activities. In the meantime, I want all the core-sampling reports, maps and any other geological items you can supply me so I can begin studying the mining situation in Silla de Montar Valley."

Slade's face softened and he took a step toward her. "Cat—"

She stepped away, arms rigid at her sides, her chin raised, eyes defiant. "No."

Slade froze, all hope shattering like an emerald struck by a pickax. When he finally spoke, his voice was charged with feeling. "I have a spare office in the west wing of the house. I can have all those things brought to you."

"Fine."

"Look, you don't have to jump into this with both feet. Kai said you still needed rest. I don't want you working eight hours a day—"

"My life for your mine. That's the way you wanted it, wasn't it?" Cat's jaw tightened. "I'll work however long I want. Don't try and set how many hours a day I can work even if I'm still mending." Her chin quivered. "I'm surprised you waited this long. It was probably killing you to wait six weeks—six weeks that could have been spent down in Colombia instead."

Slade's eyes narrowed with barely contained fury. "That's unfair, Cat. We need to talk."

She smiled wearily, some of her anger dissipating. "Nothing's fair in life, is it? You were raised with rocks. Well, so was I. I'll be just as tough as the situation demands. If you've got all the core and mining information I need, you'll have a rough blueprint for a mine in two weeks."

Slade opened his hands. "Cat, I didn't mean to make it sound as if you owed me. What I said was a mistake."

Her smile was brittle, her eyes dangerously bright with unshed tears. "We all make mistakes, Donovan. My mistake was in trusting you and your intentions. You've made it clear what you want and I'm prepared to give it to you. Your mine for my life. Okay, you've got a deal."

"Damn it, will you give me a chance to explain, Cat?"

"No!"

Slade wanted to strangle her. He also wanted to take Cat into his arms and erase the anguish he saw so clearly in her haunted expression. Her act was all a bluff on her part, and he knew it. And so did she. She was like brittle glass ready to explode right in front of him. But he didn't dare call her hand, or she might run away. No, he'd have to play by her rules, allow her to retreat and hold him at arm's length and maybe, just maybe, she'd gradually lower that shield she had in place and allow him a second chance. "All right," he rasped, "you've got a deal."

Cat swayed slightly, feeling light-headed. She took a step away, covering up her reaction by walking to the door. "Fine. Get me what I need to figure out a construction blueprint for you."

He followed her out to the patio. "Come with me," he said, trying to keep his voice steady.

Cat nodded and walked a few paces behind him as they crossed to the western wing of the ranch house. She tried to contain her surprise when he opened the door to a spacious office replete with several personal computers, calculators and drafting board. Everything she might need to formulate the kind of mine required was present.

Slade made a slight motion toward the office. "This will be yours. The IBM PC is hooked up to the data bank at Texas A & M in Houston, by phone modem, should you need more mining information."

She wondered if Slade had built this with her in mind, but bit back the question, not wishing to fight any more than necessary with him. Her strength had to be focused on the project at hand, not wasted on him. There was a cot in the corner complete with blankets and a pillow. Fine, she'd live, eat and sleep there. In two weeks, she ought to be able to come up with a decent preliminary blueprint to begin digging a mine.

"Thank you." She stepped past him, deliberately avoiding touching him.

Slade went to the drafting board, pointing to a black buzzer on the phone beside it. "If you need anything, you can ring me in my other office." He turned, pointing to a wall of cabinets opposite them. "Every core and drilling-sample spec I took on the mine is here. There are topographical maps of the valley, overburden, ore and basement-complex sample reports. I don't think you'll need anything else, but if you do, call me."

Cat refused to look at Slade and went to the cabinet. Everything had been carefully labeled, numbered and categorized. Her assessment of Slade's abilities grudgingly rose. She pulled out a roll of specs from the first cubbyhole. "I think I've got enough to keep me busy," she murmured.

Slade nodded and retreated. "Dinner's in two hours."

She went to the drafting desk, unrolling the specs

and studying them intently. "Have Pilar bring it in here, please."

Well, what did he expect—for Cat to forgive and forget? Slade shut the door quietly behind him, a bitter taste in his mouth. This was a new side of Cat Kincaid: the brilliant, tenacious mining engineer who had carved out a name for herself in one of the toughest businesses in the world. He'd have to keep reminding himself of her steel determination, because she was certainly wearing it like armor now. And he'd forced her into donning it. Damn it, anyway!

Night melded with day and day with night. Cat immersed herself in the exploration of details that would help her determine what kind of mine shaft would be best suited for the Verde Mine. Slade had named the mine at the top of all the specs. "Green Mine"—that fit, she thought. Verde to her meant growth, as did anything green. Rubbing her eyes tiredly, she pushed aside the computer keyboard and placed her pencil on the pad. What day was it? They all blended together when she attacked Verde's challenge. Looking at her Rolex, now scratched from the cave-in, she saw that ten days had passed. A slight smile cut across her lips as she slowly rose. Dawn was crawling onto the horizon as seen from the wall of windows that faced east.

Sleep.... She took snatches of three or four hours at a time. Lying down with a groan, Cat closed her eyes. When she awoke, she would go back to her room, shower and get a fresh change of clothes. As she sank deeper into the embrace of sleep, Slade crossed her mind. To her chagrin, Cat had found that if she wasn't actively pursuing her job, he would slip into her thoughts, catching her unawares. And every time that occurred, her pounding heart would underscore the wild, unnamed feelings that came on its heels. As much as Cat wanted to hate him, she could not. She was angry with him, and disappointed, and she would never trust him again...not ever.

Slade tried to contain his surprise when Cat came up to the sliding-glass door of his office on the tenth day. She had successfully avoided seeing him for nearly two weeks. Only Pilar's insistence that Cat was in the other office and appeared well had kept him from seeing for himself. Slade knew he didn't dare push Cat too far by showing up on her doorstep. He rose to open the door, but she beat him to it.

"Come in," he invited, pulling up a stool.

Cat felt the heat rush to her face. Why did she have to blush? She stood just inside the office, holding his anxious stare. Slade looked as tired as she felt. There were shadows beneath his eyes, as if he'd slept little. His clothes were rumpled, which wasn't like him. He always wore a crisp cotton shirt and dark blue jeans that outlined his beautifully narrow hips and well-formed legs. He was beautiful, Cat admitted weakly, her pulse pounding unevenly. As much of a bastard as he was, Slade still affected her physically, and she couldn't ignore the sensations racing through her even now.

"I've finished the rough calculations. I need to sit down and discuss them with you. Do you have a couple of hours to spare?"

Slade heard the strain in Cat's voice. How he had missed her! Ten days without Cat had been a prison sentence for him. He had longed for her voice, her effusive laughter, her quiet, steady presence. Hungrily, he now drank her in as she stood like a wary doe ready to flee at the first sign of danger. She was pale, he realized with a pang, and she wore no makeup to hide it. She wore a light blue short-sleeved chambray shirt, jeans and sensible brown shoes. It looked almost as if she were dressed for field work, except for the mandatory hard hat and rough boots. Her outfit didn't diminish her femininity in his eyes, though. The fullness of her parted lips sent an ache throbbing through him. Slade had often remembered kissing those lips.

"Sure, I've got the time." He sounded like an eager schoolboy on shaky ground. Well, wasn't he?

Cat turned without preamble and began the walk back to her office. Her hands were damp and she longed to rub them on her thighs to dry them off, but Slade would notice, and she didn't want to broadcast her nervousness. She almost smiled in spite of herself, though. Slade's harsh face had softened the moment he saw her. Was that an act on his part? Was it real? Cat groaned inwardly; why did she even care? Hadn't he shown his real character already?

Slade entered her office and saw two chairs sitting side by side at the drafting desk. Cat sat down, waiting for him. He wiped his sweaty hands on his jeans and then sat beside her.

"What did you come up with?" he asked. *Great, Donovan, you sound like a twelve-year-old boy whose voice is changing.*

Cat drew the first sheaf of papers between them, keenly aware of Slade's closeness. She tried valiantly to cap her own escaping feelings and cleared her throat. "I've made a study of the Chivor and Muzo mine operations before deciding what ours would be. Muzo's emerald fields are found in a loose, black shale that quite literally is on the surface. All they've had to do is clear out the jungle and go to work to reclaim the gems." She scowled, placing a paper in front of him. "Their mining operations are antiquated and, to say the least, environmentally damaging. As you can see in this color photo, they're using strip-mining techniques. They blast with dynamite and then go in with huge bulldozers, shoveling the black shale into vast washing and screening areas. Water is used to wash away the debris and leave the emeralds. What can't be bulldozed after a blast is jackhammered by miners and then pushed into the gullies." Cat glanced at him and lost her train of thought. She loved his mouth despite herself. It had ravished hers until she had melted into an oblivion of wildly boiling heat and desire. His nearness was devastating to her, and her voice faltered as she tried to pick up the reins of her conversation. "The gangue, or waste rock, is pushed into the Rio Itoco below. There the guaqueros sift through the tailings during the day, hoping to find a stray emerald."

Slade nodded, resting his chin on one of his hands. He saw her hand tremble as she turned the page of her assessment. Automatically, he wanted to reach out, take her hand and tell her everything would be all right. Miserably, he knew that wasn't true. If only he could make things right between them. With a monumental effort, he addressed her comments. "The people pan the waters of the river during the day and become tunnel rats at night. They try to either break into the terraces, which are heavily guarded by the Colombian police, or dig into the shallow mines."

"Right." Cat brought out another paper, swallowing hard. She had seen the tenderness in Slade's eyes as he locked and held her gaze. Despite everything, he did lay claim to her heart, Cat realized in anguish. She wanted to reach out and caress his cheek, to take away some of the pain that lay at the downturned corners of his mouth. Yes, they were both suffering. "Muzo's methods are outdated. Not only that, but indiscriminate blasting with dynamite is going to certainly destroy some of the emeralds."

Slade snorted. "That's already happened. At Chivor they blast cautiously and with low charges and only when necessary." Why did she have to look waiflike? It devastated him to think that he had caused Cat to appear almost a ghost of her former self. No longer was her skin that golden color, her eyes that glorious velvet green sparkling with life. When she stared at him, all he saw was fear and…was it longing? Was that possible? He clung to that possibility, barely hearing her speak about the assessment. Each word she formed with her full lips created a widening ache through him. He loved her.

Cat couldn't relax beneath Slade's intense stare and she retreated deep into her mining-engineer mode. "Your mine, on the other hand, will be a mixture of open-pit mining methods involving the terracing of the surrounding hillside, plus sinking a shaft." She cleared her throat and traced one line of figures on a core-sample readout. "My educated guess, based upon your channel samplings, is that the calcite-limestone vein surfaces here on the hill and slowly moves back down into the earth over here." Cat drew him a quick picture, showing the stratum that might hold emeralds between its thinly wafered sheets.

"What's your opinion? Are we in business or not?" he asked.

Cat straightened up, running fingers through her hair. She expelled a breath of air, taking another paper and handing it to him. "If my calculations stand up and if your channel samples were spaced properly, the Verde should yield one emerald for every twenty million particles of surrounding overburden. You're in business, all right."

Slade stared down at Cat's figures. Her numbers, all in dark leaded pencil, were agonizingly neat and precise. A slight smile hovered around the corners of his mouth. "This is even better than I had roughly figured."

"You'll have everything you want, Slade." The words had come out flat and emotionless as Cat stared at him.

Slade ground his teeth together, bristling over her unspoken accusation. Her eyes were a cool green. He tried to tell himself he deserved that from Cat because of what he'd done to her. Damn it, it hurt! And he was angry at her for prodding that festering wound that now stood between them. "Why don't you give me your mine evaluation?" he asked.

Cat slipped back into her professional mode easily, like a horse into a familiar, comfortable harness. She went over the determination factors: an estimate of future operations, a suitable production schedule, the grade, market and selling price of the product and the production life of the mine. She went into the size, shape, attitude and quality of the emerald deposit, which was determined by geologic studies and maps. She missed nothing in her smooth, methodical presentation.

At the end of the second hour, with a large flowchart concluding the final presentation, Cat wrapped it up.

"The mine itself will be tricky. Transportation of certain types of timber is going to be a problem. I'm going to need heavy equipment to get that lumber out of the jungle. And you'll need to build a good road that won't wash out in the tropical rains of winter." She shrugged and gestured toward the plans on the drafting board. "All of this is detailed and you can read it at your leisure."

Slade nodded thoughtfully, watching as Cat shoved her hands into the pockets of her jeans and walked over to the wall of windows. The sun was slanting through the glass, making her sable hair come alive with threads of gold. He had sponged in her presence in the past two hours, as if starved. God, how he had missed her.

"You've done a thorough job on this, Cat. A damn good job." His voice shook with gratitude and pride in her abilities. Slade managed a tight smile, holding her thawing emerald gaze, realizing he had reached inside those defensive walls and touched her, the woman. "Now I see why you've got one hell of a name for yourself in our industry. It would take most people a good month just to put a preliminary study like this together. You did it in two weeks."

"You had everything I needed here," Cat countered, feeling warm and good as his praise flowed through her. "Part of the time factor is based on how much an engineer has to run around collecting all the pieces of various data that are needed to put a show like this together. You're good at your job, too, Slade."

He arched like a cat beneath her flattery, and his mouth stretched into a smile. "What do you say we celebrate? Matt and Kai want me to fly us to Houston for dinner tonight. We'll go to a nice restaurant and relax. We both need that."

Cat stiffened. At first, she was going to say no. But Kai had been a godsend the first two weeks of her stay at the ranch, and she owed her thanks. More importantly, Kai had become her friend. But every minute spent with Slade weakened her resolve, her past hurt over his actions. Cat anguished over the decision.

"Come on, say yes," Slade coaxed. "Kai's called over here three times in the last ten days wanting to see you. She's been craving some female company. What do you say?"

Cat gnawed on her lower lip and stared down at her shoes. "Okay." There was a razor-honed edge to her voice.

"I'll keep my distance from you," Slade said, sensing she wanted to hear some sort of verbal promise from him.

"Fine." She lifted her head. "I think it's best if it's business all the way between us."

"I haven't forgotten."

Cat eyed him. At first, she had been angry with Slade for tricking her. Then, she felt childish after leveling a barrage at him—although she had gotten it cleaned out of her system once and for all. But ten days had modified her initial anger. The past week had made her aware of just how much she liked Slade, regardless of what had happened to damage their relationship. Cat was afraid of her own feelings toward Slade. The less she saw of him, the more she was able to control them. "Good. I'll see you later, then."

Slade rose. "They'll be here at six tonight."

"Is this formal?"

"Yes."

That meant a dress. And judging from the look of longing in Slade's eyes, Cat knew she was in trouble. She had tried her best for the past two weeks to dress for business, not pleasure. She didn't want any more of Slade's mesmerizing advances weakening her resolve. Wearing a dress would invite his advances, and she knew it. How did she get herself painted into corners like this? If she hadn't been angry with Slade, it would be funny. Normally, her sense of humor rescued her; this time it didn't.

"I'll be ready about five-thirty or so," she promised.

"What color dress will you be wearing?"

"Turquoise."

Slade smiled enigmatically. "Perfect," he murmured. "I'll come for you at five-thirty."

Why am I taking so many extra pains to look pretty? Cat gave herself a disgruntled look in the floor-length mirror. She wore a designer dress, a stunning turquoise creation made of rich georgette and luminous satin. Together, the materials created an elegant dress for any special occasion. The deep-draped neckline was graced with a satin camisole inset. The satin sash with a rosette emphasized her narrow waist, while the full-circle skirt flowed with breathtaking grace each time she moved. The sleeves were full and cuffed at her wrists, adding to the overall frothy look. This was a dress to dance in, no matter how poor a dancer she was. Cat sighed, running her fingers across the beautiful, wispy fabric. That was how she felt around Slade despite everything he had done—feminine and…loved.

Cat chose pearl earrings set in a circle of thin gold, but realized something was missing. She needed some kind of necklace to set off the dress. Oh, well, such was life, she admitted regretfully. Taking one more look at herself in the mirror, she decided she looked unusually attractive. Was it the soft sweep of her recently washed hair? The dress? Glumly, Cat knew that despite everything, she wanted to be beautiful for Slade. Damn his hold over her!

When the knock came at her door, Cat turned on her turquoise sandals and opened it. She was completely unprepared for what she saw. Slade was darkly handsome in a black tuxedo, white shirt and black tie. He had shaved, erasing the five o'clock shadow he grew daily, and his hair was still damp and neatly combed into place. Her lips parted as she stared helplessly up into the warmth of his blue eyes.

"You look beautiful," he said huskily, holding out his hand toward her. His heart started violently as he absorbed Cat's unparalleled beauty. The fragrance of her perfume drugged him and his nostrils eagerly drank in her scent. The design of the turquoise dress enhanced the delicious, exotic tilt of her green eyes. Never had he seen her look so desirable. She was all curves and softness and Slade fought the urge to take Cat into his arms, crushing her against him. Holding himself in check, he shared an unsure smile with her. Cat was just as nervous as he was, he discovered to his relief. Her fingers were damp as she lightly placed her hand in his.

"Thank you," Cat said a little breathlessly, walking slowly toward the living room with him.

"Kai and Matt are already here. We've got time for a drink before we go." Slade accompanied her into the living room, where Kai and her husband, Matt, were sitting on one sofa, drinks in hand. "About an hour from now I'm flying us all to Houston and we're going to have dinner at the Brownstone."

"The Brownstone?" Cat stared up at him in disbelief. That particular restaurant was the best in the city. Slade had made it sound as if the night's excursion was going to be less posh, less intimate. "But—I thought—"

Slade grinned rakishly, guiding her to the couch opposite the Travis's. "You need a break. We both do," he explained in his dark, honeyed voice, his mouth close to her ear. "Want your usual? A margarita?"

Cat stared up at him, nonplussed. She saw the glint of mischief in his eyes. If she read accurately between the lines, Slade had deliberately set up this plan and put it into motion. "No. Give me a double Scotch on the rocks," she said, at a loss to stay ahead of his surprises. It was supposed to be business only between them, not pleasure. She was frightened of her own emotional reactions to him. Ten days had not assuaged her feelings for Slade. How could she control them for an entire evening in one of the most romantic restaurants in Houston?

Slade stood there uncertainly. "A double?" he voiced.

"I'm not the one flying, Slade. You are. I want a double Scotch on the rocks."

"Twist of lemon?"

Cat gripped her clutch purse tightly, trying to look cool and collected in front of their guests. "Yes." *Donovan, I'm going to murder you when we get back. I swear I will...*

"This was a wonderful idea," Kai spoke up. She wore a white chemise that brought out the highlights of her shoulder-length auburn hair. The gold earrings and slender necklace at her throat matched the sparkle in her eyes. "Frankly, when Slade called over, we were ready to go to the city, but didn't plan on the Brownstone." She laughed delightedly. "I love the restaurant! It's so Victorian and so thoroughly romantic."

One confirmation, Cat thought. She shot Slade a withering look as he ambled back over with her drink.

"Yes, he's always cooking up something, isn't he?" Cat said, taking the drink. When Slade sat down and hooked his long arm around her, Cat fairly sizzled. No matter how black her look, Slade smiled, enjoying her predicament. He knew her well enough to know that she wouldn't embarrass herself or him in front of company.

Matt Travis was equally handsome in a white tuxedo trimmed in black. It brought out his dark attractiveness, Cat thought. And both Kai and Matt looked so happy together. She envied them their loving relationship.

"That's one of the many things this lady likes about me," Slade drawled, giving Cat a wide smile.

Cat clamped her mouth shut after she swallowed a healthy gulp of Scotch, silencing her urge to protest the game he was playing with her.

Kai leaned forward, her eyes fairly sparkling. "Slade was telling us he had a surprise for you, Cat. I can hardly wait for you to see what he's done."

"He's done enough already," Cat said, choking on the words that sounded almost sweet coming from her.

Kai shared a knowing glance with her husband. "Slade, why not give it to Cat now? We saw what he's made for you and I'm just dying to see the look on your face when you get it. Slade? Please?"

Slade groaned. "Kai, when you give me that pleading look of yours, how can I say no?" He got up, setting his drink on the coffee table.

Matt grinned, putting his arm around his wife, giving her a warm embrace. "See why I fell under her spell, Slade? I told you before, you can't resist those beautiful eyes of hers."

Slade tilted his head, meeting and holding Cat's gaze. "I don't want to take anything away from Kai, but this exotic beauty over here has the most beautiful emerald eyes I've ever seen."

Cat felt heat rise in her face as his compliment reached through her like a caress.

"Agreed!" Kai said, smiling.

"Exotic's the right word," Matt said thoughtfully, studying Cat.

"Well, wait here, gang. Since Kai can't stand the suspense, I guess I'll have to give Cat her present now, rather than after dinner."

Cat nervously cleared her throat as Slade left the room. She looked at them. "What's he talking about, Kai? What's going on?"

She smiled warmly. "Oh, Cat, don't you know?"

Cat wished she did. Trying to hide her desire to escape, she shook her head. "No, I don't."

Matt patted his wife's hand. "Slade's sort of like a brother to us, Cat. Ever since he brought you here, we've seen a tremendous change in him—a good, positive change. We've watched him settle down and relax, for once. He's pretty happy with you around, you know."

"And Slade is the type of man who loves to give people gifts," Kai said, a wistful look on her face. "He's given us so much over the years we've been here."

"And to our son, Josh," Matt added warmly.

"Sometimes, I think Slade collects all his strays and turns them into an extended family of sorts." Kai lowered her voice to a conspiratorial whisper. "I told Matt all along, Slade is made for marriage. Until you came he was restless, Cat. You could see it in his walk, his eyes and the way he ran his life. Now, this past month and a half, he's been so incredibly content, it's blown us away." Her voice grew husky. "I don't know what your relationship with Slade is, Cat, but he thinks an awful lot of you." And then Kai traded a merry look with Matt. "We're keeping our fingers crossed for the two of you!"

"Now what's all this whispering about?" Slade entered the room, carrying a dove-gray velvet jewelry case.

Cat nearly dropped her drink. "Uh, nothing, just girl talk," she stammered. "You know…"

Matt and Kai chuckled like indulgent parents as Slade came and sat down next to Cat.

"Girl talk, hmm?" Slade's blue eyes glimmered with mirth. "If I know Kai, she's up to no good again."

"That's not fair, Slade!" Kai protested laughingly. She got to her feet and so did Matt, coming to stand near Slade. "Go on, show her!"

Cat gripped the tumbler as if it were her last hold on life. Slade set the gray velvet box on the couch between them.

"I will. Patience, pretty lady." Slade devoted a hundred percent of his attention to Cat, his smile waning. He soberly held her nervous gaze. "Ten days ago I started a project in my hobby shop. I wanted to make you something that would somehow tell you how I felt about you. I wanted a gem that would show you what

I saw in you, Cat." Slade reached over, gently unclipping her pearl earrings. "You won't be needing these tonight," he told her.

Cat swallowed hard, swayed by the huskiness in Slade's tone. She heard the unsureness in his voice and saw it in his cobalt eyes. And suddenly, Cat wanted to reassure him that she would not reject him or make him feel embarrassed. Ever. "Ten days ago?" she whispered, an ache in her voice.

Slade's mouth twisted into a grimace. "Yes." He glanced up at Kai and Matt. "We had a big fight then," he explained to them, leaving out the details. He pried open the spring-latched lid.

Cat gasped, her hand flying to her breast. There, nestled on a deep-blue velvet cushion, was a set of opal earrings, a pear-shaped necklace on a delicate gold chain and a cocktail ring. The silence was eloquent as Slade, whose fingers were scarred and huge in comparison, gently took the necklace from its placement on the velvet.

"People remind me of gems," Slade told Cat in a low voice fraught with emotion. "To me, the opal is the most complex of all gems, like you." He settled the stone around her neck, easing the clasp closed. The huge pear-shaped opal, almost the size of a nickel in diameter, nestled into the hollow of her throat. Then Slade dared to meet Cat's eyes for the first time, afraid of what he might see and praying for the opposite. The words died on his lips as he drowned in the shimmering emerald of Cat's eyes, now filled with huge, luminous tears. In their depths he saw her incredible fire and warmth toward him. He didn't deserve this kind of a reaction from Cat after all the blundering mistakes he'd made with her thus far.

Suddenly, Slade wished Kai and Matt weren't there. The open invitation in Cat's gestures made him want to lift her up into his arms and carry her off to his bedroom to seal their fate. He wanted to make her his own, to drink her into his thirsty, starving soul. Cat could give him the serenity he sought. She was peace, he realized, as he gently cradled her hands. There was so much he wanted to blurt out to her, to apologize for. He longed to ask forgiveness. But now was not the time. If the compassionate look in Cat's eyes was any kind of a promise, she would yield despite the pain he'd put her through, and allow him to explain…to forgive him and start over with a clean slate.

As Slade clipped each of the opals to her earlobes, the iridescent layers of the precious gems gleamed with the fires of emeralds, rubies, topaz, and sapphires. The colors brought out the natural beauty of her eyes and he silently thanked God and Cat for giving him a second chance he didn't deserve.

Slipping the ring on the fourth finger of her right hand, Slade said quietly, "There's a matchlessness to opal, Cat. The layers of color change as you turn your hand one way or another. You're like that—you have so many brilliant facets that change, depending on your mood. You keep me enthralled to the point where nothing else exists for me." He held her gaze, his hands tightening slightly on hers. "You've become my day, my night, sweetheart. Nothing else comes close to you in importance. You've got to believe that. Richness from the heart outstrips monetary concerns. The color of your eyes when you look at me gives me a wealth of feelings and emotions that no emerald mine or money could ever give me. Do you understand?"

Shyly, Cat touched the opal at her throat, all of her disappointment and hurt melting away beneath Slade's beautiful words. He meant them with every fiber of his being, she realized, completely dissolved by his admittance. Placing her fingers in his hand, she gravely met his anxious look. Her voice came out in a husky, quivering whisper. "Yes… I understand, Slade."

He squeezed her fingers gently, a powerful wave of relief smashing through him. And when he dared to look into her green eyes, bright with tenderness and awash with tears, he knew she did.

Chapter 9

"Are you enjoying yourself, Cat?"

Slade's words, whispered lightly against her temple, caused Cat to tremble. He held her close as the quiet music fell over them on the dance floor. "I shouldn't be, but I am."

His chuckle was a deep, pleased sound. Slade held her a little more tightly, aware of how her soft pliant curves fitted against his harder, unyielding body. "I took a big risk," he admitted, pressing a kiss to her hair.

"I'm still upset with you, Slade."

One eyebrow cocked and he looked down at her. If that was true, he didn't see anger in Cat's eyes. Instead, he saw the molten gold desire in her dark green gaze. "For what? Arranging this weekend in Houston with Matt and Kai?" he asked innocently.

She laughed and shook her head. "You're such a rascal, do you know that? One minute you're Peck's Bad

Boy. The next, you've made up for what you caused by giving me the most beautiful gift I've ever gotten. And then you have Pilar pack a suitcase for me and hide it on the plane. If Kai hadn't told me on the way to Houston that you were planning a weekend here and not just the evening, I'd probably have dropped my soupspoon when you blithely announced it at dinner."

He grinned engagingly, whirling her around, the airy folds of her dress moving like the wind around her tall, graceful body. The night was turning into magic, Slade thought, unable to contain his joy. "You'd never drop a soupspoon in front of anyone," he drawled. "You're too cool to do that."

"Being around you is like running a big risk without insurance, Slade."

He smiled. "Thank you."

"That wasn't a compliment."

"Am I a risk?"

"You know you are, Slade Donovan. So quit giving me that engaging little-boy look. It won't work."

"It's worked so far..."

Admittedly, he was right, Cat thought, unable to resist his smile. "What else do you have planned?"

He looked above her head, noticing Kai and Matt dancing nearby on the crowded dance floor. "Actually, Kai begged me to fly her to Houston to shop. I got to thinking about it and called her back and asked her if she and Matt would like to make it a weekend with the four of us. She thought it was a great idea. I've made reservations at the Westin Hotel over at the Galleria. Saturday morning, if you want, you and Kai can go shopping. Matt and I are going to do a little golfing. That evening, we'll go to an excellent French restaurant." He looked down at Cat, devilry in his eyes. "Then, we'll go to an amusement park nearby. They have one of the best bumper-car rides around."

Cat gasped. "An amusement park?"

"Sure. Kai wanted to do something different. I figure it's been at least twenty years since any of us went on a merry-go-round or tried to win a stuffed toy. It ought to make for a fun night."

Cat laughed delightedly. "It sounds wonderful. What else?"

"Brunch on Sunday morning. I figure we'll get up late and then reward ourselves by crawling into the hot tub in my suite. We'll sip champagne, have eggs Benedict and generally pry our eyes open. Then, around oneish, we'll head back out to Del Rio. How does the game plan sound?"

Cat tried to hide her enjoyment and didn't succeed. "It sounds great and you know it."

"Remember, this was Kai's idea, originally."

"Slade, one of these days your cleverness is going to catch up with you."

He sobered. "Yeah, I know. Contrary to what you might think, I got two rooms at the Westin for us. They're both suites and are joined by a door."

Relief flooded Cat. "Thank you, Slade…"

"I didn't want to," he admitted softly, trailing a slow series of kisses along her hairline, "but I did."

"It probably killed you," she said wryly, her knees weakening as each of his kisses melted her a little more.

Slade had the good grace to chuckle. "Yeah, I really fence-sat on that one." He eased Cat away from him, staring darkly down at her. "Look, after dancing when we get over to the hotel, we need to sit down and talk."

"Yes, about a lot of things."

"I've been a real bastard, Cat. I'm sorry. I didn't mean to hurt you like I have." Slade drew in a breath and forced a slight smile. "Tonight, come to my suite when you're ready."

Cat lifted her chin, lost in the warming cobalt of his gaze, her pulse unsteady. "I will."

Pilar had packed with great care, Cat discovered as she opened her luggage. The peach silk nightgown and accompanying robe had been carefully folded on top of everything else. She held up the shimmering gown. Should she wear that over to Slade's suite? Or should she go over dressed as she was? Indecision warred with what her heart desired. "Oh, to hell with it," Cat muttered, heading to the shower.

Slade was standing by the window overlooking the scintillating lights of Houston at one o'clock in the morning. He had gotten rid of his tie and opened the throat of the shirt. The jacket had been shed on a silk settee and he'd eased out of his shoes. In a spasm of nervousness, he'd poured himself a snifter of brandy. He held the glass in his left hand as he stared out at the sleeping city. He and Cat had sobered as the evening wore on, realizing the coming confrontation between them. Slade expected to be justly brought to task by Cat. What he wanted was to make love with her, to apologize that way, instead. But that wasn't a reasonable solution to everything. No, this talk had been long overdue between them, and he was willing to endure it if it would give him hope of a future with Cat. Any future was better than none.

A faint knock at the adjoining door made him turn.

Slade's eyes widened appreciatively as Cat silently walked into the room. A flood of heat uncoiled deep within him as he stared at the huge fuzzy white hotel robe she wore. Her hair was damp at the ends, indicating she'd just taken a shower.

"Come in," he said, motioning for her to sit on the pale blue Oriental couch nearby. He saw the high color in Cat's cheeks and her unsureness. She was just as scared as he was. A load slid off his shoulders when he realized that, and Slade poured her some brandy, handing her the crystal snifter after she had sat down. Cat curled up, her long, coltish legs tucked beneath her body. Her hair was newly brushed and he could smell her showered freshness.

"Thank you," Cat murmured, lifting the snifter to her lips. The apricot scent flowed across her tongue, warming her mouth and going down smoothly, relaxing her in its wake. Cat watched as Slade sat down, his hip only inches from her knees. A hesitant smile touched her lips. "I think we both needed this."

"Yeah," Slade agreed. He noticed that Cat still wore the opal ring and that gave him hope. "You're wearing the ring."

Cat smiled gently, lifting her hand to study the iridescent colors of the oval gem. "How could I not wear it?" She held Slade's gaze. "You didn't have to make all this jewelry for me."

"Why do you think I did it?"

The silence wove between them as Cat considered his quietly asked question. She struggled to answer. "I honestly don't know, Slade."

"Guess."

She grimaced. "I'm not very good at guessing games. Why don't you just tell me why you did it?"

"Because I want to know what you thought my intentions were toward you."

Cat closed her eyes, pain in her voice. "Slade, you don't make this easy on me. The worst possible reason you might have done it was to buy my forgiveness for tricking me into doing something you wanted from me." She opened her eyes, meeting his opaque stare. "You know that, if nothing else, I try to be an honorable person. My word is my bond. You knew that by saving my life I would owe you. And you used that knowledge in a way that I'd never have expected."

He turned the snifter slowly around between his large hands. "All right, that's the worst scenario. Any others?"

"That the gift was a way of apologizing to me?"

"Possibly. What else?"

Cat heard the strain in his voice. "No. None that I can see. Is there another, Slade?"

He nodded. "Yeah. All my life I'd been bitten by green fire, the dream of finding an emerald mine. There's just something about the gem that fascinates me. I'd set up my entire life-style and reason for being a geologist to make the big find." Slade pinned her with his gaze. "It wasn't for the money, but just for the sheer challenge of finding such a rare gemstone. I got close in Brazil when I discovered the tourmaline deposits at El Camino. That just made me that much more determined and thirsty to find green fire. I knew it was close; I could feel it in my bones like a gold prospector can feel when he's approaching a vein. I could taste it. And then, it happened: that poker game in Bogotá changed my life. Or I thought it had," he added wryly.

Slade held her unwavering gaze. "I then went in search of the very best mining engineer I could find. I sought you out. When I first saw you in that shack, Cat, I didn't know what to expect. I never realized how beautiful you were, besides being accomplished and an expert in your field. The magazine photos didn't do you justice. Anyway, when that cave-in occurred, I was worried for you. And those next three days of staying in contact with you on the radio slowly began to change me. It was subtle at first, and I can't exactly find words to tell you how you began to affect me and my objectives. And then I found myself wanting you to myself for more than just professional reasons."

Slade placed the snifter on the coffee table in front of them and stood up, thrusting his hands deep into the pockets of his trousers. His face was etched harshly with conflicting emotions as he turned and continued in a low timbre. "For eight weeks, you lived with me. Until the day of our argument and my blunder trying to play amateur psychologist with you, I never realized just how much you had come to mean to me." He ran his fingers through his hair. "I guess I had given up finding a woman to share my world. It took something like this to make me discover it, Cat.

"When I came back to the ranch, I went to my office and searched through every gemstone I'd collected over the years. I wanted to find something that would reflect to you just what you had become to me in this past month." The tension in Slade's face dissolved. "I didn't make the opals as an apology or to buy anything from you, Cat. I was hoping they would show you what I hadn't been able to do with any success, to tell you that you mean far more to me than green fire…"

Cat touched the warm, fiery-colored opal, tears blurring her vision. "I'm sorry I thought the worst, Slade. I didn't know..."

He shrugged almost painfully and sat down next to her. "I haven't exactly been good at expressing myself, either, Cat. And for that, I also apologize." He reached out, capturing her right hand, holding her luminous gaze. "You were hurting so much inside from the trauma and the mine accident that I wanted to help you, and I blurted out the first half-baked idea that came to mind. I figured that if I could set you up under a condition where you'd be forced to face your fear, it would work out fine. I could see my idea wasn't having a positive effect on you. I got panicky." His words came out low and tortured. "The last thing I wanted from you was a payment of your life for the mine. My good intentions to get you to conquer your fear backfired. Sometimes, my mouth gets ahead of my thoughts. Or, at least, dealing with you it does."

Cat murmured his name softly, sliding her hand along his sandpapery cheek. "I shouldn't believe you, Slade, but I do. There's something that keeps drawing us back to each other no matter how much we've hurt each other. What is it about you that makes me believe you? What?"

Slade closed his eyes, feeling the warm caress of her hand across his flesh. He brought Cat into his arms and she sank against him, trusting him once again. Nuzzling her neck and shoulders with a flurry of moist kisses, he inhaled her feminine fragrance. "I don't know, sweetheart, I don't know." He felt Cat stiffen as he pressed a kiss between the cleavage of her taut, firm breasts before he raised his head. Reading her tender expression, he saw her eyes were lustrous and warm, with invitation in their green, sultry depths.

"The past ten days have been hell on both of us," Slade told her thickly. "You're under no obligation to me for saving your life, Cat. I would do it a hundred times over. This mine down in Colombia has no strings attached to you or me. I don't want you captive to me out of guilt. If you choose to become involved with it, it's because you want to. I'm going to fly to Colombia Monday morning. If you want to fly down with me, fine. If you don't, I'll understand." Slade stared down at her widening eyes. "No more pressure on you, Cat. Kai made me realize that no one has the right to tell you how to live your life. If you're afraid to go back down in a mine, that's something you have to deal with in your own way and time. I can't force you back into a shaft before you're ready. As much as I wish your life was in my hands, it's not." He feathered a kiss across her parting lips, tasting the apricot brandy on them.

"Wait..." she pleaded breathlessly, palms flat against his powerful chest. "Slade...who would you get to put that mine shaft in for you, then?"

"I don't know yet. It doesn't matter."

"But it does matter!"

Slade's mouth curved upward and he slid his hands up the sleeves of her arms. "Not right now, it doesn't."

Cat licked her lips, trying to pull from the heated cocoon spinning around both of them. "Slade, listen to me. We're not done talking."

He released her, sensing her concern. "All right, go ahead."

"You're really serious about this, getting another engineer?"

"Yes."

Cat muttered something under her breath, searching Slade's features. "Look, that mine is going to be tricky to build. You've got very movable layers of shale and limestone that can quiver like a dog's back if there's even a slight earthquake tremor. Not every mining engineer has the experience that I have in building one to withstand that kind of unexpected stress."

Slade wanted to embrace her, realizing she was putting his safety above her own fear. "I'm aware of that. And I'll find someone who can do it."

Getting up, Cat paced the suite for several minutes. Finally, she turned to him, her face set. "Slade, I care what happens to you. I've just spent ten days preparing blueprints for the Verde. And frankly, there isn't anyone who can build that mine more safely than I can."

"I believe you, Cat. But you don't have to go. I don't want you down there unless you're sure you're ready to tackle mine entry."

She gave him a frustrated look. "Damn it, Slade, if I didn't know any better, I'd say you were using reverse psychology on me to get me to go down there with you!" She stamped her bare foot to underscore the depth of her feeling. "Not only that, you make me feel like a child! And no one has ever brought out those feelings in me like you have." She knotted her fists. "I can't live with you. I can't live without you. On the other hand, I'm so damned scared of having to go into a mine that I turn icy cold all over."

He rose, barely aware of most of what she'd said. "You can't live without me?" Slade asked, coming up and placing his hands on her shoulders.

Petulantly, Cat shot him a withering look. "I said it, didn't I?"

"Really? You kinda like being around me despite everything that's happened?"

"I can't live with you either, Slade. You drive me nuts. I used to be a stable, steady, sane person until you dropped into my life. I don't know which way is up anymore. Or down. Or sideways. When I get around you, everything else just kind of fades and there's only you..."

His smile increased like the radiance of the sun rising as he brought her to him. "There's you and me, Cat. Just you and me," he whispered, molding his mouth against those provocative lips that were just begging to be tamed. "That's all that matters..."

A soft moan slid up her throat as Cat melted a little more beneath Slade's caressing kiss. So much was happening at once. She could barely think coherently beneath his fiery, coaxing touch. A shiver of need jolted through her as his tongue stroked each corner of her mouth, a tantalizing promise of more to come if she wanted him. An ache grew deep within her and Cat realized that only Slade had the magic to bring her to surrender. He was barely caressing her and she could feel him controlling himself for her sake.

Breathlessly, Cat eased away, seeing how his hooded eyes smoldered with a vibrant blue fire of their own. A delicious warmth flowed down through her as Slade lifted her into his arms. Cat sighed, resting her head against his, closing her eyes. "You're not an easy man to understand," she murmured.

Slade looked down at Cat as he carried her into the darkness of his bedroom. "I know that, sweetheart. Let's heal some of the wounds that still stand between us. When the sun rises tomorrow, we'll both be the better for it."

Cat smiled as he gently laid her down on the quilted satin surface of the huge king-size bed. As she awaited him, he slowly undressed. Like the mountains carved out of the enduring earth, he was beautiful to behold. Every angle of his darkly bronzed body slipped like a well-fitted plane into the next. Slade's chest was covered with a mat of dark, fine hair. His shoulders were broad, thrown back naturally, shouting of his rugged heritage. A sleek torso flowed smoothly into narrowed hips and long, muscular thighs to lean but finely sculpted calves. As Slade moved to her side, Cat whispered, "You're beautiful…"

She ran her fingers lightly across his shoulders, feeling his silent, coiled strength. Slade's hands settled around her, moving slowly and sending a sheet of prickling fire outward toward her tightening belly.

A growl reverberated in Slade's throat as she slid her hand across his chest, following the wiry carpet of hair down across the slab hardness of his stomach to—

"Cat," Slade growled savagely, pulling her tight against him. He gasped, unprepared for the caress of her warm fingers around him. As he crushed her hard against him, he branded her lips with a fiery kiss, stealing the breath from her. The pebbled hardness of her nipples pleasantly chafed the wall of his chest, taunting him. In one motion, he slid his hand beneath the terry-cloth robe revealing first one breast and then the other. Slade gave her no chance to protest, smothering her full, glistening lips with another kiss. His long, teasing kiss demanded that she submit fully beneath his onslaught.

Tonight, he wanted to please Cat as he had no other woman. Tonight was for her; tonight was for healing…

Dizziness sang through Cat as she lay helplessly in the path of Slade's ravishment. His lips created a trail of blazing fire from her earlobe, down her neck, across her collarbones and then… A gasp tore from her as his mouth settled over the first nipple. Reflexively, Cat's fingers dug into his bunched shoulder muscles, and she arched her entire body against him. Fire rippled outward, as if a stone had been tossed into the quiet surface of a deep pond, until a powerful, aching sensation gripped her loins. Each sucking motion drove her farther and farther from rational thought. She was flung into a universe where only emotion ruled.

Slade felt Cat's surrender to him, the discovery filling him with potency. She trusted him entirely. He lay on his back and pulled her gently on top of him. The instant her hip brushed his aching body, a hiss of air came from between his clenched teeth. Her eyes were barely open, her lips wet with further invitation as he settled her above him. Slade saw vague confusion register in her desire-clouded emerald eyes. He kept his hands on each of her arms to prevent her from falling.

"Your ribs," he explained thickly. "If I lie on you, I could hurt you. And I don't want to do that. For now, this is best." Slade smiled up into the shadowy planes of her radiant face and placed his hands on her hips, helping to guide her. "Come to me, sweet Cat, woman of the earth, my woman…"

A cry of pleasure tore from her as she settled down on him, her fingers digging into his arms. The fire that had simmered so long within her finally burst into brilliant life. One twist of his hips sent such a power-

ful tidal wave of pleasure that Cat sobbed. Together
they were fused like molten, volcanic lava, each stroke,
each movement a little deeper, more giving, taking and
melding than the last. He whispered her name like a
prayer given those who hold the earth in reverence. She
felt him return all she meant to him in those shattering moments that tore a cry from within her. Cat went
spinning off in a directionless universe of splintered
sunlight. And then, precious moments later, Slade stiffened, groaned and clung to her as if to life itself. As
she leaned down on him, her cheek against his warm,
damp chest, she knew they had given each other the
most precious gift of all.

Slade absently ran his fingers over her drying back,
marveling at her natural beauty. Cat lay beside him,
one hand across his chest, one leg across his. He smiled
into the darkness. "Has anyone ever told you how giving and loving you are?"

A quiver of pleasure spun through Cat as she languished in the timbre of his voice. "Not like you have,"
she whispered, incredibly satiated and fulfilled.

"Every time I hold a handful of warm earth in my
hands, I can feel the life in it." Slade splayed his hand
across her shoulder, pressing Cat gently to him, kissing
her damp temple. "I like you; you're the earth. You're
warm, yielding, fertile and incredibly alive."

A soft smile played on her lips as she weakly ran her
hand across the drying hair of his chest. "Then you're the
ocean: quixotic, mysterious and powerfully emotional."

Slade turned thoughtful as he eased to his side so
that he could see her. He cupped Cat's cheek, watching
as her eyes barely opened and focused on him. "Believe

me when I tell you that I've never made such incredible love with a woman as I have with you."

Cat felt euphoric. "Do you always have the right words?" she asked in a wispy voice, content to close her eyes and simply drink in his touch, his honeyed tone and male essence.

Slade's chuckle was derisive. "No. You know that better than anyone. I've blundered and tripped all over myself with you. And like the earth, you've forgiven me." He reached down, pulling up a sheet to cover them. He drew Cat into his arms, holding her gently for fear of putting too much pressure on her recently healed ribs. "My beautiful earth mother," he teased her huskily. "Let me hold you close to my heart."

Cat nuzzled beneath Slade's jaw, content as never before. For once, she was washed free of all her anxieties and fears. Slade had cleansed her; he had filled her with himself and given back to her. The last words she spoke before everything receded were, "You're healing me, Slade…"

The sun had barely edged along the horizon when Cat slowly awoke around six o'clock, unsure why she had left the cradling embrace of her euphoric dreams. She lay quietly in Slade's arms, a soft smile touching her mouth as he occasionally snored. One lock of dark hair had dropped across his smooth brow and she gently coaxed it back into place. For no reason, Cat was glad she was awake and Slade was still asleep. It gave her a chance to study him in the morning light.

Where are we going with one another? she wondered as she lay in his arms. *We have such a roller-coaster relationship. You lift me up higher than I've ever been and yet, like the restless ocean you are, you have the capacity to hurl me deeper into a morass than anyone ever has.* Cat studied Slade intently, trying to find the answers she sought. Last night, when he'd told her she didn't have to build that mine, she had felt a deep sense of relief. Slade had no ulterior motives where she was concerned, and he had proved it by releasing her from any obligation to him. She didn't want anything to happen to Slade. And yet, until that moment, Cat hadn't realized just how much he meant to her.

What was that saying? You must love someone enough to let them go, and if they come back to you it's from love. But if they leave and don't return, perhaps love was never there, anyway. Cat's eyes darkened as she focused on Slade's features. *Do I love you? I don't know. I'm not sure.* And then she almost laughed aloud because Slade had admitted as much to her last night: that she had somehow become more important to him than anything else in his life. Did he love her? He hadn't said so. And she was old enough to know that if Slade did, he'd tell her in time. Yes, time…time would yield what was and was not between them.

Cat found herself wanting a chance to find out where life would lead them. They'd had a rocky start with one another, and she knew it would become rockier because they had another equally powerful test before them: entering a mine. Now, however, Cat no longer struggled with the fear because she knew that when the time came, Slade would be there to help her.

Suddenly shaky at the thought, Cat grew uncomfortable. Slade would receive nothing from her, while she would be taking from him. Well, she must trust Slade on this point, let him guide and help her. All she had to do was communicate when she was in trouble. Somehow, Slade made her feel relaxed, almost eager to work with him, no matter what dangers the mine posed to either of them.

"Are you ready?"

Slade's tone was filled with amusement as he held Cat with one arm, his other hand wrapped around the pole of the carousel horse they sat upon.

A peal of laughter burst from Cat as she felt the merry-go-round gently start to move. She cast a look over at Kai and Matt, sitting haphazardly on another horse ahead of them. "Ready," she promised. Rich, warm feelings flowed through Cat as the memory of their night and day together came back to her.

Slade grinned happily. "After this, how about a round of bumper cars?" He kept a firm grip on Cat so she wouldn't fall as the horse moved up and down in time with the music. "Where's that sense of challenge you always like to grab by the horns, Kincaid?"

"Challenges, not death-defying feats, Donovan! Agh!" She nearly lost her balance when Slade moved around on the rear of the horse. Cat clung to the pole, but the carousel horse simply wasn't big enough for both of them. Still, she enjoyed Slade's closeness. She leaned back, catching his dancing sapphire gaze. "No bumper cars. Do you want me to crack my ribs again?"

Slade looked crestfallen. "Oh, sorry. I forgot." He brightened. "The Ferris wheel, then?"

With a moan, Cat said, "I'll think about it."

"I'll buy you cotton candy as a bribe. No Ferris wheel, no cotton candy," he teased, nibbling gently on her exposed earlobe.

With a laugh, Cat dodged his moist, tantalizing tongue. "You're such a rogue, Slade Donovan! You and

Matt go on the Ferris wheel. Kai and I will find something tamer to ride.

"Come on, Kai," Cat said, as they walked out the exit. She pointed toward the merry-go-round again. "I think we girls ought to stick together. Men can take all the wild rides they want, just like how they drove cars when they were eighteen: without us."

Kai giggled and followed Cat after the men were safely aboard the huge Ferris wheel. "I think we ought to have liability insurance around Slade and Matt," Kai said good-naturedly.

Cat couldn't stop laughing as they made their way back up to the brightly painted horses. The men had bought them each cotton candy and they sat aboard their chargers waiting for the music and movement to begin.

Kai's eyes gleamed with humor. "It feels strange to be at an amusement park again. I haven't done this since I was a kid of fourteen."

"I suspect Slade never grew up," Cat pointed out dryly, watching the Ferris wheel slowly start rotating in the distance.

"Ever since Slade bought the ranch, things haven't been the same out in Del Rio, either." Kai chortled. Slowly, the horses began to rise and fall beneath them, the music lilting and infectious.

"I can imagine. Slade constantly catches me by surprise," Cat agreed.

"Welcome to the club!" Kai's smile was warm. "Matt and I have been hoping for such a long time that Slade would find someone like you, Cat." She reached out, squeezing her hand for a moment. "We can tell Slade loves you."

Shock almost made her fall off her horse. Cat stared at Kai. "Slade loves me?"

"You know that misunderstanding you two had two weeks ago?"

"Yes?"

"Slade came over that day, Cat. He wanted to talk so I dragged him into the living room to tell me why he was so moon-eyed."

"Moon-eyed?"

Kai grinned. "A Texas expression. It means sad."

"I see."

"I pulled everything out of Slade, piece by piece," Kai went on. She flashed Cat an understanding look. "He felt terrible about what he said to you. I don't want to seem like a nosy neighbor or anything, and I know it's none of our business, but Slade sometimes, in his haste to make something right that's going wrong, digs himself a deeper hole."

Cat nodded. "He did, Kai. But he apologized, too."

"Then things are better between you?"

Better? Cat thought, a rush of heat suffusing her. "Yes, much better," she reassured Kai.

"Oh, wonderful!"

Fifteen minutes later, Slade and Matt swooped up from behind them, each grabbing his respective woman.

"Gotcha!" Slade growled, whisking Cat off the horse and into his arms.

Her eyes widened considerably as they wobbled off balance for a second before righting themselves. "You're going to kill me, Slade Donovan!"

He chuckled and gently lowered her to the ground. "Have I yet?" he demanded archly.

"It's just a matter of where and when," Cat muttered

as his large hands spanned her waist and he slipped behind her.

"Trust me," he coaxed near her ear, kissing her quickly.

Cat smiled, melting all over again at his nearness. "I do and you know it."

"Mmm, do you ever."

For the next three hours, Cat felt like a teenager again. The fact that they were one of the few older couples at the amusement park that Saturday night didn't bother them. She and Kai watched the men ride the bumper cars, Slade trying to show off for her by outmaneuvering Matt on the slick steel surface of the arena. The safety of the rail was comforting as Slade missed Matt and collided with two ten-year-olds because he couldn't control the direction of his car. Cat howled with laughter until her ribs started to hurt. But it was worth it just to laugh freely again. The ten-year-olds quickly disengaged themselves from Slade's plodding car and he waved to her. Only his pride had been impaired in the melee. Matt hustled his bumper car through an opening and smashed Slade's car from the other side of the enclosure. Slade spent the remainder of the ride backing out of the corner, only to be hit and driven back into it by every gleeful kid around. The entire rink broke into cheers as Slade drew a white handkerchief from his back pocket and waved it above his head in surrender, bowing to his ill-begotten fate.

Afterward, they drove to a nearby A & W. Cat had to laugh. Somehow a silver Mercedes-Benz just didn't look at home among all the souped-up pickups and gussied-up vans that jammed the place. But Slade was oblivious; he was having too much fun ordering from the machine. Soon a waitress on roller skates came out with a tray loaded with hamburgers, icy glasses of root beer and hot french fries for their late-evening snack. The car rang with nonstop laughter, and most of the time, Cat was laughing so hard that tears came to her eyes.

"Honestly," Cat told everyone, "I can't ever remember having had a better time."

Slade was pleased and fed Cat some more french fries.

"My stomach aches from laughing so much," Kai confided.

"My rear is bruised," Matt added dolefully, giving Slade an accusing look.

"My ribs hurt," Cat said, smiling at Slade, "but it was worth it."

Kai prodded Slade. "Come on, big guy, something has to hurt on you, too. After all, you were the one who thought he was a kamikaze pilot dive-bombing all those poor, defenseless kids out there in the bumper-car ring."

Slade's laughter was deep and rolling. He threw up both his hands in a gesture of peace. "Hey, what can I say? I'm just a kid trapped in a thirty-five-year-old body." He showed them a scraped elbow. "See? Do I get a Purple Heart for all my efforts?"

The car rocked with more laughter. An intense feeling of warmth encircled Cat as she met Slade's cobalt eyes and his roguish smile. So much was happening so quickly. One night in his arms had deeply changed her, for Slade made her feel good about herself, despite everything.

"Happy?" Slade asked later, pulling her into his arms.

Cat contentedly fitted herself beside him, the satin of her apricot silk gown molding against his heated, hard body. She sighed, glad to be in his arms, his breath moist across her cheek.

"Happy?" she murmured throatily, sliding her arms around his neck. "I'm floating."

He chuckled, kissing her cheek, eyes and nose, and then rested his mouth against her smiling, lush lips that parted to his advance. "Even with that bruise I found on your pretty derriere? What did you do, fall off the carousel horse?"

Cat leaned up, molding her lips to his strong, male mouth, lost in the heat of their tender exchange. His jaw was rough against her cheek, his skin smelled of soap and his hair was damp beneath her gentle fingers. "You know I got it when you dragged me off the horse," she teased. Slade's lips caught hers in a devouring kiss, and she melted as his knowing touch set her on fire again. "Oh, Slade, somehow you take the hurt away from me…" Cat rested against him, staring up into his smoldering blue eyes as he lay above her.

"Don't sound so surprised, sweetheart. Occasionally, people can do good things for one another."

"You make me feel magical," Cat said, cupping his stubborn jaw. Then with a tremulous sigh, she whispered, "I don't know when I've ever felt happier, or laughed so much. You're good for me."

"We're good for each other; it's not a one-way street, Cat." Slade tunneled his fingers through her silky hair, his voice deep with emotion. "We've had a rough and, if you'll pardon the pun, rocky start." He grimaced. "And it can get rockier."

She frowned, hearing the worry in his voice. "What do you mean?"

"Are you planning on going down to Bogotá with me on Monday?"

"Yes."

Slade rested his hand against her back and hip. "Look, I meant what I said about your not going. You could stay at the ranch, if you want or—go to another job assignment." It hurt to say the last of that sentence. "I think too much of you, Cat, and what might be, to have you go down to Bogotá unless you're very clear as to why you're going. I don't want you to go out of guilt. The slate is clean between us."

The troubled look in Slade's eyes made her heart wrench, and Cat offered him a slight smile. "I'm very clear about why I'm going down there with you, Slade. It's not out of guilt."

He accepted her explanation. Cat and their relationship were more important to him than the mine. The softness of her skin as he stroked her cheek sent another wave of exquisite longing through him. "It's going to be dangerous, Cat."

"What mine isn't?"

"I mean outside the mine. You'll have to wear a pistol at all times, and we'll be followed and watched. You'll have to have eyes in the back of your head."

"I've been in some pretty tense situations before, Slade. I'm no stranger to carrying a pistol when I have to. My dad taught me how to hit what I aimed at."

"Those guaqueros are tough and dangerous. They've been bred and raised in the back alleys of Bogotá's slums. If they think you're carrying an emerald on you, they'll slit your throat to get it."

Cat gave an exasperated sigh. "Slade, why, all of a sudden, are you trying to scare me out of going?"

"Because," he said thickly, leaning down to capture her lips, "your life means more to me than green fire."

Chapter 10

Pools of sweat had darkened the color of Slade's khaki short-sleeved shirt, and Cat wiped her brow with the back of her hand, grimacing. For seventy-five miles, they had bumped along in a ten-year-old Jeep on the only rutted dirt road leading from Bogotá to the emerald fields of the Muzo Valley. They passed several motley-looking groups of men, all stripped to the waist, their coffee-colored skin glistening from the harsh sun overhead and the humidity of the surrounding tropical forest. When they were near the guaqueros, Cat placed her hand over the handle of her revolver. The guaqueros glared, their dark, narrowed eyes quickly appraising Cat and Slade, trying to determine whether they were carrying emeralds.

Cat glanced over at Slade. All his attention was focused on keeping the Jeep on the miserable excuse for a road they were on. It had been washed out due to an unexpected thunderstorm the day before. Mud was everywhere. The guaqueros were covered with mud; only the whites of their wary eyes were visible. Despite the hardships, however, Cat was happy. She was back in the field once again, braving the inhospitable elements that seemed to come with sinking a shaft in some remote part of the world. Only when she thought about having to go in and inspect the mine shaft soon to be under construction did the black fear envelop her.

They crossed the brackish Rio Itoco on their way past Muzo Valley. The river's once-clear waters had turned black with gritty shale washed down into it by the heartless bulldozers. Cat saw hundreds of guaqueros in the river at the V of the valley, backs bent as they sluiced through the river's lifeblood. They sought the one precious pebble that would bring them a better life. Slade had told her that if a guaquero found one emerald a year he was lucky. In the same breath, he'd said: "The instant the emerald is found, the smart guaquero will hide it. If others have seen him discover it, they'll ambush him on the only road to Bogotá. If he's smart, he'll sell it to one of the esmeralderos who wait on the banks of the Rio Itoco."

Her heart went out to the treasure seekers. Cat saw not only men, but women and children amongst those who crowded in the Rio Itoco's shallow waters.

"You never said there were women and children out here, Slade."

It was his turn to grimace. He took off the baseball cap he wore to protect himself from the overhead sun. Blinding shafts stole in between the straight *pao d'arco* trees swathed in reptilian-looking vines. "Didn't want to depress you, Cat. It's a sad state of affairs down here. The women and even the children dig tunnels into Muzo's shale mountains at night. Sometimes they suffocate because of lack of oxygen in the longer tunnels. Sometimes they die in cave-ins." He glanced at her, seeing the anguish register on her features. That was one more thing he liked about Cat: she was incapable of hiding her reactions. He gripped her hand momentarily, giving it a squeeze. "It's a perilous life at best, looking for green fire," he said.

The jungle closed around them once again and the frequent foot traffic of guaqueros in the Río Itoco area shrank as the miles fell away. Humic acids of decayed vegetation surrounded them and Cat spotted a white monkey above them on one of the cable-strong vines before he went into hiding. The macaws' brilliant reds, blues and yellows made the dark, almost forbidding jungle come alive. Ferns, some as high as a man, cluttered the jungle floor, as did ringworm cassia and angel's trumpet shrubs. Perhaps most beautiful of all were the multicolored orchids, peeking out in breathtaking splendor to relieve the green walls on either side of the thin ribbon of a dirt road.

The odors of life and death clung to Cat's nostrils as Slade swung the Jeep up and out of the Muzo valley. The air was fresher and less humid as they traversed a shrinking road across the ridge, heading for Gato Valley. Compared to Muzo, Gato was spared man's plundering. No human beings were in sight. Gato, named after the jaguars that ruled the valley, seethed with wildlife and birds. Cat began to relax and let go of her pistol. Slade had given her stern warning that if a guaquero made any kind of move toward them, she was to draw the gun and ask questions later.

By the time they reached the third and final valley,

Silla de Montar, the sun was a red orb hanging low on the horizon. Cat was bruised and banged from the tortuous ride. From the rim of the valley, she saw the two peaks that created the saddle for which the valley had been named. On the left was Caballo Mountain, where Slade and Alvin owned the Verde mine land. Clothed in the green raiment of jungle, Caballo gave no hint of what lay beneath its verdant mantle. Cat smiled, thinking how skillfully the earth hid her treasure from passersby. Only Slade's patient, methodical channel samplings had hinted of the wealth that lay on Caballo and down into the mountain's heart of limestone and shale.

"It's beautiful here," she told him, meaning it.

"The air's a little less humid over here than at Muzo," Slade commented, aiming the nose of the sturdy Jeep down a steep incline toward the valley floor. "I think it's because of the higher elevation." He flashed her a tired smile. "We'll be working up on Caballo and not down in the valley. That's a plus, believe me."

"More like Chivor's mines," Cat agreed. Her short-sleeved cotton shirt gave her some relief from the static heat and sweltering humidity. She took the red neckerchief she always wore out in the field and wiped the latest layer of grit and sweat off her face. In the distance, she could see the faint outline of two tented camps. Halfway up Caballo sat a smaller camp with three olive-drab tents and one fire. About a quarter of a mile below that was a small city of tents, bustling with men and activity. Construction machinery sat behind the main camp, steel chargers that looked dark and forbidding in the jungle twilight. In the valley, Cat could barely make out huge, neat piles of posts and stulls to be used in the

creation of the mine shaft. Electricity was provided by
a number of diesel generators, now heard faintly in the
distance. All the comforts of home, Cat decided with
satisfaction. Suddenly excited, she looked forward to
meeting Alvin Moody, Slade's partner.

Cat couldn't resist a smile when she saw Alvin. He
was stooped over a fire, stirring the contents of a black
kettle, when he saw them. Slade hadn't exaggerated the
facts, she saw as Alvin rose to his full height. He looked
like an honest-to-God Texas legend come to life: a ten-
gallon straw hat was angled low on his silver hair and a
caterpillar mustache sat above his lean mouth. A long,
brown, chewed-up cigar was clamped between his teeth.
Cat turned to Slade as he braked the Jeep to a halt.

"Alvin looks like a page torn out of the 1860s," she
said.

Slade grinned, shutting the Jeep off. "That's Alvin,
all right."

"He's dressed like a marshall from Dodge City—
leather vest and two six-shooters low on his hips," she
pointed out gleefully.

"This is Dodge City and he is the sheriff, for all in-
tents and purposes of this camp," Slade growled. "Those
two pearl-handled Colts he carries are the real thing.
He's used them a time or two, believe me."

Cat gratefully slid out of the Jeep, her muscles protesting as she stretched to unknot all the kinks in her
back and rear. "Where's his badge?"

"Those Colts are his badge and they do all the necessary talking for him." Slade came around the Jeep,
sliding his hand beneath her left elbow. "Come on, he's
been waiting to meet you."

She laughed. "The big question is, am I ready to meet him! My God, he's a giant of a man!"

"Texas born and bred, sweetheart. In that state, they don't do anything on a small scale."

Cat agreed. As they drew up to Alvin, who stood with his large hands resting comfortably on the handles of his low-slung Colts, he grinned.

"Say," he crowed, sweeping off his hat in a courtly gesture, "you ugly-lookin' rock hound, you never said how purty this little filly was."

"Hi, Alvin. The name's Cat, Cat Kincaid." She extended her hand, grinning broadly.

Alvin gripped her hand, refusing to relinquish it as Slade stood nearby.

"If I'd told you how pretty she was, Alvin, you'd have left this pit and come back to Texas," Slade said, slapping him on the back.

"That's for sure, Slade. Miss Cat, welcome to the Verde mine," he told her, sweeping his arm toward Caballo Mountain just above them. His pale blue eyes twinkled. "We're right glad you're here to help us."

"Thanks, Alvin." Cat cast a glance over at Slade. "Your partner had to do a lot of talking to get me out here."

Alvin chortled and finally released her hand. He settled the huge hat back on his head. "This Texan's got more ways to twist a cat's tail than even I do. I figured if anyone could talk you into consulting for us instead of that kangaroo outfit in Australia, Slade could do it. By Gawd, I was right. You're here and that's all that matters."

Slade looked around, taking off his cap and stuffing it in the back pocket of his jeans. "What's cooking, Alvin?"

Alvin gave him a hint of a smile from beneath his mustache. "In my kettle or around Caballo?"

Hunkering down over the kettle, Slade stirred it briefly. "Both."

Alvin motioned for Cat to sit down on a log near the fire. "We got us some sidewinders prowlin' around, Slade." He patted his Colts affectionately. "Nothing I can't take care of."

"How many?"

"About half a dozen guaqueros have been hoverin' around since the mining equipment and workers was brought in." He pointed to the left, toward the shadowy mountain. "Everything you ordered is here—bulldozers, backhoes, shaft equipment. The whole kit and caboodle. That pack of guaqueros came with it." He squinted to the east of them. "As far as I can tell, they're makin' camp up there on Lazo Mountain and waitin'."

Cat glanced at Slade, watching the frown on his face deepen. "Waiting for what, Alvin?" she asked quietly, almost afraid to hear the answer.

The Texan joined them, pulling three tin plates from a nearby wooden trunk that had seen better days. "They smell green fire, Miss Cat. This bunch has a nose for emeralds like a starvin' coyote does for meat on the hoof. Right now, they're being real patient and checkin' us out." Alvin cocked his head in Slade's direction. "El Tigre is headin' up that bunch of no goods."

Slade scowled. "Him?"

"Who's El Tigre?" Cat asked, suddenly interested.

Alvin heaped a tin plate with the vittles. "One of

the meanest two-eyed snakes in the business of being a guaquero. He's a puny little bastard. Lean as a whippet, with eyes like a viper. He got his nickname over at Muzo because of his reputation of jumpin' other guaqueros after they've found green fire."

With a muttered curse, Slade stood and came over to where Alvin was doling out the food. "He's been accused of kidnapping, raping and thievery. Not necessarily in that order."

Her eyes widened. "Raping?"

"Sure," Alvin snorted, handing her a plate. "Men ain't the only ones to hunt for green fire. We got some tough women who pan right alongside the other guaqueros. El Tigre doesn't care if it's a male or female who has the emerald on them. He treats both sexes equally. If they don't give 'em the green fire, he'll do whatever's necessary to get it. That can be anything from torture to murder. If the guaquero's smart, he or she will hand over the loot and thank God for getting away alive. Sometimes, just for the hell of it, El Tigre will butcher his victim anyway as a warning to other guaqueros. There's a hundred-thousand-peso warrant out for his arrest by the owners of the Muzo mines." Alvin snorted. "El Tigre was born and raised in these mountains. Ain't no one gonna catch that oily weasel alive." He patted one Colt. "That's why you wear these at all times, Miss Cat. You eat, live and sleep with 'em."

Cat took the tin plate, now covered with beans and something with a red sauce on it. She sniffed it cautiously.

"That's rum beans for a main course," Alvin explained, "and sourdough bread and the tomatoes with biscuits is called pooch. It'll stick to your ribs."

Cat grinned. "As long as it doesn't grow hair on my chest, Alvin."

Alvin slapped his thigh, his laughter sounding like the rumble of thunder in his large chest. "Spunky little filly, ain't she? I like her, Slade. She's got a down-home sense of humor."

With a grin, Alvin served up a heaping plate for Slade and himself. The Texan sat across from them at the fire, wolfing down his portion of the food. "All I cook is cowboy food served on the open ranges of Texas. Rum beans has some bacon, molasses, mustard and a half a cup of good hundred-and-eighty-proof rum in it. Pooch is an old cowboy dessert."

The beans were tasty, maybe because she was starved. Alvin was a fine cook, Cat admitted. She smiled at him. "Well, I know you aren't going to try and poison me with your cooking, Alvin. This stuff is pretty good."

Alvin gave her an effusive grin, pleased by her praise. "I'll make you a real 'welcome to the Verde mine meal' tomorrow night, Miss Cat. I'll even throw in the horse-thief special for dessert. Hell, there ain't a cowboy alive who wouldn't ride hard like a horse thief to get a bowl of it." He winked conspiratorially at Slade. "We'll have her puttin' a few pounds on that skinny frame of hers in no time."

"Alvin, I'm not a heifer to be fattened up," Cat warned. "I like being thin."

"I like her that way, too," Slade agreed, laughing.

Alvin looked at them and said nothing, a knowing gleam in his eyes. "I'll only make half the amount of horse-thief special, then."

"No, make all you want," Slade countered quickly. "I'll eat the leftovers."

"See what I mean, Miss Cat? Men will do anything to get that dessert."

"I can hardly wait until tomorrow night," she promised him.

Conversation gradually drifted to the equipment, the work timetable and a long business discussion. The sun dropped behind the saddle formed by the two mountains, and the surrounding jungle suddenly came alive with the songs of insects. The mosquitoes had been pesky earlier; now they were vicious. The trio saturated themselves with insect repellent so they could sit around the fire without being attacked by the bloodthirsty insects.

By eleven o'clock, Cat was barely able to keep her eyes open, despite the interesting conversation. She got up, brushing off the seat of her pants.

"Which way is my cot, Alvin?"

Both men stood. "You and Slade share that larger tent on the left. The smaller one on the right is mine. Slade says you know how to live in jungles."

She smiled. "As long as you've got a mosquito net over the cot, that's all I'll need."

"You got it, Miss Cat."

"Are the guards set?" Slade asked.

"Yeah."

"Can they be trusted?"

Alvin grinned tightly beneath his silvery mustache. "Didn't I tell you? I brought some of my boys down from one of my Texas ranches."

"How'd you get them to come?" Slade asked admiringly.

"I'm payin' them double what they'd get to sit on a cow pony back home. They don't mind totin' around a rifle and standin' watches to make sure we don't get our throats slit."

Cat shivered as unpleasant reality settled over her. Seeing her shiver and rub her arms, Slade came over, placing an arm around her waist.

"We'll see you in the morning, Alvin."

"G'night, you two."

"Good night," Cat responded, casting a worried look up at Slade. Even so, she felt safe with him near. He guided her over to their tent, which was illuminated by a lantern hung inside.

"I told you this was going to be a rough place," Slade warned her in a low voice. "You can still back out, Cat."

She shook her head. "A Kincaid never backs out. We only know one direction, Slade: forward."

He opened the flap for her and ducked in after she entered. The floor was made of plywood in an effort to keep most of the insects, snakes and rodents out. A cot sat on either side and Cat tested the sturdiness of one of them, then sat down, unlacing her boots. A porcelain basin filled with warm water sat between the cots.

"I hadn't counted on El Tigre being here," Slade muttered, stripping off his damp, sweaty shirt. His chest gleamed with perspiration as he quickly washed up.

"Can't you call in the Colombian police to capture him?"

Cat sat there watching Slade, realizing once again how beautiful a man he was. Then she smiled, because Slade didn't like that term applied to him. Nudging off her boots, she peeled off the heavy white cotton socks, waiting until Slade had finished with his spit bath.

Slade scrubbed his face vigorously, the cooling water a blessing against the humid heat. "Alvin and I are going to try and operate Verde like Chivor: a private mine with no state influence." Drying his face and arms, Slade threw the water out the door and refilled the basin from a five-gallon plastic jug that sat beneath the rickety table. He motioned that it was her turn to wash up.

"We haven't even begun mining operations, so what is El Tigre going to do?" she wondered, sending a worried look to Slade.

But Slade's mind was on other things. Taking off his khaki trousers, he dropped them at the end of his cot. Cat had shed her blouse, revealing her golden tan now deepened by the kerosene lamp above them. His body hardened for her all over again. Their living quarters might be spare, but that wasn't going to stop him from loving her. He'd like to time a trip to Bogotá after the mine was under construction, taking Cat back to civilization every once in a while. That way they could spend a night in a real bed with sheets, a hot shower and air-conditioning. Now, all that seemed like real luxury. Slade smiled, watching as she washed her arms and shoulders. His gaze moved slowly up and then down her tall, graceful body, and the stirring heat in his lower body became an aching reality. Slade was amused at himself. Cat made him hungry no matter what she was or wasn't wearing.

"El Tigre will watch, catalog and send his spies down to talk with our newly hired miners," Slade said, sitting down on his cot. "He's going to see who's the boss and who might know where the emeralds are located."

Cat toweled off, standing on the wooden floor in only her lingerie. She saw the cobalt flare in Slade's eyes and swallowed hard. How was it possible that only one smoldering look from him set her on fire? No man had ever made her feel her feminine power as he did. No man had ever made her feel so cherished. Shakily, Cat placed the folded cotton towel near the basin. Before she could turn, Slade had captured her hand, pulling her over to him. He guided Cat to his lap and she smiled languidly, placing her arms around his neck.

"Let's forget about the bandits, sweetheart," he told her thickly. "This is more important…"

As his hand slid lightly up her rib cage to cup her breast, Cat gasped, dissolving into his arms. Desire coursed through her as his thumb caressed her nipple, and she was lost to his warm, knowing mouth. Cat hungrily matched Slade's mounting desire with her own.

With a groan, Slade eased his lips from hers. Cat's languorous smile went straight to his heart as she rested weakly in his arms. "I want you," he growled.

"I know…" With a sigh, Cat sat up, running her fingers through his unruly hair.

Slade patted her nicely rounded rear, the silk of her panties driving him closer to total loss of control. He saw the exhaustion in her eyes and admitted he was equally fatigued by the long trip. As much as his heart and mind were willing to carry Cat over that delicious edge and love her, Slade put a check on his desires. He didn't want to take her to his bed when he was this groggy. No, he wanted both of them awake and eager. Right now, they were both ready to keel over. He contented himself with holding and sharing this precious time with Cat instead. Moments later, he whispered, "Come tomorrow morning, we're going to be putting in twelve- to sixteen-hour days. I may not be able to hold or kiss you out there, but remember how I feel about you. We'll make up for it here in the tent every night. Deal?"

With a small laugh, Cat embraced him. "Deal. But by the time we drag ourselves into the tent to sleep, we might be too tired to do anything."

"No, we won't," Slade promised, trailing a series of moist kisses from her throat to the provocative swell of her firm breasts. "Even when I'm eighty, you'll still turn me on. Come on, let's get some sleep. We're going to need it."

Reluctantly, Cat knew he was right. Slade's words filled her heart with unexpected joy. "I'll see you in the morning, Slade," she said, rising from his cot to return to hers.

After getting the mosquito netting in position, Cat settled down to sleep. Slade turned off the lantern, and a consuming blackness quickly descended on them. The sounds of insects mingling with the howl of monkeys provided a strange symphony. Cat barely heard them, since her head and heart centered on Slade's last comment. They were growing closer to one another, and Slade was becoming her friend as well as her lover. As her eyes closed, Cat recognized that theirs was an ideal combination. She had known men in the past who only wanted her as a lover. Others she had liked well enough to call friend, but they hadn't stirred the embers of her heart or body to vibrant life. Slade did both. She felt a never-ending thirst to satiate herself with him in every way possible. As Cat sank into the oblivion of sleep, she found herself glad, despite her own personal fears about entering a mine, that she had come to Colombia.

Cat silently asked the earth to forgive their invasion as the first bulldozers roared to life. They would clear away the jungle over the site of the open pit location for the Verde mine. She stood on a small rise, white hard hat in place, watching as the powerful, growling noise of the huge machines reverberated through the surrounding jungle. Slade was down there with the dozer operators, making sure each man knew what he was doing. Alvin was coordinating other activities with the hired miners. As soon as the earth had her green mantle scraped free, the miners would carefully go over the newly shorn earth and walk it, an inch at a time. They would be looking for emeralds before another foot of overburden was scraped away.

Cat turned and went back to the newly erected shack, which would serve as her headquarters during the entire venture. The Indians had built her a small building composed of *pao d'arco*, or trumpet tree. The wood from the sometimes-two-hundred-foot giant would be the prime source for shoring beams in the mine. As Cat spread out her next blueprint on the roughened drafting-board surface, she smiled. Some of her fear left as she focused on the complexities of starting up such a project. With the throaty sound of bulldozers in the background, Cat took off her hard hat and sat down on the stool. Her final calculations would prepare for the excavation that would eventually become the mouth of the Verde mine shaft.

Night did not fall until after nine o'clock. Cat was still in her office on the hill, struggling with figures on her calculator, when the door opened. Thinking it was Slade, she turned, squinting from the light of the lantern that hung on the wall in front of her. She froze, her hand automatically moving to the Colt she carried on her hip.

"Do you want to die, *señorita*?"

Cat's mouth went dry as she stared at a dark-skinned

man barely her height. He was dressed in black-and-gray military fatigues. Two bandoliers of ammunition crisscrossed his thin chest and an array of knives, grenades and other military hardware were held in web belts. Two more men, less well equipped, slipped inside, shutting the door quietly behind them. Her gaze moved back to the leader.

"What's going on?" she forced out. Her pulse was racing, her throat growing dry. The look on the leader's oblong face was anything but friendly.

He smiled, showing his crooked yellow teeth. Motioning to the maps, he said in halting English, "These are the maps where the emeralds are?"

Cat's fingers closed over the handle of the Colt, but she knew she would be foolish to try anything. All three soldiers carried weapons.

"No," she lied, "I'm an engineer. I build mines. These are construction blueprints."

His smile remained fixed as he slowly approached her. "I'm El Tigre, *señorita*. You have heard of me, no?" He twisted one drooping end of his greasy mustache, which hung down over his mouth.

Cat nodded carefully. "Yeah, I've heard of you."

"Then you know enough not to lie." He let his hand fall on an eight-inch sheathed blade in a black leather belt at his waist.

"I'm not lying."

El Tigre's brown, feral eyes glittered and he ruthlessly assessed her in the thick, mounting silence. "No? Then who knows where the emeralds are to be found?"

Cat slowly turned, letting her hand move away from her pistol. "Listen, the owners don't even know if there are emeralds here, Señor Tigre."

He laughed; it was a curt, harsh sound. "No one gathers this kind of equipment and men if there aren't emeralds, *señorita*. Don't think me stupid!"

There was no way to escape; only one door had been built into the shack. The portable radio was set on the drafting board, but she couldn't signal Slade or Alvin that she needed help. Cat had the feeling if she made even the slightest move to escape, the Colombian guaquero would turn violent, like a rabid dog.

"I've been hired to build, that's all. I'm not a geologist."

El Tigre stepped up to her. "Then who is?"

Cat winced, assailed by the sour, unwashed smell of his body. "The geologist is still up in the States."

"Maybe, maybe not..." He reached out to touch her cheek.

Cat reacted out of instinct. The sound of the slap she delivered to the man shot through the shack. She scrambled out of the chair, her back against the wall, braced for whatever retribution might come.

El Tigre cursed, holding his injured jaw, glaring at her. "You," he snarled softly, "will live to regret this. I'm not done with you, *señorita*." He grabbed several sets of blueprints, turned and snapped orders to his men. They opened the door, disappearing into the gathering night. Before he left, El Tigre lifted his finger, waving it at her threateningly. "No one touches me, especially a gringo woman. Sleep lightly, *señorita*, for I'll be back. And next time, have the information I want or your pretty face will look like this." He jerked the knife from its scabbard and stabbed it into the drafting board, tearing long, deep scars through the remaining maps and wood.

* * *

Slade had noticed three men go up to the construction shack on the hill. He had climbed down from the bulldozer he'd been manning to give the driver a break. By the time he had gotten to the Jeep and driven up the rutted excuse of a road, they were gone. He walked in the open door and immediately saw Cat slumped against the drawing board, her head resting in one hand. And then he saw the destroyed blueprints beneath her elbow and the damage made by the knife.

"Cat? What happened?"

She looked up, giving Slade a wobbly smile meant to neutralize the concern in his voice.

"El Tigre and two of his men dropped in for a chat—of sorts."

Slade was instantly at her side, anxiously turning her toward him. "Did he hurt you?"

"Scared the hell out of me, but no, he didn't hurt me." She leaned against Slade's powerful chest, sinking into his arms. Only then did Cat release a shaky sigh, showing just how scared she had been.

"Tell me everything," he ordered harshly.

Afterward, Slade gathered up the rest of the blueprints, rolled them and stored them in the Jeep. The scowl on his brow had deepened as Cat had relayed the sequence of events. As they bumped on down the road toward base camp, he muttered, "I didn't think he'd jump us this soon."

"We should probably thank him, Slade."

"Why?"

"If he's got that good a nose for green fire, then your mine is a success even before we get a chance to start looking for the calcite matrix."

With a snort, Slade agreed. He gripped the steering wheel hard, his knuckles whitening. "You think on your feet pretty good. Telling him the geologist was in the States was an excellent idea."

Cat traded a glance with him. "Only if he believes it." She tried to quell her own fear that if El Tigre knew Slade was the geologist, his life, too, was in very real danger. She tried to shove back the nightmare played out by her overactive imagination. El Tigre would torture the information out of Slade, and she knew it. After having met the bandit, there was no doubt in her mind that he'd kill Slade after he got the information. An icy shiver moved up her spine.

"There's no safe place, is there?" she asked hollowly.

Slade brought the Jeep to a halt near their tent. He reached over and covered her hand, now clenched against her thigh. "No, there isn't. Come on, let's tell Alvin what happened. We'll figure something out."

The next week went by without incident. Two of Alvin's cowboys guarded Cat at all times while she worked at the shack. The jungle was removed, leaving the black overburden of soil. Almost immediately, a thin white vein of exposed limestone was discovered by the miners. Cat had watched in fascination as Alvin and Slade went down with the miners, gently breaking up the soft limestone with crowbars, prying it apart to see if they could find the telltale white calcite. And all the time, her gaze moved restlessly across the wall of jungle surrounding them. Somewhere in there were El Tigre and his cutthroat band.

The five or six hours Cat slept, with Slade nearby, became important. She rarely saw him during the day, although he would drop in unexpectedly to see her. The stolen kisses, unseen by anyone in the privacy of the shack, became her sustenance. At night in the privacy of their tent Slade's hands would slide knowingly down her damp body, filling her with the fire of their longing and erasing her fears. The mine became secondary to the threat El Tigre presented. Cat lived with the terror that the guaqueros would capture Slade.

Going back into the shack after dinner one night, Cat focused on her next project: getting the hardwood tree, *pao d'arco*, cut and brought down from the hillsides of Caballo so the beams could be cut and measured for use. The numbers before her blurred and Cat squeezed her eyes shut. You're tired, her mind screamed. Yes, she was tired. Sleep came grudgingly, if at all. She tossed and turned on her cot, El Tigre's viperlike eyes haunting her. *If nothing else,* Cat thought as she opened her eyes, pulling the hand calculator toward her, *it's made me own up to the fact that I'm in love with Slade.*

One week later, it happened.

"Pay dirt!" Slade breathed. The three of them crouched on the ground over a partially exposed limestone vein halfway up Caballo's western flank. A miner had discovered the white, flaky calcite matrix in the oppressive afternoon heat. Slade had called Alvin and Cat on their radios. They stood nearby while he patiently pried the matrix, as large as his hand, out of the embrace of the limestone. Pleasure wreathed Slade's features as he held the matrix up for them to see.

Cat gasped. Alvin gave a pleased chortle. Slade grinned rakishly, holding the white calcite in his palm. There, in its center, were four hexagonal green crystals varying in height from one inch to six inches. None of them was less than a quarter of an inch in diameter. Stunned, Cat watched as the rays of the sun glinted through the emerald crystals, showing their clarity.

"Green fire," Slade said hoarsely, holding the crystals up toward the sun. The molten emeralds gleamed like living beings, catching and refracting the light.

"My gawd," Alvin whispered, "look how clear they are."

Slade's face glistened with sweat, his teeth white against his darkly tanned flesh. "Muzo's deep color and Chivor's clarity. This is what I had been hoping for..."

Word of the find spread through the miners like a ripple of wind through a field of wheat. Cat stood back, watching the spectacle unfold. For a week, they had carefully poked and prodded through the limestone vein without success. A six-foot-high cyclone fence topped with barbed wire had been erected around the pit. As she stood watching the hope suddenly come alive in the Indians' faces, Cat felt frightened. El Tigre was out there, watching them—she could feel his eyes. She turned away, heading back to her shack on the hill. By four o'clock, the first of the dynamite that had been drilled into the limestone face would be triggered and an opening would be made. The mine—her mine—would begin taking shape, and soon she would have to go back inside the earth.

Despite the hundred-degree heat and ninety-percent humidity, Cat was cold. She took off her white construction hat, wiping the sweat from her brow with the back of her hand. The day she had been dreading had come. Part of her was happy about the emerald find, and Cat was sure there were more stones to be discovered. Taking a breath to support her deteriorating courage, she plunged ahead with her plans. A dynamite expert from the U.S., Tony Alvarez, was standing at the door to her shack when she arrived.

"We're ready when you are, Cat."

Cat forced a slight smile, then went inside to grab her portable radio and hook it on her web belt.

"What have we got?" she asked, getting into the Jeep.

Tony hopped in. "I prepped the area after I got rid of the overburden." He used his long, expressive hands. "The shot holes are drilled and loaded with dynamite. The blasting caps are in place and my crew has just collared each of the holes with clay."

Cat glanced at him as she drove the Jeep down the dusty road toward the valley. "Are you going to use millisecond delays between detonations to produce maximum fragmentation of the rock?"

"Sure am, boss. I'm using a four-hole, pyramid-cut pattern. It will give us a seven-by-seven-foot entrance and blow out rock seven feet behind it. We're using low charges so we won't destroy any emeralds that get in the way of our creating an opening into Mother Earth."

"Good," Cat said. She parked the Jeep a good distance from where the series of blasts would take place in the hill. All jungle growth and soil had been removed, exposing the pale green limestone. From her vantage point, using binoculars, Cat could see that Tony had set up the wall for detonation. She signaled Tony to set off the siren. The high-pitched wail shrieked over the area of the Verde, alerting everyone that blasting was going to take place. Tony raised his arm, alerting his two men who stood by the plunger.

Her mouth was dry as she lowered the binoculars. "All right, Tony, give them the signal."

The plunger was shoved down, making electrical contact with the pattern Tony had drilled into the limestone face. Ten explosions rocked Caballo, each seconds apart. Limestone spewed outward in fragments, and a huge, roiling white cloud of dust rose in the wake of the detonations. Cat's ears ached from the puncturing, thunderous roll that each one had caused. The air was pregnant with humidity and swallowed up the sound. Ears ringing, Cat lifted the glasses to her eyes. The dust slowly cleared and, as it did, she got the first look at the opening.

"Looks good, Tony," Cat praised. She had chosen a slope mine, using a slanting entry to follow the vein of limestone that carried the calcite and emerald. The dynamite had done its job, creating the entry, or adit, into the hillside. Now excavation of the debris would begin and the first of the *pao d'arco* beams would begin to be shored into place. The Verde mine had just been born.

Chapter 11

"Come on, I'll go in with you." Slade rested his hand on Cat's shoulder, feeling her tension. He saw the distraught look in her eyes and smiled. "What's this? Did you think I wouldn't escort you into the Verde mine?"

Cat relaxed beneath the massaging power of Slade's fingers on her shoulder. She had stayed away from actually entering the new mine shaft as long as she could. The last time she had seen Slade, he had been far above them in the pit, working side by side with the miners, looking for another calcite nest. A good, warm feeling flowed through her as Slade matched her slow walk toward the maw.

"I thought you were busy elsewhere," she said, knowing her voice sounded strained.

"Remember?" Slade said, becoming serious, settling his hard hat on his head. "I told you that you were more important than green fire."

A tremulous smile fled across Cat's mouth. "Judging from the look on your face earlier when you held that calcite bearing the emerald, I wondered, Slade."

His smile was devastating. "Don't. I promised you I'd be here when you needed me."

The shadow of the hill enveloped them, and Cat slowed to a stop a few feet from the shaft entrance. Already, wooden forms were being erected to create a permanent opening to the Verde. Once the forms were in place, concrete would be poured into them. Thick, rectangular beams of *pao d'arco* lay in huge, neat piles nearby. Some were already being hauled over to the mouth of the shaft.

Cat felt her stomach shrink into a knot. Her lips felt dry. She didn't dare hesitate in front of the miners who covertly watched her. The limestone was jagged from the explosions and would have to be knocked off the walls to prevent injury. She stepped into the mouth, vaguely aware of a minimal temperature drop. Slade remained at her side as they walked back the first seven feet. They stood in the center of the footwall where the rubble had been removed, both looking overhead, studying the manging wall.

Slade glanced down at her. Even in the shadowy grayness of the mine, he could see how pale Cat had become. Small beads of sweat stood out on her wrinkled brow as she assessed the ceiling with a critical eye. A fierce wave of pride overwhelmed him. Despite Cat's fear, she was holding her ground.

"We're going to need rock bolts," she said, pointing to the spiderweb pattern on the ceiling where the rock had been fractured.

Slade nodded in agreement. Often, the systematic

use of rock bolts reinforced roofs of mines that might cave in, or they strengthened existing walls in case of earthquake. "We've got an ample supply," he said.

Suddenly, Cat wanted to run. She wanted to scream. Swallowing hard, she forced herself to measure off the distance to where the first post and stulls would be set. The activity helped keep her fear contained, and as she talked with the Indian foreman in Spanish, a little more of the fear receded.

"I want those rock bolts under high tension, Pablo."

The foreman, a man close to fifty with graying hair beneath his red hard hat, nodded. *"Si, Patrona."*

"I'll be testing them," she warned him.

Slade smiled to himself. Cat would, too. That would mean she'd be spending a hell of a lot of time in the mine measuring them with a torque meter. Much later, Slade followed Cat out of the mine. He traded a knowing glance with her as she took off her hard hat, wiping her sweaty features.

"Congratulations," he told her in a low voice, "you did it. First time's always the toughest."

With a weary smile, Cat threw the hat back on her head. She watched the beams being hauled to the entrance. From here on, the building of the mine would continue for twenty-four hours a day with three crew shifts working. She would be up sixteen of those hours to keep pace with the rapid expansion of the mine until they hit a vein with calcite in it. Then, work would slow accordingly to open up the vein and hunt for the emeralds.

"I'm so shaky, my knees are knocking, Slade."

"How about if I hold you tonight?"

The gritty warmth of his lowered voice washed

through her and Cat shared a soft smile with him. The words *I love you* were almost torn from her. "Sounds wonderful, fella."

"Hey, this evening, Alvin's celebrating the mine start-up by making a special dinner for us."

Alvin was a fine cook and Cat eagerly looked forward to most of his cowboy meals. "What's on the menu?"

Slade chuckled. "Texican beef, hunkydummy, potato dumplin's and apple pan dowdy. A meal fit for a king and queen, believe me. My mouth's watering already."

Cat's wasn't. "Hunkydummy? What's that?" Alvin had a couple of other cowboy recipes she'd just as soon forget about. Every night when they settled around their campfire where Alvin was fixing the vittles, Cat went over every item he was cooking before she ate it.

"It's a kind of bread with raisins and cinnamon sprinkled over the top of it."

"Oh, that sounds pretty good."

Slade laughed. "You're such a sissy," he chided.

"I'm from Colorado, Slade, not Texas. Some of the wild food Alvin whips up could only be consumed by a Texas cowhand. Give me a break!"

Back at the shack, Cat sat down at her drafting board. Her hand shook as she picked up a blue pencil. Closing her eyes, she dropped the pencil and sat there, allowing the cold wash of fear to drench her. After a few minutes, she lifted her head, a wry smile on her lips. How could she have lived so long and not known real fear?

Absently, she picked up the pencil, going through the motions of making notations on the blueprint. The fear wasn't all negative, she mused, nearly awed by that realization. No, it had shown her that another person could give her the necessary strength to press forward.

Had Slade's love given her that support? Cat hesitated over the blueprint as she centered on that question. He had never said he loved her, nor had she told him. Nevertheless, she felt whole as never before, regardless of the fear that stalked her about mine entry. With a soft laugh, Cat shook her head. So, was this real love, this feeling of completeness that Slade automatically gave to her? Cat couldn't imagine life without Slade's presence. He made each minute, each hour important. And they were, with him.

Eventually, Cat returned to the demanding work in front of her. But numbers, formulas and figures couldn't compete with the powerful sensations in her heart. Cat allowed the full gamut of her emotions to surface and be felt. She could barely breathe for the sheer joy of being alive in every sense of the word.

Near four o'clock, Slade knocked on the door and entered. He saw Cat bent over her drafting board, hard at work. A swell of pride and love overwhelmed him as he stood in the open doorway, watching her. As she turned, he saw the sudden happiness in her green eyes because he was there. Slade was deeply moved. With a smile, he held his hand out toward her.

"Come on, I'm taking you someplace special."

Cat stared at his large, powerful fingers; they were dirt-stained and his nails worn to nothing from prying calcite apart, looking for green fire. Without a word, she slipped her hand into his.

"Where?" Her voice was breathless with anticipation.

"While El Tigre is busy watching Alvin and his men digging for green fire, you and I are going to slip off to share some well-deserved time together. What do you think? Are you ready to be carried off by your knight on his white charger?"

Gladly, Cat put down her hard hat and followed Slade out the door. "More than ready, my lord. Lead the way."

Slade gave the Jeep an apologetic look as they climbed in. "Not exactly a white charger, but it'll have to do. Still game?"

"You bet. Is this a surprise or can you tell me where we're going?"

He wanted to ruffle her hair, run his fingers through it and feel the silk of her skin beneath his hands. His voice husky, he traded a tender look with Cat. "I want it to be a surprise. I've been planning this a long time before we came down here. Just sit back and enjoy the ride, my lady."

With a sigh, Cat nodded and leaned back. The movement of the Jeep as it took them up and out of the mining area cooled her sweaty skin. She felt Slade's hand cover her own and she squeezed it. "I love you," she almost whispered. Cat had trouble not saying it out loud to Slade. The adoration in his dark sapphire eyes made her tremble with need.

As they crossed the only road up and out of the valley, Slade turned off, heading down a little-used path. The foliage and low-hanging vines swatted at them and the Jeep cautiously crept forward. Brightly colored macaws ranging from blue and yellow to a garish crimson and purple cawed raucously, their late-afternoon siesta disturbed by the noise of the vehicle. Cat filled her senses with the heavy, intoxicating smell of orchids hanging in patches of brilliant color against the jade jungle.

"If I didn't know better," she confided to Slade, "I'd say this was a slice of heaven tucked away by Mother Earth."

"It is. All right, close your eyes before we go around this bend in the path. I'll tell you when to open them."

Heartbeat escalating, Cat heard a distinctly different sound ahead and to the right of them as they rounded the corner. The Jeep came to a halt and she felt Slade's arm around her shoulder, drawing her close. His voice was low and dark next to her ear.

"Now you can open them. Welcome to our heaven, Cat."

A gasp of pleasure escaped from her as she stared at a small waterfall sitting thirty feet above them. Slade had brought the Jeep to a halt at its base in a small grassy clearing, complete with brilliantly colored flowers of all varieties. A circular pool of an inviting aquamarine color held tiny white suds floating at the foot of the waterfall. Deep green moss hugged small gray boulders along the bank. At the quietest point were several pink-and-white water lilies floating like crown jewels on the surface.

"Slade...this is incredible!" Cat whispered, struck by the beauty surrounding them.

He got out, pleased. "It's all ours. And," he emphasized, helping Cat from the Jeep, "private." He halted near the lip of the bank and turned, placing his hands on her shoulders. As she lifted her chin, her emerald eyes lustrous, Slade groaned softly, capturing her. He claimed her pliant, welcoming lips beneath his, reveling in the scent of her hair and damp skin. Fire tore wildly through him as she melted willingly against him, her arms coming around his shoulders. Slade couldn't get enough of her, ever.

Tearing his mouth from her lips, he rasped, "Today… out there at the mine, Cat…"

Dizzy with the scent of his virility, Cat forced her eyes open. "Yes?" She clung to him, wanting nothing more.

Slade framed her darkly tanned face between his hands, absorbing Cat's sultry look. "I wanted to kiss you, to tell you how damned courageous you were. It's one thing to live through a cave-in. It's another to walk back inside again. You did it, and I'm so damned proud of you."

She managed a tremulous smile, sliding her fingertips across his shoulders. "Be proud of us. I was glad you were there, believe me."

"You were going in whether I was there or not. That's what counted." He leaned down, capturing her mouth again, drowning in the only taste and texture that could satisfy his yearning.

Gradually, Cat broke away, heart racing wildly, her breasts swollen and nipples taut. She wanted Slade's touch so badly, it had become a craving. Barely able to think after his exquisite assault upon her senses, Cat whispered, "I'm discovering I can't live without you, Slade."

He grinned, kissing her lashes, nose and mouth. "Nothing wrong with that, my proud beauty."

She smiled as his tongue lazily traced her lips, sweetly sipping from each corner until crazy tingling sensations shot through her, intensifying her ache for him. "I didn't realize how lonely I was until you came into my life," she admitted softly.

Raising his head, Slade melted beneath the tender flame deep within her eyes. His fingers trembled as he sifted strands of her hair through his hands. "I've been looking for you a whole lifetime, Cat. Come on, let's take a well-earned bath. I want to love you afterward…"

Everything else ceased to exist as Cat allowed Slade to unbutton and peel off her damp cotton shirt. Drowning in the love she saw in his blue gaze, she then helped Slade undress. No longer was she aware of the grit or dirt as he led her into the cool embrace of the waist-deep water. She watched as Slade took a handful of moss from the bank. It had a soft, slightly abrasive texture as he sluiced water over her shoulders and across her breasts and gently began to wash her. For the next ten minutes, he did not speak. Instead, each touch became his focus. Then Cat took the damp moss and washed him.

"I found this place a week after we came up here to the Verde the first time," Slade explained as he took the moss and allowed it to float away from them. His hands stilled on her glistening shoulders as he looked around them. "This is a place out of time, Cat. It's special. You can feel it."

Placing her palm against the matted hair on his broad chest, she murmured, "There are some places on the earth that have their own unique vibration." She leaned forward, slowly placing kiss after kiss along the hard, uncompromising line of his jaw. "Just like the vibration beneath my hand is special." She ran her tongue across his mouth, tasting the salt of his sweat and his male earthiness. "You are one of a kind, Slade," she whispered, claiming his mouth with all the fire she possessed.

A tremor shook him as her slick, warm breasts pressed against his chest. The sweet demand of her hips against his own powerful hardness sent a tumult of raw desire coursing through him. Cat was willing, pliant and so much woman that it brought tears to his eyes as he swept her against him, holding her forever. Hungrily, he claimed her mouth, lost in the primal senses that she stirred within him. As her thighs joined his beneath the water, his control was shattered.

Cat swam in the molten heat of their desire, barely aware that Slade had slipped his arm beneath her. Then he lifted her, carrying her from the pool to a carpet of grass. Cat relaxed into the verdant expanse and welcomed him back into her arms. Never had she wanted a man more. Never had Cat wanted to share the unleashed love that throbbed through her. She felt Slade's hand slide across her hip, gently parting her thighs. The mere touch of him against her damp, waiting core brought a gasp from her. Arching, she pulled Slade down upon her, welcoming him.

Patches of sunlight laced and danced through the heavy jungle canopy overhead. The ripeness of the grass aroused her, as did Slade's masculine scent. Nostrils flared, she met each of his powerful thrusts, responding wildly to his primal demands. Sunlight and darkness, day and night, loneliness and love. All those feelings, words and sensations spun through the hallways of Cat's emotions as Slade carried her beyond any pleasure she had ever experienced. White-hot fusion exploded violently within her and she cried out, sinking her fingers deeply into his taut shoulder muscles.

"Yes…" Slade cried hoarsely, gripping her tightly, twisting his hips to give her every bit of pleasure. "Feel me, Cat. Feel how much you mean to me..." Unable to stop his own need to claim her, he gripped her hard and buried his head next to hers. Explosion after explosion tore through him, ripping him apart and putting him back together again. The French called it *la petite mort*, "the little death." He called it love. With Cat, the meeting of their bodies was an overwhelming symbol of the love he felt for her. He didn't die that small death the French referred to. No, he never felt more alive, more joyous or more sure of his destiny as when he was buried within the yielding core of Cat's body.

With a sigh, Cat sank back into Slade's embrace, floating on a wave of sensations within her. A slight, tremulous smile pulled at her well-kissed lips. She ran her fingers through his dark hair, reveling in the cobalt fire banked in his eyes.

"You take my breath away..." she murmured.

Slade laid his head on her breast, holding her, listening to the ragged pound of her loving heart. "You make me feel so deeply that I can barely breathe...or think..." He laughed softly. "You make me feel whole, Cat."

She continued to smolder beneath his husky compliments, content to lie there with him forever. "I've never flown like this," she admitted, her voice throaty. "You free me, Slade. I didn't know how chained I was until you came and unlocked so many secret places within me..." Gently, Cat ran her hand across his drying flesh, reveling in both his power and his tenderness for her.

Barely opening his eyes, Slade moved his hand down her hip and across her finely curved thigh. "Love has a way of releasing the best in all of us," he murmured.

Cat turned, meeting his eyes as he raised his head to look down at her. "You've taught me so much in such a short amount of time, Slade. You made me aware of how alone I've been. You've made me hungry for you in a way I've never experienced." She cupped his sand-papery cheek. "You've got the keys to my heart. You know that, don't you?"

Gravely, he turned, kissing her palm as if she were fragile glass. "No one's more aware of that than me, sweetheart." He watched as a cloud marred the joy in her eyes. "What is it?" he coaxed. "Are you frightened?"

"Y-yes."

"Me, too. Let's be scared together, okay? Misery loves company and no one cares for you more than I do…"

With a muffled laugh, Cat embraced him. "You crazy Texan! What did I ever do before you crashed into my life?"

Matching her effusive laughter, Slade rolled over on his back, bringing Cat on top of him. She fitted against him perfectly and he absorbed the happiness that had returned to her face. God, how fiercely he loved her. *Soon,* he promised Cat silently, *you and I are going to show our hands; we're going to admit that we love one another.*

"I can say one thing," he stated out loud.

Cat leaned down, kissing the tip of his nose, euphoria making her feel giddy with joy. "What?"

"Life hasn't been dull since we met."

"That's an understatement, Slade Donovan!"

"Well," he said in a pleased tone, "when you consider we met at a cave-in, that's pretty symbolic."

She nipped playfully at the cords of his neck, inhaling his wonderful scent. "In what way?"

"I've always believed life speaks to us in symbolic terms. For instance, a bird can mean news."

"How do you interpret a cave-in?" Cat wondered, planting her hands on his chest and smiling into his warm blue eyes.

"What's a cave-in do?"

She wrinkled her nose in distaste. "Changed my life, that's for sure."

Slade grinned. "Exactly. It symbolized that each of us would have a devastating effect on each other. It was also an opportunity for a new beginning, together."

Cat grew thoughtful, then met his warming smile. "I like the way you see life, Slade. I've never thought of it in those terms, but it's provocative."

Running his hands suggestively up across her hips and back, he murmured, "And so are you."

Chapter 12

Cat walked down into the Verde mine. After three weeks of blasting and setting up posts and stulls, the tunnel now stretched almost a third of a mile into Caballo mountain. Rock bolts screwed into the limestone ceiling hung like silent baubles above her head every few feet. The chut-chut-chut of several portable generators hammered through the tunnel, providing electric light for the miners removing rubble and those shoring up the beams. The fear was still with her, but less a monster than before. The first week, Slade had miraculously appeared at her side every time she had to go in. Cat didn't know how he knew when she would go into the mine, but she was grateful for his unexplained presence.

As she walked along the adit, a coolness enveloped her. Her main concern was installing proper ventilation through the roof of the mine to the air outside. Exhaust from the generators fouled the air with colorless and odorless carbon monoxide. If it wasn't properly managed, it could eventually kill an unsuspecting miner. The footwall beneath her feet was swept free of all debris, something she had demanded. Dust in any form in a mine ate away at everyone's delicate lung tissue. At first, the workers begrudged the amount of cleanliness she wanted in the adit. Cat stood her ground with them and they finally did as they were ordered.

Gangue, or worthless material, was now being pried off the walls at the end of the tunnel. Cat had discovered a limestone vein bearing calcite yesterday and everyone's hopes had risen to almost a fever pitch. Every shift worker who entered the mine worked in silent tension as he walked the distance of the adit to where the vein was located. There was little talking as sweating men, stripped to their waists, worked. Crowbars in gloved hands, they carefully began to chip away at the vein, searching for green fire.

Cat felt excitement thrumming through the Verde as she checked the next set of posts, stulls and rock bolts. She slid her fingers across the limestone surface of the manging wall. From all appearances, as they went deeper, following the vein, the walls would strengthen, because the rock was more compact. That was good, since they needed all the help they could get from possible earth tremors.

It was nearly 1:00 a.m. when Cat left her shack and drove back down to base camp to call it a night. Everywhere she looked, the garish flood lamps lit up the blackness. Diesel-fueled generators ceaselessly supplied the necessary light so the graveyard shift could work throughout the night, hunting for emeralds in the open-pit area. Cat dropped off her two guards at their camp and swung the Jeep down the rutted road to their private camp that stood an eighth of a mile away.

Slade was standing by the fire beside Alvin while he stirred one of many kettles. He saw Cat's Jeep approaching when suddenly, out of the jungle, four shadowy shapes emerged behind the Jeep. Cold terror raced through him and he raised his hand to warn Cat. Too late! He saw the guaqueros leap into the rear of the vehicle. The first held the blade of a knife against her ribs. Slade took two steps forward, his hand moving to his pistol.

"Now," El Tigre breathed close to Cat's left ear, "you will continue toward the encampment." He took her pistol and handed it to one of his other men. With an icy smile, he pressed the point of the blade a little more firmly against her ribs. *"Comprende?"*

Cat kept her booted feet down on the brake and clutch. *"Si..."*

"Bueno. Drive slowly, now."

Cat nearly gagged on the sour smell that assailed her nostrils as El Tigre leaned over the seat, his body pressed against her back and left shoulder. Her heart pounded heavily and she wondered who he wanted. Slade? Alvin? All of them? Cat saw several guards running down toward the camp and Slade's tall figure silhouetted against the fire. As they drove within twenty feet of the camp, El Tigre hissed, "Halt!"

Slade saw the guaquero take the black-bladed knife and press it to Cat's slender throat. The vicious blade looked stark against the whiteness of her flesh. His fingers wrapped around the pistol's handle.

"Whatever you want, you can have," Slade shouted to them in Spanish, "just let her go."

"*Señor!* I am El Tigre. Your woman here has met me before. Come!"

Slade's eyes narrowed and he barely turned his head to Alvin, who was standing there scowling.

"Follow us, if you can," Slade growled over his shoulder and then walked quickly toward the Jeep. He saw Cat's eyes widen as she sat frozen in the Jeep. Anger coursed through Slade as he saw El Tigre press the blade even more against her flesh.

"Stop there, *señor*," El Tigre commanded. He grinned tightly. "You are the geologist, *si?*"

"*Si.*"

With a chuckle, El Tigre glanced down at Cat. "Your woman led us to believe you were in Texas. She is wily like a jaguar. But we wait and we watch. We see you out in the pit every day. If there is an emerald find, you are always called. Not her, not the gringo with the white hair. But you."

Slade held Cat's frightened gaze. "What do you want?" he ground out.

"Both of you. Come, sit here in the jeep." El Tigre's eyes glittered. "One wrong move and she is dead, *señor*. Watch."

Cat felt the razor-edged blade sink into her flesh. Her eyes bulged and her breath lodged in her throat as she felt the trickling warmth of blood running down her neck, soaking into her shirt. She closed her eyes, fighting off sudden faintness. Slade's savage curse startled her.

"That's enough!"

El Tigre smiled mirthlessly, easing the pressure on

the knife. "Enough for now, *señor*. This blade has killed many. It doesn't care whether it's a man or woman. Nor do I. Now, drop your holster and pistol at your feet, then join us. And warn your men that if they try to shoot at us when we leave or try to follow, your woman will breathe her last gulp of air through her windpipe."

Slade slowly unbuckled the holster, letting it drop around his feet. He turned toward Alvin, telling him of El Tigre's orders. Immediately, all the guards lowered their rifles. Slade made his way to the Jeep and halted in front of it.

"Why don't you put that blade on me instead of her?"

"I think not, *señor*. No more talk! Get in!"

The moment Slade slid into the passenger seat, one of the guaqueros came forward. He immediately bound Slade's wrists with hemp rope. Satisfied, El Tigre eased the knife from Cat's throat.

"Drive, *señorita*. Turn around and take the road leading back toward Muzo."

Cat's mind spun with options and possibilities. She jammed the Jeep into gear and they headed out of the well-lit area, swallowed up by the shadowy jungle on both sides of the narrow, bumpy road. As soon as they were out of sight of the Verde, El Tigre relaxed, laughing.

"*Aiyeee, compadres!* I told you how easy it would be to capture them."

Thomas, his second-in-command, whose weapon was trained on Slade's back, nodded, a half smile on his mouth. The other two men cheered in unison, waving their weapons above their heads.

El Tigre rubbed Cat's right shoulder in a provocative motion, his dirty fingers trailing down her arm to the elbow. Cat jerked her arm away.

"Leave me alone!"

"This one has claws," the leader crowed.

Slade turned, his eyes a deadly black color, settling on the bandit. "You lay another hand on her, and you'll answer to me."

El Tigre smiled slowly. "You'll talk to me anyway, *señor*. You will tell us where you keep all those emeralds you're finding. If they are in a safe, you will give me the combination."

"Over my dead body."

With a chuckle, El Tigre pointed to Cat. "No, *señor*, over her dead body. She is how you say it, insurance? If you do not talk, she will die an inch at time."

Cat's skin crawled over the frigid tone in El Tigre's voice. He meant business. The twin beams of light from the Jeep stabbed through the darkness. There was no moon as they drove on, mile after mile, the blackness embracing them until Cat thought she was back in a caved-in mine once again. They had to escape! If El Tigre got them to his camp, they were as good as dead. She didn't dare look at Slade or the guaqueros might suspect something. Her mind raced to remember the road back to Muzo. Right now, they were climbing steadily out of the valley. Soon, they would be following the nose line of several ridges before dropping into the Gato Valley. Slade's hands were tied in front of him. Grimly, Cat wiped the sweat stinging her eyes.

Slade braced himself as Cat pressed down the accelerator once they had bridged the hill. The road was rocky and rutted. What the hell was she doing speeding up like this at this time of night? Didn't she know there was a series of sharp S-turns up ahead? The gravelly surface of the road would make the Jeep slide if she took them too fast. Slade glanced at Cat. Her face was grim and barely outlined by the dashboard lights. Then, realizing what she was going to do, he almost smiled. In those split seconds before they raced down on the first set of curves, Slade promised himself that if they escaped this with their lives, he'd tell Cat how much he loved her.

"Slow down!" El Tigre shrieked in her ear, pounding her right shoulder sharply with his fist.

Cat winced as his knotted fist struck her twice with hard, well-aimed blows. The lights from the vehicle outlined the first turn. She jammed her boot down on the accelerator. The Jeep lurched forward, careening toward the first curve. El Tigre cursed and was thrown backward. He fell into the two men who sat squeezed in the back, and Cat wrenched the nose of the Jeep toward the cliff. One man tumbled over the side, the gun flying out of his hand. Another fell off with a scream. For terrifying seconds, the Jeep slid sideways and then, as Cat wrenched the wheel back to the left, the heavily treaded tires screamed in protest.

"Jump, Slade!"

Everything was a blur as Slade threw himself out of the Jeep. He struck the road with his left shoulder, rolling instinctively into a ball to lessen the shocking impact. Flesh was torn from him, but he felt little pain. He heard the vehicle roar off the road, sudden silence, and then a crash as the Jeep smashed and tumbled down the steep cliff. Cat! Where was Cat?

Drunkenly, Slade got to his feet, searching the choking dust and darkness. He stumbled across unconscious guaqueros. Nearby was a rifle. He picked it up. Had everyone else gone over with the Jeep? Where was she—

"Slade!"

He jerked to the left, crouching. Cat was running toward him, her face smudged with dirt, her blouse ripped and bloodied. Both had paid dearly for landing in the gravel. Her fingers closed around his arm.

"Come on!" she gasped.

"Where are the—"

"Two went over the cliff with the Jeep," she sobbed. "Come on, we've got to get away! Give me the rifle."

There was no time to stop and untie his wrists. Slade nodded and they took off at a dead run down the road, heading back for the Verde camp they had left at least ten miles behind. Every once in a while, Cat would look back. The rifle's safety was off and she held it close, ready to fire if necessary. After running a mile they were both gasping and gulping for air. Slade angled them off the road and into the foliage of the jungle.

"Come here," he panted, holding out his hands toward her. "Get these ropes off me."

Cat came and crouched at his side. She set the rifle nearby and shakily began to untie the knots. "I—I think we're safe."

"Don't count on it," Slade said grimly, sweat streaking down his dirty, bloody face. "Those bastards have nine lives."

She grinned tightly, the adrenaline high, keeping her mind sharp as a steel trap. "So do we. There."

Slade rubbed his raw wrists tenderly. Then he turned his attention to Cat. "How are you?"

"Cuts, bruises...nothing that won't heal. I'm just scared spitless."

His grin was wobbly. "Makes two of us. All right, come on. Those four guaqueros, or whoever is left, won't let us go easily. We've got to make it back to camp or—"

Cat stood, nervously watching the dark road, expecting to see shadowy shapes emerge from it at any moment. "I know. Here, you take the rifle. I'm not sure I could shoot straight if I had to. My hands are shaking like leaves."

With a nod, Slade guided her over the bank of the road. "You run in front of me. Keep your eyes peeled and ears open. If you hear anything, signal me. Don't talk. We can't afford to make any more noise than necessary."

The construction boots felt like lead on Cat's feet. She wasn't in the world's greatest shape, but not the worst, either. After jogging another two miles, she had to ask Slade to halt. Her throat was burning and her lungs felt ready to burst. They found sanctuary in a banana-tree grove, the huge, long fronds covering them so they couldn't be seen from the road. Slade knelt near her, his concentration aimed behind them. Cat felt safe, falling back against the trunk of a tree, taking huge gulps of air.

"You—never told me about this, Donovan."

Slade wiped his face, glancing over at Cat. "I told you it would be rough. This is the Dodge City of the eighties. It's wide open, and the only law is the gun you carry. You let it do the talking for you."

"I'm demanding hazardous-duty pay," she whispered, finally sitting up.

Slade reached out and gripped her hand, squeezing it gently. "If you've accidentally killed El Tigre, you've got a hundred-thousand-peso reward coming from the Muzo mine. Is that enough?"

Cat shivered, suddenly cold. The adrenaline that had given her the courage to deliberately wreck the Jeep and leap from it deserted her. Miserably, she shook her head. "I hope I didn't kill him..."

A flat snort came from Slade. "I do. That bastard was going to kill us."

She believed him, but it still didn't make her feel any better that she had possibly killed one or more men. Slade got up, bringing her to her feet. Cat felt dizzy and leaned against him.

"All right?" Slade asked huskily, pressing a kiss to her dusty hair.

"Yes... I'm whipped."

"Adrenaline letdown. We'll jog, walk, jog. We can't afford to dally."

The fifteen-minute rest hadn't been a good idea after all, Cat discovered. Every bone and socket in her body was beginning to ache in earnest. The scrapes on her arms and shoulder smarted. The boots she wore felt like twenty-pound weights on each foot. Lift them up, put them down, she instructed herself.

Five miles had fallen away under their jog-and-walk routine. Slade kept looking back, never dropping his guard. Cat kept angling toward the center of the road, where it was less rutted. He kept pulling her back, forcing her to walk on the side where it was hard to maintain a balance. If they had to dive for cover, Slade wanted to get into the jungle with one leap. He didn't try to explain to her, realizing Cat was close to exhaustion.

The bark of a rifle silenced the jungle sounds around them. Slade cursed, throwing his full weight forward, landing on top of Cat. They hit the ground hard and he rolled them into the foliage. More bullets spit up geysers where they had stood seconds before. Slade threw Cat off him, scrambled to his knees and hid behind a trumpet tree, both hands on the rifle. There! He saw the figures of two men weaving steadily toward them.

"Son of a bitch," he muttered. He jerked around to look at Cat. She was lying nearby, the breath knocked out of her. "Cat!" he hissed between clenched teeth. "Get up! Hurry!"

With a groan, Cat blindly scrambled to her knees and dove into the brush.

Slade aimed, drew a bead on the lead guaquero and fired twice. The second shot felled one bandit. Then, he had to duck as a spate of savage automatic-rifle fire spewed into his position. Bark exploded and splintered in all directions. Slade lunged for the earth, crawling away from the tree. He got to his knees, scuttling forward in the same direction Cat had gone.

The damp humid jungle floor smelled like so much rotted flesh to Cat. She fell and tripped numerous times over unseen tree roots or vines that snaked across her path. She had heard the gunfire, and adrenaline shot through her, giving her the second wind she needed to escape. Slade! Where was Slade? Had he been wounded? Cat turned, almost running into him. Slade gripped her tightly, his breath hot against her face.

"I got one of them. The other will trail us."

With a groan, Cat clung momentarily to him. "Wh-what can we do?"

He gripped Cat's shoulder firmly. "Listen to me, Cat. Aim yourself east, toward the camp."

She looked up at him, her face blank. "What about you?"

"I'm going to lie here in wait for him. That's the only way we're going to get out of this alive."

"But—"

"Go on and don't argue."

"No, damn it! I'm staying. I can't go into the jungle at night, Slade. I'll get lost!"

His face was glistening with sweat, eyes narrowed dangerously in the direction from which the guaquero would be sure to come. "At least you'll be alive in case that bastard gets me first. Now, go on. And stop arguing with me."

Cat stood her ground, her jaw set. "I'm staying, Slade."

With a curse, he jerked her to a trumpet tree, forcing her to sit down behind it. "You stay here and don't breathe. You understand me?"

She nodded, her eyes growing large. He started to turn away and she gripped his hand. "Slade?"

Impatiently, he twisted his head in her direction. "What?"

"I love you—"

The harshness on his face melted for a split second. "I know you do. Now just lie low and stay still."

Cat nodded and scrunched herself behind the girth of the tree. How long she sat there, frozen like a fawn while a predator stalked nearby, Cat did not know. She muffled her breathing, hand over her mouth, eyes and ears focused on the path they had made coming into the jungle. Cat quickly lost sight of Slade, who had moved out into the darkness. Time drew to an excruciating halt as the noises of insects covered all other sounds. Who

was left? El Tigre? Thomas? Cat shivered. The guaqueros would be excellent trackers and hunters, having
been raised in these jungles.

And then Cat's hunting instincts came back to her.
She remembered her father teaching her and Rafe how
to hunt and stalk food. Cat grew very still, breathed
shallowly and listened carefully. There! She detected a
faint, perceptible change in the number of insects singing. Cat gripped the tree trunk. Was it because Slade
was still moving around, or was it a guaquero? In the
minutes that followed, Cat had no doubt someone was
coming in her direction.

Her heart beginning to pound in dread, Cat pressed
one hand against her breast, wondering if everyone else
could hear it pumping as loudly as she could. Could a
heartbeat give her away? A soft crunching sound to her
right made her jump. She froze, her nostrils flaring. A
sour smell reached her. El Tigre! She'd recognize the
odor anywhere. Oh, no! His shape melted out of the surrounding foliage, no more than ten feet from where she
crouched. Where was Slade? Was he even aware of El
Tigre's presence? The guaquero turned, the automatic
weapon ready to fire in his hands, walking toward Cat.

A scream welled up from deep within her. Cat felt a
trickle of sweat run down her temples. Her fingers dug
convulsively into the tree trunk and she leaned down,
face and body pressed against the rough bark, willing
herself to become part of the tree. He was only five feet
away. Did he see her? If he caught her, he would show
no mercy. Cat's eyes grew huge as he took another careful step in her direction, the ugly muzzle of his military
weapon pointed right at her.

Suddenly, the night exploded around her as Slade's

dark shape lunged from the left. Both men fell heavily, grunting and groaning. Cat leaped to her feet the instant El Tigre's weapon flew out of his hands, and she scrambled for the weapon as the men wrestled on the jungle floor. The sickening sound of bone breaking beneath the power of a fist tore into her shock. Cat lurched to her feet, screaming at them. She shoved the muzzle of the gun down into El Tigre's heaving chest and Slade got off him.

"Don't move," she warned the guaquero harshly. "Slade?"

"I'm all right," he rasped, coming to her side. "Get up!" he ordered El Tigre.

The man glared at Cat, his eyes feral with hatred as he held his injured jaw. Cat slowly removed the muzzle from his chest and handed the gun to Slade. The roar of vehicles shattered the jungle. Cat looked toward the road.

"Alvin?" she asked.

"Yeah. Get up there and flag them down. I'll bring our friend here in tow."

Cat crashed through the thick barrier of leaves, vines and roots. She finally made it to the road as the first Jeep passed by her. Waving her arms, she managed to flag down the second one. It was loaded with armed guards from the Verde mine. Tony Alvarez was driving.

"Man, you're a sight for sore eyes!" he said, getting out. "Where's Slade?"

Cat gave him a weary smile. "Coming with El Tigre."

"You two gave that snake a run for his money, eh?"

"I guess we did. There's Slade."

The next hour became a blur for Cat. The guards were enthusiastic that El Tigre had been captured alive. Slade sat behind her on the way back to their camp, his hand resting protectively on her shoulder. Alvin was like a mother hen, insisting on scrubbing their cuts and bruises with soap and water plus a healthy dose of iodine. Tears had watered in Cat's eyes when he had plastered her injuries with the yellow tincture, and she wasn't sure if the tears came because of the pain or the fear of what might have happened if El Tigre had made good his escape with them.

Slade watched Cat out of the corner of his eye as she slowly began to undress in their tent. She sat wearily on her cot, her fingers trembling as she tried to unlace her boots.

"Here," he said, crouching down in front of her and removing her hands, "let me do that."

Cat straightened up. Her shirt was unbuttoned, revealing the lace and silk of her lingerie. "Thanks. I think I'm falling apart now that it's over."

"I know you are. Just sit and relax, the worst is over."

"Why aren't your hands shaking? Aren't you feeling torn up inside?"

Slade grimaced, gently removing the first boot and tackling the second. "This isn't the first time something like this has happened to me, Cat. Maybe I'm more used to violence than you are. It comes with the territory when you get into gem mining."

"I've never seen it this bad, Slade." Cat swallowed a lump in her throat. "You can taste the violence in the air." She shivered as he pulled the second boot off.

Slade slid his hands up her curved thighs and looked at her in the flickering light shed by the lantern. Her left cheek had a cut on it and was slightly puffy. He knew she had landed on her left side, and luckily her shoulder, upper arm and elbow had received the brunt of the punishment.

He tenderly framed her face and said, "The next few days are going to be hectic. I'm going to take El Tigre over to Muzo. From there, I'm sure the Colombian police will be more than happy to take him into custody."

A tremulous sigh broke from her lips. "But that doesn't promise an end to the violence, does it?"

Slade sadly shook his head. "No. As long as there's green fire, you've got men who will do anything to get it, legally or otherwise." He brushed away the first tear that rolled down her cheek. Cat was having a natural letdown after their narrow escape, and he leaned forward, molding his mouth lightly against her lips. He felt her tremble, her arms moving around his shoulders to draw him nearer.

"God," he groaned against her soft, yielding mouth, "you taste so good..."

"Hold me, Slade. Just hold me, please..."

In one motion, he got to his feet and joined her on the cot. Cat blindly found his arms as the first sob wrenched from her. Slade murmured her name brokenly, burying his head beside hers as she cried. He rocked her gently, whispering words of comfort.

"We're good for each other, sweetheart," he told her comfortingly. "Sometimes I'm weak and you're strong. Sometimes I'm strong and you're weak. Like tonight; you took one hell of a risk on that curve. You could have turned the wheels too sharply and that Jeep would have rolled over instead of sliding off the cliff. You knew what you were doing."

Cat sniffed, trying to wipe her nose. "It was pure luck, Slade," she said, hiccuping through her tears. "I'm not a racing-car driver." She looked up at him, taking the clean handkerchief he tucked into her hands. "I never even thought about the Jeep flipping over."

He grinned, running his fingers through her freshly washed hair. "What matters is the outcome, Cat. You made a perfect skid, giving both of us the time we needed to jump clear. In my eyes, you're the female equivalent of Parnelli Jones."

Cat laughed, but it came out as a hiccup instead. "I was scared to death, Slade. I-I didn't know if you'd caught on to what I was going to do. I didn't dare look at you…"

He held her lightly against him, allowing Cat to bury her head beneath his chin. "Must have been mental telepathy. One look at the set of your jaw and I knew you weren't going to go down without a fight." Slade pressed a kiss to her clean-smelling hair. "More important, this has taught me a lesson, Cat."

She closed her eyes, reveling in Slade's protective arms around her. Now she felt secure and safe. "What?" His heartbeat was slow and strong beneath her ear, soothing away the remnants of her emotional storm.

"You remember out in the jungle, when you told me you loved me?"

Cat was afraid to nod her head, but she did. Automatically she rested her hand against Slade's chest, as if to steel herself against what he might say. "I didn't know if we'd live or die, Slade," she began in a hoarse tone. "I know you may not feel the same, but that doesn't matter to me anymore."

"How long have you loved me?"

Cat closed her eyes. "I don't know. You just kind of grow on a person, Slade."

"Like mold?"

She laughed, her hand slowly unclenching. "You make loving another person sound like a virus."

"Isn't it?" And then he chuckled, pressing a kiss to her hair.

"No."

Slade closed his eyes, relief washing through him. "What I feel for you, Cat, I've never felt with another woman."

She pulled away from him and sat up, looking deep into his eyes. "Think we've got the same virus?"

A grin tugged at his mouth. "I don't know. Maybe we ought to compare symptoms. What do you think?"

Cat couldn't help but match his widening smile. The warmth and tenderness in Slade's eyes made her feel cherished. "This is a hell of a way to find out we love one another."

With a shrug, Slade picked up her bruised right hand, cradling it in his own. "People like us have to be hit over the head with a sixteen-pound sledgehammer, sweetheart."

"You made me aware of how lonely I'd been, Slade. And despite our shaky beginning, I really enjoyed your company those two months I spent at your ranch. I liked talking to you."

"And I liked just looking at you." Slade grazed her cheek with his. "Do you realize how beautiful you are to me? Every day, I'd count the hours between breakfast and lunch until I could see you again. And then I'd count them between lunch and dinner."

"You didn't have to hole up in that office of yours, Slade."

"At the time, Alvin and I were coordinating all

equipment details being moved from the U.S. to Colombia. I was getting men from his ranch and working with the State Department on visas and passports. It was a couple of busy months for me."

She gave him an accusing look. "If you weren't in your office, then you were in your hobby shop grinding those gems."

He held up both hands, laughing. "Guilty as charged. I wanted to spend more time with you, but I felt if I did, you'd interpret it as me wanting something from you. Your health came first, not the project I had wanted to discuss with you."

"Touché," Cat murmured, realizing Slade was right.

"Still," Slade murmured, cupping her chin to make her look up at him, "I fell in love with you anyway."

"Because of my looks?"

"Other things, too," he said patiently. "I like the way your mind works. I was as starved as you were for those times when we could sit and simply share time and space with one another, Cat." Slade leaned over, his mouth caressing her parted lips. "And more than anything, I like you, Cat Kincaid. You make no apology for being yourself."

Cat quivered. "A lot of men are threatened by me."

"That's their problem, sweetheart. If they can't deal with an intelligent woman, let them turn and tuck their tails between their legs and run."

Laughter bubbled up in her throat and Cat rested her head tiredly on his broad shoulder. "I love you, Slade Donovan. For better or worse."

"It's gotten worse lately, hasn't it?"

She nodded, exhaustion flooding her as Slade held

her. "I thought my fear of the mine was my worst enemy. Now I know there's something worse—guaqueros."

"Things will settle down now, Cat," he promised her. Slade gently positioned her on the cot and he lay down beside her. Pulling the protective mosquito netting over them, he murmured, "Just keep Bogotá in mind. If we're lucky, we'll get there in less than a week."

"What's in Bogotá?" Cat asked, her voice slurred with exhaustion.

"A surprise for you. It's something I've been planning all along..."

Chapter 13

Cat stood out in the burning sun. It melted the knot of fear that insisted on staying inside her every time she had to step into the Verde. In her hand was the torque meter, ready to test rock bolts recently secured in the newest section of the mine. It was a crosscut sheering off to the left that would follow the vein. Yet something was nagging Cat and she tried to pinpoint the unsettling feeling. The sky was an unusual pale yellow, something she'd not seen before over the Colombian jungle. Then she smiled to herself: Colombia had taught her a lot of new things.

As she walked into the shadow of the busy mine, Cat centered on its positives. Slade had promised her a weekend in Bogotá more than a month ago. That hadn't materialized because he'd ended up having to take El Tigre to the capital and file charges against him. Slade had returned a week later, after they had finished dynamiting into the crosscut to follow the abrupt turn of the vein. They had dug almost three-quarters of a mile into Caballo when the vein suddenly plunged down and to the left. Up to that point, very little emerald-bearing calcite had been found. Verde was looking like a lost cause. The open pit, on the other hand, was rich with emeralds. The mine was not.

Cat nodded to a group of sweaty, dirty miners as they trudged out toward the entrance. It was noon, and time to eat. Her stomach growled, but she ignored the signal. Testing the rock-bolt tension was more important, and with the miners out of the way, she could do it more quickly. The darkness between the electric lights strung on each side of the adit always reminded her of the fear. At times claustrophobia nearly overwhelmed her, but she fought it. Her fingers tightened around the torque meter, and Cat moved her gaze up and down, automatically checking posts and stulls.

The crosscut came into view and she slowed. Standing at the Y, she was reminded of the mine in Maine that had nearly claimed her life. Lips compressed, she began to check each one of the newly placed rock bolts on the manging wall, concentrating on her job with one part of her mind, and thinking of Slade with another. He would be back today! He had been gone for three days, testifying once again in El Tigre's case in Bogotá. Cat smiled, remembering Slade's disgruntled comments that if he'd known about all the governmental red tape awaiting him, he'd have let the guaquero go. *Soon,* Cat promised herself, stretching up to place the torque meter on the next bolt, *soon we'll have that weekend together.*

Their relationship had subtly changed since the night they had admitted their love for one another, Cat thought. They had grown closer, establishing a friendship so powerful that she was sometimes awed by what they had created. It was a good feeling, Cat admitted, hearing the telling click, and checking the meter to read it. Making a note on the pad she always carried with her, she moved on to the next bolt. How she ached with love for Slade. Stolen kisses and passion shared late at night, bone-weary with exhaustion, was their only consolation. Soon…

"Cat?" Slade's voice echoed off the light green walls of the shadowy Verde.

Cat gasped and spun around. He was back! Before she could leave the crosscut, she saw him appear far above her at its lip. Despite the shadows, she saw his mouth turn up in a devastating smile of welcome. Her heart wrenched powerfully in her breast and she set the torque meter down as he approached.

Taking off his hard hat, Slade lifted Cat into his arms, crushing her against him.

"Mmm, sweetheart, you not only smell good, you feel good," he growled.

Her laughter was silvery as she threw her arms around him. "Slade! You're back early."

He sought and found her ripe mouth, then allowed Cat to slide down across his body. "I missed you," he said thickly, claiming her.

Slade's breath was moist against her cheek and she returned his hunger with hers. "I need you," Cat whispered huskily, holding him tightly.

With a groan, Slade held her. "No more than I need you, my beautiful lady."

Alone in the silence of the shaft, Cat languished in his arms, smothered with his volcanic desire, wildly aware of his hardened body against her own. Just the salty taste of his skin and the odor that was uniquely his overwhelmed her senses until she was dizzy with need.

Shuddering with a primal urge, Slade gently eased Cat from him. His eyes were burning with undisguised hunger as he stared down at her. "We're going to take off for Bogotá tomorrow morning. How does that sound?"

With a cry of elation, Cat hugged him. "Wonderful! Then this court business with El Tigre is wrapped up?"

Slade grinned. "Finally. He's getting twenty-five years at hard labor."

"Good."

"How's the crosscut looking?" Slade wanted to know, reluctantly releasing her.

"No better than the rest of the vein, so far," Cat admitted, motioning him to follow her to its end.

Slade scratched his head, then settled the white hard hat back on as he listened to her explanation of the recent dynamiting. The Verde itself was a major disappointment. Millions of dollars had already been sunk into securing the mine. He watched as Cat ran her fingers over the vein, which disappeared into the seven-foot-wide limestone wall that signaled an end to the crosscut until they could do more blasting.

"I'm having the miners on the second shift come down here with picks and crowbars to try and find some calcite." She motioned to the pile of tools and the five safety lamps placed there earlier that day.

Slade ran his hand over the vein, shaking his head. "I just don't understand this, Cat. I did extra channel sampling over this area to determine its feasibility." He glanced at her, his brows knitted. "Those small emeralds I showed you from the pouch were from this vein.

It doesn't make sense that we haven't run into the calcite again."

"Listen," Cat explained reasonably, "you know gem mining isn't a very safe bet. Maybe your Texas luck held and you tapped into the only nest of calcite and emerald the vein carried when you made your channel sample. That's happened before."

He grimaced, his face glistening with sweat. "Ouch. Don't even say it."

"Well, if this crosscut doesn't yield something soon, I'm going to recommend shutting this portion of the mine down, Slade. You can't keep funneling money into a worthless operation. We both know that."

Slade stared at the limestone wall in front of them, his mouth twisted. "Yeah, I know it. Damn! I've just got a sixth sense about this vein. I know there's emeralds somewhere in this thing. I can almost taste it."

With a gentle smile, Cat reached over and touched his sun-darkened arm. "You've got green-fire fever, Slade. That's all."

"We're doing so well out in the pit. Matter of fact, what we're finding out there is keeping us from going into the red with the mine."

Cat gave him a sympathetic smile. "Count your blessings, Slade. At least the pit is yielding. One out of two isn't bad. You could have gone bust on both, you know."

He smiled and took Cat into his arms, kissing her long and tenderly. "You're my blessing, sweetheart," he told her thickly. "Green fire is one thing, but you're far more important to me—"

Slade's head snapped up, his arms tightening protectively around her. Cat felt the earth quiver once. A sound like a freight train started deep in the bowels of the earth, rolling toward them with frightening speed. Cat's eyes widened.

"Slade—"

"Son of a bitch!"

The earthquake struck with lightning fury. In seconds they were both knocked off their feet as the earth buckled and groaned. Cat struck her head on the footwall and was knocked semiconscious. Slade was hurled over her as the second wave of the quake shuddered through the mine. Rock began to fall from the manging wall as rock bolts snapped in half like guns being fired at close range. Dust spewed through the crosscut behind the avalanche of rock that fell to the footwall.

After the last of the tremors, Slade got to his knees, cursing and coughing violently. He reached out to find Cat, panic eating at him.

"Cat?"

"I-I'm okay," she said, and she struggled to her knees, wiping blood from her mouth. The dust was suffocating and Slade fumbled with the handkerchief she had around her neck.

"Lie down," he gasped.

Cat lay on the pebbled hardness of the footwall, the cotton handkerchief folded across her nostrils and mouth to act as a filter against the deadly dust. Slade joined her, his body against hers, to protect her from further injury. She hugged the wall, trying to stop hyperventilating. Trapped! They had been trapped by an unexpected earthquake! The grayish light on her hard hat was the only source of illumination in the chamber.

"I wonder how much rock fell?" Slade muttered, all

the while listening for other sounds. It had been a sharp quake, and there were bound to be aftershocks.

"Not much, I hope. Are you okay?"

He heard the terror in Cat's voice, and kept his arm wrapped tightly around her. "Yeah. Hurt feelings more than anything else. You?"

"Bump on the head, nothing more."

"You've got a hard head."

"Yeah." She snorted. "Slade?"

"What?"

"How much rock do you think fell behind us?"

He tried to keep his voice cool and free of his own fear. "Probably not much. If we're lucky, most of those rock bolts held. Don't worry, Alvin will have us out of here pronto." He forced a laugh for her benefit. "He doesn't want to lose his chief geologist and the best mining engineer in the world."

"No, he'll come and dig us out because we appreciate his cowboy cooking so much," Cat rallied.

Slade chuckled. "Lady, I love the hell out of you."

Tears tracked through the dust on her face, but Cat didn't want Slade to know she was crying. When she spoke, the words came out staccato. "I love you too."

"We'll get out of this, Cat, I promise you." Slade slowly got into a kneeling position, keeping a hand on her shoulder. He located his hard hat, plugged the jack into the battery pack he carried around his waist and turned on the light. "Stay here by this post. We're bound to get aftershocks. I want to see just how far up the crosscut that cave-in occurred. Do you have a portable radio with you?"

Cat automatically patted her side. "Yes. I'll try and contact Alvin while you check out the wall." The gloomy darkness swallowed up Slade's tall figure. Cat licked her lips, realizing that this time there was no water to slake her thirst. She pulled the dusty radio out of its protective leather case at her side. Her heart sank as she switched it to the On position. The red light did not blink to indicate it was working properly. Then she remembered hitting the footwall first with her hip and then her head. The radio, when she held it directly up into the light from her hard hat, had a large crack running vertically through the tough plastic casing. Alvin wouldn't know if they were alive or dead...

She pushed trembling fingers through her dust-laden hair and returned the useless radio to its case. Cat rose to her feet. Oddly, she was calmer than she would have thought. As she turned to examine the damage to the end of the crosscut, a gasp tore from her.

"Slade! Slade, come here! Quick!"

He came on the run. "What?"

Cat grabbed him by the arm and dragged him over to the wall. "Look. My God, look at this, Slade." She pointed toward the vein.

Slade's breath jammed in his throat as he lifted his head and settled the light on the area she was pointing out. The quake had opened up the vein, exposing what appeared to be an endless green crystalline structure more than two feet long, which disappeared into the wall where blasting hadn't yet taken place.

"Green fire," he whispered hoarsely, reaching out and tentatively touching the nearest emerald crystals.

Cat's laugh echoed in the chamber. "There must be millions of dollars' worth in this one vein alone."

"Look at their color," Slade breathed. "Dark green and clear. Look at this!" He took off his helmet, casting the light directly on the emeralds that glittered fiercely back at them. "They're so clear, Cat. I've never seen anything like this…"

She shook her head in disbelief. It was as if the earth had opened up her most precious treasure chest and allowed them to see her finest gems. Reverently, Cat touched one of the crystals. "They're magnificent."

"You're right, they'll be worth millions," Slade confirmed, his voice hushed. "And I'll stake my life on the fact that the emeralds here are of better quality than those of any other mine in the world. I don't believe it… This is a miracle, a miracle…"

Nodding mutely, Cat agreed. Oh, she'd seen gems in calcite matrix before, but they'd been in single nests once every hundreds of thousands of tons of earth. She'd never seen a long, continuous vein like this. No, this was one of a kind, just like Slade, and his belief that something special—green fire—lived here in the earth.

As if shaking his head from a dream, Slade turned to her. "They're the color of your eyes," he said huskily. "Clear and beautiful and exotic."

Cat walked over and threw her arms around him. Words were useless compared to what she was feeling for Slade. "I'm happy for you, Slade. Your dream has come true. It's paid off."

He managed a soft laugh as he slowly released her. "Sweetheart, when I met you, my most important dream came true." He looked at the emerald vein. "I have you, and we have a mine that's going to yield the world's highest-quality emeralds ever seen by man."

Cat smiled grimly, looking toward the dust-laden crosscut. "Only if we get out of here, Slade. I don't want to be a wet blanket, but—"

"I know. Come on, pick up a crowbar. I'm getting a pickax."

She followed Slade to where the manging wall had fallen. The snapped rock bolts were scattered around like so many toothpicks, shattered by the force of the quake. Slade pointed up at the manging wall and shrugged out of his shirt.

"If you hadn't spaced those rock bolts so closely together, even more would have come down, burying us."

Cat shuddered. "We're not out of this yet, Slade."

"Wet blanket," he teased, handing her his shirt and hard hat. In the semigloom his massive chest and shoulders gleamed with sweat as he hefted the ax in his large hands. "What I want you to do is focus both hard-hat lights here. I'm going to start digging. We can't wait for Alvin to start because we've only got so much oxygen left."

Cat nodded, standing out of the way. "Slade, I can take a crowbar and—"

"Not yet. Let me work at this wall, then I'll let you clear away the gangue and I'll go back to work."

Biting her lower lip, Cat nodded. No holes were visible through the rubble blocking their escape and Cat didn't know how thick the wall was. If too much had fallen down, they could suffocate before getting rescued. As Slade began to swing the head of the pickax into the limestone, she prayed that the rock bolts had prevented a massive cave-in. Each rhythmic swing of the ax echoed throughout the chamber. The limestone crushed easily, powdering beneath Slade's swings. His body looked like burnished metal beneath the light. Sweat ran off the bunched muscles of his back and shoulders, and his dark hair clung to his head as he heaved the pick savagely into the wall over and over again.

How long Slade worked, Cat did not know. Minutes grew into hours, and his facial expression never altered. His jaw was set, lips pulled away from his clenched teeth, eyes narrowed as he glared at the wall that prevented their escape. Cat saw his rugged jeans darken with sweat and cling to his long, firm thighs as he began to make progress into the wall. The limestone was no match for steel and brawn. Each precise swing exploded into the wall, loosening a little more debris, moving them inches closer to freedom. Finally, Slade stopped. He wiped his wet brow with the back of his arm. Dust caked his massive chest, his hair and face.

Cat gave him the shirt so he could wipe his face. She set the lights down, and went to work with the crowbar to clear the gangue out of the way. Slade's incredible strength gave her strength. She knew she could not match his physical power, but she doggedly labored at clearing a space for him to work in. Her shirt clung damply to her body as she lifted some of the larger rocks, throwing them behind her. Sweat stung her eyes and she shook her head to clear them. After half an hour, most of the debris had been moved aside so that Slade could take over.

"You did a good job," he told her, coming up and sliding his arm around her shoulders.

Cat leaned against him and slid her hand across his chest, feeling the mat of wiry hair beneath her fingertips. "Aren't you tired?"

"Not when I consider the alternative," he told her, wrapping his long, callused fingers around the wooden handle of the pick. Leaning over, Slade kissed her cheek, then sought her lips. A satisfied growl rumbled from him as he kissed her quickly and hard. Reluctantly he released her and went back to work.

Glumly, Cat thought about what he'd implied: the air was growing more sparse as time went on. Each breath lessened the oxygen content. Each breath brought them closer to death's embrace. She shifted her attention back to Slade, who had resumed his rhythmic attack against the wall. If possible, he seemed to be exerting even more energy and concentrated power against their foe, death. Huge chunks of limestone flew around him, and sparks flashed as steel bit into rock. The chamber echoed with the tortured crack of rock pulverized beneath his Herculean strength. With each swing of the pick, Cat held her breath. How long could Slade sustain his backbreaking pace? His muscles bunched and released, bunched and released. Looking at his set features, Cat knew she needn't give up hope. Ever.

Five hours had passed and they sat huddled together in the pitch blackness. They had to save the battery-powered light for Slade to work by. The safety lamps required oxygen to remain lit and Slade didn't want their precious supply to be eaten up. The electrical lamps on their hard hats would have to suffice. Cat wiped Slade's shoulders and back with the wet shirt. She splayed her hands on his flesh, feeling an almost imperceptible tremor beneath her palm. He was close to exhaustion. Any other man would have quit hours before, physically unable to go on as long as he had.

"Let me massage you," she whispered, positioning herself behind him. "You're going to get cramps if I don't."

Slade nodded wearily and rested his brow on his

arms, which hugged his drawn-up knees. "Thanks," he murmured hoarsely. God, what he'd do for a glass of water right now. He said nothing, realizing Cat had to be as close to dehydration as he was. Her clothes were wet and clung to her like a second skin. He groaned as her fingers worked over his weary, protesting back muscles, helping them relax from the brutal workout he had given them. For almost fifteen minutes, Cat worked out the kinks and knots.

"Thanks, sweetheart," he muttered, patting her thigh.

Cat laid her head on his back momentarily, shutting her eyes. "I love you, Slade. You're incredible."

He snorted softly, rubbing his hand up and down the length of her thigh. "I love you, too. But incredible? Hardly."

"Your strength is unbelievable."

"It's called fear of dying. That's what keeps me going right now."

Cat wrapped her arms around him, feeling the ragged pound of his heart beneath her palms. "You must have moved a ton of gangue from that wall. That's a lot."

Slade knew what she had left unspoken: it was looking more and more as if a huge section of the manging wall had fallen. They were going to be trapped for a long time. Maybe longer than they had oxygen to last them. He wiped the accumulated sweat off his face.

"Come around here. Sit between my legs."

Cat moved carefully in the darkness. She nestled between his thighs, one arm around his waist, and her head resting against his hard, flat stomach. "At least you're with me this time," she uttered tiredly. "Sharing a mine cave-in takes away some of the fear."

Slade curved his palm against her cheek, savoring her warmth and softness. "Not as scared as before?"

"No." Cat managed a choked laugh. "Maybe I'm getting used to them, Slade. I don't feel that overwhelming fear."

He glanced around, unable to see anything. "Yeah, this is my fourth one. They get to be pretty routine after a while. Only one thing occupies your mind, and that's how much oxygen you have left."

Cat pressed a kiss to his slick flesh. "That and water. What I'd do for some water for both of us."

"I'd trade that vein of emeralds for a glass for both of us right now."

She laughed with him. "Amazing how some events in life can put everything into very sharp focus, isn't it, Slade?"

"Yes." Silence settled over them. "Cat?"

She closed her eyes, her arm tightening around his waist, hearing an unexpected tremor in his deep voice. "What is it?" Was he going to tell her that they didn't stand a chance? That most likely, they would die in here together? A fierce love for Slade welled up through Cat like a fist, taking her breath away as she prepared herself to hear those words.

"Marry me."

"What?"

"I know it's a little soon and we haven't talked about it before this, but I want you to marry me." Slade's hand came to rest on her hair. "I can't imagine life without you, lady." There was a long silence and then he felt the wetness of her tears beneath his fingertips. He leaned over, holding her tightly, anguish soaring through him. His voice cracked as he brought her up against him.

"Damn it, I know life isn't fair, but when I've finally found you, it could be too late."

Cat stubbornly shook her head, burying her face next to his and trying to stop her tears. "No, it's never too late—never!"

"I love you, Cat."

"I'll marry you, Slade..."

"You will?"

She managed a half sob and half laugh. "Of course I will!" Cat traced trembling fingers through his sweat-soaked hair, kissing his brow, eyes and finally his mouth.

Savoring her flurry of kisses, Slade held her even closer to him. "It'll be a hell of a marriage."

Cat groaned. "Tell me about it!"

"I'll have your Kincaid stubbornness to contend with."

"You're not exactly a willow in the wind, Slade Donovan," she pointed out archly.

He chuckled, the rumble moving up through his chest. "But we both have a good sense of humor. We know how to take a joke."

"Only because I'm the straight person and you're the comic of our team."

Slade nuzzled his face between her breasts, absorbing her scent. "I need you, Cat," he whispered thickly. "Now, forever. Living with you those months made me realize just how much I liked having you underfoot."

A smile touched her tear-wet lips and Cat closed her eyes, realizing the futility of their situation. "What made you suddenly ask to marry me, Slade?"

He caressed her waist, then settled his hand on her hip. "Sweetheart—" he paused and swallowed "—if I can't break through that wall, I wanted you to know just how damn much you mean to me."

How long they held one another, Cat didn't know. It no longer mattered. The chamber was stiflingly hot and stuffy; the ripe smell of their sweat assailed her nostrils along with the chalky limestone dust that still hung in the air and caked their mouths. Just as Slade took up the pickax and walked to the wall, she heard a distinct drilling noise from the other side.

"Slade!"

He turned, relief etched on his exhausted features. "I hear it…"

Cat clutched the hard hat, the light trained on the wall. "Alvin…he's coming through. That's an auger bit!"

A grin creased Slade's face as he stepped back and joined Cat against the far wall. He slid his arm around her shoulders and pulled her to him. Leaning down, he kissed her hard and long. Releasing her, he murmured, "Well, gal, it looks like you have to make good on that promise to marry me now."

She laughed, sinking against Slade, dizzy from joy that they were going to be rescued. "You mean asking me to marry you wasn't a sham, Slade Donovan? Some last-minute admission before you said hello to your maker?"

His grin widened against his stained face. "Come to Bogotá with me and find out," he challenged.

When they entered the Bogotá Hilton together, nearly every patron sitting in the lobby turned and gawked at them. Slade grinned at Cat as they came to a halt at the desk.

"I think we're a sight for sore eyes."

Cat grimaced, looking down at her disheveled appearance. "I think we're a sight, Slade." Although they'd washed and changed after they'd been rescued, they had come straight to Bogotá afterward, leaving the clean-up and newly discovered emeralds in Alvin's capable hands.

Slade's eyes sparkled as he took the registration card and signed them in. "We'll buy any clothes we need," Slade said, pulling out his wallet. He gave the clerk his credit card. Within minutes, Slade had the key to their room. "Come on, Cat. You and I are going to take a very long, hot shower. Together…"

From the balcony of their air-conditioned room, a flaming orange sunset bid them good-evening. Cat had groggily awakened from a much-needed sleep and gotten up, wrapping the thick white hotel robe around her. She looked over her shoulder; Slade was still sleeping soundly. A tender smile pulled at her lips as she sat down in the ivory satin settee facing the king-size bed where he lay.

Tucking her legs beneath her, Cat was content to simply watch Slade. She smiled softly. Once they had gotten beneath the hot, pummeling streams of water, their hunger for one another had been tempered. Pure exhaustion combined with the relaxing massage of the water had made them both too drowsy to think of anything else but sleep.

They had curled up in bed on the white cotton sheets, their bodies hot and moist against its cool, crisp texture. Nothing had ever felt so good, and Cat vaguely remembered curving into Slade's waiting arms and promptly falling asleep. Now she looked at her watch; it was almost nine o'clock. They'd slept a long time. Her stomach growled, reminding Cat that she hadn't eaten all day. Quietly, she rose and went to the phone to order dinner.

Slade awoke to the mouth-watering smell of beef-steak. He groaned and rolled onto his back, the sheet covering him from the waist down in twisted disarray.

"Slade?" Cat walked to the bed and smiled down at him, thinking how boyish he looked. She sat on the edge of the mattress, one arm across him, watching him awake. "Come on, time to rise and shine."

Groaning, Slade dragged an arm across his eyes. "What time is it?" he asked thickly.

Cat leaned down and kissed his petulant mouth. "Ten o'clock. Time to get up and eat."

Slade slid his hand up her long, robed thigh. "You have great legs. Did I ever tell you that?"

"I thought all such admissions were given in the crosscut."

A grin tugged at his mouth and Slade moved his arm and opened his eyes. Cat's hair was long, nearly touching her shoulders, and was shot through with gold from the light above. She looked like a ragamuffin in the oversize robe. "Spunky gal, aren't you?" he challenged, sitting up and leaning against the headboard. The sheet pulled away, leaving him nearly naked, but he didn't care. All of his attention was centered on Cat's shining green eyes. Her smile made him go hard and hot inside.

"You wouldn't want me any other way." Cat patted his flat, hard stomach. "Come on, I ordered us a Texas-size meal. I'm starved."

Slade glanced past her at the sumptuous meal over-flowing from the cart behind them. "What? No spotted horse thief? Where's my stewed kidneys? My johnny-cake?"

Giving him a playful pat on the hip, Cat rose, laughing. "If you're expecting Alvin's cooking, forget it." She went to the cart and drew up two chairs.

Slade got up and padded to the bathroom to retrieve his robe. He had an odd look on his face as he came back out with it. "Let's trade robes, Cat. You've got mine and I'm sure as hell not going to be able to fit into this one."

Nonplussed, her silverware poised above her thick, medium-rare steak, Cat grimaced. "Oh...sorry. I thought they were all the same size." She got up and came around the table, struggling out of the robe, revealing her nakedness.

"I lied." Slade grabbed her and carried her to the bed.

Cat laughed, throwing her arms around Slade as he settled down beside her. "You're such a joker, Slade Donovan."

Slade's smile grew wide as he leaned over and kissed her laughter-touched lips. "But you love me anyway?" he coaxed thickly, tasting her sweetness.

With a tremulous sigh, Cat slid her fingers across his shoulders. "Yes...yes, I love you anyway."

"Enough to marry me tomorrow morning?" He trailed a path of nibbling, moist kisses from her earlobe down the length of her neck, feeling her pulse flutter wildly at the base of her throat. Her fingers were wreaking havoc on him, too, as she followed the curve of his chest, brushing his nipples.

Closing her eyes, she arched against Slade as his mouth found the valley between her breasts. "Y-yes."

Slade continued his gentle assault. "God, you smell and taste good. Are you sure? You sound a little doubtful."

An exquisite ache was building in her and Cat moaned,

her mind fleeing as his knowing fingers gently parted her thighs. "Slade…." His name came out like a breathless prayer. "Love me, just love me. Now. I need you so much…"

With a smile, Slade brought a hardened nipple into his mouth and sucked gently, feeling Cat press against him.

A cry of pleasure tore from her as Slade moved one hand down across her belly, finding the rich carpet below to coax the smoldering fire to life within her. She sagged against him, jolts of such magnitude rushing through her that she was helpless in his arms. The ache intensified and Cat moved against his palm.

"Yes," Slade said in a rough whisper near her ear, "show me how much you need me. Show me, my lovely lady…"

The shattering gift of fulfillment rippled through her, and afterward, Cat lay in Slade's arms, unable to move as wave after wave of melted heat flowed through her. Her lips curved into a smile and she barely opened her eyes. The immense satisfaction on Slade's face reflected how she felt and Cat weakly lifted her arms, pulling him on top of her. "Let me give to you as much as you've given to me," she whispered huskily.

Slade's smile was pure male as he slid his hand beneath her hips and watched her eyes close as he slowly moved into the depths of her warm, rich body. His fingers froze against her hips as her fire touched him and drew him more deeply into her. His breath was torn from him, followed by a groan born deep and low in his chest. Sunlight, she was sunlight on the cool water's surface, he thought raggedly. Then reality became a blur as Slade fell beneath Cat's magical spell. Never had another woman loved him so thoroughly or with such consuming passion. Like the handfuls of warm soil he had held so often in his hand, she reminded him that she was of the earth: warm, fertile and all-encompassing. With a groan, Slade gripped her in release. Sunlight and earth once more touched as he reemerged in the magic that was Cat.

Spent, he lay against her damp breast, aware of the uneven beat of her heart. Sweat trickled down his jaw, but Slade didn't care. Gently, he ran his hand up her torso, and cupped her breast. Cat's fingers moved slowly through his hair, and he closed his eyes in contentment. Words were useless for what he felt toward Cat. Instead, he held her for a long time, caressing her and letting her know just how much he loved her.

Finally, Slade rose. On his return, Cat smiled and curled up again in his arms. He moved his fingers along the satin curve of her back.

"Every time we love, it's better," he told her.

"Every time is like the first time," Cat whispered, kissing his stubbled jaw. "You make me feel like the earth touched by rain and sunlight: a rainbow of colors and sensations."

"You're the earth, sweetheart. Giving and holding the warmth within you and giving it back when I need it."

"I never thought this kind of love or contentment was possible, darling."

"Neither did I."

Slade settled one hand behind his head and stared up at the gray ceiling. "Matt once told me he didn't believe in dreams ever coming true. Kai changed his mind, of course. But in a lot of ways, I was like him.

I never thought the woman of my dreams would ever become a reality."

"But you dreamed, Slade. And that was important."

He grinned. "But both of us doubted our dream would come true." He sat up and leaned against the headboard, bringing Cat into his arms. "And we were wrong."

"Men," Cat muttered darkly. "Can't live with 'em…"

"Now, now, be kind and patient to us Neanderthal types. We might be a bit slow, but once we're taught, we come around."

Cat sat up facing Slade. He looked so young. There was a rebellious lock of hair on his brow, as usual, and his cobalt eyes were bright and warm with amusement. "Neanderthal," she chortled. "You're hardly that. A smooth operator would be closer to the truth."

Slade raised his hand against his heart, trying his best to look wounded. "I'm Texan. That says it all."

She gave him a dirty look. "That's barely scratching the surface. Coming out of the bathroom and saying the robe was too small was a rotten trick, Slade Donovan, and you know it!"

A grin edged his mouth. "That was the easiest way I could think of to get you out of that robe and into my arms."

"Did you ever stop to think that asking might have gotten the same result?"

He quelled a smile and shrugged. "I didn't think you'd leave that steak for anything."

"Well, you were probably right. I was hungry."

Slade gave her an impish smile, obviously pleased with the success of his escapade. Cat got off the bed and pulled on a robe. As she handed him the other one, she noted the one-size-fits-all tag on the inside. With a shake of her head, she moved the table. Slade grabbed her hand and pulled her back into bed with him.

"Come here," he growled, wrestling with her until she was effectively trapped beneath him. "I'm not done with you, my proud lady."

Cat laughed, hotly aware of his naked body against her. "Now what have you got cooked up? I see that look in your eyes."

Slade rolled off her and kept a restraining hand on her while he reached in the drawer of the bed stand. "See? There you go again accusing me of being up to something."

Cat waited expectantly as he settled a folded piece of tissue paper the size of a quarter on her robed breast. "You've got that gleam in your eye again, Slade. What do you expect me to think? What's this?"

"Open it and find out. Careful…it might bite you."

Meeting Slade's smile, Cat slowly unwrapped the white tissue paper. It crinkled between her fingers. She glanced up at Slade's expectant features. "You're such a rogue, Slade Donovan."

"And you love me for it."

"Yes, I do." Cat pushed aside the outer wrapping. There was a second layer of paper. "What did you do? Spend hours wrapping this?"

"You'll see why," Slade said, his hand resting on her hip.

Cat's eyes widened as she pulled the last of the paper away. There, nestled in the center, was a thick gold ring set with a long, rectangular emerald. She gasped and struggled to sit up. Slade removed his hand so that she could.

"Slade…"

He leaned over her, resting his chin on her shoulder. "Like it?"

Cat ran her fingers lightly over the emerald. "Like it? My God, it's huge and beautiful and priceless! Look at the clarity!" She held it up for him to see.

"Of course it's clear. It's from our mine. The first Verde emerald we discovered." Slade glanced at her, tenderness in his blue gaze. "And it's priceless, like you are to me, Cat."

With a cry, Cat turned, throwing her arms around Slade. "You wonderful romantic. I love you so much!"

Slade held her tightly. "You and I, sweetheart, are going to have one hell of a happy life together. You know that, don't you?"

Cat smiled, kissed his cheek, then eased away from him. Tears made her eyes luminous as she met and held Slade's sober expression. She held the ring between them. "You and I will live life as never before," she promised. "Because now, we've added love to our existence. I'm looking forward to each new day with you, Slade."

His heart wrenched and he cradled Cat's face gently between his palms. "Green fire can't compare to how you've set my soul on fire, my love. You've captured my heart. Forever."

* * * * *

A career Air Force officer, **Merline Lovelace** served
at bases all over the world. When she hung up her
uniform for the last time, she decided to try her hand
at storytelling. Since then, more than twelve million
copies of her books have been published in over thirty
countries. Check her website at merlinelovelace.com or
friend Merline on Facebook for news and information
about her latest releases.

Books by Merline Lovelace

Harlequin Special Edition

Three Coins in the Fountain

"I Do"...Take Two!
Third Time's the Bride
Callie's Christmas Wish

Harlequin Romantic Suspense

Course of Action (with Lindsay McKenna)

Course of Action
Crossfire
The Rescue

Harlequin Desire

The Paternity Proposition
The Paternity Promise

Duchess Diaries

Her Unforgettable Royal Lover
The Texan's Royal M.D.
The Diplomat's Pregnant Bride
A Business Engagement

Visit the Author Profile page
at Harlequin.com for more titles.

TEXAS HERO

Merline Lovelace

This book is dedicated to my own handsome hero, who I first met in the shadow of the Alamo. Many thanks for all those wonderful San Antonio memories, my darling.

Prologue

"Thank God for air-conditioning!"

Swiping a forearm across his dirt-streaked forehead, the tall, flame-haired grad student followed his team leader into the welcoming coolness of San Antonio's Menger Hotel.

"If I'd had any idea how muggy it gets down here in July," he grumbled, "I wouldn't have let you talk me into assisting you on this project."

"Funny," the woman beside him responded with a smile, "I seem to recall a certain Ph.D. candidate *begging* me to let him in on the dig."

"Yeah, well, that was before I realized I'd be branded as a defiler of history and practically run out of Texas on a rail."

Elena Maria Alazar's smile faded. Frowning, she shifted the strap of her heavy field case from one aching shoulder to the other and stabbed at the elevator buttons. Eric's complaints weren't all that exaggerated. He and everyone else working the project had come under increasingly vitriolic fire in recent days.

Dammit, she shouldn't have allowed the media to poke around the archeological site, much less elicit a hypothesis as to the identity of the remains found in the creek bed. She was an expert in her field, a respected member of the American Society of Forensic Historians, for pity's sake! She headed a highly skilled team of anthropologists and archeologists. She knew better than to let her people discuss their initial findings with reporters. Particularly when those findings held such potentially explosive local significance.

She couldn't blame anyone but herself for the howls of outrage that rose when the *San Antonio Express-News* reported that Dr. Elena Alazar, niece of Mexico's President Alazar and professor of history at the University of Mexico, was rewriting Texas history. According to the story, Ellie had found proof that legendary William Barrett Travis, commander of the Texans at the Alamo, hadn't died heroically with his men as always believed. Instead, he'd run away from the battle, was hunted down by Santa Anna's troops and was shot in back like a yellow, craven coward.

Ellie and her team were a long way yet from *proving* anything, but try telling that to the media! The *Express-News* wasn't any more interested in running a disclaimer than a correction to identify her as a professor of history at the University of *New* Mexico. Never mind that Ellie had been born and raised in the States. To the reporter's mind—and to the minds of his readers—she was an outsider attempting to mess with Texas history.

Thoroughly disgruntled, she made another stab at

the brass-caged elevator. It was an antique, like every-thing else in the hundred-year-old hotel located just steps from the Alamo. Until the story broke, Ellie had thoroughly enjoyed her stay at the luxuriously appointed establishment. Now, she felt the weight of disapproval from every employee at the hotel, from desk clerks to the maid who cleaned her room.

She didn't realize just how much she'd earned the lo-cals' displeasure, however, until she unlocked the door to her suite. Startled, she stopped dead. Behind her, Eric let out a long, low whistle.

"Folks around here sure let you know when they're not happy. I haven't seen a room trashed this bad since pledge week at the frat house. Come to think of it, I've *never* seen a room trashed this bad."

The two-room suite hadn't been just trashed, Ellie soon discovered. It had been ransacked. Her laptop com-puter was gone, as was the external drive that stored the data and thousands of digital images her team had collected to date.

The loss of her equipment was bad enough, but the message scrawled across the mirror above the dresser made her skin crawl.

Mexican bitch.
I've got you in my crosshairs.

Chapter 1

Washington, D.C., steamed in the late afternoon July heat. On a quiet side street just off Massachusetts Avenue, in the heart of the embassy district, the chestnut trees drooped like tired old women and tar bubbled in the cracks of the sidewalk. The broad-shouldered man who emerged from a Yellow Cab took care not to step in the sticky blackness as he crossed the sidewalk and mounted the front steps of an elegant, Federal-style town house located midway down the block.

He paused for a moment, his gaze thoughtful as he studied the discreet bronze plaque beside the front door. The inscription on the plaque identified the three-story town house as home to the offices of the President's special envoy. Most Washingtonians considered the special envoy's position a meaningless one, created years ago for a billionaire campaign contributor with a yen for a fancy title and an office in the nation's capital. Only a handful of insiders knew the special envoy also served as the head of a covert agency whose initials comprised the last letter of the Greek alphabet, OMEGA. An agency that, as its name implied, was activated only as a last resort in instances when other, more established organizations like the CIA or the Department of Defense couldn't respond for legal or practical reasons.

This was one of those instances.

Squaring his shoulders, the visitor entered the foyer and approached the receptionist seated behind a graceful Queen Ann desk.

"I am Colonel Luis Esteban. I'm here to see the special envoy."

"Oh, my! So you are."

Elizabeth Wells might have qualified for Medicare a number of years ago, but her hormones still sat up and took notice of a handsome man. And Colonel Luis Esteban, as OMEGA agent Maggie Sinclair had reported after a mission deep in the jungles of Central America, was gorgeous—drop-your-jaw, boggle-your-eyes gorgeous.

Elizabeth managed to keep her jaw from sagging, but the colonel's dark, melting eyes, pencil-thin black mustache and old-world charm did a serious number on her heart rate.

"I believe the special envoy is expecting me."

"What? Oh! Yes, of course. Mr. Jensen's in his office. With Chameleon, as you requested."

"Ah, yes." A small, private smile played about the colonel's mouth. "Chameleon."

Elizabeth's pulse tripped again, but not with pleasure this time. Having served as personal assistant to both Maggie *and* her husband, Adam Ridgeway, during their separate tenures as director of OMEGA, Elizabeth wouldn't hesitate to empty the Sig Sauer 9 mm tucked in her desk drawer into anyone who tried to come between them. With something very close to a sniff, she lifted the phone on her desk and buzzed her boss. Her gaze had cooled several degrees when she relayed his reply.

"Go right in, Colonel."

"Thank you."

Luis walked down a short hall, opened a door shielded from attack by a lining of Kevlar, took one step inside and plunged into chaos. There was an ear-shattering woof. A flash of blue and orange. A chorus of shouts.

"Dammit, he's doing it again."

"Radizwell! No!"

"Shut the door, man!"

A hissing, bug-eyed lizard the size of a small hound darted between Luis's legs. A second later, a huge sheepdog tried to follow. Knocked sideways, Luis grabbed the door handle while the furiously barking hound raced after the iguana. Doubling back, the lizard leaped for the safety of a polished mahogany conference table. Once there, it whipped out a foot-long tongue and spit at the jumping, madly woofing hound.

"Nick!" Half-laughing and wholly exasperated, Maggie Sinclair shouted an appeal to OMEGA's current director. "Get Radizwell out of here."

The man who answered her plea sported a lean, well-muscled body under his elegantly tailored suit, but it took all his strength to drag the vociferously protesting hound out of the office. Deep, mournful howls followed

him when he returned. Closing the door to muffle the
yowls, he smoothed his blond hair with a manicured
hand and shot Luis a wry smile.

"Nick Jensen, Colonel. I'd apologize for the noisy
reception, but..." He glanced at the still hissing giant
iguana. "I understand you were the diabolical fiend who
gave Maggie her pet in the first place."

"Yes, he was." A smile lighting her eyes, Maggie
Sinclair came across the spacious office and held out
both hands. "Hello, Luis. How are you?"

Esteban's gaze took in her glowing face, dropped to
her gently rounded stomach. Regret punched through
him. He'd had his chance with this woman a number of
years ago. She slipped away from him then, as change-
able and lightning quick as her code name implied.

Luis had come to Washington on urgent business at
the request of the president of Mexico. Only he knew
that he also brought with him the half-formed idea of
reigniting the sparks that had once flared between Maggie and him. He'd heard she'd left OMEGA to finish
writing a book and raise her two small daughters. He'd
thought perhaps she might be bored and ready for a
touch of excitement. He could see at a glance that wasn't
the case, however. Maggie Sinclair wore the look of a
woman well and truly loved.

Swallowing a small sigh, he lifted her hands and
dropped a light kiss on the back of each. "I'm well,
Chameleon. And you... You are as lively and beautiful as ever."

"I don't know about the beautiful part, but my family certainly keeps things lively." Rueful laughter filled
her honey brown eyes. "I thought you might want to
see how your gift has grown over the years. Unfortu-

nately, Terence won't go anywhere these days without his buddy, the sheepdog you just met. They're best of pals until Radizwell, er, well…"

"Gets the hots for the damned thing," the third person in the room said. He strolled forward, his blue eyes keen in his aristocratic face. "Adam Ridgeway, colonel."

"Ah, yes," Luis drawled, returning both the strong grip and rapierlike scrutiny. "Maggie's husband."

"Maggie's husband," he affirmed with a smile that sent an instant and unmistakable message. "Hope you don't mind if I sit in on your meeting. I'm told it involves one of the agents I recruited for OMEGA."

Instantly all business, Luis Esteban nodded. "Yes, it does. Jack Carstairs. I understand he's on his way to San Antonio."

"He left a few hours ago," Nick Jensen replied, gesturing the other three to seats well away from the conference table occupied by the wary, unblinking iguana. "What *we* don't understand, however, is how Renegade's mission concerns you."

"Allow me to explain. When I first met Chameleon, I was chief of security for my country. I've since retired and established my own firm. I do very private, very discreet work for a number of international clients. The President of Mexico is one of them. He asked me to run a background check on Jack Carstairs."

Nick's brows lifted. "Did he?"

"Yes. You know, of course, that Carstairs once had an affair with President Alazar's niece."

"We know. Which made us wonder why he requested Carstairs for this mission in the first place."

"He didn't, actually. The request came from his niece." Flicking his shirt cuff over his gold Rolex, Luis picked his way through a potentially explosive international minefield.

"As you're aware, Elena's father—President Alazar's youngest brother—emigrated to the States as a young man. He and Ellie's mother met in Santa Fe and married after a whirlwind courtship. Unfortunately, Carlos Alazar died before his daughter was born, but his wife made sure Ellie spent summers with her father's family in Mexico. During one of those visits, Ellie met a Marine pulling guard duty at the U.S. Embassy. Their affair was brief and, I'm told, rather indiscreet."

"Indiscreet enough to get Gunnery Sergeant Carstairs sent home in disgrace and subsequently booted out of the Marines," Nick acknowledged.

"Evidently Ellie feels a lingering responsibility for ruining the man's military career. When her uncle decided she needed a bodyguard, she insisted it be Carstairs. Which is why President Alazar hired me to check him out."

"How did you get past Renegade's cover and make the link to OMEGA?" Nick asked, not liking the idea that one of his agents had been compromised.

Luis merely smiled. "I think Chameleon will attest that I, too, possess certain skills. Suffice to say I uncovered his connection to OMEGA and advised President Alazar, who subsequently made the call to your President, requesting Carstairs's services."

"And now President Alazar's having second thoughts about the request?"

"Let's just say he's worried that Carstairs's past involvement with his niece might get in the way of his ability to maintain the detachment required for this job."

Nick Jensen, code name Lightning, didn't for a second doubt Jack Carstairs's ability to do his job. During Nick's days as an operative, he'd gone into the field with Renegade more than once and had gained a profound respect for his skills. Nick also, however, possessed a Gallic understanding of the power of passion.

Once a skinny, perpetually hungry pickpocket who called the back streets of Cannes home, Henri Nicolas Everard had been adopted by Paige and Doc Jensen, moved to the States and had grown to manhood in a house filled with love. He'd parlayed the near starvation of his childhood into a string of high-priced restaurants scattered around the globe.

Nick was now a millionaire many times over. His cover as a jet-setter gave him access to the world of movie princes and oil sheikhs. It had also led to a number of discreet affairs with some of the world's most beautiful women. A true connoisseur, he could understand why Jack Carstairs had sacrificed his military career for a fling with Elena Maria Alazar. The background dossier compiled by OMEGA's chief of communications had painted a portrait of an astonishingly vibrant, incredibly intelligent woman.

Not unlike OMEGA's chief of communications herself, Nick thought. A mental image of Mackenzie Blair replaced that of Ellie Alazar and produced a sudden tightening just below his Italian leather belt. Both amused and perturbed by the sensation, Nick offered his assurances to Colonel Esteban.

"OMEGA wouldn't have sent Renegade into the field if we weren't absolutely confident in his ability to protect Dr. Alazar. If it will ease President Alazar's mind, however, I'll pass on his concerns."

"Perhaps you might also keep me apprised of the situation in San Antonio," Esteban suggested politely.

Everyone in the room recognized that they were treading tricky diplomatic ground here. Relations between the United States and Mexico had reached new, if somewhat shaky, levels with the recent North American Free Trade Association Treaty. The last thing either president wanted right now was an ugly international incident souring an economic agreement that had taken decades to hammer out.

"Not a problem," Nick said smoothly. "Once we ascertain that's what President Alazar wishes, of course."

"Of course." Rising, the colonel dug into his suit pocket and produced a business card. "You can contact me day or night at this number."

His gaze drifted to Maggie, who rose and gave him a warm smile.

"Don't worry, Luis. Renegade's one of the best field operatives in the business. He wouldn't be working for OMEGA otherwise."

With that blithe assurance, she strolled across the office and clipped a leash on the unblinking iguana. Identical expressions of repulsion crossed the faces of Nick and the colonel as the creature's long tongue flicked her cheek in a quick, adoring kiss. Adam merely looked resigned.

"We'll walk you out," he said to Esteban. "Lightning has some calls to make."

OMEGA's acting director made the calls from the control center located on the third floor.

Mackenzie Blair ruled OMEGA's CC, just as she used to rule the command, control and communication centers aboard the Navy ships she'd served on. She loved this world of high-tech electronics, felt right at home in the soft green glow from the wall-size computer screens—far more at home than she'd ever felt in the two-bedroom condo she and her ex had once shared.

One of the problems was that she and David had never stayed in port together long enough to establish joint residency. He'd adjusted to the separations better than Mackenzie had, though. She discovered that when she returned two days early from a Caribbean cruise and found the jerk in bed with a neighbor's wife.

She'd sworn off men on the spot. Correction, she'd planted a very hard, very satisfying knee in David's groin when he'd grabbed her arm and tried to explain, *then* sworn off men.

Lately, though, she'd been reconsidering forever. Her itchy restlessness had nothing to do with her boss. Nothing at all. Just a woman's natural needs and the grudging realization that even the most sophisticated high-tech gadgets couldn't *quite* substitute for a man.

Which was why goose bumps raised all over her skin when Lightning strolled over to her command console with the casual grace that characterized him.

"Patch me through to the White House."

She cocked a brow. She wasn't in the Navy now.

"Please," Lightning added with an amused smile.

All too conscious of his proximity, Mackenzie transmitted the necessary code words and verifications, then listened with unabashed interest to the brief conversation between Lightning and the Prez. When it was over, she leaned back in her chair and angled OMEGA's director a curious look.

"Sounds like Renegade's got the weight of the free world riding on his shoulders on this one."

"The weight of North America, anyway."

His gaze lingered on her upturned face. Mackenzie had almost forgotten how to breathe by the time he murmured a request that she get Renegade on the line.

His eyes, narrowed and rattlesnake-mean behind his mirrored sunglasses, Jack Carstairs snapped shut the phone Mackenzie Blair had issued him mere hours ago. The damned thing was half the size of a cigarette pack and bounced signals off a secure telecommunications satellite some thirty-six thousand kilometers above the earth. Lightning's message had come through loud and clear.

Renegade was to keep his hands off Elena Maria Alazar.

As if he needed the warning! He'd learned his lesson the first time. No way was he going to get shot down in flames again.

Hefting his beat-up leather carryall, he walked out of the airport into a flood of heat and honeysuckle-scented air. A short tram ride took him to the rental agency, where he checked out a sturdy Jeep Cherokee.

The drive from the airport to downtown San Antonio took only about fifteen minutes, long enough for Jack to work through his irritation at the call. Not long enough, however, to completely suppress the prickly sensation that crawled along his nerves at the thought of seeing Ellie Alazar again.

His jaw set, he negotiated the traffic in the city's center and pulled up at the Menger. Constructed in 1859, the hotel was situated on Alamo Plaza, right next to the famous mission. The little blurb Jack had read in one of the airline's magazines during the flight down indicated the Menger had played host to a roster of distinguished notables. Reportedly, Robert E. Lee rode his horse, Traveller, right into the lobby. Teddy Roosevelt tipped a few in the bar while organizing and training his Rough Riders. Sarah Bernhardt, Lillie Langtry and Mae West had all brought their own brand of luster to the hotel.

Now Elena Maria Alazar was adding another touch of notoriety to the venerable institution. One Jack suspected wasn't particularly appreciated by the management.

He killed the engine, then climbed out of the Cherokee. A valet took the car keys. Another offered to take his bag.

"I've got it."

Anyone else entering the hotel's three-story lobby for the first time might have let their gaze roam the cream marble columns, magnificent wrought-iron balcony railings and priceless antiques and paintings. Six years of embassy guard duty and another eight working for OMEGA had conditioned Jack to automatically note the lobby's physical layout, security camera placement and emergency egress routes. His boot heels echoing on the marble floors, he crossed to the desk. There he was handed a message. Ellie was waiting for him in the taproom.

After the blazing sun outside and dazzling white marble of the lobby, the bar wrapped Jack in the welcoming gloom of an English pub. A dark cherry-wood ceiling loomed above glass-fronted cabinets, beveled mirrors and high-backed booths. A stuffed moose head with a huge rack of antlers surveyed the scene with majestic indifference, wreathed in the mingled scents of wood polish and aged Scotch.

Instinctively, Jack peeled off his sunglasses and recorded the bar's layout, but the details sifted right through his conscious mind to be stored away for future reference. His main focus, his only focus, was the woman who swiveled at the sound of his footsteps.

His first thought was that she hadn't changed. Her mink brown hair still tumbled in a loose ponytail down her back. Her cinnamon eyes still looked out at the world through a screen of thick, black lashes. In her short-sleeved red top and trim-fitting tan shorts, she looked more like a teenager on vacation than a respected historian with a long string of initials after her name.

Not until he stepped closer did he notice the differences. The Ellie he'd known nine years ago had glowed with youth and laughter and a vibrant joy of life. This woman showed fine lines of stress at the corners of her mouth. Shadows darkened her eyes, and he saw in their brown depths a wariness that echoed his.

She didn't smile. Didn't ease her stiff-backed pose. Silence stretched between them. She broke it, finally, with a cool greeting.

"Hello, Jack."

He'd expected to feel remnants of the old anger, the resentment, the fierce hurt. He hadn't expected the punch to his gut that came with the sound of her voice. His head dipped in a curt nod. It was the best he could manage at the moment.

"Thanks for coming," she said cooly.

He moved closer, wanting her to see his face when he

delivered the speech he'd been preparing since Lightning informed him of the nature of his mission.

"Let's get one thing straight, right here and right now. My job is to protect you. That's the reason I'm here. That's the *only* reason I'm here."

Her chin snapped up. The fire he remembered all too well flared hot and dark in her eyes.

"I didn't imagine you'd make the trip down to San Antonio for any other reason. We had our fun, Jack. We both enjoyed our little fling. But that's all it was. You made that quite clear when you walked away from me nine years ago."

His jaw tightened. He had no answer for that. There *was* no answer. Eyes hard, he watched her slide off the bar stool. Her scent came with her as she approached, a combination of sun and the delicate cactus pear perfume she'd always worn. It was her mother's concoction, he remembered her telling him. He also remembered that he'd been nuzzling her neck at the time. Deliberately, Jack slammed the door on the thought.

When she raised a hand to shove back a loose tendril of hair, however, the gleam of silver circling her wrist brought another, sharper memory. The two-inch-wide beaten silver bracelet had cost him a half-month's pay. He'd slipped it onto her wrist mere moments before her uncle's police had arrived to arrest him.

"Let's go upstairs," he instructed tersely. "I want to see the message your friend left you."

Chapter 2

Wrapping her arms around her middle, Ellie stood just inside the door of the trashed suite.

"I moved to another room. The hotel wanted to clean up the mess, but I asked them to leave it until you got here."

His face impassive, Jack surveyed the mess. "Did the police find anything?"

"They dusted for prints, interviewed the hotel staff and asked for a complete inventory of the missing items, but as far as I know, they haven't come up with any concrete leads. In fact..."

"In fact?"

Her shoulders lifted under the chili red top. "The detective in charge was somewhat less than sympathetic. Evidently he read the story about me in the *Light* and doesn't take kindly to Mexicans determined to rewrite Texas history. It doesn't seem to make a whole lot of difference to some folks that I'm as American as they are."

"No, it wouldn't."

Jack had seen more than his share of bigotry during his overseas tours, both in the Marines and as an OMEGA agent. It didn't matter what a person's race, creed or financial circumstances might be. There was always someone who hated him or her because of them. With a mental note to establish liaison with the detective handling Ellie's case as soon as he conducted his preliminary assessment of the situation, he eyed the message on the mirror.

The wording suggested a man, someone familiar with weapons and not afraid to let Ellie know it. The obvious inference was that the threat stemmed from her work. Jack never trusted the obvious.

"I want a complete background brief on the members on your team," he told her, making a final sweep of the premises. "Particularly anyone who might or might not have a grudge against the team's leader."

Startled, she dropped her arms. "You think one of my own people is responsible for this?"

"I don't think anything at this point. I'm just assessing the situation."

Her eyes huge, she stared at him. Jack could see the doubt creep into their cinnamon brown depths, followed swiftly by dismay. Only now, he guessed, was it occurring to her that the leak to the press might have been more deliberate than accidental. That one of her team members might, in fact, be working behind the scenes on some hidden agenda of his or her own.

The years fell away. For a moment, he caught a glimpse in her stricken face of the trusting, passionate girl she'd once been.

He'd come so close to loving that girl. Closer than

he'd ever come to loving anyone who didn't wear khaki. Until Ellie, the Marines had been his life. Until Ellie, the Corps had constituted the only family he'd ever wanted or needed. He'd never known his father's name. He'd long ago buried the memory of the mother who left her four-year-old son in the roach-infested hotel room and drove off with some poor slob she'd picked up in a bar. After years of being passed from one foster home to another, Jack had walked into a recruiting office on his eighteenth birthday, signed up and found a home.

He shot up through the ranks, from private to corporal to gunnery sergeant in minimal time. He learned to follow and to lead. Because of his outstanding record, he was selected for the elite Marine Security Guard Battalion. His first tour was at the U.S. Embassy in Gabon, Africa, his second at the plush post in Mexico City.

The debacle in Mexico City had ended his career and destroyed all sense of family with the Corps. Thankfully, he'd found another home in OMEGA. This one, he vowed savagely, he wouldn't jeopardize by tumbling Ellie into the nearest bed.

"I also want a copy of your list of missing items."

The dismay left Ellie's face. Stiffening at his curt tone, she gave him an equally succinct response. "I'll print you out a copy. It runs to more than fifty pages."

"Fifty pages!"

The exclamation earned him a condescending smile. "My team's been on-site for almost a week now. We've recorded hundreds of digital images, cross-indexed them and made copious notes concerning each. The data was all stored in the external FireWire drive that was stolen. Thank God I backed the files up via the university's remote access mainframe!"

With that heartfelt mutter, she led the way down the hall to the new set of rooms the hotel had assigned her. Jack followed, forcing himself to keep his gaze on her back, her hair, the stiff set to her shoulders under her top. On anything, dammit, but the seductive sway of her hips.

A swift prowl around the spacious corner suite she showed him to had him shaking his head. "Pack your things."

"I beg your pardon?"

"I'll call the front desk and get them to move us."

"Why?"

He dragged back the gauzy curtains covering the corner windows. One set of wavy glass panes fronted the street. The other set faced the brick wall of the River Center complex next door.

"See the roof of that building?"

"Yes."

"It's on a direct line with these windows. Anyone with a mind to it could get a clear bead on a target in this room. Or climb up on the roof of that IMAX theater across the street and stake you out."

The color leached from her cheeks. "If you're trying to scare me, you're doing one heck of a good job."

"You should be scared. That wasn't a valentine your visitor left on that mirror, you know."

"Of course I know! To paraphrase your earlier remark, the viciousness of that threat is the reason, the *only* reason, I agreed to the nuisance of a bodyguard."

Hooking his thumbs in his jeans pockets, Jack tried to get a handle on the woman who'd emerged from the girl he'd once known.

"So why are you hanging around San Antonio, Ellie?

Why offer yourself as a target to the kook or malcontent who issued that warning?"

"Because I refuse to let said kook or malcontent interfere with my work. In all modesty, I'm good at what I do. Damned good." She speared him with a hard look. "You predicted I would be. Remember, Jack? Right about the time you and Uncle Eduardo jointly decided finishing college was more important to me than my... Let's see, how did he phrase it? My passing infatuation with a hardheaded Marine."

They'd have to scratch at the old scars sometime. Better to do it now and give the scabs time to heal again. If Jack was to protect her, he needed her trust. Or at least her cooperation. He wouldn't gain either until he'd acknowledged his culpability for the hurt she'd suffered all those years ago.

"You were only nineteen, Ellie. I thought... Your uncle thought..."

"That I didn't know my own mind." Her chin came up. "You were wrong. I knew it then. I know it now."

She couldn't have made her meaning plainer. Jack Carstairs wouldn't get the chance to wound her again. He accepted that stark truth with a nod.

"Why don't we get settled in different rooms, and you can tell me exactly what it is you're so good at. I need to understand what you're doing here," he said to forestall the stiff response he saw coming, "and why it's roused such controversy."

The hotel staff moved them to adjoining suites two floors down. The rooms looked out over the inner courtyard of the hotel instead of the street. Like the rest of the historic hotel, they were furnished with a combination of period antiques and modern comfort. A burned-wood armoire held a twenty-seven-inch TV and a well-stocked bar. The wrought-iron bedstead boasted a queen-size mattress and thick, puffy goose-down comforter.

While Jack checked phones, door locks and ceiling vents, three valets transferred boxes of files and equipment on rolling dollies. Ruthlessly rearranging the furniture to meet her work-space needs, Ellie promptly turned her sitting room into a functional office. She'd already replaced the stolen computer and hard drive, which she now hooked up to an oversize flat LCD screen.

A smaller unit sat beside the computer. Jack studied it with a faint smile. Mackenzie Blair, OMEGA's chief of communications, would light up like a Christmas tree if she caught sight of all those buttons and dials and displays. The palm-size unit was probably crammed with more circuitry than the Space Shuttle.

Evidently Ellie Alazar shared Mackenzie's fascination with electronic gadgetry. She gave the small metal box the kind of pat a fond mother might give a child.

"This holds the guts of a technology I developed the summer after we..." Her brown brows slashed down. Obviously impatient with her hesitation, she plowed ahead. "The summer after I met you. I didn't make the trip to Mexico City that year. I didn't go down for several years, as a matter of fact."

Jack wasn't surprised. Elena's emotions ran close to the surface. In the short months he'd known her, she'd never once reined them in. Looking back, he could see that was what had drawn him to her in the first place. Everything she thought or felt was all there, in her eyes, her face. Impatience, passion, anger—whatever emotion gripped her, she shared. Honestly. Openly.

She'd certainly shared her feelings the day her uncle sent his police to arrest Jack. She'd been furious with Eduardo Alazar. But not half as angry as she'd became with the Marine who refused to stand and fight for her.

"You didn't go to Mexico that summer," Jack acknowledged, steering the conversation to less volatile subjects. "What did you do?"

"I worked for the National Park Service on a dig in the Pecos National Park. We were excavating the site of the battle of Glorietta Pass. The battle took place in 1862 and was one of the pivotal engagements in the Civil War."

"The Gettysburg of the West. I've heard of it."

She gave him a look of approval. "Then you know the battle turned the tide against Confederates and sent Silbey's Brigade scuttling back to Texas in total disarray."

Another Texas defeat. Evidently Ellie had started her career at the site of one disastrous conflict for the Lone Star state. Now she was up to her trim, tight buns in controversy over another. No wonder some loyal local citizens wanted to roll up the welcome mat and send her on her way.

"We used metal detectors to locate shell casings at the battle site," she explained, warming to her subject. "We marked their location on a computerized grid, then categorized the casings by make and caliber. We also analyzed the rifling marks on the brass to determine the type of weapon that fired them."

"Sounds like a lot of work."

"It was. Three summers' worth of digging and mapping. Plus hundreds of hours of detailed research into the weaponry of the time. The Confederates tended to carry a wide variety of personally owned rifles and side arms. Union weapons were somewhat more standardized. By matching spent shell casings to the type of weapon that fired them, we were able to map the precise movement of both armies on the battlefield. We also built a massive database. For my Ph.D. dissertation, I expanded and translated the raw data into a program that allows forensic historians to reliably identify shell casings from any era post-1820."

"Why 1820?"

"The copper percussion cap was invented in the 1820s. Within a decade, two at most, almost every army in the world had converted its muzzle-loading flintlocks to percussion. More to the point where my research was concerned, the copper casing retained more defined rifling marks, which aided in identification of the type of weapon that fired it."

Jack was impressed. He could fieldstrip an M-15, clean the components and put it back together blindfolded. He'd qualified at the expert level on every weapon in the Marine Corps inventory, as well as on the ones OMEGA outfitted him with. Yet his knowledge of the science of ballistics didn't begin to compare with Ellie's.

"So how do we get from the invention of the percussion cap to your finding that the hero of the Alamo deserted his troops and ran away?"

"It's not a finding." She shot the answer back. "It's only one of several hypotheses I surfaced for discussion with my team. Honestly, you'd think simple intellectual curiosity would make folks wait to see whether the theory is substantiated by fact before they get all in a twit."

"You'd think," Jack echoed solemnly.

Flushing a bit, she backpedaled. "Sorry. I didn't mean to snap. I'm just getting tired of having to deal with outraged letters to the editor, picketers at the site, skittish team members and a nervous National Park Service director who's close to pulling the plug on our funding."

There they were again. The fire, the impatience. She hadn't learned to bank, either. Jack found himself hoping she never did.

"And this hypothesis is based on what?" he asked, the evenness of his tone a contrast to hers. "Start at the beginning. Talk me through the sequence of events."

"It would be better if I showed you." She speared a glance at her watch. "It's only a little past two. If you want, we can start here at the Alamo, then drive out to the site."

"Good enough. Give me ten minutes."

With the controlled, smooth grace that had always characterized him, he executed what Ellie could only describe as an about-face and passed through the connecting door. It closed behind him, leaving her staring at the panels.

The old cliché was true, she thought with a little ache. You can take a man out of the Marines, but you never quite took the Marine out of the man.

Like dust blown by the hot Texas wind, memories skittered through her mind. She could see Jack the night they'd met. She'd accompanied her aunt and uncle to a formal function at the American embassy. As head of the security detail, Gunnery Sergeant Carstairs had stood just behind the ambassador, square-shouldered, proud, confident. And so damned handsome in his dress blues that Elena hadn't been able to take her eyes off him all evening.

She'd been the one to ask him to dance. *She'd* called him a few days later, inviting him to join her for a Sunday afternoon stroll through Chapultapec Park. *She'd* let him know in every way a woman could that she was attracted to him.

And that's all it was. A sizzling, searing attraction.

At first.

How could she know she'd fall desperately in love with the man? That she'd find a passion in Jack's arms she'd never come close to tasting before? That she'd swear to give up everything for him—her scholarship, her family, her pride—only to have him throw them all back in her face.

If she closed her eyes, she could replay their final scene in painful, brilliant color. Jack was already under house arrest. Her uncle's overly protective, knee-jerk reaction to his niece's affair had forced the U.S. ambassador to demand Sergeant Carstairs's immediate reassignment and possible disciplinary action.

Steaming, Ellie had ignored her uncle's stern orders to the contrary, marched to the marine barracks and demanded to see Jack. He'd come to the foyer, stiff and remote in his khaki shirt and blue trousers with the crimson stripe down each leg. With brutal honesty, he'd laid his feelings on the line.

Ellie still had a year of college and at least three years of grad school ahead of her. He was going home to face a possible court-martial and an uncertain future. He refused to make promises he might not be able to keep. Nor would he allow her put her future on hold for his.

He was so noble, Ellie had railed. So damned, stupidly obstinate. Traits he continued to demonstrate even after they both returned to the States.

Cringing inside, Ellie recalled the repeated attempts she'd made to contact Jack. He wouldn't return her calls. Never answered her letters. Finally, her pride kicked in and she left a scathing message saying that he could damned well make the next move. He never did.

Now here they were, she thought, blowing out a long breath. Two completely different people. She'd fulfilled the early promise of a brilliant career in history. Jack, apparently, had bottomed out. Despite his extensive training and experience in personal security, he'd evidently drifted from one firm to another until going to work for some small-time operation in Virginia. Ellie wouldn't have known he was in the bodyguard business if one of her colleagues hadn't stumbled across his company on the Internet while preparing for a trip to Bogotá, Colombia, the kidnap capital of the universe.

It was guilt, only guilt, that had made her insist on Jack when her uncle urged her to accept the services of a bodyguard. She'd caused the ruin of his chosen career. Her own had exceeded all expectations. The least she could do was throw a little business his way.

From the looks of him, he could use it. She didn't know what was considered the appropriate uniform for bodyguards, but her uncle's security detail had always worn suits and ties and walked around talking into their wristwatches. She couldn't remember seeing any of them in thigh-hugging jeans or wrinkled, blue-cotton shirts with the sleeves rolled up. Or, she thought with a small ache just under her ribs, black leather boots showing faint scuff marks.

More than anything else, those scratches brought

home the vast difference between the spit-and-polish sergeant she'd once loved and the man in the other room. Her throat tight, Ellie turned to gather her purse and keys.

Jack flipped open the palm-size phone and punched a single key. One short beep indicated instant connection to OMEGA's control center.

"Control, this is Renegade."

OMEGA's chief of communications responded with a cheerful, "Go ahead, Renegade."

As little as a year ago, operatives at the headquarters stood by twenty-four hours a day to act as controllers for agents in the field. Mackenzie Blair's improvements in field communications allowed for instant contact with headquarters and eliminated the need for controllers. Instead, Mackenzie and her communications techs monitored operations around the clock.

Mostly Mackenzie, Jack amended. The woman spent almost all her waking hours at OMEGA. She needed a life. Like Jack himself, he thought wryly.

"I've made contact with the subject."

The terse report no doubt raised Mackenzie's brows. After all, the background dossier she'd compiled had included a summation of Elena Maria Alazar's affair with Sergeant Jack Carstairs.

"Tell Lightning I'm working the preliminary threat assessment. I'll report back when I have a better feel for the situation."

"Roger that, Renegade."

After signing off, Jack slid the small, flat phone into his shirt pocket and hiked his foot up on a handy footstool. His movements were sure and smooth as he drew a blue steel short-barreled automatic from its ankle holster. He made sure the safety was on, released the magazine, checked the load and pushed the magazine back in place. A tug on the slide chambered a round. With the 9 mm tucked in its leather nest, he shook his pant leg over his boot and rapped on the door to Ellie's room.

"Ready?"

Pulling on a ball cap in the same chili-pepper red as her top, she hooked a bag over her shoulder.

"Yes."

Chapter 3

Outside, the July sun blazed down with cheerful brutality. Exiting the hotel, Ellie turned right toward Alamo Plaza. Jack walked beside her, his eyes narrowed against the glare as he scanned the crowd.

It included the usual assortment of vendors and tourists, with a heavy sprinkling of men and women in Air Force blue. They were basic trainees, released for a few precious hours from the nearby Lackland Air Force Base. With their buzz-cut hair and slick sleeves, they looked so young, so proud of their uniform. So unprepared for the crises that world events could plunge them into at any moment.

What they didn't look like were riled-up patriots seeking vengeance on a historian who dared to question the courage of a local legend. Nonetheless, Jack didn't relax his vigilance.

"What do you know about the Alamo?" Ellie asked as they approached the mission.

"Not much more than what I absorbed from the John Wayne movie of the same name."

And in the data Mackenzie had pulled off the computers. Jack kept silent about the background file. Right now, he was more interested in Ellie's version of the Alamo's history.

"It's one of a string of five missions located along the San Antonio River, founded in the early 1700s," she informed him. "Originally designated Mission Antonio de Valero, it didn't become known as the Alamo until much later."

With a sweep of her arm, she gestured to the adobe structure dominating the wide plaza ahead.

"There it is. The shrine of Texas liberty."

The distinctive building stirred an unexpected dart of pride in Jack. As a symbol of independence, its image had been seared into his consciousness. Of course, all those John Wayne movies might have had something to do with the sensation.

"Originally the mission compound sat by itself, well across the river from the settlement of San Antonio de Bexar," Ellie related. "Now, of course, the city's grown up all around it."

They wove a path through sightseers snapping photo after photo. A red-faced, grossly overweight candidate for a stroke backed up to frame a shot, banging into several fellow tourists in the process. Swiftly, Jack took Ellie's elbow to steer her around the obstacle.

Just as swiftly, he released her.

Well, hell! Here it was, going on nine years since he'd last touched this woman. Yet one glide of his fingers along her smooth, warm skin set off a chain reaction that started in his arm and ended about six inches below his belt.

For the first time since Lightning's call some hours ago, Jack conceded maybe Eduardo Alazar had reason to be concerned. The fires weren't out. Not entirely.

Jack had been so certain the embarrassment he'd caused Ellie and himself had doused any residual sparks. The sudden flare of heat in his gut screamed otherwise. Clenching his jaw against the unwelcome sensation, he tried to concentrate on Ellie's recitation.

"A series of droughts and epidemics decimated the mission's religious population," she related. "In 1793 the structure was turned over to civil authorities. At that point, Spanish cavalry from Alamo de Parras in Mexico took occupancy, and the fort became known at the Pueblo del Alamo. When the Spanish were driven out of Mexico, Mexican troops moved in. About the same time, the Mexican government opened the province of Texas to foreign settlers."

"Foreign meaning Americans?"

"Americans and anyone else who would put down roots and, hopefully, help stem attacks on settlements by the Commanches and Apaches. Given the proximity to the States, though, it's only natural that most immigrants were Americans. Led by Stephen Austin, they flooded in and soon outnumbered the Mexican population five to one. It was only a matter of time until they decided they wanted out from under Mexican rule."

"Those pesky Texans," Jack drawled.

"Actually," she replied with a smile, "they called themselves Texians then. Or Tejanos. But they *were* pretty pesky. Tensions escalated, particularly after General Antonio Lopez de Santa Anna seized control of the Mexican government and abrogated the constitution. In the process, he also abrogated most of the rights of the troublesome immigrants. There were uprisings all over Mexico—and outright rebellion here in Texas.

"After several small skirmishes, the Americans declared their independence and sent a small force to seize the Alamo. When Santa Anna vowed to march his entire army north and crush the rebellion, the tiny garrison sent out a plea for reinforcements. William Travis, Jim Bowie and Davy Crockett, among others, answered the call."

The names sounded like a roll call of America's heroes. Jim Bowie, the reckless adventurer as quick with his wit as with his knife. Davy Crockett, legendary marksman and two-term member of Congress from Tennessee. William Barrett Travis, commander of the Texas militia who drew a line in the sand with his saber and asked every Alamo defender willing to stand to the end to cross it. Supposedly, all but one did so.

Those who did met the fate Ellie related in a historian's dispassionate voice.

"When Santa Anna retook the Alamo in March, 1836, he executed every defender still alive and burned their bodies in mass funeral pyres. Or so the few noncombatants who survived reported."

"But you think those reports are wrong."

"I think there's a possibility they *may* be."

With that cautious reply, she led the way through the small door set in the massive wooden gates fronting the mission. Inside, thick adobe walls provided welcome relief from the heat. A smiling docent stepped forward to greet them.

"Welcome to the Alamo. This brochure will give you... Oh!" The smile fell right off her face. "It's you, Dr. Alazar."

"Yes, I'm back again."

"Our museum director said you'd finished your research here."

"I have. I'm playing tourist this afternoon and showing my, er, friend around."

The docent's glance darted from Ellie to Jack and back again. Suspicion carved a deep line between her brows. "Are you planning to take more digital photos?"

"No. I've taken all I need."

"We heard those were stolen."

"They were," Ellie replied coolly. "Fortunately, I make it a practice to back up my work."

The volunteer fanned her brochures with a snap. "Yes, well, I'll let Dr. Smith know you're here."

"You've certainly made yourself popular around here," Jack commented dryly.

"Tell me about it! The exhibits are this way."

Exiting the church, they entered a long low building that had once served as the barracks and now housed a museum of Texas history. Ellie let Jack set the pace and read those exhibits that caught his interest.

They painted a chillingly realistic picture of the thirteen-day siege. There was Santa Anna's army of more than twelve hundred. The pitiful inadequacy of the defending force, numbering just over a hundred. Travis's repeated requests for reinforcements. The arrival of the Tennesseeans. The wild, last-minute dash by thirty-two volunteers from Goliad, Texas, through enemy lines. The final assault some hours before dawn on March sixth. The massacre of all defenders. The mass funeral pyres that consumed both Texan and Mexican dead. The pitiful handful of non-combatants who survived.

The original of Travis's most famous appeal for assistance was preserved behind glass. Written the day after the Mexican army arrived in San Antonio, the letter still had the power to stir emotions.

Commander of the Alamo
Bexar, Fby 24th, 1836
To the People of Texas and All Americans in the World
Fellow Citizens & Compatriots

I am besieged by a thousand or more of the Mexicans under Santa Anna. I have sustained a continual bombardment & have not lost a man. The enemy has demanded a surrender at discretion, otherwise the garrison are to be put to the sword if the fort is taken. I have answered the demand with a cannon shot, and our flag still waves proudly on the walls. I shall never surrender nor retreat.

Then, I call on you in the name of Liberty, of patriotism, & of everything dear to the American character, to come to our aid with all dispatch. The enemy is receiving reinforcements daily & will no doubt increase to three or four thousand in four or five days. If this call is neglected, I am determined to sustain myself as long as possible and die like a soldier who never forgets what is due to his own honor & that of his country.
Victory or death

William Barrett Travis
Lt. Col. Comdt
P.S. The Lord is on our side. When the enemy
appeared in sight, we had not three bushels of
corn. We have since found in deserted houses 80
or 90 bushels & got into the walls 20 or 30 head
of Beeves.
Travis.

"Whew!" Jack blew out a long breath. "No wonder the mere suggestion that this man didn't die at the
Alamo has riled so many folks. He certainly made his
intentions plain enough."

Nodding, Ellie trailed after him as he examined the
exhibits and artifacts reported to belong to the defenders, among them sewing kits, tobacco pouches and
handwoven horsehair bridles and lariats. A small, tattered Bible tugged at her heart. It was inscribed to one
Josiah Kennett, whose miniature showed an unsmiling
young man in the wide-brimmed sombrero favored by
cowboys and vaqueros of the time. Silver conchos decorated the hatband, underscoring how closely Mexican
and Tejano cultures had blended in the days before war
wrenched them apart.

When Jack and Ellie emerged into a tree-shaded
courtyard, the serene quiet gave no echo of the can-
nons that had once thundered from the surrounding
walls. Tourists wandered past quietly, almost reverently.

"Okay," Jack said, summarizing what he'd read inside. "Susanna Dickinson, wife of the fort's artillery
officer, said that Travis died on the north battery. Travis's slave Joe said he saw the colonel go down after
grappling with troops coming over the wall. They make

a pretty convincing argument that William B. stuck to his word and died right here at the Alamo."

"An argument I might buy," Ellie agreed, "except that Susanna Dickinson hid in the chapel during the assault. After the battle, she reportedly saw the bodies of Crockett and Bowie, but never specifically indicated she saw Travis's. She probably heard that he died on the ramparts from other sources."

"What about Joe's report?"

"Joe saw his master go down during the assault, then he, too, hid. Travis could have been wounded yet somehow survived. The only document that indicates his body was recovered and burned with the others is a translation of a report by Francisco Ruiz, San Antonio's mayor at the time. Unfortunately, the translation appeared in 1860, years after the battle. The original has never been found, so there's no way to verify its authenticity."

She knew her stuff. There was no arguing that.

"On the other hand," she continued, "rumors that some of the defenders escaped the massacre ran rampant for years. One held that Mexican forces captured Crockett some miles away and hauled him before Santa Anna, who had him summarily shot. There's also a diary kept by a corporal in the Mexican army who claims he led a patrol sent out to hunt down fleeing Tejanos."

Her eyes locked with Jack's.

"Supposedly, his patrol fired at an escapee approximately five miles south of here, not far from Mission San Jose. The corporal was sure they hit the man, but they lost him in the dense underbrush along the river."

"Let me guess. That's the site you're now excavating."

"Right."

It could have happened, Jack mused. He'd experienced the confusion and chaos of battle. He knew how garbled reports could become, how often even the most reliable intelligence proved wrong.

Still, as they moved toward the building that housed a special exhibit of weaponry used at the Alamo, he found himself hoping the theory didn't hold water. A part of him wanted to believe the legend—that William Barrett Travis *had* drawn that line in the sand, then heroically fought to the death alongside Davy Crockett, Jim Bowie and the others. Texas deserved its heroes.

The museum director evidently agreed. Short, rotund, his wire-rimmed glasses fogging in the steamy heat, he stood in front of the door to the exhibit with legs spread and arms folded and greeted Ellie with a curt nod. "Dr. Alazar."

"Dr. Smith."

"Were you wishing access to those artifacts not on public display?"

"Yes, there's one rifle in particular I want to show my, er, associate."

Jack flicked her an amused glance. Obviously, Ellie wasn't ready to admit she'd been intimidated into acquiescing to a bodyguard.

"I'm sorry," the director replied with patent insincerity. "I must insist that you put all such requests in writing from now on."

Ellie's eyes flashed. Evidently Smith had just drawn his own line in the sand.

"I'll do that," she snapped. "I'll also apprise my colleagues in this and future endeavors of your generous spirit of cooperation."

She left him standing guard at his post. Jack followed, shaking his head. Elena Maria Alazar might be one of the foremost experts in her field, but she wouldn't win a whole lot of prizes for tact or diplomacy.

"Damn Smith, anyway," she muttered, still fuming. "I suspect he's the one who raised such a stink with the media. He seems to think I'm attacking him personally by questioning his research."

It sounded to Jack as though the man might have a point there. Wisely, he kept silent and made a mental note to have Mackenzie run a background check on the museum director.

"I'll show you the images of that shotgun later," Ellie said as they retraced their steps.

"Why is that particular weapon so significant?"

"It's a double-barreled shotgun, reportedly recovered after the battle. Records indicate William Travis owned just such a weapon, or one similar to it. It's almost identical to the one we recovered at the dig."

Tugging her ball cap lower on her brow to shield her eyes against the blazing sun, she wove a path through the milling crowd outside the Alamo and made for the elaborate, wrought-iron façade of the Menger.

"I wish I could convince Smith that I'm still wide open to all possible theories. And that I have no intention of caving in to threats, obscene phone calls or petty nuisances like putting my requests for access to historical artifacts in writing."

Her mouth set, she rummaged around in her shoulder bag, dug out a parking receipt and approached the parking valet.

"Why don't I drive?" Jack said easily, passing the attendant his receipt instead. "I want to get the lay of the land."

He also wanted to make sure someone skilled in defensive driving techniques was at the wheel whenever Ellie traveled.

She didn't argue. When the Cherokee came down the ramp, its tires screeching at the tight turns, she tossed her bag into the back and slid into the passenger seat. The ball cap came off. With a grateful sigh for the chilled air blasting out of the vents, she swiped the damp tendrils off her forehead.

"Which way?" Jack asked.

"Take a left, go past the Alamo Dome, then follow the signs for Mission Trail."

Propping her neck against the headrest, Ellie stared straight ahead. For the second time in as many hours, Jack sensed the accumulated stress that kept the woman beside him coiled as tight as a cobra.

"Tell me about these obscene phone calls. How many have you received?"

"Five or six." Her nose wrinkled. "They were short and crude. Mostly suggestions on where I could stick my theories. One of the callers was female, by the way, which surprised the heck out of me."

Nothing surprised Jack any more. "Did the police run traces?"

"They tried. But the calls came through the hotel switchboard, and there's something about the routing system that precluded a trace."

Jack would fix that as soon as they returned. The electronic bag of tricks Mackenzie had assembled for this mission included a highly sophisticated and not exactly legal device that glommed onto a digital signal and wouldn't let go.

"See that sign?" Ellie pointed to a historical marker

in the shape of a Spanish mission. "This is where we pick up Mission Trail. You need to hang a left here."

"Got it."

Flicking on his directional signal, Jack turned left. A half mile later, he made a right. That was when he noticed the dusty black SUV. The Ford Expedition remained three cars back, never more, never less, making every turn Jack did. Frowning, he navigated the busy city streets for another few blocks before spinning the steering wheel. The Cherokee's tires squealed as he cut a sharp left across two lanes of oncoming traffic.

"Hey!" Ellie made a grab for the handle just above her window. "Did I miss a sign?"

"No."

He flicked a glance in the rearview mirror. The SUV waited until one oncoming vehicle whizzed past, dodged a second and followed.

Ellie had figured out something was wrong. Craning her neck, she peered at the traffic behind them while Jack whipped around another corner. When the SUV followed some moments later, he dug his cell phone out of his pocket and punched a single button.

"Control, this is Renegade."

"Renegade?"

Ignoring Ellie's startled echo, Jack waited for a response. Mackenzie came on a moment later.

"Control here. Go ahead."

"I'm traveling west on…" He squinted at the street sign that whizzed by. "On Alameda Street in south San Antonio. There's a black Expedition following approximately fifty meters behind. I need you to put a satellite on him before I shake him."

"Roger, Renegade. I'll vector off your signal."

"Let me know when you've got the lock."

"Give me ten seconds."

Jack did a mental count and got down to three before Mackenzie came on the radio.

"Okay, I see you. I'm panning back... There he is. Black Expedition. Now I just have to sharpen the image a little..." A moment later, she gave a hum of satisfaction. "He's tagged. I'm feeding the license plate number into the computer as we speak. How long do you want me to maintain the satellite lock?"

"Follow him all the way home. And let me know as soon as you get an ID."

"Will do."

"Thanks, Mac."

"Anytime," OMEGA's communications chief answered breezily.

Jack snapped the transceiver shut and slipped it into his shirt pocket. A quick glance at Ellie showed her staring at him in astonishment.

"Your company has a satellite at their disposal?"

"Several. Hang tight, I'm going to lose this joker."

Jack could see the questions in her eyes but didn't have time for answers right now. The first rule in personal protective services was to remove the protectee from any potentially dangerous situation. He didn't know who was behind the wheel of the SUV or what his intentions were. He sure as hell wasn't about to find out with Ellie in the car.

Stomping down on the accelerator, he took the next intersection on two wheels. Ellie gulped and scrunched down in her seat. Jack shot a look in the rearview mirror and watched the larger, heavier Expedition lurch around the corner.

Two turns later, they'd left the main downtown area and had entered an industrial area crisscrossed by railroad tracks. Brick warehouses crowded either side of the street, their windows staring down like unseeing eyes. Once again, Jack put his boot to the floor. The Cherokee rocketed forward, flew over a set of tracks and sailed into an intersection just as a semi bearing the logo of Alamo City Fruits and Vegetables swung wide across the same crossing.

"Look out!"

Shrieking, Ellie braced both hands on the dash. Her boots slammed against the floorboards.

Jack spun the wheel right, then left and finessed the Cherokee past the truck with less than an inch or two to spare. Smiling in grim satisfaction, he hit the accelerator again.

The bulkier Expedition couldn't squeeze through. Behind him, they heard the squeal of brakes followed by the screech of metal scraping metal. Still smiling grimly, Jack made another turn. A few minutes later, he picked up Mission Trail again, but this time he headed into the city instead of out.

"We'd better put off our visit to the site until tomorrow," he told Ellie. "By then I should have a better idea of who or what we're dealing with."

"Fine by me," she replied, wiggling upright in her seat.

Actually, it was more than fine. After that wild ride, her nerves jumped like grasshoppers on hot asphalt, and her kidneys were signaling a pressing need to find the closest bathroom.

Jack, on the other hand, didn't look the least flustered. He gripped the steering wheel loosely, resting one arm on the console between the bucket seats, and divided his attention between the road ahead and the traffic behind. She couldn't see his eyes behind the mirrored sunglasses, but not so much as a bead of nervous sweat had popped out on his forehead.

"Do you do these kinds of high-speed races often in your line of work?" she asked.

"Often enough."

"And you've been in the same business since you left the Corps?"

"More or less."

"How do you handle the stress?"

He flashed her a grin that reminded her so much of the man she'd once known that Ellie gulped.

"I'll show you when we get back to the hotel."

Chapter 4

"Yoga?"

Ellie's disbelieving laughter rippled through the sun-washed hotel room.

"You do yoga?"

"According to my instructor," Jack intoned solemnly, "one doesn't 'do' yoga. One ascends to it."

"Uh-huh. And who is this instructor?" she asked, forming a mental image of a tanned, New Age Californian in flowing orange robes.

"One of the grunts in the first platoon I commanded."

"You're kidding!"

"Nope. Dirwood had progressed to the master level before joining the Corps."

She shook her head. "You know, of course, you're blowing my image of United States Marines all to hell."

"Funny," Jack murmured, "I thought I'd pretty much already done that."

He peeled off his sunglasses, tucked them in his shirt pocket and propped his hips against the sofa back. His blue eyes spent several moments studying Ellie's face before moving south.

She withstood his scrutiny calmly enough but knew she looked a mess. Sweat had painted damp patches on her scoop-necked top, and her khaki shorts boasted more wrinkles than Rip Van Winkle. She was also, as Jack proceeded to point out, a bundle of nerves.

"You're wound tighter than baling wire. You have been since I arrived."

No way was she going to admit that a good chunk of the tension wrapping her in steel cables stemmed as much from seeing him again after all these years as from the problems on the project.

"I've had a lot on my mind," she replied with magnificent understatement.

"It takes years to really master yoga techniques, but I could teach you a few of the basic chants and positions to help you relax."

Somehow Ellie suspected that getting down on the floor and sitting knee-to-knee with Jack would prove anything but relaxing. Part of her wanted to do it, if for no other reason than to test her ability to withstand the intimacy. Another part, more mature, more experienced— and more concerned with self-preservation—knew it was wiser to avoid temptation altogether.

"Maybe later," she said with a polite smile.

"It's your call."

"So what do we do now?"

"We wait until I get a report on the SUV."

Sitting twiddling her thumbs with Jack only a few feet

away didn't do any more to soothe Ellie's jangled nerves than getting down on the floor with him would have.

"Since we've got the time now," she suggested, "why don't I show you some of the digital images I took at the Alamo and at the excavation site?"

"Good enough."

"I'll boot up the computer. Drag over another chair."

More than agreeable to the diversion, Jack hooked a chair and hauled it across the room. It was obvious why she'd shied away from his offer to teach her some basic relaxation techniques. She was jumpy as a cat around him. Not a good situation. For either of them.

A tense, nerve-racked client could prove too demanding and distracting to the agent charged with his or her protection. Jack's job would be a whole lot easier if he could get her to relax a little. Not enough to let down her guard. Not so much she grew careless. Just enough that the tension didn't leave her drained of energy or alertness.

Still, he had to admit to a certain degree of relief that she'd turned down his offer. The mere thought of folding Ellie's knees and elbows and tucking her into the first position was enough to put a kink in Jack's gut. Breathing in her potent combination of sun-warmed female and cactus pear perfume didn't exactly unkink it, either. Scowling, he focused his attention on the long list of files that appeared on the computer screen.

"We'll start at the Alamo," Ellie said, dragging the cursor down the list. "I want to show you the shotgun I was talking about."

"The one the museum director refused to let us see this afternoon?"

"Yes. I think the armament images pick up right

about…" The cursor zipped down the indexed files. "Here."

Brilliant color flooded the seventeen-inch active matrix screen. There was Ellie in the Alamo's courtyard, smiling at the short, rotund director who gestured with almost obsequious delight to the entrance of the building housing his prized arms exhibit. Tourists crowded the courtyard around and behind them. One mugged at an unseen camera. Another waited with an expression of impatience for Ellie and Smith to move out of the way. But the shot of Smith's face was clear and unobstructed.

"I'd like to send a copy of this image to a security analyst," Jack said. "Can you flag it for later reference?"

"Yes, of course. But…" Looking uncomfortable, Ellie turned to face him. "Smith is just trying to protect his turf. I don't like the idea of invading his privacy or compiling a secret file on him. Or on any of my colleagues, for that matter."

"We won't be compiling secret files," he answered mildly. "Merely exploiting those that already exist. You'd be amazed at how much data is floating around out there about John Q. Public."

"Yes, but…"

"Flag the image, Ellie."

With obvious reluctance, she went to the menu at the top of the screen and bookmarked the file.

Jack leaned forward, peering intently at the images that flashed by after that. More shots in the courtyard. The interior of the museum, with room after room of weaponry of the type used during the siege of the Alamo. The special exhibits, not open to the public.

"For the most part," Ellie explained, "these are pieces that have yet to be authenticated. They were either excavated in or around the Alamo or donated by descendants of the combatants."

A click of the mouse brought up a vividly detailed image of a long-barreled rifle.

"This is a Brown Bess, so known because the troopers allowed the steel barrel to burnish and thus prevent glare that could distort their aim. This smooth-bore musket served as the standard infantry rifle carried by the British during the Napoleonic Wars. After the war, the Brits sold their excess inventories to armies all over the world."

"Including the Mexican army?"

"Yes, well, Mexico was still ruled by Spain then. When it won its independence, its army pretty well retained the standard-issue armaments. Historical documents indicate Santa Anna's infantry was armed with the Brown Bess. Most had been converted from muzzle-loading flintlock to percussion by then."

She flashed up another image of the musket and highlighted the differences in the firing mechanism.

"By contrast," she continued, "the Tejanos who fought at the Alamo carried weapons as diverse as the defenders themselves. They weren't members of a regular army, remember. They were settlers—farmers, ranchers, doctors, lawyers, ministers and slaves—all rebelling against Santa Anna's edicts dispossessing them of their rights under the former Constitution. They were also adventurers like Jim Bowie. Patriots like Davy Crockett and his Tennesseeans. Slaves, like Bowie's man Joe. They came armed with everything from Spanish blunderbusses to French muskets to long-barreled Kentucky hunting rifles, fowlers and shotguns."

She ran through a series of images, identifying each

weapon as it came up. When the image of a particular shotgun filled the screen, her voice took on an unmistakable hint of excitement.

"We know from various accounts that Travis arrived at the Alamo armed with a double-barrel shotgun like this one. He'd written several letters to Stephen Austin, advocating the gun as the standard weapon for the newly organized Texas cavalry. It didn't have the range of a long rifle, of course, but it provided lethal firepower at closer range."

With a click of the mouse, she rotated the three-dimensional image.

"Note the stock. It's made of curly maple, sometimes called tiger tail or fiddleback."

Another click zoomed in on the silver inlays on the side of the stock.

"See the gunsmith's mark on the butt plate? It traces to a gunsmith in Sparta, South Carolina."

Close at her shoulder, Jack could feel her controlled excitement straining to break loose as she returned to the index, scrolled down several pages and clicked on another file.

An outdoor scene was painted across the screen. A narrow creek twisted through the background, its banks almost lost amid a dense tangle of cottonwoods. A small group stood at the edge of one bank. Ellie and her team, Jack guessed, scrutinizing each of their faces in turn.

"Flag this photo, too," he instructed.

Her lips thinned, but she bookmarked the file. That done, she zoomed in on one of the objects lying on a piece of canvas at the team's feet. It was a shotgun, similar to the one she'd brought up on the screen moments ago. But this barrel sported a thick coat of rust.

The silver mountings had tarnished to black, and wood rot riddled the stock.

Ellie enlarged the image again. "Look at the butt plate on this one. The gunsmith's mark is hard to read, but it's there."

Jack leaned closer, squinting at the screen. "Looks like the same mark."

"It is. Did I mention the gunsmith lived in Sparta, South Carolina?"

"You did."

"And that William Barrett Travis grew up, went to school and opened his first law practice in Sparta?"

"No, You saved that bit for last." Grinning at her air of triumph, he played devil's advocate. "Okay. I'm a betting man. I'd say you could lay odds Travis carried a gun made for him by a smith in his hometown *into* the Alamo. But someone could have picked up the gun when Travis went down and carried it *out,* including any one of a thousand Mexican soldiers."

"As a matter of fact, Deaf Smith, a scout for Houston, captured a Mexican courier a month later using saddlebags monogrammed W.B. Travis."

She swiveled her chair sideways, her eyes alive with the enjoyment of an intellectual debate.

"Who's to say those saddlebags weren't taken off a horse found wandering beside a creek five miles south of the Alamo? We're, uh, hoping DNA testing will help…you know…confirm…"

She stuttered to a halt. They were close. Too close. Almost nose to nose. Jack could see the gold flecks in her eyes. Feel the warm wash of her breath on his skin. If he leaned forward an inch, just another inch…

Abruptly, he jerked back in his seat.

Ellie made the same move at precisely the same moment. Chagrin, dismay and a touch of irritation chased across her face. She opened her mouth, only to snap it shut again when the small device in Jack's shirt pocket gave off a high-pitched beep. He pulled out the phone, glanced at the digital display and swung to his feet.

"Renegade here. Go ahead, control."

Mackenzie Blair came on the line. "I ran the Expedition's tag. It's registered to a Mr. Harold Berger, 2224 River Drive, Austin, Texas."

"What have you got on the man?"

"Nothing much, seeing as Mr. Berger died two years ago. His wife reports that he never owned an Expedition, black or otherwise."

Jack's glance went to Ellie, still seated in front of her computer. The tension that had jolted through him seconds ago returned, doubled in intensity.

"Interesting," he muttered.

"Isn't it?" Mackenzie replied. "I did a screen of credit cards issued to Mr. H. Berger at his Austin address. I found an American Express and a Visa card, issued six months after he died."

Jack paced the sitting room, the phone tight against his ear. "What about the Expedition's driver? Did you get a picture of whoever emerged from the vehicle after it hit the truck?"

"Negative. He didn't get out of the vehicle. Not at the scene, anyway. He backed up, peeled off and squealed into a five-story parking garage about a mile away. Unfortunately, our spy satellites can't look through five layers of concrete, so I didn't get a shot of him exiting the vehicle. I contacted the San Antonio police and asked them to check it out. They found it abandoned and wiped clean of prints."

"Figures."

"I thought you should know one of their gun-sniffing dogs alerted on it. They found traces of gunpowder residue in the front seat."

Jack wasn't liking the sound of this. A stolen identity. Gunpowder residue. No prints. His gut told him they weren't talking a short, balding museum director here. Or a highly credentialed member of a scientific team. They were talking a pro.

"I'm going to send you a batch of digital images," he told Mackenzie. "We'll put names to the folks we know. I want you to run complete background checks on them and screen the rest for anyone or anything that looks suspicious."

"No problem."

"When can I expect results?"

"I don't know. How many images are we talking about?"

"Hang on." He cut to Ellie. "How many digital files have you got stored on the computer?"

"About six hundred."

"How many of those do you estimate include images of people?"

Her forehead wrinkled in concentration. "Live persons, I'd guess about two hundred. If you include the skeletal remains, another hundred or so."

"We'll start with those folks who are still breathing," Jack drawled. "Get ready to send copies."

Her brows soared. "Of all two hundred?"

"All two hundred."

"Two hundred!" OMEGA's chief of communications

gave a groan. "And here I actually planned to beat the traffic home tonight, order a pizza and sneak in a little tube time."

"Sorry, Mac. Have your pizza delivered to the Control center and charge it to me."

"Don't think I won't," she grumbled. "Okay, I'll stand by to receive. Tell Dr. Alazar to fire off those files when ready."

They started popping up on the Control Center's screens fifteen minutes later. Dr. Alazar had converted the images contained in each file to JPEG format, thank goodness. JPEG files took a little longer to load but produced clear, sharp pictures.

Mackenzie worked the easy ones first, those with flags indicating Dr. Alazar had identified the individuals in the photos. One by one, she fed the names into a program linked to financial, government, merchandising and criminal databases worldwide. Within moments, she'd know whether any of these scholarly looking individuals had ever been cited for jaywalking, rented porn movies or fudged on his income taxes.

"Anything I can help you with, chief?"

Dragging her eyes from the screen, Mackenzie glanced at her subordinate. John Alexander had put in at least five more years at OMEGA than she had but cheerfully cited his wife and four kids as reason for remaining as a mid-level tech with semiregular hours instead of moving up to the chief's job when it had come open. With all his experience, John was a good man to have at headquarters and a wizard in the field when it came to planting bugs that absolutely defied detection.

"As a matter of fact," Mackenzie said with a grin,

"I was just going to send the cavalry to search for you. Renegade sent us a tasking."

She got him started on the unflagged files. Since they didn't have IDs on the folks in those photos, John would have to scan the images one by one and run them through a program that captured each subject's skin, hair and eye color, estimated weight and height and any discernible scars, tattoos or disfigurements. The physical characteristics would then be fed into FBI, CIA and national crime information center computers for potential matches. Information extracted by this method wasn't as accurate as fingerprints, DNA sampling or retinal scans, but the matches ran something close to seventy percent. If nothing else, they provided a starting point.

"Geez," John muttered as he opened the first file. "There must be ten or twelve people in this shot. They look like a bunch of tourists. Do you want me to scan all of them?"

"Let me see."

Mackenzie rose out of her seat and bent over the console to view his screen. That was how Lightning found her when he strolled into the control center a moment later, a pizza carton held shoulder-high and balanced on his fingertips.

He paused for a moment, unabashedly enjoying the view. Most days, Nick looked, acted and thought like an American, but he'd been born in Cannes and possessed a Frenchman's esteem for the finer points of the female form. And Mackenzie's round, trim rear certainly qualified as fine.

Unfortunately, the same rules that prohibited an agent from becoming involved with a subject during operations applied in triplicate to OMEGA's director and his chief of communications. As long as one of his agents was in the field, Lightning couldn't allow himself or anyone on his staff to become distracted. Still, his eyes glinted with masculine appreciation as he made his way across the control center.

"This was just delivered downstairs," he said casually. "I assume you ordered it."

Mackenzie scrambled off the console. "If it's a sausage, double pepperoni and jalapeño special, I did."

Nick's eyes closed in something close to real pain. Dear Lord. Sausage, double pepperoni and jalapeño.

"Have you ever tasted pizza the way they make it along the Riviera?"

"My last cruise in the Navy was to the Med," Mackenzie informed him, lifting the lid to sniff appreciatively. "We dropped anchor just off San Remo. As I recall, the northern Italians doused everything, including their pizzas, in white cream sauce. Yuck!"

"A good cream sauce can be one of life's most decadent pleasures," Nick replied with a lift of one brow. "You'll have to let me take you to one of my restaurants sometime so you can sample it done right."

And that would be, Mackenzie thought, right about the time she developed a severe death wish.

She didn't play in Nick Jensen's league and knew it. If her short, disastrous marriage had taught her nothing else, it was to avoid smooth, handsome charmers like this one at all costs. Now if only she could keep her nerves from crawling around under her skin when he came to stand beside her.

"What are you working?"

"A request from Renegade. He's forwarded a series of images and asked for IDs and background checks."

Nick's blond brows drew together. In the blink of an eye, he transitioned from every woman's ultimate sex fantasy into OMEGA's cool, take-charge director.

"I don't like that business with the Expedition this afternoon. Give Renegade whatever he asked for and then some."

Whipping to attention, Mackenzie snapped him a salute. "Aye, aye, *sir!*"

He eyed her for a moment, his expression inscrutable. She held the exaggerated pose until he left the control center, then turned to her assistant with a wry grin.

"Guess that answers your question, John. Scan every warm body in those photos."

Chapter 5

Ellie's team returned to the hotel from the excavation site a little past six that evening. The first team member to rap on her door was a tall, rangy, twenty-something male with a shock of dark red hair. He looked surprised when Jack answered his knock. Even more surprised when Ellie introduced the newcomer as an old friend.

"Jack's in the security business," she explained. "He flew in this morning to help us deal with some of the nastiness we've been subject to recently. Jack, this is Eric Chapman. He's one of my graduate students at the University of New Mexico."

Chapman's handshake was casual enough, but Jack picked up on the subtle signals that only the male of the species would recognize. Unless he missed his guess, the kid had a bad case of the hots for his professor and didn't particularly like the idea of another man poaching on his territory.

"So are we having a team meeting tonight, Ellie?"

"Yes. Eight o'clock, here in my room. Pass the word along to the others, would you?"

"Sure. How about dinner? Want to go down on the river and grab a quick bite?" His glance drifted to Jack. "If you two don't have plans, that is."

"We do," Jack answered, preempting Ellie's response.

She threw him a cool look but didn't contradict him. "I'll see you at the meeting, Eric. Tell the team I'd like a complete report of the afternoon's activities."

"Right."

When the door closed behind him, Ellie returned to the sitting room and regarded Jack with a slight frown. "I think we better establish some ground rules here, the first being that you consult with me before making arbitrary decisions."

"Like where you'll have dinner and who you'll have it with?"

"Exactly."

"Were you really that eager to go back out in the heat and chow down with the kid?" he asked, suddenly, acutely curious.

The intensity of his need to know whether she reciprocated Chapman's interest both surprised and irritated Jack. Somehow, he'd just skidded right past professional into personal. Very personal. Why the hell should he care if Ellie was providing the kid with private instruction after hours? Unless their relationship impacted Jack's ability to protect her, it wasn't any of his business. Technically.

Ellie evidently shared that opinion. Her voice chilly, she set him straight.

"No, I'm not all that eager to go back out in the

heat. I simply prefer that you not make decisions for me. Or undermine my authority with my team," she added pointedly.

"Then you'd better make up your mind how you want me to interact with them. As your bodyguard or as old friend."

The chill didn't leave her eyes. If anything, it deepened. Toying with the silver bracelet banding her wrist, she debated her response.

Jack understood her hesitation. He'd piled up enough experience as an embassy guard and as a freelancer after leaving the Corps to appreciate how much take-charge executives hated to admit their fear. Hated, too, the helplessness that came with becoming a walking target. People in Ellie's position were used to calling the shots, not dodging them.

"Why don't we just stick with the explanation I gave Eric?" she suggested after a moment. "You *are* an old friend. You're also an expert in the security business. You flew in to assess the seriousness of the threats against me and my team."

"Fine. We'll go with that. Now, about dinner. Mind if we order room service? I want you to give me a complete rundown on your team members before they assemble."

Mackenzie would provide in-depth background dossiers once she'd screened the files they'd sent earlier, but Jack wanted Ellie's take. She'd worked with these people. She knew their strengths and weaknesses.

Now that she'd had time to think about it, she might also have some insight into whether one of them had deliberately leaked her controversial preliminary hypothesis to the media.

* * *

She didn't.

Flatly rejecting the idea that that a member of her group might be trying to sabotage the project, she spent the next two hours alternately detailing their impressive credentials and passionately defending them.

She hadn't changed much in that regard, Jack thought when he left her to prepare for the meeting and went next door to grab a quick shower. She'd defended a certain hardheaded Marine just as fiercely to her uncle… until Jack killed her arguments and her passion by rejecting both.

He'd taken the right stand, he told himself as he leaned against the shower tiles and lifted his face to the stinging needles. The *only* stand he could have taken, given the circumstances. Ellie had been so young then, with her whole future ahead of her. Jack couldn't see any future beyond being sent home in disgrace to face a possible court-martial, with all its potential for publicity.

The paparazzi would have eaten it up. The niece of the president of Mexico. An American Marine with a father whose name was a question mark and a mother who could be turning tricks in Detroit for all Jack knew. He'd never cared enough to track her down.

Then there were those searing, stolen hours in Mexico City. If the sensation-hungry media had gotten wind of those, the shinola would have hit the fan for sure. Jack had been insane to give in to Ellie's urgings, crazy to think he could give her release while holding back his own. On fire with impatience and need, she'd taken matters into her own hand. Literally. Even now, Jack could remember how her hot, eager fingers had brushed his aside and tugged at his zipper.

The memory slammed into him, hitting like a fist to the gut. He stiffened, felt himself get hard. Painfully hard. Cursing, he reached out and gave the shower knob a savage twist. Ice cold pellets shot into his skin from his neck to his knees. Gritting his teeth, Jack ducked his head under the stream.

His skin still prickled when he rapped on the connecting door fifteen minutes later. So did his temper, but he disguised his edginess behind a bland expression as Ellie's team began to congregate.

There were three besides Chapman. Orin Weaver, a noted forensic anthropologist who, Ellie explained, frequently acted as consultant for local, state and national law enforcement agencies. Janet Dawes-Hamilton, an archeologist from Baylor University. Sam Pierce, a field archeologist on the staff of the National Park Service, which owned the land on which the remains were discovered.

All except Chapman possessed Ph.D.s and an impressive string of published credits. All, including Chapman, eyed Jack with varying degrees of wariness. Like Ellie, they seemed to think the addition of a security specialist to their little group added a disturbing note of authenticity to the ugliness swirling around them.

"Sorry I didn't make it back to the site this afternoon," she said once the team had made themselves comfortable. "We were on our way but got involved in a high-speed chase through the streets of San Antonio."

The dry announcement produced the expected reactions. Gray-whiskered Orin Weaver blinked. The red-haired Chapman demanded to know if she was serious.

"Who was chasing whom?" Dr. Dawes-Hamilton asked in a cool, clipped voice.

"Person or persons unknown were after us," Jack answered. "We don't know who or why. Yet."

Pierce frowned and leaned forward, his callused hands clasped loosely between his knees. The National Park Service staffer didn't come across as a man out to harass his colleague into abandoning a dig or a particular theory, but Jack wasn't going to cut him any more slack than the others.

"I'll have to notify my headquarters about this latest incident," he said to Ellie. "They're already concerned over the adverse publicity our project has generated. One more mishap or media frenzy and...well..."

"The director may decide to shut down the dig," she finished for him. "With funding for future projects up before Congress," she explained to Jack, "he's nervous about offending the powerful Texas Congressional delegation."

"Not to mention the equally powerful President, who just happens to hail from the Lone Star state," Pierce put in dryly.

Jack kept to himself the fact that it was the President who'd requested OMEGA send an agent to San Antonio with instructions to protect Dr. Alazar and defuse the situation, if at all possible. From what he'd observed in the past eight hours or so, it might not be defusable.

Which is what he reported to Lightning later that night.

It was late, well past midnight. The meeting had broken up a little past ten. Jack waited until he was sure Ellie had settled into bed before slipping out to make his rounds. By the time he'd tested the hotel's security systems and satisfied himself as to the night staff's alertness, he was ready to drop into the rack himself.

First, though, he gave Lightning his initial take on the situation.

"It's not smelling right. I'll make contact with the San Antonio police tomorrow to see what they've turned up, but that business about the Expedition being wiped clean bothers me."

"Me, too."

"How's Mac coming on those IDs and background checks?"

"Last time I checked, her pizza had gone stone cold and she had some rather uncomplimentary things to say about you."

"I'll bet."

"Hopefully, she and her folks will complete the runs within twenty-four hours. I'll stay on her."

Jack cocked a brow at the odd note in Lightning's voice. He'd dodged bullets and side-stepped pit vipers with the man during one memorable mission but still couldn't quite read him. None of the OMEGA agents could. Jensen came across as smooth and sophisticated, yet no one who'd ever witnessed his skill with a knife would willingly go blade-to-blade with him.

After signing off, Jack set the phone on the nightstand beside his bed and unbuttoned his shirt. His thoughts drifted to the time Lightning had lived up to his name and saved Jack's life with one lethal throw. Jack had returned the favor some months later while helping take down a band of gunrunners. Grunting with satisfaction at the memory, he shucked his shirt and had just reached to unbuckle his ankle holster when he heard the crash of metal and shattering glass next door.

Ellie's cry came through the wall, sharp with distress. Jack hit the connecting door a half second later, swearing viciously when he found it locked on the other side. One brutal kick with his heel splintered the wood and sprang the lock, slamming the door against the wall.

He dived through. Hit the floor in a roll. Came up in a crouch, the blue steel automatic aimed squarely at the woman who shrieked and stumbled back a few steps.

"Jack! Good God!"

Her obvious astonishment eased his blood-pumping tension a fraction. Only a fraction. Heart hammering, Jack swung in a full circle. There was no one else in the room. Only then did he straighten and record two separate impressions.

The first was an overturned room service tray, spilling the dinner Ellie had hardly touched across the carpet.

The second was her sleep shirt.

At least, that's what Jack assumed it was. It looked like a man's white cotton T-shirt, cut off a good six inches above the skimpiest damned pair of bikini briefs he'd ever laid eyes on. If that bite-size bit of nylon and lace wasn't a thong, it was close enough to raise an instant sweat on his palms.

Which, he realized belatedly, still gripped the automatic.

Swinging the barrel away from Ellie's midsection, he thumbed the safety. His breath came fast and hard through his nostrils, and his voice was distinctly unfriendly when he demanded to know what the hell she was doing.

"I was hungry," she fired back, shaken but recovering fast. "I intended to finish the salad I didn't eat earlier and tipped over the tray. I'm sorry I woke you."

Her stiff apology didn't cut it.

"I'm not talking about the damned tray! Why did you lock the door?"

His snarl snapped her chin up. Lips thinning, she speared a glance at the shattered wood.

"I wasn't afraid you were going to pay me a late-night visit and jump my bones, if that's what you're thinking."

He wasn't. Now that she'd planted the idea, though, he knew he'd have to pry it out of his head with a crow-bar. Along with the all-too-vivid image of her bare belly and long, slender flanks.

"Evidently an unlocked door is one of those ground rules we didn't cover," she said stiffly. "Maybe we'd better sit down and spell them all out."

Yeah. Right. With Jack stripped down to the waist and her in a scrap of nylon and last.

Not hardly!

"We'll spell them out tomorrow. For tonight, leave the door propped shut. And for God's sake, don't trip over any more trays."

"I'll do my best."

The sarcasm didn't win her any points. Shooting an evil look across the room, Jack made sure the dead bolt on the door to her suite was set, checked the window locks once more and retreated. His side of the connecting door closed with a small thud. A few seconds later, the shattered door on her side hit with a bang.

He was up before dawn the next morning. Showered and shaved, he took perverse pleasure in rapping on the door just past seven.

Some moments later, Ellie yanked it open. She'd pulled a short silk robe over her T-shirt, thank God. Her hair spilled over her shoulders in a rumpled free fall. Sleep added a hoarse note to her voice when she croaked at him.

"What?"

"I'm going to make a quick visit to the San Antonio police department. Don't leave the hotel until I get back."

Still groggy, Ellie grunted an assent.

Never a morning person, she felt about as fresh and perky as last week's leftovers. Her eyelids scraped like sandpaper. Her mouth had that cottony fuzz that cried for Scope. The fact that Jack was wide awake, showered and looking lean and tough in snug jeans and a black knit shirt that stretched taut across his shoulders only added to her disgruntlement.

As she closed the door behind Jack, though, she would have traded mouthwash and toothpaste *and* half her next month's salary for a cup of black coffee. She considered calling room service to order a pot, but the prospect of explaining the broken dishes and shattered connecting door nixed that notion. Any more damage to their historic hotel and the Mengers' management would probably call in the sheriff to escort her out of town.

Shaking her head, Ellie padded into the bathroom and turned the shower to full blast. Steam soon wreathed the room. After shedding her robe and undies, Ellie stepped into the stall and waited for the hot jets to work their restorative magic.

By the time Jack returned, she was dressed in a fresh pair of khaki shorts, a tan tank and a sleeveless khaki vest that came equipped with a half dozen handy pockets. With her hair tucked under a ball cap and a thick slathering of insect repellent coating all exposed areas of skin, she once again felt ready to take on all comers.

Jack included.

Chapter 6

"The police don't have anything on the Expedition yet."

Ellie accepted Jack's terse report with a nod. After her less than positive experience with the detective investigating her ransacked hotel room and the threats scrawled across her mirror, she hadn't really expected much.

"Have you had breakfast?" she asked, trying to tamp down her impatience to get out to the site. She'd already lost almost a whole day of work. With the National Park Service director waffling over the funding for the project, she didn't want to lose any more.

"I downed a cup of coffee and a breakfast burrito while I was waiting for Detective Harris to put in an appearance at the precinct," Jack replied. "How about you?"

"I'll grab some coffee on our way through the lobby."

"You need more than that."

"That's all I ever have in the mornings."

Draping her heavy canvas bag over her shoulder, Ellie waited for him to join her at the door. Jack went out first, armed the anti-intrusion devices he'd installed and followed her down the hall.

Thankfully, the hotel provided complimentary coffee for its guests. Downing the hazelnut blend in quick, grateful gulps from a cardboard cup, Ellie settled into the passenger seat of Jack's rented Cherokee. This time, the drive down Mission Trail proved uneventful. No dusty SUVs with darkened windows chasing after them. No high-speed twists and turns. Only Ellie and Jack, thigh-to-thigh in the close confines of the rental vehicle.

By the time they pulled into the parking lot of Mission San Jose, she felt the need to put some immediate distance between her and the hard, muscled contours of his body.

"We could drive around to the dig," she informed him, shouldering open her door, "but I thought you might want to see the mission compound first. It'll give you a better sense of what the Alamo was like back at the time of the siege."

Slinging her canvas field bag over one shoulder, Ellie led the way down a gravel path. As always, Mission San Jose's tranquil setting and superb restoration thrilled both the historian and the aesthete in her. San Jose had been the largest and most active of the Texas religious settlements and, in her considered opinion, richly deserved its title as the Queen of the Missions.

The church boasted a large cupola dome, an exquisitely ornamented façade and the beautiful but curiously misnamed Rose Window, with elaborate carvings not of flowers but pomegranates. A rectangular granary with an arched roof dominated the opposite side of the compound from the church. The walls surrounding both were twelve feet thick, a potent reminder that these missions served secular as well as religious purposes.

"San Jose was founded in seventeen twenty," Ellie told Jack, their boots crunching the gravel path in a synchronized beat. "Just a few years after the Alamo. Like the other Texas missions, its purpose was to convert the local population to Catholicism, extend Spanish civilization in the New World and buttress the northern frontiers. At one time, the mission housed a population of more than three hundred priests, soldiers and Coahuiltecan Indians."

Signs spaced at intervals on the path pointed to various points of interest, including the park headquarters and gift shop. Ellie steered Jack past the main structures toward a gate in the far wall.

"The Indians farmed the surrounding countryside, producing corn, beans, potatoes, sugar cane and cotton, among other crops. They also maintained large herds of cattle, sheep and goats. Naturally, a rich settlement like this made for an irresistible target for hostile raids. When the Apache or Comanche threatened, the residents would drive their livestock inside the compound and hunker down behind San Jose's massive walls. Reportedly, they were never breached."

"Unlike those at the Alamo," Jack commented.

"Also unlike the Alamo, San Jose is still an active Catholic parish. Masses are said in the church, and I'm told it's a popular spot for weddings. The diocese maintains the church, and the National Park Service is responsible for the other structures and the outlying grounds."

Once through the small gate, they faced a wide,

grassy field banded on three sides by a split rail fence. A twisting line of cottonwoods defined the fourth. As Jack and Ellie crossed the field toward the tree-lined creek, grasshoppers buzzed in the early morning heat and leaped out of their way. About halfway across the grassy field Ellie pointed out a series of small squares dug in the earth. Staked strands of wire surrounded each square. Red tags dangled from the wire.

"We've been using metal detectors to scan this field. Each of those tags marks a spot where we found spent cartridge shells. Most of the shells have rifling marks which suggest they were fired from Brown Besses similar to those used by the Mexican army. We also found several we think were fired by the shotgun we excavated down by the creek. We won't know for sure until we run a full ballistics analysis."

She tried to keep her voice properly dispassionate, but the thrill of discovery added a vibrancy she couldn't quite disguise. "Notice how those digs run in almost a straight line from north to south?"

Jack took a quick fix on the sun and nodded. Carefully, Ellie emphasized her point.

"The trail of expended bullets extends from the far corner of the Mission San Jose Park almost to the creek."

"By extrapolation," he said slowly, picking up on her lead, "from the Alamo to this spot five miles south, where a desperate defender might have raced for the tangle of trees to escape his pursuers, firing as he rode."

She beamed at him. "Exactly!"

His instant grasp of the significance of those small digs didn't surprise her. Jack Carstairs was no dummy.

Except, she amended, when it came to his long-ago relationship with a passionate nineteen-year-old.

"The bullets track right to the spot where the skeletal remains were found," she related.

"Who found them?"

"The bullets or the bones?"

"The bones."

"A couple of boys. They snuck out of Sunday Mass and slipped away to play by the creek. When they spotted the bones, they ran yelling for their mom."

"Probably had nightmares for a month after that."

"I don't think so," Ellie replied, laughing. "I saw the news cam videotapes taken right after the find. The boys mugged like mad for the cameras. They seemed to think they'd landed right in the middle of a grand adventure. Even more so after the police and ME determined from the artifacts found with the bones that the find had historical significance."

"Is that when you were called in?"

"Yep. Because I'd done so much work for and with the National Park Service, the director contacted me and asked me to head up the team. He hasn't said so," she added with a wry grin, "but I'm pretty sure he's regretting his choice."

They were almost to the creek when Eric Chapman stepped out of the shadows and into the blazing sunlight. A metal detector extended from his left arm like a long, mechanical claw. When he spotted Ellie, a look of profound relief crossed his face.

"Hey, boss lady. You got here just in time."

"Uh-oh. What's up?"

"Another TV reporter, with cameraman in tow. Sam's trying his best to fob her off with the press release we hammered out last night, but she wants down and dirty details."

Ellie threw a glance at the trees. Just what she needed to start her day. A camera crew and more adverse publicity. Swallowing a sigh, she eyed the detector strapped to Eric's arm.

"We've pretty well covered this open field. Work the grids closer in to the mission today."

"Will do."

Jack's knowledge of metal detectors was thin, at best, but even with his limited frame of reference, he could tell the piece of equipment cuffed to Chapman's arm was no ordinary treasure hunter's toy.

"It's my own design," Ellie told him, noting the direction of his gaze. "Remember that little black box that contained the database I developed after those summers at Glorietta Pass?"

"Yes."

"It's a duplicate of the one that fits right here, on the neck of the metal dectector."

She signaled Chapman to raise the instrument for Jack's inspection. Grunting, the grad student lifted the heavy wand to waist level.

"I call this baby Discoverer Two," she said with a touch of proprietary pride. "Discoverer One was the prototype."

Like most metal sweepers, Discoverer came with a large, flat disk at the bottom end of its arm. At the top, where the wearer could comfortably read it, sat the computerized brain box Ellie referred to.

"One ping gives you a good idea of what you've found," Chapman added. "A low tone indicates iron, gold and nickel. A medium tone, lighter metals like aluminum pull tabs and zinc. Brass, copper and silver return a high pitch."

"In addition to the type of metal found," Ellie elaborated, "Discoverer will tell you how deep it's buried. The built-in computer also uses the signal return to paint a picture of the object here on this little screen. When we lock on something that looks, sounds and smells like a shell casing, the preprogrammed data from my prior research gives us a pretty good indication what type."

His arm sagging with the weight of the wand, Chapman waited patiently for her to finish describing some of the more technical aspects of the equipment. Once the grad student had trotted off to begin his sweeps, Ellie drew in a deep breath, braced herself and plunged into the shade of the cottonwoods.

The rest of her crew was there, doing their best to dodge the questions of a news reporter with a waist-length curtain of black hair and an air of dogged inquisitiveness. Sam Pierce stood solidly in front of the camera and greeted Ellie's arrival with barely disguised relief.

"Here's Dr. Alazar now. She can give you a better estimate of when we'll release our findings."

Jack stepped to the side and out of the picture as the camera locked onto Ellie.

"Dr. Alazar. Deborah Li, Channel Six news. We understand you've sent bits of bone from the remains you recovered to the police lab for DNA sampling."

"That's correct."

"When will you have the results?"

"Hopefully, by the end of the week."

"Then you're going to run a match against a sample from one of William Travis's descendents?"

"A great-great-grandniece has volunteered a sample," she confirmed. "So have descendents of several other Alamo defenders."

After all the bad press, Ellie only hoped the donors would still provide the samples as promised. Several had already voiced doubts. She didn't share that bit of information with the reporter, however.

"What if there's no match?" Li asked. "Pardon the pun, but won't that shoot your theory that the remains might belong to William Barrett Travis all to heck?"

"At this point, it's only a theory," she reminded the reporter with unruffled calm. "One of several we're working. If you like, I'll show you around the site. There's not much to see at this point, though," she warned. "We're almost finished here. By next week, we hope to switch from field to full laboratory mode."

As curious as the reporter, Jack trailed along. It was quite an operation, he discovered. Two vans held racks for the team's equipment, which included an impressive array of computers, field microscopes, digital imaging cameras and chemicals for sampling soil, wood and metal fragments. The excavation site was cut into the bank of the creek. It formed a flat, level bed where what looked like a hundred or so cubic yards of mud and debris had been removed bit by careful bit.

"As I said, there not much to see at this point. The major artifacts we recovered have been photographed, catalogued and shipped to Baylor University, where Dr. Dawes-Hamilton and her assistants will complete the authentication process. The skeletal remains were transported to the San Antonio morgue pending DNA identification and possible burial by family. If we make no ID, the bishop of the diocese has agreed they should be buried here, in San Jose's old mission cemetery."

At this point, Ellie explained, the team was working the final phase of on-site activity. Reconfirming exact coordinates of the finds. Digging additional exploratory sites up and downstream to make sure they hadn't missed any artifacts. Making last, expanded sweeps with the metal detector.

Jack found the excavations fascinating, the decisive authority Ellie projected even more so. She was at once coolly professional and vibrantly passionate about her work. She never allowed the reporter to throw her off stride or pull information she preferred not to give.

When the news crew departed a half hour later, her skin wore a pearly sheen of perspiration and her boots were caked with mud, but no one viewing her on the news tonight could doubt her credentials or the intellectual honesty she brought to the project.

Not that either would protect her from a nut bent on safeguarding his preferred version of history. Or a professional hired for the same purpose.

His senses on full alert, Jack turned his attention to the group who remained after the TV crew departed. In addition to the professional members of the team, a number of amateur archeologists, high school students and interested volunteers had turned out to help.

"We don't have as many volunteers as we did at the start of the project," Ellie explained. "As a result of the adverse publicity, a number have defected."

Those who hadn't were already hard at work. As Jack soon discovered, even the last stages of fieldwork involved labor-intensive effort. He wasn't quite sure how Ellie roped him into it, but by mid-morning he was up to his knees in creek mud, digging an exploratory site alongside Sam Pierce and a fresh-faced sophomore.

Later that afternoon, he tried a turn with the metal detector. It took a few swipes to get into a smooth rhythm, keeping the bottom flat to the ground and the swing in a controlled arc. It also took muscle power. The contraption weighed only about eight or ten pounds, but felt more like twenty or thirty after Jack had covered the length of the compound's south wall a half dozen times.

True to Eric Chapman's predictions, the digital displays lit up like fireworks at any hint of metal. The number and variety of objects buried beneath the earth astounded Jack. Discoverer Two hit on bridle bits, nails and barrel hoops from the nineteenth century, beer cans, bobby pins and dimes from the twentieth, and just about everything in between. His prize find was a blackened, dented silver disk.

"It's a concho," Ellie informed him after scrutinizing the object. "From the size of it, I'd say it's most likely off a bridle or sombrero. The concho was the decoration of choice on hats favored by both Mexicans and Tejanos. At least until a New Jersey hatter by the name of Stetson traveled west for his health and produced his version of the ten-gallon hat."

"I always wondered if those things really held ten gallons," Jack mused, recalling once again the Westerns he'd seen, where scouts and cowboys poured precious canteen water into their hats for their panting ponies.

Smiling, Ellie shook her head. "Only about three, actually, although that had nothing to do with the name. Gallon is a derivation of the Spanish word *galon,* which means braid. A ten-gallon hat simply refers to the amount of braiding around the brim."

"Another Hollywood myth shot down in flames," Jack muttered, shaking his head as she added the metal disk to the inventory of historical artifacts to be turned over to the National Park Service.

All too aware that they were working on borrowed time, the team remained at the dig until seven that evening. Once back at the hotel, Ellie conducted a quick wrap-up before sending her crew off to hit the showers and find dinner.

Jack was ready for both. When he knocked on the connecting door a half hour later, his stomach rumbled like a '56 Chevy with bad pipes. His hunger took on a whole different edge, however, when Ellie answered his knock. She'd changed into a long, gauzy flowered skirt in shades of green and lavender, topped by a lilac scoop-necked top. A silver crucifix on a thin chain circled her neck. Silver hoops dangled from her ears. As always, Jack noted with a kick to his gut, the bracelet he'd given her so many years ago banded her wrist.

But it was her hair that drew his gaze. She'd caught it back with combs at either temple and left the still damp, shining mass to tumble down her back, the way she used to when they'd first met.

Like hard right jabs, the memories hit him. Of tugging those combs free. Burying his face in that fragrant mass. Tunneling his fingers through the silky curtain to bring her mouth down to his.

Christ!

Clenching his fists, Jack managed to ask in a relatively normal voice where she wanted to have dinner.

"After last night's fiasco with room service, I suggest we go downstairs. Or better yet, out on the Riverwalk. I'll take you to my favorite Mexican restaurant. It's only a block away."

"Lead the way."

As Ellie had indicated, Casa del Rio was only a short walk from the hotel. They could have covered the distance in five minutes if not for the crowds jamming the popular Riverwalk.

"I've never seen it this packed," she told Jack as they took the stairs down to the river and plunged into the ebb and flow.

Crowded was an understatement. Tourists strolled shoulder-to-shoulder along the stone walks lining both sides of the placid green waterway. Many toted plastic drink cups and called to friends on the opposite side of river, pitching their voices to be heard over the music that spilled from the hotels and outdoor restaurants crowding the flagstone walk. A good number of the revelers wore wide-brimmed sombreros. Unlike the hats Jack and Ellie had discussed only this afternoon, these were cheap straw imitations decorated with red and green pom-poms instead of leather braid or silver conchos.

"There must be a convention in town," Ellie murmured, surveying the sea of straw.

"There is."

The comment came from a tourist decked out in an ankle-length red sundress and one of the distinctive sombreros. Dipping her head, she pointed to the lettering on the high-peaked crown.

"The American Travel Agents Association annual convention. Tonight's our big opening gala. You'll see the fireworks shooting up from the convention center later on."

Smiling her thanks, Ellie wedged sideways to make way for the woman and her companions. The movement brought her close to the river. Too close. Her heel caught on the edge.

"Careful!"

Jack's hand whipped out and caught her arm. He spun her away from the murky water. She landed awkwardly against his chest. Fingers splayed against his shirtfront, she blinked at him.

Ellie had never believed the silly cliché about time standing still, but for some reason the moment seemed to stretch forever. She could feel Jack's heat and the strong, steady beat of his heart under her fingertips. Her pulse skipped a beat, two, then drummed like thunder in her ears.

She didn't expect the hunger that leaped up and grabbed her by the throat. Wasn't prepared for it. Yet everything in her burst into a fever of need.

"Jack…"

He must have felt it, too. His muscles tensed. The arm he'd slipped around her waist to steady her tightened to a steel band. Ellie strained against him, aching, wanting, only to crash back to reality at the sound of a chuckle.

"Excuse us, folks. Hate to intrude on your little tête-à-tête, but we need to get by. Don't want to be late for the opening gala."

A glance over her shoulder showed a circle of grinning travel agents. Her cheeks warming, Ellie pulled out of Jack's arms. "Sorry."

"No apologies necessary, sweetie!" The woman in the red knit sundress laughed and let her gaze drift over Jack with unabashed feminine appreciation. "If a world-class hottie looked as hungry for me as this one just did for you, I sure as heck wouldn't be sorry."

Her glance dropped to Ellie's left hand. Grinning, she dug into her straw tote.

"Here's my card. Give me a call when you two are ready to make it legal, and I'll get you a heck of a deal on a honeymoon package."

Ellie's cheeks went from warm to downright hot as she accepted the card the woman pressed on her and slipped it into her skirt pocket. Mute, she steered through the crowds toward the restaurant.

Jack kept his jaw clamped shut and his hand on Ellie's arm. *Not* because he couldn't bring himself to let her go. And certainly not because the press of her body against his for those brief moments had set spark to a fire in his belly he was doing his damnedest to douse.

The fact was he didn't like these crowds. Liked even less the advantage the restaurants and hotels on either side of the walkway gave a shooter. Anyone could check into the Hyatt or Hilton. Take a room on one of the upper floors. Line up a clear shot at the merrymakers flowing by below. His nerves crawling, Jack tucked Ellie closer to his side. She frowned when their hips bumped a time or two, but said nothing.

The restaurant she'd selected didn't provide any better cover. Case del Rio sat right on a bend of the river, its open-air patio a kaleidoscope of umbrellas and colored lights strung from tree to tree.

"Let's eat inside," Jack muttered, guiding Ellie away from the exposed patio and into the air-conditioned interior. Only after the waiter had showed them to a booth set well away from the windows and he'd scoped out the clientele did he allow his shoulders to slump against the back of the booth.

Ellie's brown eyes met his. He knew she'd felt it, too. The way his muscles leaped under her touch. The instant heat every time they came in contact. He read the question in her eyes but didn't have an answer that would satisfy either one of them. He thought he caught a flash of disappointment, maybe even regret, before she picked up the menu and used it as a shield between them.

"I'll have combination number three," she told the waiter who plopped down a basket of chips and cups of salsa. "And a margarita."

"Same here," Jack said, tossing aside his menu. "No margarita, though. Just water."

"Just water?" Ellie echoed when the waiter departed. "As I recall, your drink of choice used to be an icy cold Corona."

"It still is, but not while I'm on duty."

"That's right." Frowning, she stabbed a chip into the salsa. "How could I forget? You're on duty."

The word hung between them, as solid as a brick wall and twice as impenetrable. In her last, furious tirade all those years ago, Ellie had accused him of caring more about the Corps than he did about her. Of letting his sense of duty take precedence over what they had together. What they could have together.

Like an uninvited guest who wouldn't take the hint and leave, the echoes of that ugly argument stayed at the table all through the meal. As a result, conversation was stilted, at best. Ellie shook her head when the waiter asked if she wanted another margarita, then abruptly changed her mind.

By the time she slurped up the last of her drink and they left the restaurant, dusk had softened to night, and colored lights twinkled all along the river. The late hour hadn't diminished the foot traffic. If anything, the crowds had increased. Barges filled with sightseers jammed hip-to-hip floated over the dark water. From another barge, a mariachi band poured a soaring rendition of "Una Paloma Blanca" into the night. The music drew cheers and applause from the appreciative crowd, most of whom, Jack noted, sported straw sombreros. The travel agents had descended on the Riverwalk en masse.

His muscles tensed in instinctive response to the crowd. Throngs like this could provide an excellent protective shield. Conversely, they could also mask the approach of unfriendlies.

Jack kept Ellie on the inside, away from the river, and forged a path toward the stairs leading up to street level. They were just a few feet from the steps when he heard a muted pop and the crack of rock splintering.

He took Ellie down in one swift lunge, covering her body with his on the way down. Before they hit the ground, the night exploded around them.

Chapter 7

Pinning Ellie to the stone, Jack yanked out his automatic and twisted around. In the heart-pounding seconds that followed, he registered the startled faces of tourists. The lights strung through the trees. The deafening booms that exploded into starbursts of glittering red and green.

"Hey!" one of the bystanders exclaimed over the flashes of color. "What the heck do you think you're doing?"

With a snarl, Jack whipped his weapon toward the source of the shout. The man's face went chalk white beneath his sombrero. Stumbling against his companions, he jerked up both palms.

"Take it easy, pal! Take it easy!"

There was another earsplitting series of pops. Red and green balloons pinwheeled through the sky. As the sound faded, Ellie gasped and wiggled under the dead weight pinning her to the flagstones.

"What's going on?"

Jack didn't take his eyes from the crowd. "I heard a gunshot."

"That—that was the fireworks," the white-faced travel agent stuttered, his hands still high. "Really, pal, all you heard was the fireworks."

As if to add emphasis to his nervous explanation, another series of booms exploded right overhead. Rockets of brilliant red and green shot into the night sky, trailing long, sparkling tails. A chorus of oohs and ahs rose from the spectators not engaged in the small drama occurring at the foot of the stairs.

"Jack." Ellie panted, wiggling frantically. "Please! I can't breathe."

He had to get her out of here. The single thought hammered in Jack's head. He rolled to his feet, the automatic tight against his thigh. Wrapping his free hand around Ellie's arm, he hauled her up.

The travel agent and his friends gaped as Jack hustled Ellie up the stone stairs. She was panting when they gained street level and decidedly unhappy when they arrived at the Menger. While the elevator whizzed them upward, she collapsed against the brass cage.

"That's twice now you've pulled that gun and scared the dickens out of me. Tell me you haven't gone all Rambo since leaving the Marines."

"I haven't gone all Rambo."

"Then what's with the rather dramatic reaction to a few fireworks?"

"I recognize the sound of a gunshot fired from a silenced weapon when I hear it."

Ellie opened her mouth, snapped it shut again. She didn't say a word during the walk down the hall to her room or while Jack checked the intrusion detection devices he'd set when they left the hotel. Satisfied no one had been in the rooms, he turned to face her.

She stood in the middle of the room, hugging her crossed arms. Her face and throat showed a decided pallor against the soft lilac of her top.

"If you did hear a gunshot," she said slowly, "it was timed perfectly to go off with the fireworks."

"That's what I'm thinking."

"So if there *was* a shooter, he's not some nutcase trying to scare me away." A shudder rippled down her body. Her fingers dug into her arms, making white marks in the tanned skin. "He's planning each move."

As much as Jack wanted to shield her from the ugly suspicions he'd been harboring for the past twenty-four hours, he knew he had to level with her. She wasn't the young girl he'd once dreamed of keeping safe and warm in his arms. She was Dr. Elena Maria Alazar, the woman he'd been sent to protect. As such, she had to understand the nature of the threat as he perceived it.

"I think we're dealing with a pro, Ellie. Someone who knows exactly what he's doing."

Briefly, he related the information he'd received from Mackenzie yesterday. Ellie's eyes narrowed as he detailed the assumed identity, the gunpowder residue, the Expedition carefully wiped clean of all prints.

"Why didn't you tell me all this before now?"

"I should have," he admitted.

She was furious, as she had every right to be. Eyes spitting fire, she marched up to him and jabbed a blunt-tipped finger into his chest.

"I'd suggest you remember who hired you, Carstairs."

"Your uncle, I was told."

"Wrong!" Her finger struck again. "Uncle Eduardo insisted I have a bodyguard. I insisted it be you."

"You were behind this job?" His hand closed over hers, stilling it before she could take another jab. "Why?"

"I felt guilty."

"Guilty?" That threw him. "For what?"

"For causing you to be sent home in disgrace," she snapped. "For ruining your military career. For making you start over as a hired hand with some obscure company no one's ever heard of."

Jack couldn't tell her OMEGA worked very hard at remaining obscure. He was still absorbing the fact that Ellie had carried around a load of guilt all these years almost equal to his own.

"None of what happened was your fault," he countered fiercely. "I knew the risks when I took you to bed. Given the same circumstances, I'd do it again. In a heartbeat."

Her breath caught. She stared at him, her anger suspended, her hand fisting into a tight ball under his.

"What about—?"

She stopped. Drew her tongue along her lower lip. Forced out a ragged question.

"What about *these* circumstances?"

Jack barely swallowed his groan. He wanted her. God, he wanted her! The hunger was like a wild beast, clawing at his insides to get out.

This time there was more at stake than his career and her reputation, though. This time, her life might well depend on his ability to remain detached and alert.

"As you said, I'd best remember I'm a hired hand. I was sent here to protect you, Ellie."

Disgust flickered in her eyes. Or was it disappointment? Before Jack could decide, she yanked her hand free of his.

"We've already had this discussion."

"Yes, we have."

"Do you have anything else to tell me about this phantom who may or may not be stalking me?"

"I wish I did."

She nodded. One quick, regal dip of her chin. "Then if you'll excuse me, I have work to do."

Jack took the hint and beat an orderly retreat. Somehow, he'd come out on the losing end of this discussion.

Ellie paced the sitting room, glaring at the computer sitting on the table, at the stacks of field notes waiting for review, at the closed connecting doors. Despite her icy request that Jack make himself scarce, work was the farthest thing from her mind at the moment.

What was the matter with her! Hadn't she learned her lesson nine years ago? Why in the world was she twisting herself into knots like this?

Over Jack Carstairs, for pity's sake! The stubborn Marine who'd considered her too young, too starry-eyed, to know her own mind. The noble idiot who'd walked away from her. The man who'd already broken her heart once.

If she let him do it again, she'd be a fool! A total, one-hundred-percent, feather-headed fool!

No way was she giving in to the heat that had flamed under her skin at his touch. *Or* following up on his startling admission that he'd take her to bed again in a heartbeat, given the same circumstances.

She had herself convinced, completely convinced, until she shoved her hands in the pockets of her skirt and felt a slip of pasteboard. Her throat tightening, she pulled out the business card the travel agent had pressed on her earlier. She stared at the embossed printing until it blurred. Crumpling the card in her fist, she whirled, crossed the room and yanked open the connecting doors.

Jack was standing at the window, hands shoved in his back pockets, staring out at the darkness. Her abrupt entrance spun him around.

"I have to know." She bit the words out. "Did you ever love me?"

"What?"

"Tell me, dammit. Did you love me?"

So bad, he'd hurt with it. In every inch of his body. Jack couldn't admit the truth then. And it was too late now. Far too late.

"What difference does it make?" he said quietly. "What's done is done."

"Bull!" She flared up, as fiery and passionate as the girl he'd once known. "It makes all the difference in the world. I want to know. I need to know."

"What you need is to go back to your room before one of us says something we might regret."

"Like what?" She advanced on him, her chin tipped to an angle he recognized all too well. "That we still want each other? That you still get hard and I still get hot every time we bump knees or hips or elbows?"

"Ellie, for Christ's sake!"

"What? Are you worried I'll bring up the fact that you wanted to kiss me down there on the river before dinner? Or admit that I *ached* for you to do it?"

She stopped in front of him. Her breasts rose and fell

under the scoop-necked top. A pulse beat wildly in one side of her throat.

"I'm still aching, Jack."

Her total honesty humbled him, just as it had nine years ago. She held nothing back. She never had. Desire jolted into him, as hot and fierce as any he'd ever felt for her. He went rigid, fighting the shock, fighting himself.

Ellie couldn't miss his reaction. Triumph leaped into her eyes. She moved closer, determined to get at the truth whether he wanted it out or not.

"I have to know."

She raised her arms, slid them around his neck. Her breasts flattened against his chest. Her hips canted, pressing her belly into the bulge that pushed hard and hurting against his zipper.

"Did you love me?"

He couldn't lie to her. He'd never lied to her. But neither could he fully articulate the tangle of emotions she'd roused in him. He hesitated for long moments, then offered her the only answer he could.

"I would have laid down my life for you."

Her throat closed. He *had* laid down his life for her. The only real life he'd ever known. At the same time, he'd spurned her offer to do the same.

"But you wouldn't let me sacrifice my reputation or my career for you."

His jaw locked. "That was different."

She stared at him, torn between a sharp, sudden urge to whack him alongside the head and the overwhelming need to kiss the mule-headed stubbornness right off his face.

She waffled between the contradictory impulses for several moments before muttering a curse that would have shocked her students and her colleagues. Tightening her arms, she hauled herself up on her toes and fastened her mouth on his.

Jack stood stiff and unyielding under her assault, but he didn't break the contact. He didn't even *try* to break the contact. Her pulse leaping, Ellie angled her head to fit her mouth more fully against his.

Memories of other nights and other kisses exploded inside her head. Deliberately she blanked her mind and concentrated fiercely on this moment.

When she finally pulled away, Jack might have been carved from gray Texas granite. His jaw was set. The cords in his neck stood out in stark relief. His blue eyes were dark, shuttered, hiding his thoughts.

Ellie felt the first twinge of remorse, followed swiftly by self-disgust. She'd done it again! Thrown herself at the man. Shame coursed through her, but pride kept her head high as she offered a stiff apology.

"I'm sorry, Jack. That was stupid of me. I had no business complicating an already awkward situation."

His stony silence signaled complete agreement.

Ellie forced a smile. "You'd think I'd have learned to exercise some restraint in nine years."

Actually, she had. She'd acquired a good deal of patience and restraint. She'd dated a fair number of men over the years. Had even thought she could fall in love with one or two. Yet she'd never *attacked* any of them.

Only Jack.

God, she was such a fool!

"I'm sorry," she whispered once again.

Writhing inside, she kept the smile plastered on her face and her chin high as she turned and headed for the connecting doors.

Let her walk.

The words thundered in Jack's head. He had to let her walk. If his years of experience as an undercover operative hadn't already underscored the need to maintain a clear head, Lightning had laid the issue square on the line. Jack was to keep his mind on the mission and his hands off Ellie. Period. End of discussion.

She got one step, maybe two, before he made a sound halfway between a snarl and a curse and went after her. Snagging her elbow, he yanked her around.

"We can both be sorry."

The force of his kiss bent her backward. For a moment, Ellie thought her spine might crack. Recovering from her startled surprise, she threw her arms around his neck and fit her body to his.

Unleashed, his hunger was like a live, ravaging beast. It devoured Ellie. Consumed her. Thrilled her to her core.

This was a different Jack, she thought on a rush of wild excitement. Not the tender, passionate lover who'd teased and tormented her. Not the skilled tutor who'd schooled her in pleasures she'd never imagined. This Jack made no attempt to disguise what he wanted.

Ellie.

Naked.

Under him.

Afterward, she could never say who dragged whom down to the plush carpet. All she knew was that she was on fire by the time they hit. Every inch of her body flamed with heat. The areas Jack paid special, savage attention to blazed white-hot. Her lips. Her breasts. Her belly. The tight, aching nub between her thighs.

He stripped off her clothes first, then his own, all

the time doing things to her that had Ellie alternating between groans and breathless little pants.

She didn't lay passive. Submissiveness didn't form any part of her character. Her hands kept as busy as his. So did her mouth and tongue and teeth. Awash in a sea of sensations, she rediscovered the texture of his skin, the wiry tickle of his chest hair, the satin-smooth heat of his engorged shaft.

When he worked his hand between her thighs, she was wet and ready. So ready. Still, he primed her. The heel of his hand exerted exquisite, maddening pressure on her mound. His fingers worked a steady rhythm inside her. Ellie stood it as long as she could before lifting her body in a taut arc.

"Jack! Now!"

"No." Deliberately, he eased the tormenting pressure. "Not yet, Ellie. I've laid awake too many nights remembering how you—"

With a muttered curse, he bit off the rest of the sentence. A red flush mounted his cheeks.

Stunned, Ellie stared at the rugged planes of his face. He'd thought about her. Dreamed about her. Laid awake remembering her touch and her taste. The realization melted away the years. With them went much of the long-buried hurt and anger.

"I've laid awake, too," she whispered. "Too many nights to count."

His eyes searched hers. His jaw was clenched so tight Ellie thought it might crack. Just when she thought she'd have to take the initiative again, he groped for his jeans. For an awful moment, she thought he'd changed his mind. Frustration and chagrin welled to fill her throat with a taste like chalk.

To her infinite relief, he'd only paused to dig a condom out of his wallet. He'd protected her all those years ago, she remembered on a warm rush of emotion. He was still protecting her.

He sheathed himself with quick, jerky strokes, then rolled back to her. One hand tangled in her hair, bringing her head up for his crushing kiss. The other parted her legs and positioned his rigid member. Ellie opened for him joyously, eagerly, her heart singing a welcome even as her hips lifted to meet his initial thrust.

They made love with all the fury and twice the skill of their youth.

The first time was fast and hard. Mouths greedy, hands groping, hips grinding, they rolled over and over on the plush carpet. Ellie climaxed twice, mind-shattering orgasms that left her whimpering. Jack held back as long as he could, determined to draw out their pleasure, until Ellie took matters out of his hands. Hooking a leg, she climbed astride him, wrapped her fingers around his shaft and held him steady as she sank down, inch by satiny inch.

The second time was slower, lazier and took place in bed, thank goodness. Ellie knew she'd sport a nice complement of carpet burns in the morning.

The third time left her completely sated and limp with exhaustion. It was well past midnight when she fell asleep, her arm flung across Jack's chest and her nose buried in his neck.

She awoke the next morning to find him sitting in the chair across the room. He was dressed all in black, unshaven, and looked more dangerous than she'd ever imagined he could.

Chapter 8

One glance at Jack's tight jaw and grim expression sent a single thought ripping through Ellie's sleep-fuzzed mind.

He was going to leave. Again.

With a flash of pure pain, she sensed that he was already regretting last night. As he'd pointed out several times, he was there to protect her. Only to protect her. Getting involved with Elena Maria Alazar—again—compromised not only his ability to do his job, it could very well cost him the career he'd carved out since leaving the Marine Corps.

Her chest squeezed so hard and tight she could barely breathe. Yanking at the tangled sheet, she bunched it over her breasts and wiggled up to rest her bare shoulders against the wrought-iron headboard. With some effort, she managed to keep her crushing sense of loss out of her voice.

"You're already dressed, I see. Are you going out?"

"I've been out."

"Have you? Where?"

Her cool, almost disinterested query irritated the hell out of Jack. He'd spent three hellacious hours, first down at the river, searching for proof that someone had, in fact, fired at Ellie last night, then convincing the San Antonio PD detective honchoing her case to haul his butt out of bed. Jack wanted a cast of the fresh scar he'd found in the stone steps. Maybe ballistics could turn up information as to the type of bullet that had gouged it.

Finding evidence that a killer had taken aim at Ellie was bad enough. Seeing her naked and sleepy-eyed, sporting what looked suspiciously like a whisker burn on the curve of her left shoulder, magnified Jack's self-disgust and guilt a hundred times over.

He'd been sent to San Antonio to keep her safe, for God's sake! And what the hell did he do? Spent half the night rolling around in the sack with the woman whose life might well depend on his focus and ability to concentrate.

If the killer had tried again...

If he'd hit when Jack was otherwise occupied...

If Ellie had been hurt...

His gut twisting, he practically snarled at her. "I told you I recognized the sound of a round fired from a silenced gun when I heard one."

She looked confused for a moment, either at his savage tone or the information he'd imparted.

"Last night," he growled, "on the Riverwalk, right when the fireworks went off. That was a shot."

The fingers gripping the bunched sheet went white at the knuckles. "Are you sure?"

"I'm sure. I found the gouge in the stone where the bullet hit."

The last of the sleepy flush left her cheeks. She stared at Jack, her eyes wide with dismay. Speculating that they might or might not have heard a gunshot was one thing, he knew. Having the brutal fact confirmed was another.

He hated the fleeting look of fear and helplessness that chased across her face. Hated even more driving home the fact that she was a target.

"From the angle of the mark," he continued tersely, "it looks like the shell ricocheted off the stone into the river. Detective Harris and an SAPD crime scene crew are down there now, trying to locate the shell and run it through ballistics."

Some of the helpless vulnerability left her face. "I can help with that! I'll lay odds my team's equipment is considerably more sophisticated than the police department's."

Dragging the sheet with her, she swung her legs over the edge of the mattress and groped for her clothes. Jack's harsh voice stopped her cold.

"Someone wants you dead, Ellie. Very dead. You're not leaving this room until I find out who."

"But…"

"The matter's not open for discussion or debate. Just so you know, I've requested backup to augment your security detail. I've also called in an expert from the company I work for to provide additional electronic surveillance and defensive countermeasures. Both team members are en route as we speak."

"Jack, be reasonable. I can't just cower here in my

hotel room. Ballistics is my area of expertise. I can help. I want to help."

"I told you, the issue's not up for negotiation."

Her chin went up. "I'm not negotiating. Give me ten minutes to shower and dress."

Scooping up her clothes, she yanked the tail ends of the sheet free of the mattress and headed for the bathroom. Jack spit out a curse and followed. The shower jets were already turned to full blast when he pushed inside.

Her clothes lay in a scattered heap on the tile, along with the discarded sheet. Whirling, she snatched a towel from the nearest rack. Jack had a feeling he'd carry the image of her copper-tipped breasts, flat belly and the dark, seductive triangle between her legs around in his head for a long, long time.

"I said ten minutes!"

"And I said you're not going anywhere."

Steam curled through the open stall door. The jets drummed against the glass. Ellie made a heroic attempt at calm and reasonable. And failed.

"I'm not one of your troops. You don't bark orders at me and expect unquestioned obedience. I'm an expert in my field, just as you are in yours. I'm going to—"

"You're going to stay where I put you."

"*Put* me?"

"Don't force me take extreme measures."

Scorn flashed in her eyes. "What are you going to do? Lock me in the bathroom?"

"I was thinking more along the lines of handcuffing you to the bed."

"Oh, give me a break! I know you too well, Carstairs. You wouldn't resort to such Neanderthal tactics."

His gaze raked her near-naked form. A grim smile settled in his eyes.

"Oh, yeah, babe. I would."

Without warning, the tension in the steam-filled bathroom took on a whole different edge. Ellie felt it right down to her bones. A sudden wariness that had nothing to do with bullets or ballistics sent her back a step. A feminine instinct older than time screamed at her to cover herself, placate the angry male before her, defuse the situation.

Being Ellie, she did just the opposite. Another instinct, sharp and urgent, demanded she stand her ground. This was Jack, she reminded herself furiously. She'd let his hardheadedness defeat her once. She couldn't let him ride roughshod over her again. Not if she wanted him to consider her his equal. In *and* out of bed.

Spray from the open shower enveloped her in a fine mist. Steam invaded her lungs. Blinking away the drops that had collected on her lashes, Ellie looked him square in the eye.

"I wouldn't mind doing the bed-and-handcuff bit, as long as we take turns as the cuffee. But not right now, Jack. Right now I'm going to take a shower, get dressed and haul myself and my equipment down to the river. You can accept my decision and come with me, or…"

She let the sentence trail off, stalling for time while she tried to decide just what the heck *or* she could throw at him.

Jack obviously had a few ideas of his own. His eyes narrowed. The hot mist had soaked his hair and raised a sheen on the stubble darkening his cheeks. He looked wet and angry and menacing as he took a step forward.

"Or what, Ellie? You'll fire me?"

"Oh, no! I'm not letting you walk away from me again."

The retort spilled out before she could stop it. Recklessly, Ellie laid the rest of her tumultuous emotions on the line.

"We started something last night, Carstairs. Correction, we *restarted* something. I for one think we should see it through to the finish this time."

Her heart slamming against her ribs, she waited to hear Jack's take on the matter. He declined to give one. Instead, he spun on one heel and made for the bathroom door.

Ellie's toes curled into the tiles. Fury and pain lanced into her in equal measures. "Jack! Dammit, you can't just—"

"Someone's at the door." He threw the words over his shoulder. "I'll see who it is, then we'll finish this discussion."

She hadn't heard a thing over the pelting water and the heat of her emotions. Muttering under her breath, she kicked the bathroom door shut, then stepped into the shower stall. When they finished this discussion, she wouldn't be bare-assed and still sticky with the residue of their lovemaking.

When he peered through the peephole and identified the individual on the other side of the door, Jack didn't know whether to curse or give a heartfelt grunt of relief. He settled for twisting the dead bolt and greeting OMEGA's chief of communications with a curt acknowledgment.

"You got here fast."

"Lightning put his personal jet at our disposal."

Mackenzie Blair breezed in, toting her heavy field case. She wore the uniform she favored for traveling, Jack noted: a dark blue T-shirt emblazoned with U.S. Navy in four-inch gold letters, snug jeans and serious running shoes. Few of OMEGA's special agents could keep up with the woman when she hit her stride.

She'd have a full assortment of other garments in her case, Jack knew. He and the other males at OMEGA all harbored a particular partiality for the jumpsuit she slipped into for night operations. The black nylon zipped up to her chin and covered her slender curves like a thin coat of paint.

Taking a quick glance around the suite, she cocked her head at the sound of running water in the other room. "Did I get you out of the shower?"

"No."

One brow lifted. "There must be some other reason your clothes are soaked, then."

There was, but Jack didn't offer it. His black shirt sticking to him like wet saran, he closed the door to the suite. Mackenzie dumped her case on a handy chair and turned to face him.

"Cyrene is checking in downstairs. I came right up. I've got something for you, Renegade."

Jack's pulse jumped at the intense satisfaction glimmering in her eyes.

"We IDed some interesting characters in our screen of Dr. Alazar's digital images. One in particular will catch your attention."

Punching in a code on the digital lock, she opened her field case and produced a flat silver CD. Her gaze cut to the computer sitting on the desk.

"Will Dr. Alazar mind if I use her laptop?"

Jack shook his head, although at this point he couldn't predict Ellie's reactions to anything. She'd put his back up with her stubborn resistance to his orders and thrown him for a complete loop with that business about not letting him walk away from her again.

Elena Maria obviously hadn't figured it out yet, but he had no intention of leaving her. Or letting her leave him. Not after last night. And sure as hell not with a killer stalking her.

His mouth set, he crossed the room to peer over Mackenzie's shoulder. She drummed her fingers impatiently while the laptop booted up, then sent them flying over the keys. A moment later, a scene was painted across the screen.

It was the courtyard of the Alamo. Jack recognized the low, flat building Ellie had identified as the Long Barracks in the foreground. In the background was the massive oak that gave welcome shade to the throngs of tourists wandering from exhibit to exhibit.

"There he is."

With a click of the mouse, Mackenzie placed an arrow on one particular tourist. He wore a straw Stetson and dark glasses. A camera was slung over one shoulder. He stood in the shade at the rear of the courtyard next to another man.

"It took me a while to ID him. The glasses obscure his eyes, and the hat conceals his hair color, although I doubt it's still the same color listed on the FBI most-wanted bulletin."

Well, hell! The FBI's most-wanted bulletin. That's all Jack needed to hear. The tension coiling his muscles took another tight twist.

"I finally got a hit on the scar." Clicking away, Mackenzie zoomed in on the man's profile. "See it? Just below his left ear?"

He saw it. "Unless I miss my guess, someone once took a knife to this particular tourist's throat."

"You pegged it. According to FBI reports, he got that little souvenir from a street pimp who strenuously objected to being taken out. He's a hit man, Renegade. A real professional. Suspected of killing at least ten people, both in the States and abroad."

Jack had suspected he was dealing with a pro. Knowing he was right didn't give him so much as a hint of satisfaction.

"The man's assumed dozens of different identities over the years," Mackenzie reported. "Including, we can lay odds, Mr. Harold Berger of 2224 Riverside Drive, Austin. The FBI was *very* interested to hear he'd popped up in San Antonio. Particularly when we IDed the man standing next to him."

She zinged the pointer to a beefy, wide-shouldered man with sandy hair and a bulldog jaw.

"Meet Mr. Dan Foster. He's local, a very successful building contractor."

"What his connection to our hit man?"

"Three months ago, Foster's wife was kidnapped from their country club estate. Although there were some indications that both Fosters played around, Danny Boy appeared devastated by the kidnapping and insisted on paying the million-dollar ransom."

Eyes narrowed, Jack studied the image on the screen. Despite his size, Foster gave off a definite country club air. A designer logo decorated the pocket of his knit shirt. His khaki Dockers showed a knife crease. Gold flashed at one wrist.

"Before Foster could get the funds together," Mackenzie continued, "his wife's body turned up in a Dumpster. From the rope burns on her wrists and ankles, shredded nylons and gravel embedded in her knees, the FBI thinks she tried to escape and was shot in the process. Now, you'd expect the supposed kidnapper to bury the body or otherwise keep it hidden until after he'd collected the ransom."

"Unless he *wanted* it found," Jack said slowly.

"Right. Again, our friend Foster appeared devastated. But the Feds took note of the fact that he was sole beneficiary on his wife's two-million-dollar life insurance policy. And that he was falling behind on repayment of several major business loans he'd floated."

The pieces fell together with startling clarity. The trashing of Ellie's hotel room, her stolen computer, the attempts on her life. None of those had anything to do with the controversy she's stirred up in town, but with the fact she caught a killer and the man who could well have hired him on camera.

"Foster must have sweated blood when he read the stories about Ellie in the papers," Jack guessed. "Particularly those that went into detail about her digital scans of the Alamo and its weaponry. It wouldn't have taken more than a few calls for Foster to find out if Dr. Alazar was at the Alamo the same day he arranged to meet Scarface there."

"What I don't understand," Mackenzie said, tapping a finger on the keyboard, "is why the heck they'd risk meeting in such a public place."

"Maybe he didn't feel safe meeting with a killer anywhere else. Maybe Scarface insisted on it, intending to blackmail Foster later by threatening to reveal his shady connections."

"Then why would he care if Dr. Alazar caught the meeting on camera?"

"Scarface might not care, but Foster sure as hell would. My guess is he hired the guy to trash Ellie's hotel room and destroy her digital images. When word got out she'd backed them up, Foster would have no choice but to take out a contract on Ellie, too, hoping her death would scuttle her project—and the pictures she'd taken—before they ever saw light of day."

It was all speculation. Mere guesswork. But Jack knew in his gut they'd stumbled onto something.

"Did the Feds run a ballistics analysis of the bullet that killed Foster's wife?"

"I'm sure they did. I can e-mail my contact at the Bureau and find out. Why?"

"Because I'll bet you another dozen pizzas that the rifling marks on the bullet retrieved from her body will match those on the one fired at Ellie last night."

"Which makes it even more imperative we retrieve it from the river," a cool voice said behind them.

Jack grunted in disgust. Hell of a field agent he made! He hadn't heard the shower cut off. His only excuse was that Mackenzie's startling information had riveted his attention.

The new arrival seemed to rivet Mackenzie's. Her fascinated glance took in every detail of Ellie's fresh scrubbed face and damp hair before shifting to Jack's still wet shirt. OMEGA's chief of communications didn't say a word. She didn't have to. The deliberately bland expression she assumed said it all.

Unfortunately Lightning hadn't exercised the same restraint. When Jack reported that matters between him and Ellie had taken an unexpected and very personal turn, Nick had ripped a foot-wide strip off his agent's hide.

Jack had expected nothing less. He'd also expected Lightning to yank him off the mission and was fully prepared to tell OMEGA's director to go to hell. No way Jack was leaving Ellie. He intended to stick so close to her she couldn't tell her shadow from his until he brought her stalker down.

After that...

His stomach clenched. He couldn't allow himself to think past right here, right now. Ellie's safety demanded his total focus. After would have to take care of itself. Silently, he watched her cross the room and hold out a hand to Mackenzie.

"I'm Elena Alazar. I assume you're one of Jack's colleagues."

"That's right."

Effortlessly, Mac slipped into the cover identity designed to shield her OMEGA connection. Since her extensive network of friends and acquaintances from her Navy days all knew about her background in and fascination with electronic gadgetry, she'd set up a fictitious company. Blair Consulting was listed in the Yellow Pages. It maintained a fancy home Page on the Web. Only a handful of Washington insiders knew the company's proprietor and sole employee worked exclusively for OMEGA.

"I'm Mackenzie Blair, Dr. Alazar. I own Blair Consulting. We specialize in electronic surveillance and computerized data searches. It's a pleasure to meet the woman who designed and developed the prototype for Discoverer Two."

"You know about metal detectors?"

"I'm former Navy," she answered with a grin. "We squids all harbor a secret fascination with sunken treasure. I've done my share of beachcombing."

"Then you might be interested in watching the Discoverer Two in action," Ellie said with a smile that did *not* include Jack. "I'm going to take it down to the river to help locate the shell casing you're both so interested in."

"Great!" Mackenzie enthused before Jack could counter Ellie's flat statement. "I'd love to see that sucker in operation. I understand you've loaded twenty gigabytes of metallurgical and ballistics data into its core operating system."

"Twenty-four, actually."

"Good Lord! How did you cram all that data in a portable device?"

"By compressing the reference files and—"

"Ladies," Jack interrupted. "Do you mind if we get back to the small matter of a stalker?"

Both women turned at his heavy-handed attempt to head off what had all the earmarks of an animated and lengthy discussion of bits and bytes.

"How much did you hear of what Mac had to say about the men in this image?" he asked Ellie.

Her glance flicked to the screen. It lingered on Scarface for long moments before shifting to Foster.

"Enough to make me want to hurt those bastards," she said fiercely. "Really bad. Let's get to work, shall we?"

Chapter 9

While Ellie and the young grad student on her team assembled the equipment she wanted to divert from the archeological site to the river, Jack met with the back-up agent OMEGA had sent in. Normally, Jack worked alone. The fact that he'd requested backup hadn't surprised Lightning, coming as it did on the heels of Renegade's admission that he'd crossed the line with Ellie.

After he'd finished tearing into Jack, Nick had sent one of the best. Claire Cantwell, code name Cyrene, had lost her husband to a bungled attempt to free a group of oil executives being held in Malaysia by radical separatists. Burying her grief behind a serene façade, she'd schooled herself to become one of the world's foremost experts on hostage negotiation. A noted psychologist, she was also OMEGA's most skilled agent when it came to screening crowds and identifying potential troublemakers.

Mackenzie respected and admired Renegade and Cyrene and looked forward to providing their on-scene electronics support. She'd just checked out a super-cool lie-detecting camera being developed by the Home-land Defense folks for airport use. The handy-dandy little device spotted deceivers by recording mild facial warming when under stress. She couldn't wait to have Cyrene test it out in her crowd surveillance. But when she checked into her room and made her initial on-site report, Lightning laid another task on her.

Nick Jensen's face was displayed with crystal clarity on the small screen of her communications unit. Thought-ful. A bit grim. And so damned handsome Mackenzie was tempted to drag her thumb over the trackball to blur the image a bit. She couldn't quite handle the combined impact of his navy blazer, Windsor-knotted red silk tie and deep tan this early in the morning!

"I want Foster on an electronic leash," Nick said. "He'd going to contact his hired gun sooner or later. He'll demand a progress report, or at least an explana-tion of why the hit's taking so long. Renegade will want to hear it when he does."

"No problem." Her mind was already sorting through various technical options. "I'll look through my bag of tricks and see what we've got to play with."

"Good."

"Is that it?"

"For now."

"Roger."

Signing off, Mackenzie considered the best approach to Foster. Normally, field agents tagged targets. In fact, the unwritten rule of thumb was that *only* field agents made direct contact with targets. But Renegade needed

Cyrene for backup on the river. There was no reason Mackenzie couldn't accomplish this little task herself.

The background dossier she'd compiled on Daniel Foster indicated he was something of a playboy who went in for the coy, kittenish type. She didn't have a kittenish bone in her body, and she wasn't sure how well she could do coy, but she'd give both her best shot.

Her first step was to trade her jeans and Nikes for strappy sandals and a sleeveless, V-neck dress with a matching short-sleeved jacket. The slinky black matte jersey defied wrinkles. It also clung to her slender curves.

After unclipping her hair, Mac dragged a brush through the shoulder-length dark mass and applied more makeup than she usually wore. A quick survey in the bathroom mirror convinced her to take a page from her mentor's book.

Maggie Sinclair, code name Chamelon, could assume a completely different personality with a few strategic accessories. At various times, Maggie had gone into the field disguised as a nun, a nuclear scientist and a high-priced call girl. On one memorable mission, she'd lifted a black lace garter belt and fishnet stockings from a shop, left a note for the owner to send the bill to the American consulate and waltzed into a smoke-filled waterfront dive that catered to gunrunners and drug lords.

What she needed, Mackenzie decided, was the equivalent of a black lace garter.

She found just what she was looking for at the department store located in the massive River Center complex adjacent to the Menger. The underwire demi-bra transformed even her modest curves into plump, seductive mounds. Additional pads pushed her breasts up so high they almost spilled out of the V-neck. More than satisfied with the result, Mackenzie charged the miracle bra to her OMEGA expense account.

She returned to the Menger and waited for the sporty little Mustang she'd arranged to have waiting at the south-side airport where Nick's private plane had landed this morning. The same valet who'd parked it in the Menger's garage less than an hour ago gawked at her dramatic cleavage when he delivered the vehicle curbside.

After she slid behind the wheel, Mackenzie placed her field case on the passenger seat and flipped down its side to access the keyboard. Dan Foster would be at work by now. According to the information she'd gleaned from her FBI contact, the two million Foster had collected from the insurance company after his wife's murder got him current on his construction company's outstanding loans but hadn't paid them off by any means. The man still had to work for a living.

She accessed the address and phone number of his office, then put in a quick call. The helpful receptionist informed her Mr. Foster was on-site at a job on San Antonio's north side. Twenty minutes later, Mackenzie pulled up at the fenced construction site.

Massive steel girders shot twenty-four stories into the cloudless blue sky. Super cranes hoisted beams to workers who appeared ant-like from the ground. Trucks raised clouds of dust as they rumbled in and out of the gate in the chain-link security fence.

Once again Mackenzie reached into her case. She peeled off the adhesive backing on a tiny, transparent disc, then stuck the disk to the back of her business card. Once attached, it became invisible. No one could tell it was there without a microscope.

She had just climbed out of the Mustang when two men exited the trailer parked beside the gate. One carried a clipboard and wore a badge identifying him as some kind of inspector.

The other was her quarry.

Her stomach did a little flip. Foster's size didn't intimidate her. Nor did his rugged good looks impress her. At all. It was just that the newspaper clippings and shots of Dan Foster the FBI had compiled did *not* do him justice.

Those grainy black-and-whites had depicted the man in a tux, his wife at his side, attending some fancy do at the country club. Or in a dark suit, his face contorted in grief as he exited a limo after her funeral.

This morning he was in boots, jeans and a hard hat. His rolled-up sleeves displayed trunklike arms that could only have been acquired by manhandling the dozers and cranes he now hired others to operate. Muscle had never particularly turned Mackenzie on, but she had to admit this guy's were impressive.

"Mr. Foster?"

He squinted through the dust. She started toward him, remembered her role and altered her stride to a hip-swinging glide.

"I'm Mackenzie Blair, president of Blair Consulting."

Foster accepted the business card she held out, but his glance made a detour to her chest and lingered for several seconds before dropping to examine the engraved lettering.

"I called your office for an appointment, but your

secretary said you'd be on-site all day and suggested I catch you here."

"What can I do for you, Ms. Blair?"

"My consulting firm specializes in electronic communications. I'm looking to expand my operations in this part of the country and would like to talk to you about the communications support you plan to put in this building."

"I've already accepted a bid from a subcontractor to wire it."

He was going with hard wire. Good. That gave her just the opening she needed.

"I think you should consider fiber optics instead of wire."

"Well, I…"

"You'd be offering state-of-the-art networking capability to whoever occupies the building. And…" Her voice dropped to a throaty purr. "I guarantee I could save you a minimum of a hundred thousand dollars."

She'd pulled the figure out of a hat, a sheer guess based on the size of the project. As she'd anticipated, though, the combination of succulent Wonder curves and a possible hundred grand in savings proved irresistible.

The contractor's eyes gleamed under the rim of his hard hat. "A hundred thousand, huh?"

A teasing smile played at her lips. "I'm good at what I do, Mr. Foster."

"I'll just bet you are."

His glance dropped to her chest again before shifting to the inspector waiting patiently a few feet away.

"Look, I'm going to be tied up here for most of the

day. Why don't we get together for a drink this evening and discuss all this money you're going to save me?"

Mackenzie let her smile curve into a seductive promise. "My cell phone number's on that business card. Call me."

"I will." Grinning, he tucked the card into his pocket and gave it a pat. "Talk to you tonight, Ms. Blair."

Oh, you'll be talking to me before then.

On that smug thought, she strolled to the Mustang.

A quarter mile from the site, she pulled to the side of the road and extracted a wireless earpiece. With the plastic piece tucked comfortably in her right ear, she keyed a special code into the receiver. Foster's angry voice stabbed into her head.

"...filed for those permits two months ago. I wish to hell you folks would get your act together."

Wincing, Mackenzie adjusted the volume. She'd tagged her target, temporarily at least. She'd replace the tag with a more permanent one tonight. Humming with satisfaction, she called in a quick order to OMEGA's communications center to monitor the transmissions and drove off.

She connected with Renegade at the stairs leading to the Riverwalk. He'd planted both fists on the stone balustrade. His gaze was locked on the scene below.

The San Antonio PD had cordoned off a section of the river and commandeered one of the colorful river barges. Several uniformed and plainclothes police officers occupied the boat, which floated at the end of a long tether.

Dr. Alazar was in the barge, as well, along with her flame-haired assistant. As Mackenzie watched, Ellie slipped the heavy instrument that could only be Discoverer Two off her arm and passed it to the grad student.

"How's it going?" she asked the man beside her.

"It's not."

His face grim, Jack turned to give her a quick rundown. His startled glance zeroed in on her cleavage.

"Good Lord!"

"Hey, thanks a lot! At least Foster liked the new me."

Renegade's gaze whipped up to lock with hers. "You made contact?"

"And then some." Grinning, she tapped her ear. "He's right here, inside my head."

"Dammit, Mac, you shouldn't have tackled the guy alone. You shouldn't have tackled him at all, for that matter. That's my job, or Cyrene's."

"You were busy. And he was an easy mark. I'm a walking window into everything the man says or does. At the moment Danny Boy is… Hmm. It sounds like he's taking what we used to refer to in the Navy as a leak."

"Has he talked to Scarface?"

"No. But he wants to continue *our* conversation. We're having drinks later tonight."

"Does Lightning know about this?"

"Lightning's the one who said to tag the creep."

She was stretching things a bit there. She knew it. Jack knew it.

"Last time I checked the field manual," he drawled, "tagging didn't include dinner or drinks."

Since there was no such thing as a field manual for his line of work, Mackenzie decided to ignore the comment.

"Bring me up to speed on the salvage operation," she

said instead, turning her attention to the barge. "What's happening?"

"Ellie laid out a search grid based on the angle of the gouge mark in the stone. They've been sweeping from left to right." Frustration edged his voice. "They're almost at the end of the grid."

"They haven't found anything?"

"Are you kidding? They've found everything but the kitchen sink. That'll probably turn up, too. In the meantime, they've racked up an impressive collection of tire jacks, switchblades, car keys and coins in a dozen different currencies and denominations. But no bullets."

"Hmm. Where's Cyrene?"

"Over there, at that restaurant. Second table to the left, by the rail."

Mackenzie spotted the pale-haired agent at the open-air restaurant on the opposite side of the river. The elevated deck gave the agent a bird's-eye view of the barge as well as the curious crowd that had gathered to watch. With Renegade and Cyrene flying cover, Mackenzie opted for a closer view of the action.

"I'm going down to watch. I want to see Discoverer Two up close and personal."

She had taken only a few steps before she heard a high-pitched pinging. Dr. Alazar's assistant gave an excited exclamation.

"I've got something on the screen! The digital displays indicate it's a spent forty-one caliber hollow-point casing, two hundred grain, number one hundred. Probably a Speer, although it could be a Remington."

Brushing past Mackenzie, Jack went down the stone stairs two at a time. Part of him went tight with dread at the possibility the police might soon have evidence linking Dan Foster's murdered wife to the attempts on Ellie's life. Another part of him hoped they'd make the connection and he could convince Ellie to get the hell out of Dodge.

If he couldn't, those handcuffs were sounding better and better.

Grabbing the mooring line, Jack leaped onto the barge. It rocked under his weight and earned him a frown from the plainclothes detective and a grunt from Eric Chapman. The kid spread his legs wider to brace himself and held the detector steady over the water.

"It's showing a depth of seven and a half feet," he informed the wet-suited diver beside him.

"The water's only a little over six feet deep at this point," Ellie told Jack in an aside. "That means the bullet's burrowed into the mud."

A uniformed officer propped his elbow on the barge railing to add support for the heavy detector Eric held suspended over the river. Discoverer Two pinged noisily as the diver opened the air valve on his tanks, wrapped his lips around his mouthpiece and pulled down his face mask. Black fins waving, he went over the side with and hit with a splash. He glanced up to take a bead on the wand and dove straight down.

Shoulder-to-shoulder, Jack and Ellie peered over the railing. Mud swirled to cloud the green water. Air bubbles bobbed to the surface. The muted pops when they broke sounded so much like the silenced shot Jack had heard last night that his palms got slick with sweat where they gripped the rail.

Dragging his gaze from the swirling water, he scanned the scene. He spotted Cyrene, seemingly relaxed and at ease as she sipped a frothy pink drink at a

patio restaurant and let her glance drift over the gawking onlookers. Mackenzie was on the steps, dividing her
attention between the voice in her head and the drama
being played out before her.

Despite the added security, tension wrapped Jack in
a tight coil. Scarface was out there. In one of the high-
rise hotels overlooking the river. Lounging at a table in
one of the restaurants. Mingling with the crowd. Watching. Waiting.

Jack could feel the killer. Smell him. He just couldn't
see him. He edged closer to Ellie, angling his body
to shield hers. His nerves were stretched so tight the
whoosh of the diver breaking the surface damned near
had him flinging her facedown in the barge.

Muddied green water streamed over the diver's mask.
Spitting out his mouthpiece, he shoved his mask back
on his head with one hand and held up the other.

"Is this what we're looking for?"

The expended shell gleamed in the sunlight. Unlike
the artifacts Ellie and her team had recovered from
the archeological site, the copper casing was clean and
new and bright.

"It's a forty-one hollow point," Ellie confirmed with
a single glance.

"Same caliber as the bullet that killed Joanna Foster," Detective Harris muttered.

Flashing Jack a quick glance, he dug a plastic evidence bag out of his pocket. In their first meeting,
the SAPD veteran hadn't tried to disguise his cyni-
cism about harebrained professors who stirred up more
controversy than they could handle. He was coming
around. Fast.

"We'll run it through ballistics ASAP," he promised Jack. "Should have a comparison between it and the bullet that killed Mrs. Foster by late this afternoon. Tomorrow at the latest."

Jack grunted, not happy with the prospect of another day's wait. Ellie didn't much like it, either. Frowning, she glanced at her watch.

"It's just a little past noon. I need to go out to the dig. I don't want to waste the rest of the day."

"Sorry. Consider it wasted."

"I'll go on out," Chapman volunteered.

After unstrapping the heavy metal detector, the young grad student swiped the sweat from his brow with a freckled forearm. The sight of the gleaming copper shell casing had sobered him…and turned him into a reluctant ally.

"Carstairs is right, Ellie. You shouldn't make yourself any more of a target than you already are."

Her mouth pursed. Jack was all set to ask Detective Harris for the loan of his handcuffs when she caved.

"All right. Tell the rest of the folks I'm sorry for leaving wrap-up operations to them. We'll convene in my room at 8:00 p.m. for a team meeting. In the meantime, I'll go through yesterday's field notes and start working on the draft report."

That was the plan, anyway. She returned to her suite, took a quick shower to wash away the sweat and stink of stirred-up river water. After a quick sandwich ordered from room service, she settled in front of her laptop and attacked the field notes, but the constant comings and goings of Jack's associates played havoc with her concentration.

With her fascination for all things electronic and near genius with computers, Mackenzie Blair was certainly an interesting study. Particularly after her sudden and rather startling transition from techno-geek to femme fatale. The calm, tranquil woman Jack referred to as Cyrene proved every bit as compelling in her quiet way.

Ellie caught only snatches of their discussion of cover points and team surveillance of Mackenzie's upcoming meeting with Dan Foster. She couldn't miss, however, Blair's rueful grin when she reported the gist of her conversation with someone named Lightning.

"You were right," she told Jack. "He had a few choice words to say about me tagging Foster."

"No kidding."

"He also reminded me I'm not—" She caught herself, threw a quick glance at Ellie and obviously modified whatever she'd intended to say. "I'm not one of you field jocks. I'm to take every possible precaution."

At that point, Ellie felt impelled to intervene. Abandoning any pretense of working on her report, she swung around in her chair.

"You don't have to do this, Mackenzie. I'm the one Foster and his hired gun may be after. You shouldn't put yourself in danger."

"Hey, don't spoil my fun. I don't get the chance to come out to play with the big guys all that often." She checked her watch. "I'd better go start getting beautiful. It could take a while."

Ellie said nothing more until Blair and the woman named Claire departed. Her eyes thoughtful, she waited for the door to click shut behind them before voicing the question hovering in her mind.

"Who are those people, Jack? For that matter, who are you?"

He took his time responding. Folding his arms, he

leaned his hips against the back of the sofa. "Who do you think I am?"

"Obviously not a small-time bodyguard in need of work."

Flushing a bit at the memory of how she'd insisted her uncle hire him, believing he might need the income, she left her chair.

"So tell me. Who are you? What do you do for a living?"

"Does it really matter, Ellie?"

The question took her back nine years. She could almost hear the echo of her fierce arguments, see Jack's stony face.

"No," she said softly. "What you do for a living *doesn't* matter. It never did."

Jack took the hit without blinking. He deserved it. More than deserved it. Considering the discussion over, she started to turn.

He caught her with a hand on her arm. Drawing her closer, he curled a knuckle under her chin.

"I'm not saying I was wrong all those years ago, you understand?"

"What are you saying?"

Bending, he brushed her lips with a kiss so gentle Ellie almost melted on the spot. When he raised his head, his expression was so serious her stomach did a little flip.

"This isn't the time or the place for promises," he said, his tone gruff. "Not with everything that's coming down on you right now. But if anyone walks away this time, Elena Maria, it'll have to be you."

Chapter 10

Ellie was still thinking about Jack's *non* promise when her team arrived from the dig. They'd shut down operations early. For good, this time.

"The deputy director of the park service called," Sam Pierce related, his craggy face both resigned and regretful. "He asked for you. I gave him your cell phone number and the number here at the hotel, but he said I could relay the message."

"Let me guess. NPS has pulled our funding."

Pierce nodded. "They left just enough in the kitty to restore the site."

She'd sensed it was coming. Given the pressure exerted by the Texas congressional delegation, the park service could hardly do anything else if they hoped to fund future projects. Still, the abrupt termination stung. Fighting a crushing sense of disappointment, Ellie listened while the others briefed her.

"We packed up all the equipment," Orin Weaver advised. "Eric loaded your van. I've got mine loaded and ready to go. I'll give you my input for the final report tonight and head home tomorrow."

The forensic anthropologist had other jobs waiting, Ellie knew. He was a frequent consultant for local, state and federal law enforcement, and his services were in demand. She couldn't ask him to stay and work gratis.

"Thanks, Orin." Forcing a smile, Ellie shook his hand. "I appreciate all you've contributed to this project."

Dr. Dawes-Hamilton wasn't quite as ready to abandon ship. "I've got some grant money back at Baylor waiting to be spent," she told Ellie. "I'll press ahead with the authentication process on the artifacts we've shipped to the university and send you a copy of my findings."

If the archeologist could use her department's grant money to authenticate the rifle and scraps of clothing found with the remains, Ellie could certainly scrape together enough funds to pay for DNA testing. Assuming, of course, the donors were still willing to provide samples.

"You'll have to decide what you want done with the bits and pieces we recovered in the past couple of days," Sam Pierce said. "I imaged and catalogued them on the computer, but most of the stuff is just junk."

The bits and pieces he referred to filled a large cardboard box. At Ellie's request, Eric lugged it in and deposited it beside her computer.

"Nothing there the park service might want to add to their collection of items found in and around Mission San Jose?" she asked Sam.

"Nope."

"I'll go through the box one more time. Maybe the archdiocese of San Antonio will be interested. Or the Alamo's museum director."

"Maybe," Sam said doubtfully.

"If not, I'll dispose of the unwanted items when I make arrangements for the site restoration."

Which would take her all of a day or two.

Ellie bit back a sigh. The project she'd begun with such enthusiasm and intellectual curiosity had generated nothing but controversy and was about to ignominiously fizzle out. Adding insult to injury, someone apparently wanted to fizzle *her* out with it.

Well, she hadn't completely finished with this project yet. Or with Mr. Dan Foster and his shadowy, frightening associate.

When she indicated as much to Jack and *his* team some time later, however, he flatly vetoed her suggestion that she slow roll the cleanup and shutdown operations in an attempt to draw out the killer.

"No way! You're out of here as soon as you pack up and hit the road."

"What good does it do to leave? Scarface could easily waylay me on the road or follow me home."

"You're not going home."

"Oh?"

She threw a glance at Mackenzie and the woman they called Cyrene. Both returned it with absolutely blank expressions. Obviously, this was Jack's show. They'd take their cue from him.

"All right," she said, swinging back to the man in charge. "I'll bite. Where am I going?"

"You're taking a nice long vacation at an undisclosed location."

"Don't be ridiculous. I can't just disappear indefinitely. I've got a house, a job, students who've signed up for courses that begin in less than a month."

"They can sign up for other courses. Until we bring Scarface down, I don't want you in his line of fire."

"I hesitate to point out the obvious, but I'm *already* in his line of fire. Where I'll stay until, as you say, you bring the bastard down. Seems to me you have more chance of accomplishing that right here. It's just a matter of flushing him out of hiding."

"Yeah, right. With you as bait."

Deliberately, Ellie suppressed the queasy feeling in her stomach. She was no coward, but neither was she a fool.

"Look, I'm not proposing to stroll around town with a target pinned to my back. I'm merely suggesting we turn the termination of the dig to our advantage. We can leak rumors that I'm drafting my final report. Set up a press conference. Hint that I'm going to distribute vivid images of my research and visits to the Alamo along with copies of the report. Make Foster and his hired killer sweat and, hopefully, provoke them into doing something stupid."

"It's too risky. I won't let you stake yourself out like a sacrificial goat for a cold-blooded killer. Nor do I think it's wise to reignite the anger of every hotheaded Texan who thinks you're messing with history."

Mackenzie broke her silence. "Ellie doesn't have to actually release the report to the media. All we need to do is make Foster *think* the release is imminent. I can help there."

Jack shot her an evil look, but before he could nix the plan that seemed to be forming despite his objections, Cyrene broke ranks, as well.

"When she meets with Foster tonight, Mackenzie could also let drop something about the bullet recovered from the river," Claire said in her quiet voice. "The possibility that the police might make the connection between the attacks on Ellie and his wife's murder would add significantly to Foster's stress levels."

"The doc's right," Mackenzie argued. "I could spin all kinds of rumors. Really put Foster in a real puddle of sweat. My bet is he'll dump me like radioactive waste and head straight for the nearest phone to contact his hit man."

"Yeah," Jack snarled. "That's my bet, too."

In the face of his fierce opposition, Mackenzie backed off. Ellie, however, held her ground.

"I guess I'm taking my cue from William Barrett Travis. I'm drawing a line in the sand. I'll take my stand here, in the shadow of the Alamo."

"Right! And just look where that got Travis. Depending on how your final report reads, he either went down on the walls or was shot in the back of the head while trying to escape."

Jack regretted the scathing retort the moment it left his lips. The color leached from Ellie's cheeks. Fear flickered in her brown eyes for a moment before she resolutely quashed it. Holding his gaze, she summoned a shaky smile.

"I'm not running—or walking—away."

Jack's head jerked up. Her message came through loud and clear. To him, at least.

The other two in the room sensed the sudden charge

in the air. The women exchanged questioning glances, but neither said anything until Renegade conceded with a bad-tempered growl.

"All right. We'll play this out a little while longer. Mac, see what you can stir up tonight. First, though, I'd better advise Lightning on the change of plans."

Jack had a feeling Nick Jensen wasn't going to be happy with the latest turn of events. Not only was the niece of Mexico's president offering herself up as bait for a killer, Mackenzie Blair was making an inch-by-inch transition from chief of communications to fully engaged field operative.

Jack was right.

Lightning was *not* happy.

He'd made a call to the President to bring him up to speed on the situation in San Antonio, then advised Colonel Luis Esteban, as well.

As afternoon wore into evening, Nick reminded himself that his chief of communications had gone through much of the same training as OMEGA's field agents. All headquarters personnel took marksmanship training, endured the water, jungle and desert survival courses and learned hand-to-hand combat from experts to give them an appreciation of what operatives went through in the field.

With the added benefit of her Navy background, Nick knew his comm chief could more than hold her own in just about any environment. But the gold Mont Blanc pen Maggie Sinclair had given him tapped an erratic beat as he leaned back in the leather captain's chair just past eight Washington time.

"You're not wearing a ring." Dan Foster's disembodied voice floated through the Control Center. "Does that mean you're not married?"

Nick's pen took another bounce. Foster was about as subtle as one of his eighty-ton earthmovers.

Eyes narrowed, Nick studied the scene Cyrene was beaming to the headquarters via the pen-size camera in her purse. The wall screen displayed a detailed portrait of dim lighting, gleaming wood and the couple in the booth.

The builder had hooked an arm around the back of the booth. His white shirt was unbuttoned at the top to accommodate his bull-like neck. Gold glinted on his wrist. Pure, unadulterated male lust gleamed in his eyes.

Nick could understand why. Mackenzie hadn't opted for subtle, either. If she drew in too deep a breath, she'd fall right out of that dress.

"Isn't my marital status irrelevant to this discussion?" Her husky little laugh rippled through the control center like warm velvet. "We're here to talk business."

"I make it a point to learn everything I can about the people I do business with," Foster countered with a predatory grin. "It gives me a leg up in negotiations."

"We haven't entered into negotiations."

"We might. We just might. So what's the story? Are you married, engaged or otherwise involved?"

"At the moment, none of the above. And I'd better warn you, I'm *very* ticklish in that particular spot."

Nick's pen went still.

Mackenzie waited until the builder had brought his left hand from under the table and clasped it loosely around his drink before picking up the conversational ball.

"What about you? Are you married?"

"I was. My wife died a few months ago."

"A few months ago?" With a slight turn of her head, Mackenzie let her glance drift to the arm draped around her shoulders. "I'd offer my condolences, but you seem to have recovered from your loss remarkably well."

"Joanna and I had what you might call a mutually satisfactory arrangement rather than a marriage. She didn't ask any questions. Neither did I."

"How did she die?"

"She was kidnapped and murdered."

"Good God! How awful for her. For you, too."

"Yeah, it *was* pretty awful." Making a show of pain, Foster knocked back the rest of his drink. "I still have nightmares."

Nick just bet he did. No doubt those nightmares had started about the time reports about Elena Maria Alazar's work in and around the Alamo hit the front pages.

Tucking his pen in the pocket of his camel sport coat, he leaned forward. Cyrene was providing backup for Mackenzie, leaving Renegade to guard Elena. Nick would have trusted either operative with his life. He couldn't seem to get past the fact that Mackenzie was trusting them with hers.

Grimacing, Nick remembered the strip he'd ripped off Jack for crossing the line with Ellie. Nick had better take a dose of his own medicine. Personal and professional didn't mix in this job.

"Like any big city, San Antonio seems to have a lot of murders," Mackenzie commented. "A woman staying at my hotel was shot at just yesterday. Right on the Riverwalk."

"That so?"

With apparent disinterest, Foster signaled to the waitress to bring another round of drinks. Settling against the booth, he stroked his fingers over his companion's bare shoulder.

"I heard about it from the concierge," she continued with a theatrical little shudder. "According to him, police divers recovered the spent shell casing."

Foster's hand froze.

"I have to admit, he didn't seem all that surprised that someone had taken a shot at this woman," Mackenzie confided ingenuously. "Evidently she's been stirring up all kinds of trouble. Something to do with the Alamo. Supposedly the story made all the papers. Maybe you read it?"

"No."

"Really? Well, you might see something soon. Rumor is the woman's about to release some bombshell report."

Careful, Nick thought. *Go careful here.*

"The concierge says she's reserved the hotel's ball-room for a big bash," Mackenzie continued airily. "She's going to give some kind of multimedia presentation, complete with sound, light and digital images."

Having neatly dropped her own bombshell, she snuggled into the crook of Foster's arm.

"Now, about the presentation *I'd* like to give you on the communications for your building. If you'll tell your secretary to provide me a set of blueprints, I can work up a detailed plan."

"Yeah, I'll do that." Disengaging, Foster reached into his back pocket and dragged out his billfold. "Listen, I'm sorry to run out on you like this, but I just remembered something I have to do."

"Now?"

"Now."

Tossing a bill onto the table, he started to slide out of the booth. Mackenzie halted him by the simple expedient of hooking a hand in his belt buckle.

"I want this contract." Her voice dropped to a seductive purr. "I'm fully prepared to give you a special deal."

Foster's startled glance dropped to his belt. Whatever Mackenzie's hand was doing behind the metal buckle had snagged his serious attention. Beads of sweat popped out on the man's brow. Nick felt a few pop out on his own.

"How long are you going to be in town?" the builder asked, his voice hoarse.

"That depends on you."

"I'll call you, okay?" He patted his shirt pocket. "I've still got your card. You see my secretary, tell her I said to make you a copy of the blueprints. Tomorrow, the next day, we'll, uh, get down to business."

With a smile that hovered between a pout and a promise, Mackenzie released him. Foster slid out and disappeared from the screen.

A moment later, Mackenzie winked at the camera. Her amused voice floated through the speakers.

"He might lose my business card, but until he changes belts, he'd not going to lose the bug I just stuck to his buckle. Over to you, control."

A half hour later, the team assembled in Jack's suite.

He and Ellie had listened via satellite link to the exchange between Mackenzie and Foster. Together with Mac and Cyrene, they now waited for the builder to take care of the something he'd suddenly remembered he had to do.

Foster made the call from his home just after 9:00 p.m.

Shaking her head, Mackenzie adjusted the volume on the receiver.

"What a jerk!"

Amazed that the man would be so stupid as to risk calling from his home, she listened to the muted beeps of the dial tone. Although muffled, they were picked up by the bug she'd planted on Foster. The control center's computers would translate those beeps instantly into numbers.

"Yeah?"

"This is Foster. Things are happening. Things I don't like. You have to take care of that business we discussed. Like, now."

"I'm workin' it."

"Work harder!"

The phone was slammed down.

The four people in the hotel suite maintained their silence, hoping for something more. An indiscreet mutter. A short, angry tirade. Anything that might give them a better clue as to Foster's arrangements with his contract killer. All they got was the clink of glass on glass and the sudden blare of the TV.

"Well, Scarface didn't say much," Mackenzie told the others, "but we should be able to get a voice print out of it. Let's see if Control got a lock on the number Foster dialed."

Jack stood at her shoulder. His face darkened as he read aloud the message that flashed on her screen.

"The number was traced to the call notes for a cell phone registered to Harold Berger, 2224 River Drive, Austin."

Cyrene's silver blond brows lifted. "The dead man?"

Nodding, Jack cut a quick glance at Ellie before turning to Mackenzie.

"Can you work a satellite lock on the transmissions to and from that cell phone?"

"Not unless we catch a call during a broadband sweep of the entire transmission area. The chances of that range from zero to minus zero."

Jack didn't like the answer. He could see that Ellie didn't much care for it, either.

"Control will take it from here," Mackenzie advised, shutting down her unit. "If there's any further contact tonight, they'll let us know."

She rose, as did Cyrene. The psychologist cocked her head, studying Jack's grim face.

"You're tired. I'll take first watch."

"I'm okay."

"You need sleep."

"I'm okay."

"I won't let anything happen to her," Claire said gently. "I promise. And you'll be right here, a shout away."

Jack knew damned well he was operating on sheer nerves. He also knew that he wasn't about to let Ellie out of his sight tonight. Or any other night, if he had any say in the matter.

"You stand first watch here in my room," he suggested by way of compromise. "Ellie can leave the connecting door open. I'll bed down on the couch in her sitting room."

Cyrene accepted the altered arrangements without argument. While she went to her room to collect a few things, Jack grabbed a pillow and blanket from the closet and deposited them on the rolled-arm sofa in the living room. He'd pulled out his automatic to check the magazine before he noticed the woman standing in the shadows. Hugging her arms, she stared blindly at the curtained windows.

"Ellie?"

She jumped and swung to face him. Her eyes were wide, their pupils dark pools.

"You okay?"

A shiver rippled down her spine. She didn't answer for a moment. She couldn't. The fact that she'd just heard Foster issuing her death warrant had taken some time to sink in, but sunk it had. She understood how the Alamo's defenders must have felt when Santa Anna delivered his final warning that he'd give no quarter if they continued their hopeless resistance.

Panic swept through her. She came within a breath of telling Jack that she'd changed her mind, that she wanted out of the hotel, out of the city and as far away from the Alamo as he could take her.

But she couldn't erase the mental image of that line in the sand. As much as she wanted to, she couldn't bring herself to tuck tail and run.

"I'm okay. Just a little shivery. Guess I've got the air-conditioning turned up too high."

The lie was so obvious Jack didn't bother to challenge it. Instead, he crossed the room, caught her in his arms and returned to the sofa. The cushions whooshed under his weight as he wedged his back into the corner. Settling Ellie comfortably in his lap, he gave her his warmth.

This wasn't the moment to tell her he'd also given her his heart. Not when Cyrene was moving about in the next room within easy earshot and a killer lurked somewhere in the shadows. He'd come as close to it as he dared earlier, when he told her she'd have to be the one to walk this time. She'd answered obliquely but unmistakably. That would do. For now.

Propping his chin on Ellie's head, he began to murmur the repetitive, hypnotic mantras that would ease the tension locking them both in steel cages.

For the first time in longer than he could remember, the relaxation techniques didn't work. Jack couldn't blank out the shape and scent of the woman nestled against him. Couldn't empty his mind of how near he'd come to losing her.

Again.

He didn't realize his hold had tightened around her until she squirmed and tipped her head back.

"Jack?"

Her eyes held a question, but it was her mouth he ached to answer. The tendons in his neck corded with the effort of holding back. He'd compromised her safety once by losing himself in her arms. He was damned if he'd do it again.

"Sorry," he murmured, loosening his hold. "Try to relax."

Lowering her head to his shoulder, she wiggled into a comfortable position. The movement of her bottom drove every mantra Jack had learned over the years right out of his head.

Gritting his teeth, he focused all his psychic energy on maintaining control over his body. He might not ever walk upright again after tonight, but he would keep Ellie safe at all costs.

Chapter 11

Detective Harris contacted Jack just after ten the next morning.

"We ran the bullet retrieved from the river through ballistics and sent the results to the FBI, who worked the Foster kidnapping and murder. You were right. The same gun fired both."

Jack's stomach clenched. No question now. Their conjectures had moved right out of the realm of possibility and into cold, lethal reality.

"So where does that leave us?"

"With some very excited FBI field agents who want to know just how the heck you tagged Dan Foster. They'd like to meet with both of us this afternoon. Two o'clock. Their offices are in the courthouse at 615 East Houston Street. Can you make it?"

His glance went to Ellie. She sat at the desk, a cold cup of coffee beside her. She was in jeans and a short-sleeved white shirt, its tails tucked in neatly at her trim waist. Dark circles shadowed her eyes, but her face wore a look of intense concentration.

She'd been hard at work since breakfast. Jack suspected her fierce attention to detail sprang as much from a need to keep her mind off her stalker as from a determination to tie up every loose end on her project. From the stack of field notes sitting beside the computer, he suspected she'd be at it for hours to come.

"Yes," he told Harris. "I can make it."

Cyrene would provide security for Ellie. Jack would take Mackenzie. She'd made the initial connection between Foster and Scarface and run it through her contact at the FBI. She'd also had two face-to-face sessions with Foster. The FBI guys were going to want to hear about those. And about the tag she'd put on the builder.

Mackenzie would know how to finesse that bit of electronic eavesdropping. OMEGA took its direction directly from the President and wasn't bound by the same rules and restrictions when it came to field operations as other government agencies, but it didn't hurt to head off jurisdictional disputes at the pass.

Cyrene was one of OMEGA's best. Jack could trust her to keep Ellie safe. Still, he had to force himself to the door after lunch.

With Jack gone, the suite seemed emptier, the afternoon endless.

Cyrene curled up on the sofa with a spy novel. Ellie made calls to several companies for estimates to fill in the excavation site. She also called each of the volunteers, thanking them for their assistance at the dig before putting the final touches on her report.

As she scrolled through the pages, she fought another sharp stab of disappointment. She and her team had come so close to fitting the pieces of the puzzle together. She hated to end the project by offering supposition and conjecture instead of fact.

Setting aside her personal feelings, she forced herself to take a critical eye to the report. She'd fine-tuned the sections detailing the discovery of the remains, the assembly of the team, the recovery of artifacts and the on-site authentication processes the team had employed. She'd add Dr. Dawes-Hamilton's laboratory results later.

The section dealing with the remains was the hardest to work on. She'd already incorporated Dr. Weaver's anthromorphical analysis, which included the basic physical features as extrapolated from the skeletal characteristics.

Male. Caucasian. Average height for his time. Age thirty to thirty-five. Indications of incipient arthritis, with some degree of bone degeneration in joints.

Propping her chin on her hands, Ellie stared at the terse summary. The shadowy figure of a Tejano formed in her mind. He didn't wear buckskins and rough frontier garb as depicted by Hollywood in its movies about the Alamo, but a broadcloth suit such as a doctor or lawyer might have donned. His face was shaded by a wide brimmed-hat to protect it from the fierce Texas sun. He grasped a double-barrel shotgun in one hand.

Who are you? she wondered for the hundredth time. *Did you escape the Alamo? If so, when? Before the final assault or after?*

Blowing out a long breath, she hit the laptop's keys.

By three o'clock the walls were starting to close in on her. Abandoning the computer, she decided to attack the cardboard box Sam Pierce had deposited on the floor. It took all her concentration to remain focused on the objects she pulled out to examine and verify against the inventory.

None of them appeared to hold any real historical significance. A broken snaffle bit. Several coins. A rusted tin plate. What looked like a piece of a plowshare.

At the bottom of the box, she found the dented silver disc Jack had turned up during his stint with Discoverer Two. Evidently the National Park Service hadn't considered the item worth salvaging. It was tarnished almost black, pitted all the way through and not anywhere near as valuable as the solid silver bracelet circling Ellie's wrist.

She'd never given Jack anything in return, she realized. She'd never had the opportunity. She'd only seen him once after he slipped the two-inch band on her wrist, and that was when she'd stormed into to the U.S. Embassy compound to engage in a furious, one-sided argument with a certain hardheaded Marine.

The small, dented concho wasn't in the same class as the expensive bracelet, but polished, it might make a keepsake for Jack. Something to remind him of these days in San Antonio—as if either one of them would need reminding!

Fingering the disk, she dialed housekeeping. "This is Dr. Alazar in Room two ten. Would you please send up a small jar of silver polish and a soft cloth? Yes, silver polish. Thanks."

Claire looked up from her book, her glance curious.

"Jack found this out at the site," Ellie explained, displaying the bit of silver. "I'm going to clean it up for him as a souvenir."

A maid delivered the requested items. No doubt the Menger's management was wondering just what Dr. Alazar was up to now. After passing the woman a generous tip, Ellie went to work on the concho.

Gradually, the tarnish disappeared to display an intricate pattern stamped into the silver. The design was extraordinarily artistic, with scrolls and swirls and a tiny oak leaf cut in the center. The oak leaf wasn't a traditional Mexican symbol. It struck her as more like a design a silversmith would do for one of the Tejanos.

A vague memory stirred in the back of her mind. She'd seen a design like this before. She was sure of it. But where?

Puzzled, she took it to the desk. A search of her database turned up no images that matched it. Only after a second lengthy search did she remember the design stamped into the silver work on the shotgun she'd photographed at the Alamo.

A touch of the old excitement fluttered in her veins. Pulling up the image of the double-barreled shotgun, she examined the elaborate scrollwork on the sidings and butt plate.

Yes! There it was! A small oak leaf in the center of the scrollwork.

Her excitement taking wing, she pulled up images of the gun they'd found some yards away from the skeletal remains. The silver was still tarnished, the design difficult to decipher, but Ellie could swear it was the same.

Okay. All right. What did she have here? Not a whole lot, except the possibility that the smith who worked the silver facings on both guns might very well have crafted the concho Jack had found.

Once more she attacked the computerized files. The

minutes ticked by. Undaunted, Ellie conducted search after search before she found a reference to Josiah Kennett, one of the Alamo's more obscure defenders. Or more specifically, to the silver conchos on Josiah's Kennett's hat.

Suddenly, Ellie remembered the miniature portrait of an unsmiling young man, his collar tight around his neck and his face shadowed by the wide-brimmed hat favored by Mexicans and Tejanos alike. She'd seen his miniature in the Alamo, right next to the man's tattered Bible.

The thrill she always felt when the pieces of a historical puzzle began to fall together gripped her. Closing her fingers over the silver disk, she swung around in her chair.

"When's Jack going to be back?" she asked Claire.

"I don't know. Soon, I would think. Why?"

"I need to make a quick visit to the Alamo. I think I may have a clue to the identity of the remains that my team and I recovered. I won't know until I get a shot of a portrait in the museum and enlarge it."

"It's not a good idea for you to leave the hotel," Claire countered gently. "Not until Jack gets back, anyway."

Ellie had no intention of taking a step outside the Menger without Jack. "Can you contact him? Find out where he is?"

"Of course."

Slipping a small cell phone out of her pocket, she pressed a single button.

"This is a secure instrument," she said with a smile as she put the instrument to her ear. "Mackenzie would take it as a personal insult if anyone ever eavesdropped on one of us."

Like Mackenzie herself was doing to Dan Foster. Recalling the builder's terse call last night, Ellie almost changed her mind about leaving the confines of her hotel room. A cowardly little voice inside her head whispered at her to hunker down behind strong barricades and stay there until it was safe to come out.

She couldn't cower behind drawn shades and closed doors forever, though. And a determined foe could breech even the strongest walls…as the defenders of the Alamo had learned all too well.

Shoving her hands in her pocket, she listened to Claire's side of the conversation with Jack. Evidently, she'd caught him and Mackenzie on their way back to the hotel. His first instinct was to flatly veto Ellie's request for a quick trip next door. His second, to acknowledge the bitter truth. If two OMEGA agents backed-up by their chief of communications couldn't keep her safe, no one could. Period. End of story.

"He'll meet us in the lobby in fifteen minutes," Claire advised. "Hang loose while I run a check of the halls and the elevators."

Her movements graceful and unhurried, she hooked her purse over her shoulder and exited the suite. In her gray pleated linen slacks, narrow belt and sliky green blouse, she could easily pass for one of the hotel's well-heeled guests instead of a highly specialized protective agent.

At least that's what Ellie assumed she was. One of these days, she vowed, she'd have to pin these people down on exactly who they worked for. Pacing the room, she rubbed her thumb over the silver disk and waited in mounting impatience for Claire's return.

"All clear," she advised after a short absence.

Snatching up her camera and a curled-brim crush-able straw hat, Ellie hurried out the door.

Jack and Mackenzie met them as they stepped out of the elevator. He didn't have much to say about his visit to the FBI and Ellie knew better than to probe for details in such a public place. He did, however, want to know what the hell was behind the urgent visit to the Alamo.

"This."

Pulling her hand out of her pocket, Ellie uncurled her fingers. "It's the concho you found at the excavation site. Look at the design. I've seen it before, Jack. I'm sure I have. I just need to verify where."

He shook his head but could tell from the suppressed excitement in her voice that she thought she was on to something.

"Okay. Just stay with me, and do exactly what I say the instant I say it. Cyrene, you take point. Mac, you've got rearguard."

With Claire strolling ahead and Mackenzie trailing behind, they walked outside. After the controlled chill of the hotel's air-conditioning, the muggy Texas summer hit them like a baseball bat. Hastily, Ellie slipped on sunglasses and tugged her hat lower on her brow to shield her face. Her skin began to dew before they covered half the distance to the monument next door.

The usual crowd milled around Alamo Plaza, snapping photos in from of the mission and slurping up ice-cream cones purchased from nearby vendors. The hair on the back of Ellie's neck prickled as her glance roamed over the tourists. Was Scarface lurking among these camera-laden sightseers?

Her pulse skittered when she caught a glimpse of a straw Stetson similar the one the killer had been wear-

ing when she'd unintentionally photographed him with
Dan Foster, but the face beneath the brim belonged to
a short, stocky man of Hispanic descent. He carried a
baby in one arm and had looped the other around his
young son's shoulders.

Blowing out a sigh of relief, Ellie pushed through the
door set in the massive walls. Once inside, a welcome
wash of cool air surrounded them.

"Oh-oh!"

Elle's murmured exclamation put Jack on instant
alert. Claire's head whipped around. Her hand disappeared inside her purse. Mackenzie hurried up to add
to the living shield around Ellie.

"Do we have a problem?" Jack asked softly.

"Yes," Ellie whispered, "but not the one you're worried about. See that docent?"

All three agents eyed the gray-haired volunteer
cheerfully passing out brochures.

"If she recognizes me," Ellie whispered, sliding her
sunglasses back up the bridge of her nose, "she'll call
out the palace guard. Would one of you distract her long
enough for me to slip by?"

Claire had no difficulty claiming the docent's attention. A simple question about the age of the wood
beams overhead had the volunteer craning her neck to
point out original iron nails and peg-joints. Ellie kept
her face averted and whisked right past.

Once inside the courtyard, the ripple of excitement
she'd felt earlier in her hotel room returned. History was
both her profession and her passion. Solving the mystery
of the remains found in a creek bed five miles south of
the Alamo might not rank up there with discovering
the Dead Sea scrolls or deciphering the Rosetta Stone,

but putting a name to the man who died alone and unmourned would afford her immense personal satisfaction. Consequently, she paced in a fever of impatience until Claire rejoined them.

"The exhibit I want to see is in that long, low building."

Cyrene, you stay outside and surveil the crowd," Jack instructed, slipping a hand under Ellie's elbow. "Mac, I want you at the entrance."

Nodding, both women took up their posts.

As she and Jack entered the Long Barracks, Ellie kept a wary eye out for Dr. Smith. The museum director had insisted she submit written requests for further access to the private collections. He hadn't said anything about the public exhibits, but she wasn't taking any chances.

The display case containing Josiah Kennett's tattered Bible and miniature was in a small room filled with artifacts belonging to the Alamo's lesser-known defenders. Ellie's gaze shot straight to the hat shading Kennett's young, unsmiling face.

A narrow leather strap banded the crown. Ellie's breath caught as she noted the silver conchos ornamenting the band. Given the small size of the portrait, she couldn't tell whether or not the design included a small oak leaf.

A quick glance around the room showed she and Jack were alone. A clutch of tourists peered at exhibits in the room across the hall, but for the moment at least, Ellie had Josiah Kennett all to herself.

"I just need a few pictures," she said, excitement simmering in her veins.

She was reaching for her digital camera when Jack's

cell phone gave a discreet ping. Sliding it out of her pocket, he glanced at the digital display.

"It's Mac."

Flipping open the phone, he tried to acknowledge the call. A frown creased his forehead. The static coming through the line was so loud even Ellie could hear it.

"Something's breaking up my transmission," Jack muttered. His gaze snagged on the intrusion detection device mounted above the exhibit cases. "Probably the infrared beams from those security alarms."

"Probably," Ellie agreed, absorbed by the contents of the exhibit case. "The Alamo is more wired than Fort Knox."

Jack glanced down the way they'd come. The halls were clear. The rest of the tourists had moved onto another section of the museum. Mac was right outside, ten steps away. Jack could keep Ellie in sight while he checked with Comm on the transmission problems.

"Do not leave this room," he ordered tersely. "I'll be right back."

He took two steps down the hall. Caught a faint whisper of sound. Sheer instinct spun him down and around.

There was a soft pop. A fiery explosion of pain. With a small grunt, Jack took the bullet.

Unaware of the lethal drama taking place just paces away, Ellie fiddled with the settings for her camera and snapped away. She'd have to do more research on Kennett. Verify where he came from. How he ended up at the Alamo. If possible, determine what weapons he was carrying when he joined the ranks of defenders.

Humming, she zoomed in on the miniature. Only then did the significance of the small leather pouch slung over Kennett's left shoulder sink in. On closer examination, she decided it could well be a courier's pouch, like those carried by army scouts. Identical, in fact, to one she'd seen in a portrait of James Allen, the sixteen-year-old courier who carried Travis's last, desperate appeal for reinforcements out of the Alamo on March 5th, the day before Santa Anna attacked in full force.

She knew from historical documents that Travis had sent out a number of couriers, some identified by name, some not. James Butler Bonham, a lawyer and fellow South Carolinian from Travis's home county, had tracked down Colonel James Fannin at Goliad. Captain Juan Seguin carried an appeal directly to Sam Houston. Young James Allen made that last, hopeless ride.

As she tried to recall references to the other, unnamed couriers, the possibilities burst like fireworks in Ellie's mind. Maybe Travis had gleaned intelligence warning of the imminent attack. Maybe he'd worried one courier might not get through enemy lines. Maybe he'd sent two, sacrificing badly needed firepower in the hope that one of them would make it. Maybe young Kennett wasn't fleeing the massacre on March 6th, but trying urgently to prevent it.

She'd have to go back through the inventory of artifacts recovered at the dig. Check to see if there was any bit of metal or scrap of rotted rawhide that might have come from a pouch. Snapping away, she recorded several more digital images. The creak of a floorboard behind her had her whirling to share the exciting possibilities with Claire and Jack.

It wasn't Jack who stood in the doorway, however. Or Claire. It was a tourist in mirrored sunglasses and a black ball cap emblazoned with NYPD in gold letters. Ellie took in the reassuring lettering and started to smile a welcome. Her smile turned into a sick gulp when she noticed the white scar tracing a path in the tanned folds of the man's neck.

"Hello, Dr. Alazar."

She didn't need the faint mockery in his greeting— or the long, lethal silencer screwed to the muzzle of the pistol in his hand—to know she'd come face-to-face with her stalker.

"Jack!"

Her frantic scream bounced off the thick walls.

"Your friend can't hear you," Scarface said with a grim smile. "He can't hear anything."

Despair knifed into Ellie, so sharp and lancing she almost doubled over.

"No!" she moaned. "Dear God, no!"

"Yes," the thug taunted. "And now…"

"You bastard!"

Acting from sheer animal instinct, Ellie reached behind her and smashed her digital camera into the glass exhibit case. Before the first, shrieking alarm had filled the air, she brought her arm forward and flung her camera at Scarface.

What was left of the glass exhibit case behind her shattered. Ellie didn't hear the gunshot over the screaming alarm, didn't even care that his first shot had missed. Fingers curled into claws, she launched herself at the man.

She had to get past him, had to get to Jack….

Before she reached him, there was a bright flash. An unseen force propelled her attacker into the room. He collided with Ellie, took her down. Frantic, she tried to scramble out from under his dead weight.

"Ellie!"

The hoarse croak came from above her. A fist reached down, yanked at the weight crushing her into the floor. The instant she could wiggle free, she rolled onto all fours. Broken glass cut into her hands and knees. The alarm shrieked like the hounds of hell, but Ellie felt nothing, heard nothing but a roaring rush of joy.

Jack! It was Jack! Blood flowered like a bright, obscene hibiscus on his shirt. His face was dead white. But his eyes were feral as he went down on one knee beside her, keeping his weapon trained on the man sprawled in a growing puddle of blood the whole time.

"Were you hit?"

She saw his mouth move. Saw, too, the near panic in his eyes as they raked her from head to foot.

"What?"

Mackenzie raced into the room at that moment, followed a second later by Claire. Ellie saw the weapon in their hands, saw their lips moving, but couldn't hear anything over the deafening clang.

Jack motioned to Claire to keep Scarface covered and whirled back to Ellie. "Where were you hit?"

She shook her head, unable to hear but grasping the reason for his fear. Blood splattered her white blouse and drenched her jeans from the knees down.

"I'm okay!" she yelled. "But you…" Frantic, she fluttered her sliced palms at blood-drenched shirt. "You've been shot!"

The alarm cut off abruptly. Her ears ringing, Ellie tried to understand what Jack was saying as he gently grasped her wrists.

"It looks worse than it is. Damned bullet ricocheted

off the bone and took me down for a few moments, but it went clear through."

Mackenzie's sneakers crunched on the glass as she crouched down beside them. "Just hold still," she instructed, "we'll get you patched up and…"

The sound of running footsteps cut her off. Jack chopped a hand in the air, motioning her to one side, and shoved Ellie behind him. Claire slammed her shoulder blades against the wall, where she could keep both Scarface and the door covered. Ellie tensed for another attack.

Dr. Smith burst in. His jaw dropping, the pudgy museum curator gaped in disbelief at the carnage. His wild gaze flew from the unconscious figure on the floor to Claire, to Jack. Finally, to Ellie.

Red suffused his cheeks. His eyes bugged behind his glasses. He sputtered, choked, spit out Ellie's name like a curse.

"Dr. Alazar! I should have known! What in God's name are you doing?"

The combination of stark terror and relief so deep and sharp it ate like acid into her bones had her snapping right back.

"What does it look like we're doing, you twit? We're fighting the second battle of the Alamo."

Chapter 12

Keeping a tight lid on the shoot-out at the Alamo required the combination of Renegade's forceful personality and Lightning's political influence. There was no way they wanted Foster to know his hit man had gone down. Not yet anyway.

Dr. Smith went tight-lipped with indignation and disapproval when informed that the President's special envoy had placed a call to the head of the Daughters of the Texas Revolution. She had agreed that this unfortunate attack on the niece of the President of Mexico was a matter for the police, not the press.

The various law enforcement agencies involved concurred. Wheeling Scarface out of the Alamo on a gurney, they informed the gawking tourists that there had been an accident. He died in the ambulance on the way to the hospital without recovering consciousness. His demise left a frustrated Detective Harris and two very disgruntled FBI agents with no clue to the hit man's real identity. Or with anything linking him to Daniel Foster except Ellie's photograph.

"Which," Claire said later that evening in Ellie's hotel suite, "Foster's lawyers will argue is merely a chance juxtaposition of two visitors to a popular historic landmark."

"Yeah, right," Mackenzie groused. "Some visitors."

She took a turn around the sitting room, hands shoved into the front pockets of her jeans. Her Nikes left tracked imprints on the plush carpet. The sex kitten who'd nestled up to Foster at the bar last night was gone. In her place was a woman imbued with a sense of purpose.

"We all know Foster hired that bastard to off his wife. We just can't prove it. There's no record of money transfers from his bank to suspicious accounts. No traceable phones calls besides the one we intercepted, and that was made to a cell phone we *think* belonged to Scarface but can't locate, as he didn't have it on him when he died."

Ellie sat quietly in an armchair, her bandaged hands tucked loosely around her waist. More bandages showed beneath the hem of her shorts, padding her knees. She couldn't get quite as worked up as Mackenzie over Daniel Foster's probable guilt. Not just yet. She was still recovering from the trauma of dodging the assassin's bullet.

Jack had remained quiet since they'd returned from the emergency room, too. As he assured her, the bullet had merely glanced off his clavicle. Luckily, the bone hadn't shattered. The entrance and exit wound were clear. He'd refused pain pills and now listened to the others with every evidence of attention, but his glance shifted to Ellie at frequent intervals, as if to make sure she wasn't about to keel over from blood loss or delayed shock.

"Foster's got to be a mass of raw nerves right now," Mackenzie continued. "He'll be expecting a call from Scarface with confirmation he's done the deed. Every hour that goes by without word is going to torque up the pressure on Danny Boy. Sooner or later, he's going to do something stupid. I say we make it sooner."

"I say we let him sweat," Jack countered. "For tonight, anyway."

"Yes, but—"

"I agree with Renegade," Claire said, rising from her chair with fluid grace. "As long as the incident at the Alamo doesn't leak to the press, Foster will think Scarface is still on the hunt. That puts the advantage squarely in our court. Let's use the time to think through our next moves."

Hooking an arm through Mackenzie's, Cyrene gently but firmly steered the younger woman out. Jack followed them to the door, shot the dead bolt and armed the intrusion detection alarm he'd rigged when he'd arrived. The immediate threat to Ellie had been eliminated, but he couldn't shake an edgy sense of incompleteness. She still had to wrap up the last details of her project. He still had to decide whether to go after Foster or leave him to the locals.

Then there was the small matter of where he and Ellie went from here.

Tonight wasn't the time to talk about it, though. His wound hurt like hell and Ellie looked ready to drop. Her shoulders drooped. Fatigue left shadows like bruises under her eyes. If that weren't enough to rouse Jack's fiercely protective instincts, the bandages on her hands and knees would have done the trick.

"You should get some sleep," he said, his voice gruff with concern. "You've had a hell of a day."

"It was rather eventful." A faint smile feathered her lips. "Do you think Dr. Smith will ever let me set foot inside the Alamo again?"

"I'd say you'll have to do some real sweet talking first."

"Maybe he'll relent when he hears my theory about young Josiah Kennett."

"Maybe. In the meantime, I suggest you forget Smith, forget Kennett, forget the second battle of the Alamo and crawl into bed."

"I might, if you crawl in with me."

Her smile deepened, starting an ache almost as fierce as the one in Jack' shoulder.

The docs said you should rest," she reminded him, using her bandaged hands to lever herself awkwardly out of her chair. "Let's go to bed."

Yeah, right. As if he'd get any rest lying next to Ellie. Particularly when she stopped beside the bed and lifted her hands helplessly.

"You'll have to undress me. I can't work my shirt buttons with these bandages."

Jack's throat went dry. "I think I can manage that."

"I think you can, too."

His blood was pounding, but he kept his touch gentle as he unbuttoned the linen camp shirt Claire had helped her into after returning from the E.R.

The docs had assured Jack they'd extracted all the glass shards from Ellie's palms and knees, and that the cuts weren't deep enough to require stitches. Yet the gauzy bandages were a grim reminder as he eased the shirt down past her elbows.

If he hadn't caught that faint whisper of sound and dodged the assassin's bullet, if Ellie hadn't won a few precious seconds by flinging her camera at the killer, she might have been the one wheeled out of the Alamo on a gurney. The thought made his chest squeeze so tight he couldn't breathe.

She didn't seem to notice the sudden constriction in his breathing. Heeling off her shoes, she kicked them aside and waited patiently for Jack to start on her shorts.

By the time he'd stripped her down to her bra and bikini briefs, more than just his chest was tight. Hard and aching, he skimmed a knuckle down the hollow of her belly.

"You sure you don't want another of the pain pills the docs prescribed?"

"I'm not feeling any pain at the moment. My sleep shirt is over there, on the chair."

Jack retrieved the scrap of cotton. The damned thing had put him in a sweat the first time he'd seen her in it. He was feeling pretty much the same effect now. Ignoring the painful pull in his shoulder, he eased it over her head.

"Now you," she murmured.

Ellie's throat closed as he eased off his shirt. The neat bandage wrapped around his shoulder brought the afternoon's horror rushing back. Inching sideways on the bed, she made room for him.

"Fine pair we are," he said with a wry grin. "Come here."

Slipping his uninjured arm under her, he brought her

closer. Ellie cradled her head in his good shoulder. Her palm rested on his chest. Beneath her fingers was the strong, sure beat of his heart.

"This afternoon," she whispered, "when Scarface said you couldn't hear my scream. I thought… I thought I'd lost you."

"I thought the same thing when I barreled through the door and saw you go down."

Curling a knuckle under her chin, he tipped her head up. His eyes held hers.

"A few nights ago, you asked if I'd ever loved you. I've never stopped, Ellie."

"Oh, Jack!" She wanted to weep with the joy and the sharp, stinging regret. "We wasted so many years. So many days and nights we could have shared."

"I know." His thumb brushed her cheek. "I don't plan to waste any more."

She hooked a brow. His teeth flashed in a rueful grin.

"After tonight," he amended. "Go to sleep, sweet-heart."

The bright bubble of joy was still with Ellie the next morning, when she bundled into one of the hotel's plush terry-cloth robes, made a futile attempt at wielding a hairbrush, and ambled into the sitting room in search of Jack and coffee.

She found both, as well as two other men. One was a stranger. The other Ellie recognized immediately.

"Colonel Esteban!"

"Elena. It is good to see you again."

Moving with the grace of a jungle panther, he came forward and bowed over her hand. Ellie had met him on several occasions during her visits to her aunt and uncle, yet even her awareness of the shadowy world the colonel worked in couldn't blunt the impact of his dark eyes, luxuriant mustache and Caesar Romero smile. Ellie might have fallen in love with Jack Carstairs all over again, but she wasn't blind. Nor was she oblivious to the tension in the air.

Frowning, she threw a quick, questioning look at Jack. He had obviously rolled out of bed well before she did. Showered and shaved, he filled a cup with black coffee and carefully passed it into her bandaged hands.

"How's your shoulder?" she asked.

"Hurting but healing. How are your hands?"

"The same."

Downing a grateful sip, Ellie returned her attention to the colonel. "It's good to see you, too. What are you doing in San Antonio?"

"Your uncle sent me. He was informed of the unfortunate incident at the Alamo and wishes to be assured you took no serious hurt."

"I'm fine."

The colonel's glance drifted to the white gauze.

"I just took a few cuts and bruises," Ellie said. "Really. You can tell Uncle Eduardo I'm up and walking and ready to get back to work."

"Perhaps you should tell him yourself. He would like you to come stay in Mexico until the U.S. authorities take care of this bastard who wants you dead."

"We were discussing that last night. Getting hard evidence against Daniel Foster could take months, even years. I can't—correction, I *won't*—run away and hide that long."

The stranger had said nothing, but her protest brought him forward. He was a tall man, dressed with casual elegance in knife-pleated gray slacks and an Italian knit sport shirt.

"We don't believe it will take as long as that, Dr. Alazar."

"And 'we' are?"

"Sorry. I should have introduced myself sooner. I'm Nick Jensen, special envoy to the President of the United States."

Ellie had spent enough summers with her uncle to have a good grasp of the various levels of bureaucracy inherent in any government. Despite that background, she didn't have a clue what a special envoy did.

Jensen didn't enlighten her. "Like your uncle, the President is concerned for your safety. That's one of the reasons we sent Renegade—Jack—to protect you."

"You sent him? But I thought—that is…"

"That your uncle hired him? Let's just say it was arranged through my office."

Well, she'd already figured out Jack Carstairs wasn't the down-at-heels gumshoe she'd first thought him, but the fact that he worked for the special envoy to the President of the United States took some getting used to. Struggling with the mental readjustment, she picked up on Jensen's comment.

"You said concern for my safety was one of the reasons you sent Jack to San Antonio. What were the others?"

"Quite frankly, the President also worried that the ill will displayed toward you could erupt into ugly anti-Mexico sentiments, possibly derail the North American Free Trade Association Treaty. Neither Mexico nor the United States wanted to see that happen."

A sick feeling curled in Ellie's stomach. She didn't look at Jack. She couldn't.

"Let me get this straight," she said slowly, the coffee cup cradled in both hands. "You—all of you—got involved in this mess because political issues were at play?"

"Political issues are always at play," Jensen said, "but your safety was the overriding concern, of course."

His rueful smile might have charmed Ellie under any other circumstances. At the moment, she was too numbed by the thought that she'd been a political pawn in a game she'd known nothing about.

"Of course," she echoed dully.

"It's still the overriding concern," Jensen continued smoothly. "Foster has already demonstrated the lengths he'll go to. He hired one killer. There's nothing to say he wouldn't hire another. The President thinks you should consider your uncle's offer. Or at least let us take you to a safe house until Jack and the others put Foster on ice."

"I see."

Carefully, she placed the cup on the sofa table. She felt frowsy and frumpy and at a distinct disadvantage facing Esteban and Jensen in her bare feet and bathrobe. But those feelings paled beside the ache that formed around her heart when she turned and saw Jack's face. There was no sign of the tender lover in his stony expression. No spark of warmth in his cool blue eyes.

"What do you think? Should I leave San Antonio?"

"Yes."

She waited for some softening of the hardness in his face, some indication another separation would rip him apart as much as it would her. When he didn't so much as blink, Ellie's hurt took a sharp right turn into anger.

No! Not again! Jack Carstairs had gone all stubborn and tight-jawed and noble about what was best for her nine years ago. No way in *hell* she was going to let him do it again!

Her spine snapped straight. Matching him stare for stony stare, she made her position ice clear. "You said I'd have to be the one to walk away this time. I told you then and I'm telling you again, I'm not walking. So you can just deal with it. All three of you!"

On that note, she exited the scene. Slamming the bedroom door behind her was childish and unnecessary, but it gave Ellie intense satisfaction.

The thud reverberated through the sitting room. Esteban and Jensen stared at the closed door for some moments before turning to Jack.

"You were right," Nick conceded with a grin. "She didn't take kindly to the idea of being hustled out of town. We'll have to fall back and regroup."

Luis Esteban wasn't quite as ready to admit defeat. Smoothing a palm over his lustrous black hair, he gave the closed door a disgruntled glance. "You must speak with her, Carstairs. Convince her to leave. You and I, together we will handle this Foster."

"You and I?"

"President Alazar has suggested I remain in San Antonio to, ah, provide whatever assistance you might require."

Hell! That's all Jack needed! A watchdog hired by Ellie's uncle looking over his shoulder, second-guessing his every move. The urge to tell the colonel just what he and Eduardo Alazar could do with their so-called assistance rose hot and swift in Jack's throat.

He swallowed the words, right along with his pride. With Ellie still at risk, he wasn't about to turn away any help. Lightning made the bitter pill easier to take when Jack had assembled Comm and Cyrene in his suite some fifteen minutes later.

"Luis Esteban worked a hairy mission with Maggie Sinclair some years ago," he said by way of introduction. "She and Thunder both came to my office to meet with him a few weeks ago. The colonel's gone into the private sector now, but he's still one of us."

That was all the endorsement Mackenzie required. "Anyone Chameleon considers a good guy *is* a good guy in my book."

Her unconditional acceptance won her a quick, slashing grin from Esteban. Those gleaming white teeth and glinting black eyes sent the gulp of coffee she'd just taken down the wrong pipe. Choking, Mackenzie rattled the cup onto the table, splashing lukewarm liquid on the polished surface.

Claire was more reserved in her reaction to the newcomer. Reaching across to pound her sputtering colleague on the back, she gave the colonel a cool, assessing look.

Esteban's gaze was considerably warmer. Where in God's name did OMEGA recruit these women? Maggie Sinclair was in a class by herself. The one called Mackenzie possessed a lively animation and a quick wit. But this one, this mature, composed beauty, stirred his blood in a way no woman had since... Well, since Maggie Sinclair.

He'd have to find out more about her. His resources might not reach as deep or as far as OMEGA's, but he could still access information when he wanted it.

"So why are you and the colonel here?" the dark-haired Mackenzie asked Lightning when her fit of coughing subsided. "What's the plan?"

"The plan is, ah, under review at the moment. As to what Colonel Esteban and I are doing here... We flew down to convince Dr. Alazar she shouldn't take any more risks."

"Well, darn!" A look of acute disappointment crossed Mackenzie's expressive face. "I wish I'd been here to hear Ellie's response to that."

Even Cyrene was amused. "Renegade made the same argument. Apparently you two didn't have any more success than he did."

"We'll try again," the colonel assured her. "She must realize we have only her best interests at heart."

Her best interests.

The words clanged like a klaxon in Jack's head. He'd uttered them himself. More than once. For the first time, he recognized how pompous and patronizing they must sound to Ellie. As if she weren't intelligent or rational or mature enough to recognize her needs.

He still wanted her out of San Antonio. His overriding instinct was to shield her, to safeguard her from all harm. If anything, the shoot-out at the Alamo yesterday had reinforced the edgy feeling that she wouldn't be out of danger until they nailed Foster.

Jack had finally learned his lesson, though. He couldn't make her decisions for her. Nor could anyone else. It was time he acknowledged that fact. Past time.

"Why don't we get Ellie's input into the revised plan?"

The suggestion earned him a frown from Esteban, a curious glance from Lightning and an emphatic second from Mackenzie. Claire sent her approval in the form of a small nod.

Crossing the room, Jack rapped on the bedroom door. "Ellie? We want to talk to you."

The door swung open. She emerged from the bedroom wearing crisp linen slacks, a sleeveless turquoise top and a decided air of authority.

"I have a few things to say to you, too." She made a quick sweep of the room, nodding at Claire and Mackenzie. "Good, you're here. I won't have to repeat myself."

Moving to the center of the sitting room, she tucked her injured hands under her crossed arms.

"All right, listen up. Here's what we're going to do. I'm going to finish my research into Josiah Kennett and coordinate the final report with my team. That should take twenty-four hours, less if I get right to it. Then I'll release the team's findings. Right here, in San Antonio. We'll gather the public forum Mackenzie hinted to Foster about and blow it up big. Invite the media. The mayor. The city council. Influential members of the business community and country club set. Including," she announced grimly, "one Dan Foster."

"Oh, this is good," Mackenzie breathed. "Really good! Danny Boy will go ballistic when he gets the invite."

"We'll hold the reception here at the hotel," Ellie continued, directing her comments to the three men, daring them to object. "It's short notice, but we have to hope they can accommodate us. I'll work the crowd at the reception. I'll also contrive to get Foster alone at some point. You," she said, pinning Jack with a look that could have cut glass, "will come up with some scheme to get him to incriminate himself."

"I think I can manage that," he drawled.

"Good!" With the air of one who's firmly in charge, she surveyed the group. "Does anyone have any questions or comments?"

"Just one," Nick said in the short silence that followed.

Ellie braced herself for an argument. To her surprise, Jack stepped between her and the President's special envoy.

"We're doing this her way, Nick."

His firm, no-arguments tone had Ellie blinking. A few moments ago, he'd stated flatly that he wanted her out of San Antonio. She still hadn't quite recovered from the hurt of knowing he'd been following a political as well as a personal agenda all this time.

Now he was not only acknowledging her right to make her own decisions, it sounded as though he was fully prepared to sacrifice a second career for her. Thoroughly confused, she couldn't decide whether to whoop in delight or warn him to back off, fast.

Not that he would have listened. From the set to his jaw, it was obvious Jack had no intention of backing down.

"Ellie's had her baptism under fire," he told Jensen. "She's earned her spurs. We're doing this her way or not at all."

Once again, she was surprised. Instead of taking offense, Jensen merely nodded.

"You're in charge on this mission, Renegade. You call the shots. I was simply going to offer my restaurant as an alternative site for the big announcement. It will hold as many or more than the hotel's ballroom and give us better control over security."

Ellie blinked. "You own a restaurant?"

"Actually, I own several."

"Try several dozen," Mackenzie muttered. "Ever hear of Nick's?"

"Good heavens, yes! There's one in Mexico City. In Acapulco, too, I think."

Mackenzie held up a hand and ticked off a few others. "And Paris and Rome and Hong Kong, New York, Vegas, Palm Springs. You'll find a Nick's about everywhere the rich and famous gather."

"And none of them," he commented with a glinting look in her direction, "serve sausage, double pepperoni and jalapeño pizza."

"Too bad." She tossed the words back. "You won't get my business unless you diversify your menu."

"We'll have to talk about that. Along with the expanded operation role you've assumed on this mission."

"Uh-oh." Mackenzie's brows waggled. "This doesn't sound good."

"Let's go to my room, shall we? I had Mrs. Wells book one just in case I decided to stay." He gave the others a polite nod. "If you'll excuse us."

With the exaggerated air of a martyr about to meet her fate, Mackenzie preceded him to the door.

Chapter 13

Mrs. Wells hadn't just booked Lightning a room. She'd reserved the presidential suite.

Of course.

The palatial five-room suite took up most of the top floor and gave stunning views of the Alamo. Ornate furnishings from a bygone era made Mackenzie feel as though she'd stepped into the bustling days of Texas before the turn of the century, when cattle was king and Judge Roy Bean's Lillie Langtry thrilled audiences from coast to coast. The massive antique sideboard that housed a bar and entertainment center had been carved from some dark, brooding wood. So had the canopied four-poster she glimpsed in the bedroom. The thing looked like it could comfortably sleep six!

"Forget the ballroom and your restaurant," Macken-zie commented. "You could fit the mayor, the city council, the entire country club set and every news crew in Texas in this suite."

"Let's talk about a certain member of that country club set." Tossing his room key onto the sideboard, Nick leaned his hips against it and slid his hands in the pockets of his gray slacks. "You got pretty chummy with Foster at the bar the other night."

Airily she waved a hand. "All part of the job, chief."

"But not part of your job. When I instructed you to put a tag on the man, I didn't say to do it yourself."

"You didn't say not to, either."

"Don't play games with me, Comm."

The whip in his voice brought her snapping to attention. "No, *sir!* I would never do that, *sir!*"

Nick eyed her for long moments. The coins in his pocket clinked as he jiggled them in one hand.

"Did any of your Navy commanders ever consider a court-martial?"

"One or two." Grinning, she abandoned her exaggerated pose. "I was usually shipped out before matters reached that point."

"I may just ship you out this time, too."

"That's your option," she agreed breezily, refusing to admit this annoyed, unsmiling Nick was just a little bit intimidating. "But I was thinking our friend Foster might want a date for the big do. Someone who can give him an alibi when his hired gun shows up at the party."

"Why would he think Scarface will show?"

"Well, I sorta figured I'd tell him."

Lightning's eyes narrowed. The coins clinked again. Mackenzie held her breath until he broke the small silence.

"How?"

She was on her turf now. Confident, eager, she sketched her idea.

"We got a voiceprint on Scarface when Foster called him. It's not much. Only a few words. But we can digitize the sounds and run them through a phonetics databank, then use a synthesizer to imitate his exact intonation. Tweety Bird could chirp into the phone, and Foster would think it was his hired killer."

He didn't argue her skills. No one could. When it came to electronics, she was the best.

"Think about it, chief. Foster will want to attend the function to make sure the hit goes down *before* Ellie makes her announcement and releases her report to the media. But he'll need an alibi, someone who can swear he was otherwise engaged when it happens. I'll be that alibi. I'll also make sure we get our boy on tape when Renegade figures out how to get him to incriminate himself."

Lightning wasn't convinced. "There's a good chance Foster already paid for one death and is working on a second. I don't like the idea of my chief of communications turning up number three on his list."

"Aww. Are you worried about me, boss?"

"Worrying about OMEGA's operatives comes with the title of director, Blair, but you're adding a new dimension to the mix."

Mackenzie would have had all four incisors yanked without the benefit of anesthetic before she admitted to the thrill his sardonic reply gave her. Still, she couldn't hold back a smug little smile as she sashayed to the door.

"I'll get my folks at headquarters to work running the voiceprint through the phonetics database."

* * *

While Jack accompanied Nick to his San Antonio bistro to perform an initial security assessment, Ellie got to work. Her bandaged hands made things awkward, but she spent several hours engaged in a flurry of phone calls and e-mail exchanges with universities, libraries and genealogists. Finally, she tracked down the clerk of Kearnes County, Texas, where Josiah Kennett's family had reportedly homesteaded. After a hand search of county records, the clerk located an eighty-seven-year-old great-great granddaughter of Kennett's only sister.

Ellie got Dorinda Johnson's number from information. To her delight, the woman who identified herself as Dorrie answered the phone. She sounded frail but had no difficulty grasping Ellie's background and interest in the tumultuous events of 1836.

"I remember my great-granddad telling us about the Runaway Scrape," she said in a wavery, paper-thin voice. "That Generalissimo Santa Anna you mentioned came up with a plan to move foreign settlers to the interior, replace them with Mexicans and cut off all immigration. Said he was going to execute every foreigner who resisted. After the Alamo and the massacre at Goliad, I guess the American settlers round these parts figured he meant business. Every one of 'em, including my great-great-granddaddy, abandoned their land and skeedaddled over the border to Louisiana."

If Ellie remembered correctly, the frantic scramble labeled the Runaway Scrape took place in early April, a month after the Alamo fell and just weeks after Colonel James Fannin and his force of four hundred Texians surrendered to Santa Anna. Under the mistaken impression they would simply be expelled from Mexico, the Tejanos were marched back to Goliad, where Santa Anna had them summarily shot.

Word of the massacre spread across Texas like prairie fire. Frightened settlers loaded everything they could into wagons and rushed helter-skelter for the U.S. border. Soldiers in Sam Houston's ragtag army abandoned ranks in droves to assist their fleeing families. Houston was left with only a little over nine hundred volunteers to face Santa Anna's well trained, well equipped and—until then—victorious army.

"Great-granddaddy said his grandpa's cabin was burned to the ground," Dorrie related, "but he came back and rebuilt after Houston beat the pants off Santa Anna at San Jacinto."

"Did your great-grandfather ever mention a great-uncle named Josiah Kennett?"

"Seems like he did, but I don't recall much about him, 'cept he died at the Alamo."

"Are you sure?"

"Well, that's what we were always told. I've got some old family pictures and letters stashed in a trunk up in the attic. I think there's one in there that talks about Josiah. Might take me a while to get to it, though. Doc says this new hip of mine isn't ready for stairs yet."

"That's all right!" Ellie said hastily. "Please don't go up to the attic."

She did some quick thinking. Kearnes County was less than an hour's drive from San Antonio. She could get out there and back by late afternoon.

"Would you mind if I drove out to your place and took a look through that trunk?"

"You come right ahead, missy. I'd enjoy the company."

Snatching up a pen, Ellie jotted down directions to her place. "Thanks. I'll be there by two-thirty or so."

Trying to contain her excitement, she filled the time until Jack's return by negotiating a contract for the site restoration and drawing up a list of invitees for the reception.

Mackenzie pounded on her door just before noon, every bit as excited and even more impatient for Jack and Nick's return. They arrived at the Menger a while later. Ellie wasn't quite sure how the colonel had managed to become a permanent member of their little group, but the others seemed to have accepted his presence.

Plugging a microphone into a small gray box, Mackenzie claimed their immediate attention.

"Wait till you hear this."

Her eyes gleaming, she spoke a few phrases into the microphone. The synthesizer translated the words into a deep rasp. The result sounded so much like the man who'd attacked Ellie in the exhibit room that goose bumps raised on her arms.

When the raspy echo faded, Mackenzie looked across the mike at Ellie. "You're the only one of us who heard him live. What do you think?"

"I think it's amazing. And just a bit scary."

"Good!" Her glance went to Jack. "Want to make the call to Foster?"

"Let's work out the wording, then you can go for it."

A few minutes later, Mackenzie dialed Foster's private number. When an answering machine clicked on, she rasped out a brief message.

"Word on the street is our friend plans to release

her report tomorrow night. I'll be there to make sure it doesn't happen."

Ellie knew it was a ploy. She was standing right there, had watched Mackenzie mouth the words. Yet the threat sounded so ominous that she had to work to match Mackenzie's smug grin when she cut the connection.

"There! That'll up Foster's pucker factor. I'll wait till he gets his invitation to the soiree to make the next call."

Recalled to her part in the drama, Ellie produced the list she'd worked on earlier. "Believe it or not, I convinced Dr. Smith to help me pull it together. The man's so eager to see me leave town—and so relieved that it looks like I'm not going to rewrite the history of his Alamo—that he actually volunteered the names of the high rollers who've contributed to the Alamo Restoration and Maintenance Fund."

She met Jack's glance.

"Foster's wife was one of the contributors."

A savage satisfaction glittered in his eyes. "That gives us the perfect rationale for including the bastard among the invitees. Think you can notify everyone on the list today?" he asked Mackenzie.

"Consider it done. I'll zap the list to my people at headquarters. Given the short notice, they'll have to fax the invites. We'll make sure it looks as though they came from Dr. Alazar. As soon as they're out, I'll put in another call to Foster and offer myself as his date. Then," she announced, "I'm going shopping."

Jack hooked a brow. "Again?"

"Again. The results of my last expedition seemed to impress Danny Boy. This time, I'll pull out all the stops and knock him off his feet. Literally."

"No, you won't."

Jack's reply came hard and fast, preempting Nick's.

"Foster's mine. All mine. No one knocks him off his feet but me."

Faced with his vocal opposition and Nick's tight frown, Mackenzie backpedaled. "Okay, okay. He's all yours. But I still need to go shopping. I didn't bring anything suitable for a black-tie affair. How about you, Claire? Ellie?"

The psychologist's gaze drifted around the small group. It didn't linger on Luis Esteban for more than an instant, but whatever she saw in his face caused her to incline her head in a graceful nod.

"I'll join you."

"Ellie?"

"I can't make it this afternoon. I want to drive down to visit a fourth-generation relative of one of the Alamo defenders."

The excitement she'd felt at the start of her project seeped into her veins. Her face eager, she turned to Jack.

"She lives in Kearnes County, less than an hour from San Antonio. She thinks she has some letters in her attic that contain information about Kennett. I'm also hoping I can talk her into providing a DNA sample. Will you go with me?"

The first real smile she'd seen in days crept into his eyes. "Try going anywhere without me."

The trip through the South Texas countryside was just what Ellie needed. After the stress of the past weeks and the sheer terror of the attack in the Alamo, the wide-open plains rolled by with soothing monotony.

Jack was at the wheel of the rented Cherokee. His

eyes shielded behind mirrored sunglasses, he kept a
close watch on the rearview mirror. They weren't followed this time. Nor did they engage in any high-speed
chases. Gradually, even Jack relaxed.

They drove south on 181 for some forty miles,
roughly paralleling the course of the San Antonio River
as it meandered to the Gulf. Just past Hobson, they
turned onto a two-lane county road that ran straight as
an arrow between fields fenced by barbed wire. Ellie
consulted the directions she'd scribbled down earlier.

"Dorrie said her place was three point four miles
down this road."

Nodding, Jack took a fix on the odometer. Three
point four miles later, a dented mailbox atop a weathered post proclaimed the Johnson place.

A dirt track led to the house, perched on a slight rise
a quarter mile from the road. The Cherokee jounced
over deep ruts. Dust swirled in a long plume behind,
announcing their arrival long before they drove over a
cattle guard and pulled into the yard.

The original structure must have been constructed
in the early Texas dogtrot style, with separate sleeping,
cooking and eating quarters on either side of a walk-
through breezeway. Native stone walls enclosed the
original sections, but succeeding generations had tacked
on clapboard additions and enclosed the breezeway.

Leaning heavily on a walker, Dorrie Johnson hobbled
out to greet them. Shaded by the tin roof that extended
over the front porch, she was a tiny figure in a bright
yellow blouse, denim jumper and sturdy sneakers. To
Ellie's consternation, she'd prepared a small feast for
her visitors.

"My molasses cookies won first prize at the county

fair for near onto three decades," she announced smugly. Her walker thumping, she led Jack and Ellie into the front parlor and waved at them to have a seat. "The pecan crop wasn't all that good last year, though, so I baked up a sweet potato pie, too."

Jack didn't appear to find any fault with the pecans. He consumed a plateful of cookies, washing them down with sweetened iced tea, before tackling a hearty sampling of pie. Ellie was too enthralled by the memories Dorrie shared of her family to do more than nibble at the rich sweets.

"Salathiel Charles Kennett and his bride homesteaded this place in twenty-eight. Hauled everything they owned west in a covered wagon. Like I told you, they left in a hurry in thirty-six."

At Jack's questioning look, Ellie explained the Runaway Scrape.

"They came back, though," Dorrie continued complacently. "One of their offspring or another's been squatting on this patch of dirt ever since."

"Do you know where Salathiel hailed from?"

"He was from Alabama. Barbour County, best I recall. His wife was from Sparta, South Carolina. Dorinda. Dorinda McLaren. Want to guess who I was named for?"

Ellie jerked upright in her seat. Ignoring the playful question she fired one of her own.

"Your kin came from Sparta?"

Dorrie's eyes twinkled. "Didn't I just say so, missy? I'll admit I'm getting a mite forgetful these days, but I can pretty well remember the words that just popped out of my mouth."

"Yes, of course. I'm sorry. It's just that... Well, William Barrett Travis, the commander of the troops at the Alamo, moved to Texas from Sparta, South Carolina, too."

"You don't say!"

Carefully placing her iced tea on a coaster, Ellie scooted to the edge of her seat.

"Historical documents indicate Travis arrived at the Alamo armed with a double-barreled shotgun, among other weapons. There's one on display up there in San Antonio bearing a mark that traces to a gunsmith in Sparta. I found another buried in a creek bed some miles south of the city with the same mark. We're trying to determine who that gun belonged to."

"Don't know that I can help you there, missy. Seems I remember great-granddaddy talkin' about a shotgun *his* daddy carried west with him. Could have been made by that gunsmith you're talking about, but I don't know what happened to it."

"Could he have given it to his brother, Josiah, to take with him when he joined the Texas Army?"

"I 'spose so."

"Maybe there's something in those letters you told me about that will give us more information," Ellie hinted.

"Maybe," Dorrie said doubtfully. "You're welcome to crawl up to the attic and take a look."

The tin roof trapped the heat and held it under the eaves. Dust motes danced and swirled in the hazy light cast by the bulb dangling at the end of a long cord.

Switching on the flashlight Dorrie had provided for extra illumination, Ellie stepped over bundles of old *National Geographic*s and stacks of yellowed sheet music.

A zigzagging course through the treasured junk of several generations took her to the steamer trunk pushed under the eaves. Leather peeled in strips from its sides and humped top. The rusted hasps were sprung and hung uselessly on their hinges. Grunting, Jack used his good arm and worked it out far enough for Ellie to raise the lid.

She gasped in delight. He swiped at a trickle of sweat and groaned.

"It's going to take hours to go through all this stuff."

"It might take *you* hours," she retorted, the historian in her affronted by his lack of faith in her abilities. "I know what I'm looking for. Just pull up that crate, get comfortable and hold the flashlight steady."

Jack did as ordered. Hunkering on the sturdy crate, he planted his elbows on his knees and aimed the beam of light at the yellowed letters, old newspaper clippings and faded family photos.

Her still tender knees made kneeling impossible, so Ellie sat cross-legged beside the trunk. Despite the bulky bandages on her hands, or maybe because of them, she handled the clippings and documents with extreme care. She skimmed each with a keen eye before setting it aside. Inch by inch, the stack beside her grew.

Jack found the woman digging through the trunk far more intriguing than its contents. She probably didn't have any idea how beautiful she looked to him at this moment. Dust swirled around her. Sweat glistened on her forehead and upper lip. White streaked her hair where she'd caught a cobweb. She was totally absorbed by those yellowed scraps of paper, as thrilled by the past as Jack was nervous about the future.

He'd dropped enough hints. Hell, he'd come right out

and admitted that he'd never been able to get her out of his head or his heart. He'd had to work to say the words. He'd never told any woman he loved her, Ellie included.

He was pretty sure she loved him, too. She'd told him flat out she wasn't walking away from him. And she certainly held nothing back the night she'd flamed in his arms. Yet Jack wanted to hear the words. Needed to hear the words.

"Ellie."

"Hmm?"

"Last night…"

She glanced up then, curiosity warring with impatience to get back to the letter in her hand.

"What about last night?"

"I meant what I said. I've never stopped loving you."

The words hung on the suffocating air. Chewing on her lower lip, Ellie considered his quiet declaration.

"Last night," she said after a long moment, "I believed you. For a moment this morning, I had my doubts."

"I know. I saw the hurt in your eyes when Lightning brought up that business about the treaty. You have to know politics have nothing to do with what's between us."

"To quote your friend Lightning, political issues are always in play. They certainly were nine years ago."

"But not this time. Marry me, Ellie."

"What?"

"You said it yourself. We've wasted too many days and nights already. Marry me. Here in Texas, or in New Mexico or wherever we can get a license with the least hassle and delay."

Helplessly, Ellie gaped at him. Sweat trickled down

his temples. With the flashlight's beam backlighting his face, he looked like a character from a B-grade horror flick. She couldn't believe the man had chosen this hot, musty attic to ask for the commitment she'd ached to give him nine years ago, but she wasn't going to argue the time or the place. As she'd told Jack, she knew her mind then and she knew it now.

"Yes," she said simply. "I'll marry you. Whenever and wherever you want."

With a small, inarticulate sound, he bent to seal the agreement. The kiss left them both breathless and several degrees hotter than before.

"Better finish with that trunk," he warned with a crooked grin, "or Miss Dorinda might hear some strange thumps coming from her attic."

Chapter 14

Ellie found the prize she'd been searching for near the bottom of the trunk, tucked inside an old Bible. The yellowed, folded sheet had torn at the creases and almost came apart in her hands. Carefully lifting the bottom edge, she took one look at the signature and gulped.

"Here." Her hands clumsy and trembling in their gauze wrappings, she passed the letter to Jack. "I don't want to take a chance on tearing this further. Unfold it, will you, and hold it so I can read it."

Trading the letter for the flashlight, he lifted the folds and tilted the letter toward the beam. Ellie came up on her knees without so much as a blink at the pain and leaned on Jack's thigh. Her heart thumping, she peered at the spidery script.

March 5th
1836

Elijah—

I don't have time for more than a few lines. The colonel's sending me & another out shortly. God willing, one of us will make it through & bring back reinforcements. If there are none to be had, I'll rejoin my company here at the Alamo.

Ammunition's running low, but I still have enough for pa's short-barrel to give a good accounting. She fires as true as the colonel's. Guess she should, seeing as the same smith cast both.

They're calling for me now. I'll leave this letter with the captain's wife, as many of the company are doing. She's promised to see them delivered if she survives the attack we all know is coming.

Yr brother,
Josiah Kennett
Private
Texas Volunteers

Ellie's throat ached at the letter's simple poignancy. The satisfaction of knowing she'd found the last vital piece of the puzzle didn't begin to compare with the admiration she felt for Kennett's courage and sense of duty.

"James Allen made it to Goliad," she murmured, leaning against Jack's knee, "but Fannin delayed sending troops until it was too late. I wonder where Josiah was headed."

"Guess we'll never know." Carefully, he folded the letter. "Do you think Dorrie will agree to contribute this to the collection at the Alamo?"

"I hope so!"

Dorrie not only agreed to let Ellie take the letter, she also cheerfully provided a DNA sample. After rolling a cotton swab around in her mouth, she stared at the tip for a moment before dropping it into a plastic baggie.

"You sure that's all you need?"

"If that doesn't do it, we know where to find you."

Ignoring Ellie's protests, Dorrie thumped out to the porch to see them off. "Y'all come back any time."

"You promise to bake more of these and we will," Jack said, carrying the bag of molasses cookies the older woman had pressed on him with the same care Ellie carried her bagged letter and DNA sample.

Ellie occupied the hour's drive to San Antonio plotting how best to rush through a DNA test. Jack expressed far more interest in obtaining the blood test required for a marriage license.

He solved the first problem by swinging by the federal courthouse. Tracking down the two FBI agents he and Mackenzie had met with the previous day, he traded an update on the Foster situation for a promise to strong-arm their lab into an overnight DNA analysis.

He took care of second problem with a stop at the emergency room where Ellie's cuts had been treated two days ago. Her eyes widened when he pulled into the lot.

"Jack! You were serious? You really want to get married right away?"

"This afternoon, if we can talk the doc into doing the blood work and track down a judge to waive the three day waiting requirement. Why? Are you having second thoughts?"

"No! But my mother, my aunt and uncle… They'll be crushed if we don't invite them."

Jack gave her a wry look. "Your uncle Eduardo, huh?"

"Uncle Eduardo," Ellie said firmly. "He might not be able to rearrange his schedule and fly up here on short notice, but for all his overbearing ways, he's been as much a father to me as an uncle. I have to invite him. And, well…"

She fiddled with the plastic bag holding Josiah Kennett's precious letter. The mere thought of joining her life with Jack's sent excited anticipation racing through her veins. After so many years, so many hurts, the future held all the promise their past had cut short.

Ellie didn't want anything to spoil their day. Anything.

"Let's think about this waiting period. If we work things right in the next twenty-four to thirty-six hours, we can go off on a nice, long honeymoon with no loose ends left dangling."

"Like Josiah Kennett," he said with a smile.

"And Daniel Foster."

Jack kept the smile on his face, but it took some doing. At this point he couldn't say how much, if any, of his urgent need to make Ellie his stemmed from an instinctive, gut-deep desire to give her every protection a man can give his woman. All he knew was that he didn't like the idea of Ellie going head-to-head with Foster. At all!

From all indications, the bastard had arranged the murder of one woman. If pushed to the wall, he might take matters into his own hands. The man was big enough, ruthless enough, desperate enough to pull the trigger if he thought he could get away with it.

Jack would just have to make sure Foster knew he couldn't get away with it.

"All right," he conceded. "We take care of the loose ends, then we get married."

After that, it seemed to Ellie as though events moved with the speed of light.

Anticipating a wedding, preparing a public announcement of a major historical find and rehearsing responses to several different scenarios involving Dan Foster took up the rest of that evening and most of the next day.

RSVPs came pouring in. All the local TV and radio stations were sending crews. The mayor and most of the city council intended to make an appearance. Almost every local member of the Alamo Restoration and Preservation Foundation accepted—including Daniel Foster.

As it turned out, Mackenzie didn't have to place a second call to Foster and inveigle an invitation to be his date. He called her. Listening to the tape of their brief conversation gave Ellie a distinctly queasy sensation. If the man was driven by anything more than a desire to show up with a gorgeous female draped over his arm, he hid it well.

Gorgeous, he'd certainly get. Mackenzie had made good on her promise to do some serious shopping. The midnight blue sheath she displayed to Ellie dipped dangerously low in the front, even lower in back.

Claire, too, had found the perfect gown to complement her silvery blond beauty. The shimmering turquoise silk was strapless, banded with silver sequins at the bodice and split up one side. Ellie had no idea how the woman would hide anything, much less her neat little revolver, under that whisper of silk. Smiling, Claire admitted that a holster strapped to the inside of her thigh made gliding across a room an exercise in extreme care.

Forcefully reminded of her woefully inadequate wardrobe, Ellie coerced the two women into a return trip to the elegant little boutique they'd discovered in River Center mall. Those sixty minutes turned out to be among the most expensive of Ellie's life. She ended up purchasing not only a gown for the reception that night, but a cream-colored silk suit perfect for a wedding, a flame-colored chiffon nightdress that clung to her every curve and lacy underwear designed more for seduction than for comfort.

Mackenzie took one look at the scraps of lace and promptly bought two pair for herself. Even Claire was convinced to splurge on the outrageously extravagant panties.

"Now I really won't be able to walk straight," she said with a rueful smile.

"Maybe not," Mackenzie returned with a grin, "but you'll sure have the colonel wondering why. You notice he hasn't taken his eyes off you since he arrived?"

"As a matter of fact," the psychologist replied serenely, "I have."

The happy saleswoman was ringing up their purchases when a cell phone rang. All four women checked their phones. Ellie flipped hers open.

"Dr. Alazar. Yes, I can hold."

Gnawing on her lower lip, she waited for Janet Dawes-Hamilton to come on the line.

"Ellie?"

"Yes."

"As you requested, the FBI sent me the results of the

DNA profile their lab worked up for you. I just ran it against the samples we took from the skeletal remains."

"And?"

"We have a match, girl!"

Whooping, Ellie danced around her startled companions.

The shopping expedition and thrilling report from her colleague succeeded in holding Ellie's nervousness at bay for an all-too-brief hour. It came rushing back when the three women returned to the hotel and got caught up in the flurry of last-minute preparations for the function that night.

Jack insisted Ellie rehearse a variety of different responses for if and when she confronted Foster. The responses ranged from merely smiling and letting Foster do all the talking to dropping facedown on the floor if his hand moved so much as an inch toward his tux or pants pocket. After the third or fourth drop, she was a bundle of raw nerves. Pleading the need to review her speech a final time before dressing, she escaped to her bedroom.

Jack knocked on the connecting door at the time they'd set as the time to leave the hotel. Ellie had just finished putting the final touches to her makeup. Thankfully, the cuts on her palms had healed enough for her to leave off the bandages. A light application of pancake makeup muted most of the scabs. Fighting a panicky flutter of nerves, she tucked a stray curl into the feathery cluster on top of her head and opened the door.

"Oh, my!"

Nine years ago, she'd taken one look at a tall, broad-shouldered Marine in his dress blues and immediately decided to wrangle an introduction and a dance. When Jack had arrived at the Menger, his rugged informality had at first surprised her, then stirred her senses.

This Jack rocked her on her heels.

His tux might have been cut by the hand of a master. The black broadcloth showcased his broad shoulders. Silver studs winked at the front of his snowy white shirt. A satin cummerbund nipped in his trim waist, and a matching satin stripe ran down the outside of his pants legs. What struck Ellie even more than the elegance of the formal attire was the casual ease with which he wore it.

"Where did you get a tux to fit you on such short notice?" she asked when she recovered her breath.

"Nick had it delivered. Compliments of the same tailor who rigs out his waiters."

If Nick Jensen's employees waited tables in hand-tailored tuxes like this one, it was no wonder dinner at one of his glitzy watering holes reputedly cost more than the down payment on a four-bedroom house.

"You look incredible," Ellie murmured.

"*I* look incredible?"

Jack's glance made a slow journey down her length. Just as slowly, he brought his glinting gaze to hers.

"You're going to have every man in the room tonight wishing they could go back to school and take more history courses."

Ellie had to admit the slinky silver lamé gown was about as far from academia as anything could get. The plunging halter top left her shoulders and back bare, while the pencil-slim skirt clung to her hips and glittered with every step. Paired with the silver bracelet

Jack had given her nine years ago and dangly silver earrings, the effect was pure Hollywood.

If she'd had more time to deliberate and less on her mind, she might have chosen something more restrained, more dignified. The gleam in Jack's eyes made her glad she hadn't.

"I have something I want you to wear tonight," Jack said. Sliding his hand into his pocket, he produced what looked like a thin transparent patch.

"What is it?"

"A wireless transmitter, compliments of Mackenzie."

His knuckles warm on the slope of her breast, he stuck the tiny device to the inside folds of the halter top.

"Don't take this off tonight. For any reason."

"I won't."

He hesitated a moment, his fingers lingering on her warm skin before reaching into his pocket once more. This time he produced a little box bearing the logo of the jewelry shop just off the Menger's lobby.

"I was going to wait and let you pick out the ring you wanted, but I saw this downstairs and thought it would match your bracelet."

"Oh, Jack! It's beautiful!"

The diamonds were channel cut and set flush in a narrow platinum engagement ring. A wider wedding ring of beaten platinum nestled in the black velvet below the diamonds. Leaving the wider band in place, he popped the box shut and slipped the diamonds on her finger.

Ellie waggled her fingers, marveling at the fiery sparkle. She couldn't quite believe so much was happening so fast!

"I've got a gift for you, too," she told him. "Noth-

ing near as beautiful as this ring *or* my bracelet, but…
Well… Wait here a minute."

Hurrying into the sitting room, she retrieved the silver concho.

"I thought you might like this as a souvenir. It's the concho you found at Mission San Jose."

Pleasure softened his features as he worked his thumb over the intricate design. "Don't you need it to substantiate your findings?"

"Not with Josiah's letter and Dorrie's DNA sampling."

"Then I'll keep it."

Sliding the concho into his breast pocket, he drew her forward. His kiss was long and hard and went a long way to calming Ellie's jittery nerves. The reassuring smile he gave her helped, too.

"Time to go. Are you ready?"

She drew in a shaky breath. "As ready as I'll ever be."

Nick's more than lived up to its reputation.

The restaurant occupied the entire top floor of one of San Antonio's tallest buildings. An outside glass elevator whisked patrons upward while providing stunning views of the Riverwalk and the floodlit Alamo. Guests stepped out of the elevator into an eagle's aerie with a spectacular three-hundred-sixty-degree view of the city. Floor-to-ceiling glass panels stood open to the night to allow easy circulation between the dining area and the mist-cooled balcony.

Ellie had never been to a Nick's, but understood they were famous for incorporating local culture and cuisine. This particular establishment offered the best of Texas with a distinctly Hispanic flavor. Discreetly lighted niches displayed museum-quality pieces of sculpture and art depicting the rich heritage of the area. The wine cellar, she'd been told, stocked some fifteen hundred labels, including a number of rich, hearty Texas reds bottled in Hill County vineyards.

For tonight's bash, the lush greenery that provided diners an illusion of privacy without impeding their view had been removed, as had most of the tables. This was a stand-up reception with an open bar and a lavish spread of hot and cold delicacies, subsidized by the restaurant's owner. Good thing, as Ellie knew the pitiful bit of funding that remained in the project kitty wouldn't have covered the drinks, let alone succulent Gulf shrimp sautéed in a white wine sauce, bourbon seared beef tenderloins, and a *carne asada* with the most delicate, delicious aroma she'd ever sniffed.

A good number of guests in black tie and glittering cocktail dresses and gowns had already assembled. Conversation hummed. Ice clinked in glasses. Tux-clad waiters floated between groups refilling glasses and plates. Her palm clammy where it rested in the crook of Jack's arm, Ellie skimmed a quick glance over the assembled guests in search of Mackenzie and her escort.

Foster had picked Mac up at the hotel twenty minutes ago. Ellie had been kept out of sight, but Nick, Jack, Claire and Colonel Esteban had observed the pickup from different vantage points. Claire and Luis had trailed the couple in Luis's rented Lincoln. Both couples should have arrived by now.

A fact that obviously played on Nick's mind when he greeted Ellie and Jack.

"Comm's playing her part to the hilt," he informed them. "She managed to talk Foster into a detour on the way here, ostensibly to show her another building he constructed."

Annoyance darkening his blue eyes, Lightning flicked the cuffs of his dress shirt. If the stark black and white of formal dress tamed Jack's rugged good looks, Nick Jensen wore his like he'd been born to them.

"From the tenor of the transmissions we're receiving," he said with something less than his usual urbane charm, "she's succeeded in upping the man's pucker factor by several degrees."

She was certainly upping Ellie's. The delay set her nerves snapping and sparking like downed electrical lines. She longed to snatch one of the crystal champagne flutes from the tray a smiling waiter presented, but she knew she had to keep a clear head.

Instead, she sipped at the glass of Perrier Nick procured for her with a single word to the waiter. The overhead lights shot brilliant sparks off the diamonds on her hand as she lifted the heavy crystal goblet. Nick's glance went to the ring, then to Jack. A smile played at his eyes, but he said nothing.

"There's the mayor," he commented. "As host for tonight's event, I'd better greet him."

"And I should look over the layout for the presentation," Ellie said to Jack.

Nodding, he led her to an area cordoned off by black velvet ropes. Rows of straight-backed chairs emblazoned with a gold N faced a raised platform. A wall-size screen would be lowered from the ceiling behind the podium on the platform.

Gulping, Ellie clutched her little silver lamé evening bag. Inside were a lipstick, a compact and a CD in a thin plastic case. She'd boiled down all her weeks of work, all the hours at the dig and at the Alamo, all her team's collective research into a dramatic slide presentation. It was astounding how much history could be crammed onto a single CD.

Her fingers tightened on Jack's arm. "Do you think I'll actually get to present the findings tonight?"

"Yes. Just play this out the way we rehearsed. Exactly the way we rehearsed."

She felt like a Ping-Pong ball bouncing between the public drama of her presentation and the very private, very tense drama with Foster.

"I just hope the rest of the team arrives in time," she said nervously.

Orin Weaver had made arrangements to fly to San Antonio. Janet Dawes-Hamilton was driving down from Waco. Sam Pierce had indicated he'd show, too, and had coerced the National Park Service regional director into coming with him. Ellie had made sure invitations went to each of the volunteers, as well. The only member of the team she hadn't been able contact was Eric Chapman. The grad student was on the road somewhere between San Antonio and Albuquerque and not answering his cell phone.

If her team was still arriving, most of Jack's was already in place. Nick circulated among the crowd, greeting the mayor and other dignitaries with an ease that astounded Ellie considering the fact that he was also receiving a steady stream of transmissions from his headquarters. She couldn't begin to imagine how she separated the mayor's polite patter from the voices feeding into his right ear.

She spotted Detective Harris on the far side of the room, tugging a finger at the tight black bow tie encircling his neck. Jack had indicated upward of a half dozen more of SAPD's finest would be in attendance tonight. Ellie thought she recognized one of the FBI agents she'd met yesterday. The other was here, as well, but she couldn't see him in the growing crowd.

The media had turned out en masse. Banks of TV cameras stood ready opposite the podium. Reporters with mikes and Minicams vied for space and the best backdrops in the roped-off area reserved for interviews. They understood Ellie and her team wouldn't be available until after the presentation but were managing to capture other VIPs on tape.

"Guess we'd better circulate," she murmured, dragging in a shaky breath. "At least until Mackenzie and her date make an appearance."

They arrived less than ten minutes later. Claire and Luis Esteban drifted in almost on their heels.

Ellie sensed rather than saw their entrance. Jack's arm went taut under hers. The skin pulled tight across his cheeks. Gulping, she saw his eyes narrow as he tracked his prey.

She turned slowly, searched the crowd milling at the entrance for a glimpse of a midnight blue gown. Mackenzie floated into view a second later, clinging like a burr to Dan Foster.

The builder's face was ruddy above his black tie. Even from this distance, Ellie could see the sheen of sweat at his temples. His eyes darting around the restaurant, he dragged a folded handkerchief from his pocket and dabbed his forehead.

Across the room, his gaze locked with Ellie's. His hand

froze in mid-dab for a second, maybe two. Abruptly, he stuffed the handkerchief in his pocket and turned away.

After so many hours of clawing tension and dread, trapping Daniel Foster in the net he had woven proved embarrassingly easy. Almost anticlimactic.

Mackenzie played her role to perfection. While the entire team watched from various vantage points, she snuggled up to Foster, whispered coyly and did everything but stick her tongue in his ear to add to his obvious edginess.

Nick Jensen, Ellie saw in a quick glance, didn't appear to fully appreciate her performance. Like Jack, he tracked the builder's progress around the room with narrowed eyes.

Foster was obviously searching the crowd, looking for one face in particular, growing more tight-jawed by the moment when he didn't spot it. Since a good number of guests had drifted onto the balcony to enjoy the view, it didn't take much work on Mackenzie's part to steer her escort there, as well. With seemingly effortless ease, she maneuvered him to the corner Jack had chosen earlier. A bend in the building left that particular niche shielded from view of most of those inside. The wrought-iron lampposts scattered around the balcony cast only a dim spear of light in that direction.

It was barely enough to illuminate Mackenzie as she withdrew her arm from Foster's and pantomimed powdering her nose. Distracted, he gave a terse nod. A moment later, a stunning figure in midnight blue floated past Ellie and Jack on her way to the ladies' room.

"All right, you two. He's all yours."

Swallowing, Ellie swiped her hand down the sides of her dress. Her damp palms slid over the glittering metallic material. Too late, she realized that she'd left smears of the makeup she'd used to cover the ugly scabs on her hands.

Wondering how in the world she could even *think* about such trivia at a time like this, she started forward.

Jack held her back. "Remember how we rehearsed it. If he lifts so much as a finger, you hit the deck."

"Don't worry! I'll go down like the *Titanic*. Now let's get this over with."

The scene that followed might have been scripted. When Ellie moved into the circle of dim light cast by the wrought-iron lamppost behind Foster, the builder reacted just as Claire had predicted he would.

His eyes turned wary. His shoulders went taut under his tux. But no one watching from more than a few feet away would see anything but affability in his smile.

"Mr. Foster?"

"Yes."

"I'm Elena Alazar. I understand your wife was one of the leading contributors to the Alamo Restoration and Preservation Foundation. I just wanted to say how very sorry I was to hear about her tragic death."

"Thank you."

"I know there's been some concern on the part of other foundation members about my team's findings. I just wanted to assure you that…"

With a show of concern, Ellie took another step forward. That was as close as she dared get to the man whose knuckles had gone white where his hand gripped the balcony rail.

"Mr. Foster? Are you all right?"

His glance was riveted on something just beyond her. She didn't have to look around to know it was the gleam of a long, lethal silencer.

"Are you crazy!" Foster whispered, frantically searching the shadows behind the gun. "Not here! Not with me standing two feet away from her!"

"Mr. Foster, what in the world? Oh!"

Ellie froze as something hard jabbed into the small of her back.

"Don't make a sound," a deep voice rasped from behind her. "Or a move. One twitch and you're dead."

She didn't have to fake the ice that crystallized in her veins. The press of that gun barrel against her bare skin was all too real. The voice so eerily like the one at the Alamo that Ellie couldn't breathe, much less twitch.

Foster fed on her fear like a jackal feasted on carrion. With a snarl, he pushed away from the railing.

"For Christ's sake, keep her here in the shadows until I get across the room. Then do it right this time and blow the bitch away."

"If I blow anyone away," Jack answered in his own voice, "it'll be you."

His jaw dropping, the builder whirled back. "What the hell…?"

"Take one step." With a savage smile, Jack stepped out of the shadows. "Just one."

The beefy contractor was no fool. He froze right where he was. With a grunt of acute disappointment, Jack raised his voice.

"Did you get that, Comm?"

Mackenzie sailed through the glass door. Nick, Claire, Esteban, Detective Harris and the FBI man crowed right on her heels. Behind them, TV crews scrambled frantically to aim their cameras and lights.

"We all got it," she announced, shooting Foster a look of utter scorn. "I broadcast the murdering bastard live."

Epilogue

Washington, D.C.,'s muggy July had given way to a surprisingly pleasant August when Renegade ushered his new bride up the steps of an elegant town house set halfway down a shady street just off Massachusetts Avenue.

Ellie had already met a good number of Jack's friends and colleagues. Men and women with curious code names like Jaguar, Cowboy, Artemis, Chameleon and Thunder had converged on San Antonio, families in tow, for the wedding that had taken place at Mission San Jose the day after Ellie gave a name and a history to the solitary solider who'd died so many years ago on mission grounds. In addition to that lively group, a whole contingent of Marines showed up unexpectedly. Square-shouldered and spit-shined, they stated emphatically that they had to see their old Gunny take the plunge with their own eyes.

Jack's friends weren't the only ones who crowded into the beautiful old church. Ellie's team had showed up *en masse*. A tall, handsome Marine escorted a beaming Dorrie Johnson to her pew. The First Lady of Mexico and her sister-in-law occupied the front pew on the bride's side.

The media had turned out, too. Dr. Alazar, one was heard to proclaim, sure provided *great* copy. TV Minicams whirred and cameras flashed as the President of Mexico escorted his niece down the aisle.

The wedding supper that evening was held on a string of colorful barges floating along the San Antonio River. Candles winked in crystal chimneys. A mariachi band serenaded the guests. Nick's catered the food and wine. It was, Ellie had decided, the perfect ending to her visit to San Antonio and her quest to discover the identity of a fallen Texas hero.

It was also, she thought on a flutter of pure happiness, the perfect beginning for her new life with her own particular hero. A beginning that included a honeymoon in the Pyrenees, where she intended to entice Jack into exploring the mysteries of some recently discovered ice-age cave paintings.

First, though, he'd insisted on a stopover in Washington. It was time, he'd stated, she understood exactly what he did for a living.

The tour a smiling Nick Jensen gave Ellie of the offices of the special envoy didn't shed any particular light on the subject. Not until he ushered her and Jack into an elevator hidden behind a walnut panel fitted with a titanium insert and whisked her up to Mackenzie Blair's domain did she grasp the significance of that bulletproof shield. The door slid open to reveal a state-of-the-art war room.

"Good grief!" Stunned, Ellie took in digital displays that took up three of the four walls. "What is this? An alternate command center for the Joint Chiefs of Staff?"

"They wish!" Her eyes sparkling, Mackenzie waved a proprietary hand. "Nope, this is all mine."

She caught Nick's hooked eyebrow and made a slight correction.

"*Mostly* mine. Come on, I'll show you around."

Dazed, Ellie was treated to a detailed description of the control center's futuristic array of electronics, a visit to the field dress unit, a view of weaponry at the firing range that would have challenged even the data stored in Discoverer Two, and finally a highly sanitized briefing of OMEGA's charter.

Enough of its mission came through, though, to make her frown and swing around in her chair.

"This is what you do, Jack?"

"It's what I did," he answered quietly. "What I do from here on out depends on you."

Startled, Mackenzie and the other agents present at the briefing flashed a quick look at Lightning. He shook his head, signaling that this was news to him, too.

"I don't want you worrying every time I walk out the door, Ellie, or wondering if I'll come back. I came here today to terminate my membership in this elite club."

Relief washed through her, followed immediately by the sharp sting of regret. She'd cost Jack one career. Now he was giving up another for her. Her smile wobbly, she opted to continue this discussion without an interested audience.

"We'll have two weeks in the Pyrenees. Why don't we talk about it there?"

The wolfish grin that slashed across Jack's face said more clearly than words that his plans for those two weeks didn't include a whole lot of talking. Nodding to the others, he escorted Ellie out of the control center.

Mackenzie folded her arms. Toe tapping, she stood beside Lightning and watched the two leave. She liked Ellie. Liked *and* respected her. But she wasn't happy with the idea Renegade might not rejoin the ranks of active operatives. Mac considered each and every one of them her personal responsibility.

"Do you think he'll really give up OMEGA for her?"

Nick slanted her an enigmatic look. "Wouldn't you, for the right man?"

The glint in his blue eyes closed Mackenzie's throat. She had to take in a quick gulp of air before she could inject the right note of nonchalance into her reply.

"Maybe. Maybe not. Guess I'll just have to wait for the right man to make his move and see what happens."

Nick's amused glance followed her across the control center. "I guess you will," he murmured.

* * * * *